Nowhere Burning

Also by Catriona Ward

The Last House on Needless Street

Little Eve

Sundial

Looking Glass Sound

Nowhere Burning

CATRIONA WARD

NIGHTFIRE
TOR PUBLISHING GROUP
NEW YORK

NOWHERE BURNING

A Nightfire Book
Published by Tom Doherty Associates / Tor Publishing Group
120 Broadway
New York, NY 10271

www.torpublishinggroup.com

Nightfire™ is a trademark of Macmillan Publishing Group, LLC.

EU Representative: Macmillan Publishers Ireland Ltd, 1st Floor,
The Liffey Trust Centre, 117–126 Sheriff Street Upper, Dublin 1, D01 YC43

The Library of Congress Cataloging-in-Publication Data is available upon request.

ISBN 978-1-250-86005-7 (hardcover)
ISBN 978-1-250-86006-4 (ebook)

Our books may be purchased in bulk for specialty retail/wholesale, literacy, corporate/premium, educational, and subscription box use. Please contact MacmillanSpecialMarkets@macmillan.com.

First published in Great Britain by Viper, an imprint of Profile Books Ltd

First U.S. Edition: 2026

Printed in the United States of America

10 9 8 7 6 5 4 3 2 1

For my mother, Isabelle Ruth Learmont Ward, the first person I ever knew, whom I miss with all my heart

Childhood is the kingdom where nobody dies.

Edna St. Vincent Millay

1

Riley

Some people attract death. It loves them, twines around them like ivy, follows them all their lives. Riley has suspected for some time that death is just a step or two behind her. So when the boy in green follows her down the street that summer day she wonders – if only for a moment – whether he might be death, catching up with her at last.

Riley is on her way home – or back to Cousin's house anyway – when she feels him in her wake. He moves from shadow to shadow. He's thin, about her age, as far as she can see. Green t-shirt, jeans streaked green at the knees like he's been climbing trees or skidding down hills. He slips into the shadow of Higgers drugstore, then behind a car. Each time she turns she just catches him – a flash of thin limbs. If he wasn't trying so hard to hide Riley probably wouldn't have noticed it.

It's an unseasonably warm early summer and behind the city the white snowline has crept back up to the very tips of the mountains.

The asphalt is warm and stray dandelions poke up from the cracks in the sidewalk. People are starting to come outside, walking slowly through the heat the day has left behind, tugging their hat brims down against the sinking sun.

She leaves the avenue with the convenience store on the corner and turns down the quiet street, lined with worn-out Victorians. Riley can almost hear the paint bubbling and cracking in the heat. Like a twig cracking underfoot, she thinks. The sound comes again and Riley realises with an indrawn breath that the sound is not just in her imagination. It's out here in the world with her. It's not paint cracking in the sun. It is footsteps, someone walking with a quiet tread, in her wake. Riley turns quickly, breath held, searching the shadows thrown by fences, sheds, the tall weathered gables of the houses. The street just stares back, sun-warm. She can't see anyone. A bumblebee wavers drunkenly past her, over the fence into a nearby garden. She feels the buzz of it right through her body. Riley knows better than to believe the street, with its air of lazy summer peace. Someone is following her.

Riley turns and walks – quickly, but not too quickly. She can feel the gallon of milk she took from the grocery store sloshing in her backpack. She keeps her gaze forward and unwavering. Riley knows, as every kid knows, that ignoring fear is camouflage. Close your eyes and the bad thing – the tall thin shape in the dark at the foot of your bed, or the footstep behind you in an empty street – could miss you. It's noticing the bad thing which makes it notice you. It feeds on attention – fear and your slanted glance.

Riley turns the corner onto the street where Cousin's house sits squat at the end of the close. Riley speeds up; she strides fast, just short of running. This is another rule: you mustn't run. Only things that are prey run. There's a scent now in the air, something like charred meat, and she knows it comes from him, the boy. He's close, she almost feels his breath on the back of her neck.

Riley shoves open Cousin's rickety gate and now she is running, racing up the path, throwing herself in the front door. She slams it behind her. Riley locks the door, rests her back against the wood and breathes. She's inside now, so she's safe. Monsters can't cross boundaries unless you let them. It's important to believe that.

She settles her breath before calling out. She doesn't want her fear to touch him.

'Oliver?'

Only silence answers, but she feels her brother's warm little presence. He has three hiding places, and she knows which one he will have picked today.

'Where could he be?' she remarks as if to herself as she climbs the stairs. 'Where is my Oliver Olive?'

Oliver was scared this morning, Cousin made him do boxes for an hour. So Riley knows that Oliver will want to be in his small dark place, close to the floor. When he's happy he goes up high, crouches on top of the kitchen cupboard like an eaglet.

Riley goes to the little bathroom they share with Cousin. She pulls open the cupboard under the cracked sink.

Oliver is folded up so tight she is afraid for a moment that he can't be alive, not contorted like that, bent at angles like a folded switchblade. But his eyes are bright and dark on hers.

'Come,' she says briefly. 'Quick, his shift ends at four.'

Riley pours milk into an empty jelly jar she found under the kitchen sink. She doesn't want to touch the array of mugs and glasses in the cabinet. Cousin is very precise. He will know if anything like that has been moved.

Cousin gave them each a bowl of rice yesterday and fruit for breakfast this morning. No more. You starve a demon out, everyone knows that.

'Drink,' Riley says.

Oliver tips the gallon jug to his mouth. He drinks too quickly, coughing and swallowing air. Riley hits his back gently. 'Come on,' she says when he stops. 'More. But slowly.'

'Again,' Riley says when he finishes the jar.

He drinks the second one willingly.

'Again.'

By the end of the fifth jarful he is rubbing his stomach. 'No more, Riley,' he says. 'I can't.'

'Sure?' she asks, hearing the desperation in her voice. 'Are you sure you can't handle a little more, Oliver Olive?'

He shakes his head and burps, tears in his eyes.

'Ok,' she says. 'That's ok.' She tips the plastic gallon jug back and swallows the rest, her throat working in pulses. She fills herself with milk, tight as a drum.

'Better?' She strokes Oliver's hair.

Oliver shrugs, pale. Riley hopes he doesn't puke. He needs to keep that milk down. It's full fat, almost cream, and it will keep him going for a day or two. Oliver's knees are knobs projecting from his thin legs. His face is simian in its starved lines. A couple of his teeth are loose, she felt it while brushing them last night. Maybe it's just his age, he's losing his milk teeth. But Riley is afraid. He was so mischievous once, plump with childhood.

'Did the demon make us disobey?' Oliver asks.

Riley feels a cold moment of unease. Sometimes when she eats or drinks she can almost feel the demon inside her licking its lips, enjoying the nourishment. She shakes herself. 'There is no demon, remember, Oliver Olive? Just Cousin telling stories. Right?'

'Right, Riley.' He smiles at her and she smiles back.

Riley washes the empty plastic milk jug in the sink, then creeps out back. She puts the milk jug deep in the neighbour's trash. She breathes in and out, in and out, hand on the plastic trash-can lid which is still warm with sun. *Calm*, she tells herself. Cousin is not god or anything. He can't see everything she does.

When Riley comes back in Oliver is resting his head on crossed arms on the kitchen counter. He's tired. She has to keep him alert, at least for a little longer. Once he sleeps she won't be able to wake him up, and he has to be awake when Cousin comes home.

'Shall we read a story?' Riley asks Oliver brightly. 'Come on. Let's snuggle.' She doesn't know if she's doing the right thing, trying to comfort him – to make it normal. Shouldn't she be screaming and crying? What if Oliver comes to believe that this is what life is supposed to be like? Sometimes Riley even misses their mother.

Oliver leans into Riley on the couch, warm and solid against her side. He picks a book about a disobedient pug dog, and she reads. Oliver giggles at the jokes and points to things he likes in the illustrations. Or he follows along, sounding out the words silently. He is so smart it makes Riley want to cry. She doesn't allow her voice to catch. She keeps reading in a steady tone.

They finish that book and are halfway through a Dr Seuss when Cousin comes in. His tread is heavy like a storm, it shakes the house. He hangs his coat and takes off his tie. Riley and Oliver listen, bodies like taut wire. Riley quickly slips Dr Seuss under the couch cushion. She takes up the *Phonics are Fun!* exercise book from the coffee table and pushes a pencil gently into Oliver's hand.

Cousin stands in the doorway. He scratches his cheek and looks at them, head cocked to one side.

'Hello, Cousin,' Riley says, bright. 'How was your day?'

'Adequate,' Cousin says. He checks his wristwatch and says, gently, 'Boxes, Oliver. An hour.'

Riley sits in the room she shares with Oliver and listens to him labouring up and down the stairs, carrying the cardboard box filled with bricks. His breath comes in gasps. He stumbles sometimes and Riley's body clenches, but Oliver recovers, he does not fall. By the end of the hour Oliver is staggering.

Riley can hear Cousin murmuring, 'Come on, old chap.' Cousin likes to sound British, thinks it makes him fancy. He copies the accent from masterpiece theatre on PBS. *Bit of this, bit of that. Give and take; win some, lose some. Swings and roundabouts.* Riley wants to go out and help Oliver but she knows what will happen if she tries to help.

Riley brushes Oliver's teeth gently, trying not to move his canine and incisor, both of which are loose. There's a little blood on the toothbrush when she's finished so she washes it quickly under the tap before he can see. She doesn't know whether he's supposed to be losing so many teeth so fast. Maybe it's normal at this age, Riley can't really remember. Everything that happened before their mother died is hazy. Oliver's eyes close intermittently and he sways. With so little food and doing the boxes each day, he sometimes falls asleep on his feet.

Riley tucks Oliver in and then goes to her own bed under the window. She lies down but doesn't sleep. Instead she stares into the dark and tries, just like she does each night, to fix her mind on how they will get out. Riley is allowed to go to school, which means she'll get her GED. Oliver is home-schooled. Mostly this seems to mean boxes and the Bible, along with that old phonics book Cousin found at the goodwill. Riley thinks the only reason Cousin lets her go to school is he wants her to help at the funeral home. Bookkeeping. Riley acts like she will stay and do this. Otherwise he would pull her out of school too. Riley listens as Oliver's breath grows slow and regular. At least he can rest now.

The scent comes sudden and strong, hits her as if someone has just opened an oven door. Meat, burning, roasting. It's fainter than it was this afternoon but that's not even good because it's coming through the window, creeping through the cracks. Riley sits up. Her heart hammers. The sound when it comes shocks her, quiet though it is.

Tap, tap, tap. Riley clutches her blanket.

Tap, tap, tap. A fingernail on the glass, a summoning.

Calm, she tells herself. *Stay calm.* If it wanted to kill her it wouldn't tap at the window first, would it?

Tap, tap, tap.

The sound is growing sharper, more insistent. It sounds impatient. Riley thinks anxiously of Cousin sleeping across the hall. She wonders if you can shatter a windowpane with a fingertip.

She leans forward and looks.

Behind the glass is the boy in a green t-shirt, grinning like a mask. His bright straw hair is cropped short all over, and he's thin. Perhaps he is fifteen or sixteen. His brown eyes are wide; they should look innocent but all Riley can see in them is pleasure. The boy covers his mouth with one hand and laughs at the horror on her face. He must be clinging to the window frame with only one hand now, but he's steady, easy as if he were floating mid-air. He motions with a finger for her to raise the sash.

Riley gently slides the window up an inch or so and bends to look through the crack. She understands that events are now out of her control. There's a momentum to what's happening that can't be stopped. The scent is very strong now; the reek comes in through the window – char and flesh and smoke.

'You followed me from the store,' Riley says. 'What do you want?' She wonders exactly how the boy is going to hurt her. She accepts hurt now, as a part of things. Demons might not be real but people are.

'I just wanted to talk to you,' the boy says, startled, and hearing the voice, Riley realises her mistake. 'You looked sad. And I saw you steal the milk.'

'You're a girl,' Riley says.

'Sure,' says the girl. She touches her shorn head. 'I had to cut it off, it was knotted like a rat king.'

The smell that surrounds the girl is mostly dirt, woodsmoke and unwashed clothes, Riley realises – not meat and sulphur.

'My name's Noon,' the girl puts a hand through the open window for Riley to shake, and the gesture is so homely and regular in spite of the strangeness of it all that Riley can't help but smile. The girl's hand is warm and dirty, with the calluses and scratches that come from work. It's a normal hand. She gives Riley's hand a quick squeeze and holds on.

'How did you get up here?' Riley asks. 'What are you standing on?' She hates heights and even thinking about the girl clinging on to her windowsill two storeys up is terrible.

'I'm a good climber. So why were you sad?' Noon says. She turns Riley's hand over, palm up and looks at it, the bones protruding sharp from the wrist. She reaches for Riley's upper arm and holds it for a moment, assessing. She's gentle, Riley doesn't feel the revulsion she usually gets at the touch of others. It's like Noon is a doctor or something.

'He doesn't feed you,' Noon says. 'But he's big enough.' The house still holds the scent of the fried bacon and eggs Riley made Cousin for his dinner. In the beginning, when they first moved in with Cousin, Riley was very hungry. Now the scent of food, like fat and eggs bubbling in the pan tonight, just makes her feel sick. It's Oliver she worries about.

'Where I live,' Noon says, 'we catch fish from the streams and roast them on open fires. We grow our own vegetables. If we need something we can't grow or catch,' she leans in and whispers in Riley's ear, 'we come to town and we steal it.' Her warm breath fills the spaces in Riley's head. The scent is all around her but now it seems like sun-warm earth and something spicy.

Riley draws a deep breath, head swimming a little. 'You can't steal me.'

Noon grins her mask-like grin. 'I don't want to steal you.'

'No?' Riley feels a flutter of something, fear or something else, hard to tell.

'No. Come because you choose to. Don't you want to be free? Live in the mountains, under the sun and the stars, where everyone gets love and respect? We're all kids, we all escaped something bad. And we decided to make a better place.'

Riley's hand tightens on Noon's. 'It's a good story,' she says sadly.

'Come and see for yourself. Climb out the window right now and come.'

'I'd fall ...'

'I'd catch you.'

'I can't leave Oliver,' Riley says.

'Bring him too.'

'We can't walk through the mountains now, it's night.'

'Maybe we'll fly.'

Riley laughs. But as she looks at Noon, hanging there in the dark, she thinks she sees again that slight rise and fall to her as if she were hovering in the air.

Riley starts at a faint sound from the hallway. Cousin is going to the bathroom.

'I have to go,' she whispers.

'Here.' Noon pulls a scrap of paper from her pocket. It's smudged, laboriously written in block capitals. 'I wrote it all down. Directions.'

'Directions to what?'

'Nowhere,' Noon says. 'Come and find us.'

'That place,' Riley whispers. Her fear returns with a cold blow, it races up and down her spine with small feet. 'My mother told me about Nowhere.' She whips her hand out of Noon's grasp. 'Leaf Winham's place, where he killed those people.' She looks at Noon with dawning horror. 'How are you really staying up here at my window?'

The toilet flushes. Cousin is coming out.

'Go away,' Riley says. 'Don't follow me again. You're a dream. If you're real, I'll call the police.' She draws the window closed as quickly and quietly as she can. Riley crumples the directions in her fist and looks frantically for a place to put them. Cousin does not allow a trash can in their room. He inspects each morning, and sometimes wakes them in the night for extra checks. He looks through their drawers and smells their sheets for evidence of the demon. He checks under the mattress, the insoles of sneakers and in every pocket. If he finds food or candy or any writing or drawings that are not schoolwork, it means the quiet room in the basement. Riley doesn't want to go there. She wonders if the paper with the directions on is too big to eat and decides that it is. She tucks it quickly into her underwear.

As she hurries into bed she glances out of the window. No one is there, just the yellow circles of streetlights and behind that the dark, and the cloud-haloed moon over distant mountains.

By the time the bedroom door squeaks open and Cousin's shape fills the doorway, Riley is lying quiet, her breathing even, her body still as death. Even after the door closes behind Cousin, Riley stays still. Sometimes he listens, ear to the wood.

Under the blankets Riley raises her middle finger, as she does each night, at the old man in the sky. *Eff you*, she mouths at him. *Until I finish school I'll keep going. Only four more years. Then I take Oliver and we go.* The words beat a pulse in her brain, pounding black and white until the black takes over and they follow her into sleep.

In the morning she wakes with an unusual glow in her, a feeling she vaguely recalls from some time past. It's happiness, she realises, though that doesn't make any sense at all. She knows that the boy/girl at the window was a dream. The memory has that feel – of otherness, of being neatly lifted out of reality. But when Riley told the girl to go away she felt the flare of anger and for just a moment she was herself again.

Something feels scratchy. Riley puts her hand gently into her underwear, to find the folded paper resting against her skin.

Riley got caught, the first time she stole the milk from Mountain Foods and Goods.

Mr Assadaya's son was on the register. He was a quiet man, maybe in his early twenties. Riley had never thought about him much. But she slunk past him now, trying to be unremarkable. She had to give Oliver something that wouldn't make Cousin realise they were cheating. He palpated their stomachs sometimes. Sometimes he checked the toilet after they went. Riley had thought about it a lot. Milk was the answer.

She slid open the cold door and took the gallon jug out, silent. The store was empty, it was a good time. She had just started to slide the milk into her backpack when she glanced up.

Above her in the corner was the big convex mirror. Mr Assadaya's quiet son was looking at her, right at her. Riley froze. Their eyes held for what felt like forever. She waited for him to speak, or pick up the phone to the police, or call his dad out from the back. But he just looked. After a long moment he turned away, and started doing something with the cigarettes behind the counter. Riley shoved the milk into her backpack and walked right past him, out the store, not looking left or right. He didn't look up from the cigarettes.

Riley broke out into the cold air and into a run. No one chased after her. The milk sloshed in her backpack. The world was so full of colour. She felt it, now. She understood. There was a power that ordered the universe. It had told Mr Assadaya's son to let her leave. She laughed as she ran, panting, filled with a surge of joy, of gratitude, the knowledge of order in the universe. Riley had seen it in Cousin's eyes – belief. She had seen it in her mother's face. Why shouldn't she know it, too?

As she turned the corner, Riley stopped running. Cousin's house sat squatly at the end of the road. Riley slowed and realised, as she did each day, that she had to sleep there and live there. She remembered the alone place in the basement and that her parents were both dead. Riley fell to her knees on the sidewalk, struggling to breathe. That was when she realised how bad it was, with Cousin. No higher power had helped her steal the milk. It wasn't a sign of grace. It meant that a grownup could look at her and see right away how bad things were. Bad enough to let her steal from them.

Riley wiped her eyes and blew her nose on a receipt she found in her pocket. She pushed herself up from the sidewalk and jogged on, back towards Oliver. She had to get a gallon of milk into their stomachs before Cousin came home.

The day Riley's dad spoke to her mom through the board, she killed herself. At that time he had been dead for twelve years. Riley knows that her father never spoke to her mother through the Ouija board. Her mother just wanted to die.

There is only here, this world. Riley knows. There's nowhere else to go.

Riley is home from school a little late today so Oliver has had lots of time to hide. 'Wherever can he be?' she wonders aloud, searching through each room. But Oliver is not in his high-up place. He is not in his low-down place under the sink, either.

She keeps her voice level, calling, 'Oliver Olive!' She doesn't want him to know that she's starting to get scared. She checks the bedroom and bathroom and living room and then there's nowhere else to look except the basement.

She tries not to feel anything but each hair on her body stands up as she goes down the stairs.

The basement looks mostly ok. It's like a den with a dirty beige pile carpet, a broken couch that sinks soft in the middle, covered with an old rug. There's a TV but it doesn't work. There's a record player, records with faded sleeves falling at a slant against it. The walls are dented brown pine, the overhead bulb swings bare from a length of flex. Sometimes they get mice or rats down here, it can't be helped. It's Riley's job to fill the trays in the corners with the bright pink poison, and collect the dead.

So it looks like a regular basement except for the cubicle in the corner. It has a toilet in it, so maybe it was just a toilet once. Riley doesn't know. The door to the alone room is ajar; someone is crying quietly inside.

'Hey,' Riley says, gentle. Oliver is sitting on the punishment stool. She strokes his head. 'Come upstairs. Let's read or sing something.'

'I can't.'

'Sure you can, Oliver Olive.' She pulls him gently but he backs away, wriggling further into the alone room.

'I said I can't, Riley!' She winces at his cracked, shrill tone. 'The demon is in me so I have to stay here.'

'Cousin's not back from work for hours,' Riley says. 'He can't make you do anything.'

'He's not making me,' Oliver says. 'I have to be punished. I felt it.' He trembles, arms locked about his legs.

'Felt what?'

'The demon.'

The world shifts cold about her. 'The demon isn't real, Oliver.'

'It is,' he whispers. 'Why else does Cousin need to help us so much? It's in my head, telling me things ... just like Cousin said. It tells me to eat. To break open the lock on the cupboard.' Oliver shivers.

'You're hungry, Oliver,' Riley says. 'There is no demon.'

'Then why do I feel it?' Oliver hits himself in the head with a fist. 'Riley. Why do I hear it?' He hits himself again, once, twice. She grabs his arm and pulls him out of the alone room. 'Stop!' he screams.

'Oliver,' Riley tries to soothe him but he writhes away from her.

'I'm trying to get the demon out like Cousin said and you are bad!'

'Remember the plan, Oliver?' Riley holds him tightly, Oliver hits her with his fists. 'The plan is, we wait until I finish school. Then we go. I get a job. I take care of you. You can go back to school. You liked school.'

'No!' Oliver's back heaves with sobs. 'I just want to be good. If we had been good, Riley, and not let the demon in them Mom wouldn't have died.'

'That's not true.' Riley strokes his back, wet with tears and sweat. The centre of things has shifted. She sees that there is no more time. Oliver is breaking. They need a new plan.

Oliver tries to push her away. His arms are like sticks. 'That's your demon talking,' he says. 'Your demon wants you to disobey Cousin all the time. Anyway.' He sniffs. 'Where would we go? Not back to the home.' Oliver shivers and wipes his nose with the back of his hand. 'Not there.'

'No.' Riley is thinking hard. She holds a tissue against Oliver's nose and he blows. She strokes his hair. 'I'll figure it out.'

She goes to the cupboard and pours the pink grains of poison into the little plastic trays.

Riley fries chicken for Cousin's supper. She also makes biscuits and gravy. He likes all these things. She makes him a strawberry pie. Riley sits with him at the table, eating her crackers and her apple in small bites. Cousin likes company and he says it's good for her to watch him eat. It gives her the gifts of humility and gratitude.

The scent of sugar and pastry fill the air as Cousin cuts himself a slice of the warm pie. It's perfect, the pastry crisp and golden. The gleaming strawberry insides spill out red.

*

Riley wakes Oliver at midnight.

He always sleeps with his head under the sheets like a covered corpse. She pulls the sheets down to show his small face, tousled dark hair.

He scrubs his eyes. 'Go away, Riley.' Sisters never get any respect.

'Pants on,' she says. 'Right now.'

'Why? It's night?'

Oliver's legs are so thin. She pulls his pants on with a stab in her heart.

'Why are you inhaling like that?' Riley taught Oliver to spell 'inhale' the other day.

'The demon is coming,' she whispers. 'We have to get out of Boulder.'

He looks very little all of a sudden, way smaller than his seven years.

'My demon?' he whispers.

'Ours. But we can get away from it.'

He doesn't argue anymore.

She pulls Oliver's socks over his feet. They're his favourite; they have a goofy kind of dog on them, from some cartoon he used to watch. The dog has big lunatic eyes. It is called Banana, Nana for short. To Riley, Nana seems frightening or maybe frightened but Oliver loves her and he really loves these socks.

'Shoes.'

Riley shoves Oliver's sneakers on. She pulls a sweater over one bony shoulder then the other. 'It'll be cold out there. And we have to carry what we're not wearing.' Riley can't feel his arm anymore through all the wool. It's like he's vanished. Sometimes she gets this, the breathless panicked feeling that Oliver has gone. Evaporated into air. She touches his head quickly, warm and real. 'I packed everything we need,' Riley says. 'We have to go quiet or the demon will hear.' She can't be sure about Cousin.

Oliver is still only half awake and he weaves and falls against the wall as they go down the stairs. Riley listens for stirring but nothing comes.

'Hurry,' she says. 'It's right behind us.' She almost feels the colour drain from him. Riley feels a hot rush of hatred for herself. It hurts to use Cousin's words to get Oliver away from him. But they have to get away. She's nothing like Cousin, Riley reminds herself. She's doing this for the right reasons.

They're by the door and Riley's about to ease the bolt back when she stops. She nearly forgot it.

'We have to go, Riley!' Oliver whispers. 'Demon!' She has done her job too well, maybe.

'Just a second, Oliver Olive.'

Riley creeps on light feet to the potpourri box on the mantlepiece. It stinks sweet of fake roses. She hates that smell.

She puts a hand into the box. The dried stuff feels nasty, like dead bugs. It's at the bottom but her fingers find it. Cousin can't hide anything from Riley. She has been watching everything he does, ever since they came here. She knows where he keeps it.

The locket settles around Riley's neck, onto her breastbone, the silver cool on her skin.

'That's Mom's locket,' Oliver whispers.

'It's mine now,' she says.

They slip out into the night. Riley slides her thumbnail into the crack and tries to ease the locket open. It stays firmly closed. It has never opened, and she kind of likes that about it. She can imagine whatever she wants inside.

Oliver walks slowly. He's already tired. Riley breaks off pieces of a Powerbar and feeds him in fragments as they go. Earlier this evening, she broke the lock off the pantry and the storage cupboard and raided them.

She has made it final. They can never come back to Cousin's house.

They catch the bus on the corner of Front Street, blinking in the neon glare. The driver has a kind, pouched face like an old orang-utan. Riley feels Oliver wanting to talk to him. He doesn't get much company. She draws him gently to the back of the empty bus. 'If the demon is looking for us,' Riley says, 'we should try not to attract attention.'

It's a twenty-minute ride to the edge of the Rocky Mountain National Park. Riley feels the driver's eyes on them in the rear-view mirror. She knows that she and Oliver are too young to be out alone at this time of night. As the bus pulls up to the dark gates he looks at her and says, 'Someone meeting you?'

'Our mom's just started as a maid over there,' Riley says brightly, clutching Oliver's hand tight. She points at the blocky stack of a motel. Behind it, the Rocky Mountains rear. 'Her shift finishes now and she's got the car. Got to give the keys back to my aunt Mimi, she doesn't drive no more 'cause she don't know her left from right, never did since the boom hit her head, on that TV show she did catering for back in—'

'All right, all right,' the bus driver says hastily. Riley does have this talent – has it for days. She can lie.

Riley bends and pretends to tie her shoe until the red eyes of the bus are closed by dark distance. 'Ok,' she says. 'Time to go!' Oliver trots happily beside her. He doesn't seem to mind about the demon anymore. Real life is always half made-up for kids, anyway.

They go quickly past the empty ticket booths, the ranger station. Oliver doesn't even need to duck to walk under the traffic barrier.

Inside the park everything is different. Quiet but breathing – like it's been waiting for them. A bird calls in the night. *There won't be mountain lions this close to the gate*, Riley reminds herself. *Or bears. There won't.*

She reaches into her pack and pulls it out. Oliver gasps. He's shocked but also thrilled. 'We don't touch Cousin's gun,' he recites.

'I do. You a hundred per cent don't.' Riley has watched Cousin enter the code to the gun safe through her eyelashes, over and over. She knew she might need it.

She makes sure the safety is on and slips it into her jacket pocket. It's only a .22 but it could help. *In the dark? Against a 700-pound bear? Shut up, brain.* There were other guns in the safe, gleaming ranks of sheeny metal. Riley took this old one with its chipped wooden grip and its pitch to the left. She knows a little about how guns behave. Her mother always said, *they're always looking for something to bite and they don't much care what.* So Riley didn't take a really powerful one with big jaws.

'Is it for the demon?' Oliver asks.

'Yup. I'll shoot it dead if it follows us.'

He nods, satisfied. Riley puts on the flashlight and it throws a wide beam up the narrow trail that leads away from the road. Uphill all the way, to above the treeline, to the ridge. Out of the forest they'll be silhouetted against the moon but they'll be able to see anyone coming too.

She takes the directions carefully from her pocket. Noon wrote them on paper already soft with wear. Riley touches it with care.

DAY ONE
WEST GATE – TURN RIGHT
CLIMB UP THE MOONLIT RIDGE
FOLLOW MARKED TRAIL
TRAPPER CABIN
DAY TWO
14 MILES

STRIKE WEST OFF MAIN TRAIL. LILAC IS THE DOOR
DEER TRAIL
PASS THE CLEARING BENEATH TREE LIKE A SHIP
DAY THREE
DEER TRAIL
OVER THE MOUNTAIN PASS WHERE PEAKS HAVE
EARS LIKE CATS
CLIFF PATH
WEST, SUMMER FOREST
THE CLIFF, THE END
NOW FLY
NOWHERE

We'll never find it, Riley thinks. *Never.* And there's no way to interpret the last instruction. But there's also nowhere else to go.

You think you're such a clever clogs. Cousin's voice is in her ear, clear as anything.

Riley has known for a while that she does have a demon, really. It's Cousin, in her head. 'Shut up, you turd,' she mutters. That cheers her up a little.

'Lost my manners,' she says aloud, mimicking Cousin's voice. 'Were you born in a barn? Raised by wolves?'

'Cheerio,' Oliver says, joining in. 'Mustn't grumble.'

Sometimes making fun of people is the only power you have.

The climb is difficult for Oliver. He labours, breathing hard. The rocky slope crumbles like dry toast and more than once they slide, hands scraped bloody, scrabbling for a hold on the loose scree. 'You're doing such a good job,' Riley tells Oliver over and over, which is true. And 'This is the hardest part,' which is a lie.

Eventually they stumble out of the pine-scented dark onto the ridge. The moon lights the land grey, puddles of dark in the hollows. It's like being on the moon itself. Riley holds Oliver's hand tight.

They're the only breathing things for miles around. Or that's how it feels.

'Where are we going?' Oliver asks.

'Up and over.' She points. 'We'll be there in no time.' The wind runs its cold fingers through her damp hair, stealing all her heat. She shivers.

'Eat this and come on.' Riley throws the Powerbar wrapper aside.

'Plastic takes up to five hundred years to biodegrade,' Oliver says, kicking a rock hard up the path ahead. It skitters, the sound echoing off the rock walls around them.

'Don't do that.'

'How much further, Riley?' They're still on the main trail. Dawn is still a few hours away.

'I don't know.'

'But how much—'

'Quiet, Oliver.' She can hear how mean and stretched she sounds. She had hoped they would make faster progress but Oliver is so weak.

'I'm tired.'

'I said be quiet.' She's scared that she has brought them into the wild to die – there are so many ways to die, out here.

Oliver starts to cry and Riley stops and takes him in her arms. He pushes at her with small fists.

'Oliver Olive,' she says, but he shakes his head. It always feels like a missing limb when Oliver is angry with her.

'You're a demon, Riley.'

She catches her breath and takes a moment before she speaks. 'You need to go to the bathroom, clean your teeth, ok?'

'I don't want to!' He points at her. 'Demon!'

'Would a demon make you clean your teeth?'

She remembered to bring toilet paper. She digs a pit for them beneath a stand of briar and fills it in after. After she's disinfected Oliver's hands and given him water and another Powerbar. They eat as they walk. The moon turns their walking shadows into spindly giants.

'You still not talking to me?' They are climbing again and their breath shows white on the air. Oliver shakes his head, but maybe he's just breathless. Anyway, he will forgive her in the end. He must. They only have each other.

When Riley looks upwards she sees it sharply like a shock: the sleek form moving dark against the night. The mountain lion slinks along the ridge, keeping pace with them as they make their slow way along the trail. A single small pebble clatters from the heights above onto the path ahead, echoing through the canyon. Riley's insides are liquid now; she can almost see it, gold eyes glassy in the moonlight, coat slivered, barred with light and dark. Jaws licked by a long tongue. She catches that distinct scent of dried grass and bitterness. She caught it occasionally on hikes with Mom, back in the day – the trace of savagery on the air.

She swallows and it makes a clicking sound. 'Oliver. Stay close to me.' He mumbles something defiant but she grabs his arm hard and drags him in close. She takes the gun out slowly, trains it on the ridge. The skyline is bare. Nothing stirs.

'We have to hurry,' she says. She hopes she's right – that they're near the old trapper cabin in the directions.

Cousin whispers in her ear, '*You nitwit. You're both going to die in blood and jaws and bone and—*'

Shut up.

'Riley?'

'It's ok, Oliver Olive, talking to myself.'

Walk, don't run. She read that somewhere: running triggers the predator instinct. She pulls Oliver behind her at a brisk walk. She can feel the lion out there, she and the lion are focused on each other so tight that they seem to blaze like beacons in the night.

'Riley, don't go so fast,' Oliver says. 'My legs hurt.'

'Keep up.'

'Riley ...'

'One foot in front of the other,' Riley tells him. 'Breathe slow.'

Something gleams ahead on the trail. Riley thinks, *eyes*? But it's moonlight on glass. The trapper's cabin comes into view around the bend, night sky gleaming in the windows.

Something stirs in the boulders above, a squat shape detaches from the rocks. It moves with a tiny disturbance of air, a tail lashing.

Riley runs with her heart in her throat, half carrying, half dragging Oliver.

The hut has timbered uppers above granite walls, shingle roof, windows showing wooden shutters on the inside. *Be open,* she thinks, *that's all I ask. Let the door be open and I'll never wish for anything else again.* The latch doesn't budge when she tries and she screams, rattling it.

The door gives abruptly and they fall into the hut. Riley slams the door shut. Oliver is crying and she takes a second to hug him tight. He hugs her back this time. 'Are they here?' he whispers through his tears. 'The demons?'

'They can't get in,' she tells him. Riley drags a heavy steamer trunk from the corner of the room and rests it front of the door. She can hear her pulse in her ears.

They wait, listening. There is only the wind outside. Slowly Riley's heart settles. Maybe it wasn't even a mountain lion. Maybe it was a curious deer. Maybe it was nothing at all, just pictures in her mind, on the dark.

Or maybe it was Cousin stumbling towards them on the trail, arms swinging, white face crawling with flies, red strawberry spilling from the corner of his mouth.

No.

Riley knows that she must never think about that part. People carry their thoughts in their eyes.

Riley and Oliver roll out their packs. The canvas is waxy-smelling, good as new. Cousin talked about being a survival expert and close to nature. But he never left the city in all the time Riley and Oliver stayed with him. The packs stayed in the store cupboard.

'Oliver Olive,' Riley says, 'come over and share.'

Oliver crawls into her arms and she zips them both up. He wriggles until his body fits her contours. He's trembling. Riley breathes, draws the air down deep, so he can take the relaxation from her body.

'Remember how I tickled your toes when you were born?' she asks.

'Yes.' He always says he remembers things that happened just after he was born.

'I was sitting with you both in the hospital room. Mom was sleeping. You were awake, though. You were looking right at me. And you were confused.'

'I didn't understand how I was outside when I'd been inside.'

'I could see that. It was all too much new stuff. You thought maybe everyone was an enemy. How could you know different? So I grabbed your feet—' Riley reaches down and grabs his socked toes. Oliver squeals with delight.

'Yes, that's the noise you made! Just like that. Then I tried to eat your head ...' she snarls and gnashes her teeth on his dark hair. 'And you just laughed and laughed.' They are both giggling now, it's so stupid. 'Mom woke up, she was mad, but we were just laughing.'

'We were laughing and laughing,' he says, drowsy. She strokes his head, slowly, slowly, until his breath follows suit, and he sleeps. Despite it all he trusts her. He doesn't know any better.

It didn't really happen like that. Babies that little don't laugh. But he loves the story and it's become part of their history.

Riley doesn't sleep much. She keeps her arms free, one hand on the gun. Every now and again she thinks she hears soft breath, as though a large muzzle is pressed to the crack under the door. But either it goes away or it was just the wind.

What really happened is that Riley sat in that hospital room next to Mom, who was passed out, and she watched Oliver as he lay in his crib. He stared around, barely able to see with his little dark-blue new eyes, barely able to wave his little hands and feet, unable to move his little perfect head. She was seven. People don't think kids that young can feel things so deeply, but that's not true. Something woke in her, painful like a tear in the world. Maybe that's always how love is, Riley doesn't know. She only loves Oliver.

Riley touched the little baby's hand, his silken head. *I'll never leave you*, she told him. *I'll always be here.*

Dawn brings a freezing mist. They climbed pretty high overnight and are now at over six thousand feet. She watches Oliver's still face – his closed lids, long lashes soft and dark on round cheeks. She hopes he'll be ok. His breath seems to come a little short in his sleep. They are both hungry and tired and everything seems less and less real the higher they go.

She strokes the locket where it sits under her shirt. Her skin doesn't warm it, somehow. It rests there like a cold secret on her chest.

There was only ever one photo of her father in the house, and Riley has never seen it. It's around her neck right now. The clasp has been broken ever since she can remember. Mom wore it all the time anyway. Sometimes she would stop while she was doing the dishes or in the supermarket or on the phone, and she would just hold it in her fist, like it was warm or gave her strength. After she went to hospital the last time Riley sat with it a while on the front step, tried to slide her nail into it, pry it open. She couldn't. Riley thought about hitting it with a hammer to open it but she didn't want to do that either. She didn't give it to the funeral home, like Mom asked in the note. Riley pretended she couldn't find it. She put it under her mattress. Cousin took it on one of his bedroom searches. But now Riley has taken it back.

Maybe it's a picture of a model or a dog or a rainbow or something. Maybe there's nothing in it at all. She may never know. Riley has never seen the inside of the locket, just as she has never met her father.

They come to a stand of lilacs at around noon. Oliver is slowing, his breathing laboured. It troubles Riley. The hoarse sound, in and out. The sight of his thin legs makes her want to cry.

Riley catches the sweet mineral lick on the air. The lilacs send their perfume ahead of them. There's a buzzing in the air like machinery or a headache. A pool of purple against the green. It's a lilac tree in full bloom, clinging to the rocky side of the peak. Clouds of gnats and flies move over it. On the purple blooms butterflies open and close slow drunk wings.

Riley looks around. It can't be right, there is no trail here. But she takes a deep breath anyway and pushes into the lilac. The scent is overwhelming, almost stinging her nostrils. Behind, she hears Oliver sneeze.

On the other side she comes out coughing. At first she doesn't see it, it's so narrow and faint among the new green growth. A deer trail which cuts directly up into the mountains, into the wild.

'Ok,' Riley says. 'Ok. Lilac is the door.'

'I want to go home,' Oliver says.

'That place we came from – Cousin's place – it's not your home,' she says. 'You and me, we're each other's home.'

His mouth crumples and he pushes past her. The set of his jaw as he struggles away up the narrow trail – it makes her heart catch. He looks so small. Riley jogs to catch up.

'Let's carry on talking about how you were born. Do you remember the story Mom told?'

Oliver shakes his head, silent. But she sees his shoulders unhunch a little.

'Ok,' Riley says. 'I'll remind you. Once upon a time, there was a woman who wanted a baby so much, it filled her every moment and thought. She wanted a little boy with green eyes like this.' Riley circles Oliver's eyes with a gentle finger. 'She imagined him so clearly. A little boy with green eyes who loved to be tickled.'

She tickles his ribs and Oliver screams.

'She wished for him so hard, every morning as she walked in her garden, waiting for the roses to open.' Riley tickles harder, harder. 'The most beautiful rose of all was a blood-red bud, right in the centre. The woman was crying one morning, when the blood-red rose opened and in the centre was a little boy, a perfect little boy with eyes as green as the grass beneath her feet.' Riley pokes him in the stomach and Oliver screams with delight. He takes her hand.

'Mom and your dad were so happy to have you,' Riley says. Oliver's dad was a bartender in Ault. He even sent Mom money for child support before he died. Oliver's dad was an ok guy.

Oliver swings on her hand. 'What about your dad, Riley?'

'I don't have one. I was hatched from an egg like a chicken.'

'No,' he says, delighted. 'You weren't!'

'Swear to god. Mom was just about to make me into an omelette for breakfast, when tap tap tap, the egg cracked open and out I came.'

Truth is often overrated, Riley thinks. Oliver has enough bad stuff in his head for one small person.

Riley checks the directions. There's nothing to do but go ahead. Overhead, white magnolia blossom nods against distant snow. Summer comes later the higher you go in the mountains.

The path winds through blossom and everything smells new and green. Their spirits lift. Oliver bounces along the path. He sees a hummingbird and yells. He's only seven and there is sunlight everywhere. Riley feels a great release. She did the right thing. She knows it now. 'We would have died if we'd stayed with Cousin,' she says gently to the mountain. 'Sooner or later.'

Cousin isn't speaking into Riley's ear anymore. She doesn't believe in such things, but she has a thought she can't get rid of – that it means Cousin is dead.

A lone cedar towers ahead. Its branches form the shape of a ship with sails, rippling in the breeze.

Beneath the tree's shelter in the dusk, Riley builds a fire. She feeds kindling carefully into its small red burning heart. She rinses out Oliver's weird Nana dog socks in a puddle and lays them out to dry on a rock.

The warmth is comforting, as are the flames' crackling remarks. She feels protected here, as the sails of the ship – no, she reminds herself, the leaves of the tree – rustle above. Tall trees take care of you, everyone knows that. Riley tries to keep watch, but her eyes keep closing. The world winks out again and again. She wonders if the lion was even real. The mountains light up old wild parts of the mind. Riley gathers Oliver into her arms and thinks, *a nap. Just ten minutes.*

She wakes completely in an instant. The moon casts long stark light and shadow everywhere. The scent of bitterness and dried grass is strong in her nostrils. The mountain lion is close. No, it's already here.

The fire has burnt down to grey coal but the moon is high and bright. It shows the shape of the man crouching beside the embers. He is tall. In the flickering light he looks lean and lined with weather. He reaches into Riley's pack, going through it with expert fingers. Her mind takes a second to make sense of it – when did mountain lions learn to walk upright? Then she sees. *Oh right – it was never a lion at all, was it.*

'You been following us,' she says.

He turns and smiles and she sees the gaps in his back teeth. It makes the front ones look like fangs. 'Hello, sister.' His voice is deep like wood. 'Something for the hungry?'

Oliver is gone from Riley's arms. Half of her thinks, *where is he*? The other half thinks, *good boy, smart boy.*

Riley pulls a Powerbar from her pocket and tosses it at the man. 'There. Now leave us alone.'

'Travelling is better with company,' he says. He is close to her now though she hasn't seen him move. His breath smells of burnt hair. 'You seem like a girl who doesn't want to be found. I know the trails round here, the places no one goes. The caves, the gullies. Places no one will find you.' The reek of him is as heavy as bonfire smoke. She thinks of Noon. He smells like her, of dirt and smoke. Did Noon lure them to this place? Are they prey?

The man's hand hovers above her knee, strokes the air there, squeezes it. He's showing her what's to come. She sees the bluntness of the stump where his little finger is missing.

'Don't touch me.' She tries to keep her voice even but it comes out thready and high.

'I wasn't going to,' he says, injured. 'Just trying to help you kids out.' He's still wearing the costume of a person who's being helpful. People only wear disguises in the wild when they want to do bad things – things their real selves can't handle.

'I'll yell. I'll scream.' It is the wrong thing to say. Riley knows that as soon as she says it. He smiles. She really is prey, now.

‘Why would you do that? I’ll take care of you. No one would hear anyway. This trail is closed. Too many landslides. Nearly no one comes this way.’ He sounds genuinely sympathetic. ‘Where’s the kid?’ he asks. ‘Your brother?’

‘I don’t know,’ she says honestly. ‘He’s only seven, maybe he got lost.’ All the time she’s speaking, Riley thinks carefully about what to do next.

She waits until he moves his hand, as she knew he would, towards the knife at his belt. This is where the world will change from one thing to another. She reaches too – behind her, slowly – so slowly that she hardly seems to move. She keeps her eyes on his. The man’s face is distant, occupied, almost like he has forgotten about her.

His eyes focus all of a sudden. Now he comes in close, the big body hovers over her like a cage. She smells every thought in his head. They are all there in his sweat, his hair, his breath.

Riley keeps feeling delicately through the leaf mould with silent fingers. She keeps her eyes on the man’s wide brown ones. It’s like they’re going to kiss. Riley has only ever kissed Jared Rubenstein and it tasted like Clearasil. *What a waste*, she thinks, almost laughing out loud. *I’m going to die after just one kiss. Well that one and this one, if he kisses me.* He might not. He doesn’t need to, to do what he wants.

If this doesn’t work Riley hopes that she loses her mind. She doesn’t want to be in her body for what happens next.

Her seeking fingers brush lightly against the barrel of the gun. Her fist settles gently around the grip and she brings it swiftly forward.

He is almost too close, the muzzle brushes his nose in passing. But the movements feel smooth and easy, as if with long practice. She shoots the man twice, once in each eye. She fires a third shot which doesn’t land. The man doesn’t make a sound at first, just keels over backwards. Flat out on the ground, he twitches. Legs full of dance. Little gushes of breath come out, and the air is heavy with the scent as he soils himself. Riley doesn’t take her eyes off him, she watches as he moves from living to dead. Something red and hot is in her. *I did that.* It's terrible, but also her heart pounds with another feeling. Riley takes the flashlight from her pack and trains it on the man. She's hungry so she grabs the Powerbar from the dead man's hand and eats it in three bites watching his still face.

The stump of his missing finger twitches once, twice, faintly a third time. After it stops Riley watches for a few minutes to make sure. His eyes are red tunnels in his face. A creaking sigh comes from his mouth. It's just his lungs giving up their last. He has stopped like a clock.

She kicks his booted foot because she can. He isn't a *he* anymore but an *it.* She unwraps another Powerbar from her pack.

'You can come out now, Oliver!' she yells through her mouthful. *I'm the lion now*, she thinks. There's a kind of dead fire in her.

'Oliver!'

There's no answer. Shock is beginning to settle into Riley, cold ripples up her spine. Her teeth clench then chatter. She presses a hand hard over her mouth.

A sound comes from a clutch of alder. She goes quickly.

Oliver is curled up behind the bush.

'I hid when the demon came,' Oliver says. 'I tried to keep quiet.'

'Smart, smart boy. You did right.'

'Sorry, Riley,' he whispers. 'I didn't hide good enough.'

'It's ok,' she says. 'It's ok, Oliver Olive, he can't hurt us now.' She goes to hug him. She sees it for a couple of moments before she understands – the strange angle he's lying in, how he clutches his shin, the dark, wet stain seeping through his jeans. Riley pulls up his pants leg. The third bullet made a neat hole in the muscle.

'It's ok,' she says again stupidly. 'Don't move, Oliver Olive.' She hunts through her pack, torch beam juddering. At last she finds the little medical kit. Gauze, baby Tylenol, water-purifying tablets, antiseptic, bandaids, sterile gloves. It's not nearly enough to treat a bullet wound.

Riley pushes down her panic and puts on the gloves. The hole in Oliver's leg is leaking blood. Not a lot, but a steady, constant trickle. She can't find an exit wound; the shot must still be in there, buried in his calf muscle. He moans and weeps. 'You're brave, so brave, Oliver Olive,' she says over and over as she swabs the hole with antiseptic and covers it with gauze. She gives him a baby Tylenol with a swallow of water. She finds him a sturdy branch to use as a crutch.

'We'll go slow,' Riley says, bright. 'There's no hurry.'

'What if there are more demons?'

'There aren't,' she says. 'That was the demon. I got it.'

'Promise?'

'Promise. Hey, look at the sunrise.' Riley makes a shield of her palm, hiding the man's body from his view. 'Stay over there, ok? Look at the mountain.' She thinks. 'We have to leave some stuff behind.'

Riley supports Oliver as he hobbles back to the narrow trail. She sees how slow he goes, how much he leans on the crutch.

'Rest, Oliver Olive.' Riley sits him down on a rock. She takes the heavy stuff and throws it hard down the hill, to the bottom of the gully. The pans ring and clang as they go. Riley and Oliver can eat trail mix and dry food. Riley throws the gun down the hill too.

She looks once more at the dead man. In the pink light of dawn his face is young, much younger than it looked by the light of the moon. He's not a man, he's just a boy – not much older than her. He's shorter, thinner than he looked in the night. Riley peers at the thing the dead boy holds in his hand. It's an old-fashioned compass, gleaming silver in the dawn. It wasn't a blade after all.

This is too big to think about. Riley lifts and pushes the dead boy, turning him, rolling him down the slope. He is not stiff at all, which she had been expecting. His upper lip has receded, curled up to reveal his teeth. She looks away and rolls him. The boy's body thumps heavily down the hill – down, down into the tangle of brush. When he comes to rest Riley sees that a frond of fern has settled in his wet eye socket. She reaches out a gentle finger and removes it. Then she makes to close his eyes, to cover those staring red holes. Her fingers meet only an open gash, fast cooling. There are no eyelids to close. Riley's fingertips are red and brown with slick matter. Riley gets up quickly and stumbles as far as she can before she bends double and throws up the Powerbars.

When she's done she closes her eyes and forces it all deep, deep down, what just happened. The boy, the red holes. She pictures it like a cool, deep cave, the place where the bad things live. She puts the memories down there and there they stay, suspended in the dark.

'Riley?' Oliver calls from above, voice high, near panic.

Riley tears a handful of leaves from a bush and wipes her fingers clean of the blood. 'Coming,' she calls. 'Hold on, Oliver Olive.'

Oliver sits on the rock, mouth pursed with worry. He tries to get up and run to her. He sits down again, wincing.

'You ready to go, bud? Does your leg hurt too bad?'

She strokes his dark head and he smiles up at her. 'No,' he says. 'It's ok.'

Some problems can't be forced down into the dark place. They're happening now and all around her. Riley knows that Oliver can't walk through the wild for long. *He's going to die*, she thinks, almost marvelling. *I have killed my brother.*

2

Marc

Marc and Kimble interview the kidnapped woman under a tree, with the mountains blue and rolling behind. It makes a good background for the shot. Annie sneezes, apologetic. She's sensitive to pollen.

'My "Anniegies", my husband calls them.' Annie is diminutive, blonde, and shakes as she tells her story. She holds herself close with her arms at times, as if she is cold. Kimble asks her more than once if she would like to move inside. Annie smiles and shivers and says in a little voice that outside is best. It feels better to talk about it in the open air. After the third time Kimble stops asking. Outside is better for the shot anyway. Annie is framed by the mountains. Somewhere in those peaks lies the place where they took her that day, and kept her for three weeks.

She was in her home, asleep in her bed. She woke at the touch of something on her lips. Dimly, she realised that her husband must have come home early from his trip. Then the cloth settled gently over her mouth. She opened her mouth to scream and it clamped down hard. Annie struggled, then breathed, was pulled suddenly into the black maw of the chloroform. Gone, pecked up into darkness like seed by a bird.

After that, she says, there was dark. Weeks of dark. Then a blazing square of light. Someone cut her bonds and she was free. She was stumbling and slipping down the dew-slick mountainside until she threw herself in front of an eighteen-wheeler, waving her hands and pleading with the driver to stop.

'They took blood from me once a day,' she says.

'With what?' Marc asks.

'A knife. But apart from that they didn't hurt me. They just wanted me for – my blood.' She shivers. 'It was Nowhere, they took me – where I was kept.'

'How do you know?' Marc's warm, inviting interview voice has dropped away. His tone is sharp; he hears it and Annie does too. Her liquid blue eyes go solid, hostile. He looks at Kimble, who widens her eyes. *What are you doing?*

'They thought I was passed out when they carried me in,' Annie says. 'But I saw flashes of things. A broken Ferris wheel on the ground. Sometimes they whispered, "blood in the land". Or "blood on the land". I don't know which.'

'Cut,' Marc says. 'For a moment.'

Kimble doesn't cut. 'What does that mean?' she murmurs from behind the camera. She's talking to Annie but she stares at Marc. He has stopped doing his job.

Annie looks down, silent. Her eyelashes are dark on her cheek. She wants Marc to ask her, not Kimble. It's not unusual for interview subjects to assume that Marc is in control.

Marc takes a deep breath, slow and silent. When he's sure his voice will be steady he asks, 'Blood?'

'They took a little each day,' she whispers. 'It was the Nowhere children.' Annie shivers again, clutching herself. She pulls back her loose linen sleeve.

Kimble zooms in. Annie's skin is perfect, buttermilk, except for the red welts of old cuts, healing now to scars.

'Why do you think a group of children would kidnap you and take your blood?' Kimble asks.

'They worship him. They live up there where all those people died.'

Marc pauses, letting Annie feel what she has said. When he sees it in her eyes he says, 'Tell us about them. The Nowhere children.'

'Most is just what I've heard.'

'What have you heard?'

'Well,' Annie says. A faint flush spreads over her ivory cheeks; she's enjoying being believed. 'They're all runaways. It's a kind of cult but only for kids. They live up there on his old ranch and they worship him.'

'Him?' Kimble asks.

'Leaf Winham.'

Marc nods. For a moment which seems to last an hour, he stares at Annie.

'Did you report it to the police?' His voice sounds slow and thick in his ears.

'I filed a report but nothing happened. They think I'm lying. They think I was with my ex-boyfriend.' Annie's pink lips purse and fold in on themselves. 'I wasn't surprised, somehow, when they took me. When I woke up there.' She shrinks into the chair, becomes even more fragile and delicate, as if collapsing from within. 'Maybe all women feel this.' Annie looks at Kimble, appealing, and Kimble smiles a little, just enough to suggest empathy.

'Feel what?' Kimble asks.

'That it's your fate. Something like this. Like, *I'm just waiting to meet my killer.* I was sure every day that the knife would go into my neck. But it didn't. I don't know why not.' She gasps, wipes her eyes quickly, brushing away the tears. 'Do you know what they fed me?'

Kimble zooms in.

'Two things,' Annie says.

'What were they?' Marc tries to keep his voice level.

'Mushrooms,' Annie says. 'The kind that makes you see things. I was so hungry, I had lost so much blood I would have eaten anything. I saw – I was—' She swallows. 'And the other thing was formula. They gave it to me from a bottle like a baby.'

'I need a minute,' Marc says. Kimble nods. They have learned to give one another space when it's needed.

'Meet me in the square in an hour,' she says. 'Don't be late.'

The floor of the Dew Drop Inn is tacky. The soles of Marc's shoes stick and peel up with each step. He orders whiskey and breathes, letting the smell of stale beer and the country music and the sharp liquor burn do its work.

He calls Silvie. She is crying when she answers and that slices Marc right open. Claude comes on the line, and even though he's trying and he can tell that Claude is too, within a moment they are hissing at each other in an angry blend of languages.

'*Ta gueule*,' Claude is saying. 'You know what you are? Do you *know* what—'

'*Chiante*.' Marc hangs up. Anger courses up and down him. The bartender gives him a measuring look.

'My ex,' Marc says, easy. The bartender nods, understanding. Everyone knows what that's like.

Marc orders another drink, and then another right away to save time. The world is getting that nimbus, that halo around it. He looks at his watch. He has been here for an hour and a half. Kimble will be waiting. He thinks, *I'll just finish this then go*, but when he raises the glass to his lips it's already empty so he orders another.

A woman comes in. She is a small, brown-haired. He saw her earlier, behind the cash register of Mountain Foods and Goods.

'They were in the dumpster again last night, like raccoons,' she says to the bartender. 'Expired meat, Tylenol. The camera caught one of them.' She shakes her head. 'We're a nice town and it's not nice. Trespassing, stealing.'

The bartender gives her a small neutral smile. 'Susie.'

Marc feels the slipperiness of the round stool beneath him. The texture of the air is thick. He needs to get out of here.

'Who was in the dumpster?' he asks.

The woman looks at him, suspicious. 'Kids.'

'But not kids from Ault,' Marc says.

'I don't know where they were from.'

'I make TV shows.' Marc is careful to hit all his consonants. 'I'm making one about this place. Could I look at the surveillance footage? The cameras?'

He pulls his cell phone from his pocket. There are eighteen missed calls from Kimble. He closes his eyes, braces himself. 'Hey, listen, I had some stuff to do—'

'We were supposed to meet an hour ago and that's a pretty loud bar you're in.'

'Don't hang up,' he says quickly. She's silent, he feels her scorn crackling down the line, but she doesn't hang up. 'I've got something.'

In Mountain Foods and Goods, Marc follows Susie down the dry goods aisle. He runs a finger along the very top row of cans. His fingertip comes away feathered with dust. He nods in satisfaction. His sister taught him this. Never buy anything from the top shelf, not in these little places. These cans have probably been here for years. Always buy the things at eye level.

Marc and Kimble crouch in the tiny office at the back. The screen judders, black and white. Then it settles and there they are – at the edge of the light. They wear a hood, and on the grainy black-and-white footage it is impossible to tell much else about them. But they're thin. Marc can see the bones in the wrist poking out of a baggy sleeve. After a few moments the figure slips across the screen and lifts the lid of the dumpster. They duck their head and look around, like someone accustomed to waiting for a blow to fall. Then they lean forward and plunge both arms shoulder-deep into the dumpster.

They toss the dumpster expertly, carefully, sorting frozen meat, pizzas, canned goods, bags of rice and beans. A few vegetables that haven't rotted yet. They are tidy and don't make a mess.

They find something. Their body language changes from casual to relief. They start grabbing cans of something, shoving it into their backpack.

'What is that? he says to Kimble. 'What have they got?'

'Powdered baby formula,' Kimble says, not taking her eyes from the screen. She chews her lower lip and notes the timecode.

On screen the kid thrusts can after can of formula into their bag.

'I don't like it,' Kimble says quietly.

'Do we let the lizard go?' Marc can't tell whether the big feeling sweeping over him is relief or something else.

'That's exactly why we *don't* let go.' Kimble looks up at Susie, who is watching them. 'Can I copy this? I'll bring it back tomorrow.'

'I can't do that,' Susie says with quiet triumph. 'I shouldn't even have let you back here. I might need it for evidence. You know they kidnap people. They steal little kids to join them and take adults for their blood. I could have been killed, sitting here all on my own last night—'

'Come outside for a moment,' Kimble says to her. 'We can talk, just us girls.'

They are gone for maybe fifteen minutes. Kimble comes back holding a tape. 'Let's go.'

'We'll find a motel,' Marc says.

Kimble shakes her head. 'I'm not staying in this town.'

‘Van? Campground?’

She nods and strides ahead out of the store. ‘We’ll pick up food,’ she says over her shoulder. ‘To soak up the bourbon you’ve got on board.’

‘What did you say to her?’ Marc asks. ‘How did you get her to let us have that?’ The road snakes ahead in the low light. Kimble hasn’t said a word since she got behind the wheel.

Kimble bites her thumb. ‘She gave me a note to give to her son.’

‘Ok.’

‘He ran away four months ago. She thinks they took him, or he joined them – the Nowhere children. I told her we were making a documentary about them, that we were going up there.’ Kimble shrugs. ‘So I said I would give the note to him, if we found him.’ Kimble’s hands tighten on the wheel. Her face is calm, you wouldn’t know she was upset unless you were paying very close attention, or knew her really well. Marc can see the simmering in her, the anger in her skin.

‘And?’ he asks, neutral.

‘I’m not going to do it.’

‘Why not?’

‘She told me how to identify him,’ Kimble says. ‘It was by his scars. None on his face, his stepdaddy was careful.’ Kimble takes the note out of her pocket. ‘He had a head injury as a child so he’s slow, she said. The kid was always making trouble so his stepfather had to keep him in line. It got out of hand, sometimes, the discipline.’ Kimble crumples the note in her fist. ‘She defended him, the stepfather.’ She rolls her window down and lets the crumpled paper fly out. ‘I’m not doing anything for that woman.’

They pass the rest of the trip in silence. It’s a relief to go up towards the peaks where things are less complicated. They drive up and up.

They don't see another car on the mountain. Once a herd of deer, glimpsed to the left, melts out of view, startled into forest shadow. This road, like every road around here, feels like you're the first to travel it. Kimble and Marc drive until they find a turnout overlooking a green valley meadow. There's a dented sign with a scratched campsite logo leaning hard to the left. They pull over and sit on rocks to eat the burgers. It's difficult to shake off the day – Annie, the cashier from Mountain Foods and Goods, all the rest of it. The grass waves like silk below.

'*Merde*,' Marc says, absent.

Kimble nods, grim.

Marc screws up his burger wrapper. 'Mountains give me the creeps.'

Kimble breathes deeply. 'I'll ask again. You ok to go on with this?'

Marc realises that the cigarette in his hand has broken in two. Flakes of tobacco fall through his fingers in a gentle shower. He watches with intense regret. It's the last in the pack. He wishes his eyes could set the tobacco alight, turn it to smoke as it drifts. He'd lean in, suck the smoke right out of the air. A dragon taking back its own breath.

'It's a filthy habit,' Kimble says.

'I know,' he says.

'We're just a couple of ridges over.' Kimble points at the rise beyond the meadow, which is dark with pine and spruce. 'It's somewhere over there. Nowhere.'

'You can't know that,' he says, exasperated. 'It all looks the same. Forest, forest, mountain, mountain.'

'Don't be so French.'

'I'm Canadian,' he says, mindless.

'Then this should feel like home.'

'It gets to me. The Nowhere children, all that urban legend.'

'Urban legends tell us who we are, and what we fear.'

Marc kicks a rock like it's the rock's fault.

'I was busy while you were drinking,' Kimble says. 'Tomorrow I'll show you.' She picks up the burger wrapper Marc has dropped. She looks out over the hills, in the direction of Nowhere. 'It seems to happen less often than it did. But it's always the same. They're taken, and they are bled.'

'No access,' he says. 'No corroboration.'

'Patience,' Kimble says, turning her direct gaze on him. 'Lizard tail, Marc.'

It's their rule. Once they have a story by the tail they have to hold on at all costs. Lots of times the tail detaches and the lizard slips off into the dark. But sometimes, it doesn't. So if they get a hold, they cling. They made the rule long ago and it's a good one, most of the time.

'It's gross.' His fingers tremble on the rolling paper and he makes an ugh of frustration. 'Leaf Winham didn't die.'

Kimble's face goes hard as it does when she's confused. 'He did, Marc.'

'He's a virus. Every time someone watches one of those movies, he spreads a little more. We're keeping him alive by doing this.'

Kimble nods. 'It's terrible,' she says, emotionless. 'But it's our job to look terrible in the eye. You know that. And you owe me.'

Marc inhales. 'I don't know what you mean,' he says, distant.

'The hell you don't.'

'Have you heard from Margot recently?' Marc asks, polite.

Kimble gets up and takes the burger wrappers to the trash can. In the glimpse he catches of her face he sees that she hates him. Just in this moment, though. He's sure that it's just in this moment.

Marc finds an old grill pit in the undergrowth and makes a fire. Kimble gives him one of her long looks. 'You nearly dropped the ball back there, during the interview with Annie.'

'Bad day, I guess.'

Kimble leans in close. She smells like detergent, clean hair, healthy skin. 'You nearly lost her. Don't mess with me, Marky Mark.'

'I was waiting to call Silvie,' he says. 'I waited all day. It stole my focus.'

Kimble breathes long and slow. She's trying to push it out with her breath – the anger.

'And?' she asks.

'It's not good.' He is startled to realise that this is the truth. It's just not all of it. Kimble nods. She probably knows he's holding back but she won't push him. She's giving him privacy again. Or maybe Marc has exhausted her, emptied her of the power to care.

They met in Wichita, interviewing a man who had been a serial killer's dentist. He wanted to talk about the serial killer's teeth and his eyes, about how they looked up at the dentist from the chair, red-rimmed, over the serial killer's pink straining cave of a mouth. About how often the serial killer visited the dentist, gums bleeding with hours of brushing – because of the stress of avoiding capture or the pleasure of killing, whatever story Marc decided on in the edit.

The dentist was small and mild. He spoke quietly and precisely, gave them answers any dentist would give. Marc started to wind up. It wasn't worth wasting any more time on it. What had he expected from an interview with a dentist, anyway?

'Last question.' Marc didn't really have another question but it's a good rule, always, to ask more than you need. 'You can see stress in teeth, can't you? Grinding, clenching ...'

'Sometimes.' The man began to shake. 'There was nothing like that. But once there was this thing – I wondered what he had eaten.' Marc felt the camera operator next to him tense. Sometimes Marc gets the interview so right that it feels wrong. It feels like debriding flesh, breaking bone to reveal the chest cavity, the heart where it hides like a little naked animal.

'What did you think he had eaten?' Marc asked.

'During one check-up I found a thing in his teeth,' said the dentist. 'I thought it was tomato, then I thought it was a sliver of carrot.'

'And?' Marc's hair rose slow and gentle off the back of his neck.

'It was just a little sliver,' the dentist said, pleading. 'It could have been any kind of flesh.'

Marc turned to the camera operator to signal to her to get out from behind him, get coverage. She was already moving.

'What was it, in his teeth?' Marc kept his tone gentle.

'He came to that appointment the day after the third woman disappeared.' The dentist's voice had dropped to a whisper.

'The one he—' Marc said. 'And you think ...'

'I don't know,' the man said. 'I wonder every day.' He buried his face in his hands.

Marc wanted to tell the DOP to make sure to stay on the dentist, not to cut just because he's not talking. But then he felt her, silent and attentive at his side. She was getting all of it.

Afterwards, out on the street, Marc and the camerawoman took deep breaths, almost in unison.

'You were good back there,' she said.

'You too.' He offered her a hand. 'Marc.'

'Scheherazade.'

He laughed at the resignation in her face.

'My parents smoked a lot of weed.'

'Let's get something to eat,' Marc said. 'I've got a job coming up in New Jersey next month.'

*

Marc calls her Kimble because of her many ways of being. Like Richard Kimble in the old TV show, or the movie with Harrison Ford. Kimble seems equipped for every circumstance. Her real self is fugitive.

'I'm ok,' Marc says to Kimble now. 'Really.' The firelight cracks and dances. 'Don't worry about me, Scheherazade.'

'Don't call me that.'

'But it suits you so well.'

She snorts.

'They'll only buy this if it features him.' Marc feels the rising pressure of anger and takes a deep breath. 'Leaf Winham.'

The fire spits and they both jump.

'Maybe,' Kimble says. 'It's part of the story, after all.'

'I hate it.'

'Not everyone's like you, Marky Mark.'

'What am I like?' he asks. Sometimes it's better when other people answer this question for you. It means you don't have to do it yourself.

'Blank. It's relaxing.'

'I am not blank,' he says, irritated. 'Anyway you're so back and forth. You go away behind a camera, and then you come out and make people like you and then you go away again. You've got no centre.'

'*Au contraire*,' Kimble pokes up sparks from the fire with a stick. 'I'm just showing you all of who I am. I have layers.'

'I have layers too.'

'But your layers are all the same,' Kimble says. 'All the way down.'

'Wow.'

'It's not a bad thing. There's just no nuance to you. No complexity. You're kind of simple—'

Marc growls. Kimble is already laughing and he can't help snorting in return, because he's not really mad and Kimble's not really being mean. She often annoys him like this when he gets all twisted up inside. It gives him focus. He can never tell whether she knows this and is doing it to help him – or not.

'They don't let anyone near the gate,' he says. 'Maybe it's over before it starts.'

Kimble looks into the fire and smiles. 'I've been trying to say—'

He feels a hard stab of excitement. 'You found the back door.'

She hums, making him wait. 'I was busy while you were drinking.'

'Where is it?' His mind is turning over and over. He feels anxious, excited, sick.

'I'll show you tomorrow,' she says. 'Nighty night, Marky Mark.' Kimble stands. 'I'm taking the back seat.' Vaguely, against the sound of crickets he hears her brushing her teeth, spitting into the forest. Fireflies move above in the forest canopy.

Marc eases himself quietly into the back of the van. He lifts his trouser leg and gently removes his prosthetic and the liner. He cleans the blunt place where his shin ends with an antibacterial wipe and then cleans the socket of the prosthetic. He realises that he forgot to bring lotion. The stump aches, it tells the tale of a long day. Marc makes a small noise of frustration. The pain is deep and massaging it with lotion is the only thing that helps.

'Jesus.' Kimble's voice is thick with sleep. 'Is that a buffalo herd? Or a marching band firing guns next my head? So much noise.' Kimble doesn't like being woken up.

'Sorry.' It takes him a moment before he sees her hand sticking over the back of the seat. She groans and drops something which falls by his feet. It's her fancy mineral vitamin E lotion.

'Thanks, Kimble,' he whispers.

'Shhh please now, shut up shut up.'

*

The hardware store has a hand-painted sign out front. Inside it is deserted.

A bald guy sweeps the linoleum floor in slow, sad strokes. He's thick with muscle. A rose tattoo winds red and green around his neck. Behind him, dirty paper ribbons flutter in the wheezy air conditioning, leading to the stock room, as dark as a lion's den.

'Doesn't look like much of a back door,' Marc says.

'You haven't met him yet. Linus,' Kimble calls.

The bald man lifts his head and fixes them with a level hard gaze.

'Wait,' Marc says. 'How?' The back door is a person.

Kimble flicks Marc a look. She takes off her sweater and hands it to him. It's their code for *I got this.* She goes to the man, easy. 'Hey. Remember me?'

'No way.' The guy turns back to the dark storeroom. 'I already told you.'

'I know,' she says. 'But I have this disorder. It's a bad one.'

'Uh. I'm sorry.' He sounds it, really.

'It might finish me in the end.'

'What,' the man asks, awkwardly, 'exactly—'

'I can't hear the word no,' she smiles. 'Doesn't matter how many times someone says it I just – can't hear it. So I come back again and again, like a curse. I never leave you alone.'

He gives a reluctant cough of laughter.

'It's an affliction.' Kimble nods towards the back. 'You got time for a smoke?'

He hesitates.

'It's just a smoke.' Kimble is honey, voice dripping with it, but also giving him space, letting him feel it's his decision.

'Uh,' says Linus. 'I have a break coming up.'

The afternoon sun has warmed the red brick wall behind the store. Instinctively, they all three lean their backs against it.

'I'm Marc.'

‘Linus.’ In their handshake Marc feels the great size and strength of Linus’s fingers, the many calluses. Linus offers a pack of cigarettes and Marc takes one, grateful. Kimble shakes her head. Marc and Linus smoke.

‘People who see them say they dress like they’re from another time,’ Linus says. ‘Sneakers, flares, old football jerseys. You usually only see one at a time. Two, maybe, I’m not sure.’

‘When they come down, do they take – anything – else?’

Linus smiles. ‘Oh yeah. People, right? Every year one or two claim it. Some say it’s the runaway husband’s excuse.’ Linus draws deep on his cigarette. Smoke wreathes about his face.

‘They come back with injuries.’ Marc thinks of the healing scars on Annie’s pale skin.

‘I don’t know if they’re even still up there, the Nowhere children.’ Linus shrugs. ‘They might have all died.’

‘You just said they come down dumpster diving.’

‘Impossible things can become real,’ Linus says. ‘They exist now. We brought them to life. Even if it is them who come down to steal expired Tylenol and baby food – how are they still children? How can they still be children after all these years?’

‘They’re not the same kids, obviously.’ Even Marc hears the edge in his voice. ‘This is what you were doing yesterday, Kimble?’

‘Marc,’ Kimble says, polite. ‘You got low blood sugar? You need a snack or something?’

Marc pushes himself away from the wall, turns and grinds out his cigarette. ‘Tail’s come off. Thanks for your time,’ he says to Linus. Many people have opinions about the Nowhere children, most of them want to be on TV.

Kimble smiles. ‘Please,’ she says quietly and puts a hand on Linus’s arm. ‘You don’t have to do anything. Just tell him what you told me last night. Otherwise my boss has dragged me out here to Colorado all for nothing.’

'I guess it's the tunnel,' Linus says. 'The one Leaf Winham got out by. I think I can find it again. But don't know if I can go back there.'

'Again?' Marc asks, polite. 'Back there?'

'After last time,' Linus says, apologetic. 'Leaf Winham was trying to kill me when he died.'

Marc feels everything in his body go still.

Linus stubs his cigarette out on the wall, the black ashy stain right next to Marc's. Sunlight catches his jaw, his collarbone, the tendons of his neck. Marc sees it suddenly, like a magic eye picture – the scars. They are almost but not quite covered by the rose tattoo. They spread and branch over Linus's throat.

'People always want to talk about that day,' Linus says. 'I guess it's normal but I can't. So I keep to myself. Like I said, I want to find it – and I don't.'

'It must be hard.' Marc summons it, the shine, the thing that makes people trust and love you. He doesn't like to do it – it's manipulative, even embarrassing maybe. It raises old memories he would rather leave behind. He much prefers to let people pass on by, to be an empty house with blank windows. But right now he will do anything to get what he wants. So for a moment Marc lets himself feel all his love for Silvie, allows it to show in his face and eyes so that Linus sees it too and thinks he's a real human being. 'I'm not going to lie to you. We want to talk about it too, man.'

'I don't know.' Linus's words are slow. Marc feels it working on Linus, the magic, the sun.

'It's your call.' Marc shrugs. 'But this is your story. You should get the chance to tell it your way.'

'I don't know,' Linus says again.

'Ok,' Marc says. 'Different question. What would bring you back? What could – if you ever decided to – take us up there?' Marc asks.

'Ten thousand dollars?' Kimble says, easy.

'What?' Linus's eyes are wide.

Marc can see the child he once was. Doesn't matter, he thinks, shoving down the guilt. Lizard tail. Lizard tail.

'That's right,' Marc says. Neither he nor Kimble has ten thousand dollars but this is the kind of bridge they are used to crossing when they come to it. Though Kimble usually doesn't set such a high figure.

Linus takes another cigarette from the pack, looks at it, then slides it back in. 'Sometimes I think I dreamed it all. The fire, that day. Him, leaning over me. If the fire engine hadn't come down the road at that moment, I would be dead. Leaf Winham cut his own throat when he saw them, you know. He was right on top of me so – his blood was all over, it ran down my face. It was so hot, I hadn't expected blood to be ... I still taste it, sometimes. I dream about it trickling down my cheeks, up my nose, into the cut he made in my neck.' Linus fingers the scar at his throat. 'You don't know what it's like up there. Reality – it gets kind of – thin. Maybe I'd like proof. Witnesses. Maybe if you film it – if we find that way into Nowhere – I'll know I'm not crazy.' He looks away. 'I get stalkers, you know? Death threats. Marriage proposals. All for twenty minutes that happened so long ago.'

'You were part of something important,' Marc says. 'People respond to that.'

'I guess,' Linus says. He rubs the back of his neck so the grey hair stands up like the crest of a parrot.

'Do you mind if we shoot this conversation?' Marc asks.

'I guess not,' Linus says.

Marc nods to Kimble, who turns and runs without a word towards the end of the alley where they left the van.

'Ok,' Marc says to Linus. 'When she gets back, you're going to say all that again, exactly as you just did, for the camera.'

'I want half the money upfront,' Linus says.

'Not possible,' Marc says. 'Payment on return. Take it or leave it. We'll draw up a contract to make it official.' He smiles easily into

Linus's eyes, who smiles back in a lopsided, surprised way. Marc doesn't often smile and people are startled by it.

Kimble comes back with the gear and sets up. Linus pulls out another cigarette then puts it away again. He's nervous. Everyone is stiff in front of the camera at first. Then they get used to it, stop noticing it, even.

Kimble talks soothingly to Linus, makes him laugh a little, gets the mic under his collar. Over his shoulder she gives Marc a quick grin. Marc feels the spread of relief. It's ok, he and Kimble are on the same team again.

Marc needs Kimble. She is the only person who's ever come close to knowing who he is. It's frightening when he suspects she doesn't need him in the same way.

They set out before dawn the following day. The van climbs the steep roads, engine juddering, headlights faint and brave on the thin morning mist. Marc can feel Linus in the back seat – his unfamiliar weight, his foreign breath.

They climb and climb as the sun spreads red on the mountainside. The road winds up and up. Gradually the surface grows rougher, more broken, littered with debris, stones, pocked with holes.

'Do we—' Kimble asks.

'Keep going,' Linus says. Marc swerves to avoid a fallen limb of pine. The road is more craters than surface, now. His teeth click together on his tongue as the van dips and bounces. He winces and tastes the mineral tang of blood. On and on, they climb the flanks of the mountain.

Marc recognises it as they approach – the turnout.

'That's the place,' Linus says briefly. 'Where the cars all used to stall.'

'I'm not familiar ...' says Marc.

'Visitors to Nowhere – their cars all stalled back there,' Linus says. 'So he used to come and get them. It meant they couldn't leave.'

'We didn't stall.'

Linus shrugs, shoulders tense.

Marc watches the turnout retreat in the rear-view mirror. For a second he swears he sees a blue Mustang convertible there. He shakes his head. It's a glitch in his brain, a special effect produced by looking at all those photographs, before he saw the actual place. He has looked at pictures of Leahy's turnout a hundred times. Other people's memories are beginning to overlay reality. It happens when you get too deep into research. Staring at the past, at the faces of the dead, makes them more real than the living. Adam Leahy drove a blue Mustang.

'Are we nearly there?' Marc knows they're close. 'The gates can't be too far away.'

'We're not going to the gates,' Linus says. 'I'll tell you when to turn.'

At last Linus taps Marc on the shoulder. 'Turn up there,' he says. Marc follows his pointing finger. He doesn't see it at first. The dirt track is almost obscured by yellow flowering broom, nodding in the breeze. Marc turns the van slowly. Pollen dusts the windscreen in the late morning light.

The track narrows and narrows. Soon it has all but disappeared, and the van bounces over turf and rock.

Marc brings the van to a halt. 'I don't think we can get any further.'

'Packs on,' Linus says. 'We walk from here.' He is suffused with a strange eagerness. Marc can see him now, in the lines of Linus's sad face – the young man who tried to save Adam Leahy's life.

'How far is it?' Kimble asks, shouldering her pack.

'Half an hour maybe? If you don't walk too slow.' Linus grins wide, showing white tombstone teeth.

'I'm not slow.' Kimble gives him her most dangerous smile. Linus flinches.

They pack up and lock the van, although what's the point, up here, really, and set off up the slope. When Marc turns back for a last look, the van is covered in pine needles, pollen and dust, tyres sunk into the leaf litter. It looks like it's been abandoned for years.

After the rough road, the forest is still and quiet. Somewhere a cuckoo calls.

'GoPro,' Marc says. The three of them put on the headsets. 'We keep these on, ok? All times. Except the obvious.'

Kimble takes a deep breath and smiles at Marc. 'The air is blue and green,' she says.

'Altitude,' Linus says. 'Makes you a little loopy.'

But Kimble is right. Marc breathes deeply and his lungs fill with blue and green.

They climb through pine-scented forest, dappled in sun and shade. After a mile or so the slope levels out and they come out of the trees onto a rise. The world stretches out in every direction, green and brown and far below.

'We'll set up camp here,' Linus says. A ring of scorched stones shows that they are not the first, though it seems impossible that anyone else has ever set foot on this spot, in the deepest wild.

'Let's go tonight,' Kimble says. 'Let's get into Nowhere.' There is a set to her mouth Marc knows well. 'We can—'

'Stop,' Linus says. 'We look for the tunnel. The gate is welded shut but they still come down to Ault to raid. They must be using it.' He puts a hand to his throat. He swallows and strokes the scar with trembling fingers. 'We'll start looking tomorrow.'

'We'll find it,' Kimble says. She loosens, relaxes, stretches hard with her hands high above her head. Nothing makes Kimble calmer than the impossible.

'And I get paid the same no matter what?' Linus's face is suddenly lined and sad. There's need in it.

'Like we said,' Marc replies. He's not sure what they're going to do about that part yet, but he and Kimble always think of something.

'You sure about the gate?' Kimble asks.

'You can see it from here,' Linus says. 'Take a look.' He hands her binoculars. 'Track down from the dip between the third and fourth ridge.'

Kimble looks. Her face blanches. She hands the binoculars to Marc, guides his hand.

He sees a gap in the trees on a rise. Metal gleams in a clearing maybe half a mile away. It is reinforced with corrugated iron, topped with rolls of razor wire. It is ugly, meant to tear flesh. There are things speared on the spikes of the razor wire. They are small bodies. Birds; crows, blue jays. There's something with russet fur, maybe a polecat. A pale, larger body that Marc thinks is a possum. They are impaled, splayed in death. There are also brighter patches of colour – blue, white, green. Clothing, Marc realises. Yellow fabric that might be a t-shirt. A pair of jeans. Streaks of something the colour of rust run across all of them.

'What the hell?' he says, to no one in particular.

'That's the gate to Nowhere,' Linus says. 'We don't go near it.' He bends to his pack to put away the binoculars. 'Better set up camp.' His fingers tremble on the buckles.

In the distance, by the gate laden with dead animals, a narrow point of light gleams briefly like a star. Something reflective, a mirror perhaps, is trained into the fading light. It comes again, winking in and out, once, twice.

'What's that?' Marc snatches the binoculars from Linus and trains them on the gate to Nowhere, but by the time he's found the spot, there's nothing to be seen.

'I guess they know we're here,' says Kimble.

Linus nods, lips pressed tight.

Marc goes close to Linus. 'You're afraid,' he says.

'Yes.' Linus's gaze is direct. 'I nearly died here. It all comes back.'

'What are you afraid of?'

'Them,' Linus says. 'The Nowhere children.'

'They're just kids.' Marc welcomes the anger as it begins to stroke gently at his skull.

'I think they're like him,' Linus says.

'Yes? Who?'

'You know who.' Linus swallows. 'I think that woman you spoke to is lucky to have lived.'

'That's a big assumption.' Marc takes Linus gently by the collar. He's not sure what he's doing but Linus's words make him simmer lightly inside like water coming to boil. 'You want your fifteen minutes of fame, fine. But you've got no moral high ground here.'

'Hey, Marky Mark.' Kimble's grip is so hard on his shoulder he can feel each one of her fingernails. 'Come on. Help me weatherproof the kit. Put the tent up or whatever. I'm doing everything here.'

'Be there in a second.' For a moment he still holds the neck of Linus's t-shirt bunched in his hands. Then he lets go. 'Sorry, man,' he says, the fight they didn't have still coursing in his blood.

'You don't look sorry,' Linus says. Marc smiles. The adrenaline keeps pounding, he sees it in Linus's face too. Their bodies shift, tiny adjustments, aligning in readiness.

'Marc.' Kimble is still beside him. She fixes him with her blank grey gaze. 'The tent.'

He starts. 'Yes.'

Together Marc and Kimble put the gear into canvas and plastic to protect it from moisture and condensation overnight. Kimble reaches for Marc's hand and for a brief moment squeezes the webbing between his pointer finger and thumb. She doesn't look at him. This signal means *What the fuck are you doing?*

Marc seizes her index finger and squeezes it twice in return, which means *What the fuck have you gotten us into, Kimble, what the fuck are YOU doing?*

'Yeah, yeah, yeah,' Kimble sings to herself to the tune of 'She Loves You' by the Beatles, moving away from him and thrusting a tent peg into the ground. And that's as close to an answer as he'll get, for now.

Loneliness hits Marc, blade-like and cold. *It's just work*, he reminds himself. He always feels weird when they've been on the road for a while. He loses his centre, forgets his home. Kimble doesn't. She never loses any piece of herself that Marc can tell.

He wants to call Silvie so badly it's an ache. But phones don't work up here. *Nothing does*, he thinks, hilarious. *Minds, lives, phones.*

Altitude.

3

Linus

Linus is twenty-two, this day in October, when the sun rises in the west at around 6 p.m. He is riding the road back to the station when he sees it, the orange cast behind the mountain, warm against the falling dusk. He knows that light and what it means – a false dawn, made by flame.

Linus pulls over and gets on the radio. He's in the number two engine, his favourite, which he has just picked up from the repair shop. She's been pulling too far to the left on turns and her pump was sluggish. Number two is old but Linus likes her; she's quick and generous, not prone to those little exhaustions and stalling like some other engines. Fire engines can stall, like all engines. *They're only human.* That's a joke Linus likes to make. But number two is a good one.

'I think it's the Winham place,' the dispatcher says. Everyone knows the Winham place. It used to have another name.

Dispatch tells Linus to come back to the station. It's the right thing to do. Linus can't man engine two by himself – can't use the pumps and hose at the same time.

But Linus doesn't do that. 'Send everyone in engines three to six,' he yells back. 'I'm responding.' He swings engine two carefully around across the four lanes, turns her towards that fiery orange corner of the sky, towards the national park. He knows there isn't much time but maybe he can help, get people out. Who lives up there? Apart from him, of course – Leaf Winham. Linus has been in the fire service three years and never seen a death yet. He's been lucky. Today, he wonders, with that turning of the gut that goes with fate, if all that is about to change.

Linus puts on the siren. As he drives he scans the radio. He'll be the first there, he's by far the closest. The Winham place is over by the Never-Summer Wilderness. All the rangers are on the radio, squawking. All across the park they watch as that spot on the horizon brightens, an unnatural dawn. At the entrance gates a police car roars ahead of Linus, clearing traffic to the sides. The police radios take up the call.

Most people call it the Winham place after its famous inhabitant, but its name is Nowhere. It was an apple farm before it was *his* home. Some say before that it was built on the foundations of a Franciscan monastery. Anyhow there's always been a house up at Nowhere.

Linus loves Leaf Winham's movies. His favourite is called *Fallen Kingdom*, about two airline pilots stranded in the wild after a crash. They live in a cave together for ten or eleven years, forming a bond no one can break. When they are finally rescued, they can't adjust to normal life again. They can't handle people, except for one another. So they leave their wives and strike out together back into the forests, never to be seen again. Linus thinks about that a lot, about how if the wild gets inside you, you can't ever get it out.

The radio crackles, a high nervous voice comes across the air. The call finally came in to 911. It's official, now – code 3-25, meaning Linus will use sirens, because there is a fire. A big one.

Linus speeds up. The roads are steep and narrow but engine number two is good, she tries, she rides the steep incline with a roaring motor. The police car falls behind to clear passage for the other fire engines coming up from Boulder.

The gates of Nowhere come into view. Linus sees ash and burning debris on the wind. There is no one at the great automated gates to open them. The guard booth is empty. Linus leaps out with the crowbar. The ground is strange underfoot. He tries to pry the gates apart. He realises quickly that it's no good. He gets back into engine number two and reverses slow and careful to about a hundred feet. He hopes that will do it. Then he guns the engine until it whines and drives at the gates full speed.

He knows he shouldn't but he closes his eyes at the moment of impact. He feels the steel reverberate, as if it's inside his body, part of his bones. The gates part with a crash. Linus and engine number two fly into the grounds of Nowhere.

On either side of the road are split-rail fences. Horses gallop along their length, screaming. 'Sorry,' Linus whispers as he speeds past. The fire will reach them soon enough. The grass is dry, it will go up like tinder, but there's no time to stop. Dark, glistening wide eyes shine in the headlights as he guns the engine. 'I'm so sorry.'

In his rear-view mirror Linus sees a bay mare jump, clearing the posts with ease. A heavy dapple grey with a hogged mane follows suit. His hooves clip the top rail, cracking it. Now horses crowd round the broken fence, pour out and over, their hide shining in the firelight. They gallop out through the steel gates, onto the mountain, into the night. Linus is so glad. 'Run, horses, run,' he screams at them in the rear-view mirror, beating the dash with his fist.

The world lightens as he goes; a moment or two later there's no need for headlights anymore. Shadows stretch long in the orange light. Linus is heading to the centre of it all, the heart of the burning star – Nowhere House.

To the left, through the smoke, something black and spectral is backlit against eerie red. A terrible metal circle. Even in his panic

Linus draws in his breath. They always said there was a Ferris wheel at Nowhere. He takes a corner too tight. Engine two crashes into something that looks like a Wendy house, knocking it onto its side, staving in the roof. A flock of doves bursts from the cote into the black sky. Some of them are alight. All Linus can see through the dash is burning feathers, like fingerpainting on the air. Linus chokes on the scent. Some of the birds get high enough so the fire on them goes out and they fall earthward like comets. One lands on the windshield of engine two. It lies there for a moment, a black skeleton in a ball of fire. Then it is gone. Linus drives.

In the orchard some apple trees have been set alight by the sparks and embers that rain slowly from the sky. The air is full of burning leaves and smoke. Under it is the scent of warm apple pie.

Beyond the orchard the house rears into view, a great timber skeleton against the sky, lit up and beautiful with flame. The first floor is ablaze. For a moment he sees, or thinks he sees, a head silhouetted in the upstairs window. A hand, spread and pleading.

Linus drives engine two even harder, getting ready to unload the ladder. He leaps out, keeping his eyes on the window above, on the fragile, spider-like silhouette. It's the second floor, ok, he can reach that with the ladder on his own. At least, he thinks so. Smoke billows; he reaches, coughing, to release.

In the distance there is the sound of sirens. Linus feels the collapse of relief. The adults are here. They will take care of things now.

'Leaf Winham's up there!' Linus yells. The officer jumps out of a cruiser. Linus knows Lloyd, he's a good guy. 'I saw him, he was waving ...'

Officer Lloyd follows Linus's finger. He looks, expressionless, at the burning casement. Flames lick.

The house is ringed with engines. The fire rages on. By 4 a.m. the water reserves of the forestry service are exhausted. Then the pumps and water tanks along the service roads are all used up. More engines come from Denver. Through the night Nowhere smoulders, flame reviving in unexpected spurts. The firefighters have been unable to reach the window where Linus saw the man waving. Leaf Winham is probably dead.

Linus's chief tells him to go home. He's been on for nearly twelve hours.

'Please,' he says. 'Let me stay.'

Chief Renwick puts a hand on his shoulder and turns Linus about-face towards the patrol cars. His touch is not unkind. 'Get a ride with one of the patrol cars, they're changing shifts.'

Linus nods and Chief Renwick turns away. Linus is already forgotten.

Linus doesn't go towards the patrol cars. Instead he wanders eastwards, around the smouldering house, through the scalded trees. He doesn't know where he's going. He thinks of that head silhouetted in fire, that desperate waving arm. He clutches his helmet in both hands. He's surprised to find that his face is wet, and realises that tears are making their way down his soot-blackened face.

Leaf Winham was Linus's closest companion while his brother had cancer. He watched *Fallen Kingdom* every day. One scene in particular, where the pilots begin to pretend that they are actually half-brothers who grew up together. They invent a childhood for themselves, talking under the trees, in the cold clear forest air. Linus cried, hugging his knees in front of the TV, watching those scenes over and during Matthew's chemo, rewinding and watching, watching and rewinding. Linus's brother recovered. Matthew is married now with three loud kids and a harassed expression and far less hair on his head. Linus loves every part of that.

Linus has not been a firefighter long but he has an idea of what it's like – to burn to death. Flesh blackening, splitting and crackling. At school in history class he could never listen to the descriptions of witches being burned. It's part of why he chose this job, maybe. And the idea of Leaf Winham being gone makes Linus afraid. Maybe the magic can now be reversed, and his brother can be taken from him after all. If Leaf Winham can die eaten by fire then anyone can die, including Linus and everyone he loves. He staggers on through the forest, his boots catching on root systems and fallen boughs. He can't get in a patrol car and go home. If he leaves that's an ending, and if there's no ending there's still hope.

Beside the house is a low, gentle hill topped by a graveyard, marked with small white crosses. Linus had something similar down the bottom of the garden when he was growing up. A pet cemetery. Most houses where kids and pets have lived will. Leaf Winham doesn't have any kids. Linus recalls what they say about him – that he's like a child himself. He looks at the white crosses and thinks, *this whole place is a graveyard now.*

Linus walks. He goes back through the orchard, past the empty paddocks, and out the gate. When he reaches the road he strikes out for higher ground. He needs to stay in constant motion, to feel his legs, to climb the rise. He must be tired, he knows he is, but the chemicals of emergency are still surging in his blood. It's better to be in the dawn forest, to hear a woodpecker drum its tattoo, to leave the scent of ash and death behind. He doesn't know how long he walks, and he doesn't care. He knows these mountains. If he needs a compass point Nowhere is behind him, sending a black cloud of smoke into the pink-blue sky.

'It will be ok,' Linus tells himself, aloud. His voice sends a startled wood pigeon flapping for the rafters of the trees. He's thinking of his brother Matthew, of the pain he was in. It's almost as if he can hear his brother's groaning now.

Linus stops. The sound is not in his mind. Someone is groaning nearby. Linus hears the unmistakable note of pain, injury.

'Call to me,' he shouts, the first responder instinct kicking in. 'Keep talking.'

‘He,’ the man says, voice weaving faint through the trees. ‘Me …’

‘Keep talking.’

‘He … No, he …’

Linus follows the voice, treading gentle. The mountain is deceitful. It has pockets and gullies and secrets. You can walk right past someone and if you’re on the wrong side of a stand of brush you’ll never see them. So Linus goes slow and velvet-soft. He listens so close it’s like he’s hooked to the man’s breath.

So he sees the bear trap when many others wouldn’t. It lies a few feet ahead on the deer trail, half hidden by leaf mould, rusty teeth poking through. Linus takes a deep breath. It’s the old kind with a vicious spring mechanism – what they used to call a shin-breaker. Some of the traps left in these remote parts are a hundred years old. The trappers who set them are all dead but the traps wait in the forest anyway, rusting in the sun and the rain. Some still work. They can bite through to the bone. The traps are often laid in groups along animal trails. Those trails haven’t changed too much in a hundred years so hunters still track them and occasionally someone triggers an old shin-breaker whose jaws lurk deep in the mulch. One guy lost a leg last summer.

‘Keep talking,’ Linus calls, breaking a long branch from the nearest tree. The man – he’s pretty sure it’s a man – groans. He’s close. Linus follows the sound, probing and sweeping the path before him carefully with the tree branch.

The man lies propped against an oak trunk, head lolling. His face is milk-pale beneath dark blond hair. His clothes are spattered with blood, it’s hard to say where it’s coming from.

Linus kneels by him. ‘What’s your name?’

‘Adam,’ the man says.

‘Ok, Adam, I’m going to see where you’re hurt, ok?’ Linus lifts the man’s pants cuff, one then the other. Both his legs are whole. Maybe he fell and his hand triggered the trap. But his arms and wrists are unharmed too.

Adam is panting. 'Have to go. Coming.'

'Who's coming?' He pries Adam's hand away from his throat. At first he doesn't understand what he's seeing. There is a smile there, a bloody mouth in his neck. Someone has slit it. The incision is deliberate but not deep; it's ragged at one end as though Adam pulled or rolled away as the cut was being made. It has been a very bad day but a cold spike is building in Linus, a certainty that it is about to get a lot worse. A person did that, not a bear trap.

'Murderer,' Adam whispers.

'You're ok,' Linus says, soothing.

Under the blood, Adam is covered in smoke marks and soot. He smells strongly of the acrid burning that Linus has just left behind.

'You were at the house,' Linus says slowly. 'You were at the fire. How did you get here?'

'Tunnel,' Adam says. 'Not my fault.' His face is pale and sorry. 'Not my fault.'

'Let's figure out all that later.' Linus puts a shoulder under Adam's and helps him up. His heart is chopping like an axe at what the man has just said. But people say all kinds of things when they're hurt, Linus knows this, even after just a couple of years in the service. He doesn't like the way the wound in Adam's throat is opening and closing as he moves, leaking more blood. He takes his handkerchief from his pocket and ties it around Adam's neck.

'Hurry,' Adam says. His voice is growing dryer and hoarser. 'He's coming. *Tunnel.*' They hobble through the dawn forest, Linus trying to support Adam over the uneven ground. He has lost a lot of blood.

There will be time for questions later, Linus tells himself once more. Tunnel from where? He doesn't want to think about it, or what parted Adam's neck like a slit peach. Tunnel from where? Adam has lost a lot of blood.

Linus finds himself walking faster, almost carrying Adam on his shoulder. He thinks his way to the nearest road, which lies downslope a quarter of a mile away. If he aligns their path east and downhill, in line with the defile between the nearest two peaks, they should hit it soon.

They walk, both breathless. Adam seems almost unconscious at moments. Linus sets their course as true as he can but something isn't right. His head is all messed up. He could have sworn he knew this place like his backyard, but now the trees and land all look the same and he can't seem to figure out the compass points in relation to the sun. The peaks will not stay in place, they're shifting each moment. Are they walking in circles? *Shock*, he tells himself. *It's just shock.* But the feeling will not leave him – it's not just that. The mountain is resisting. Adam now leans almost entirely on Linus. He has begun to make choking, sobbing sounds.

Linus looks behind them, uneasy. Under the noise of their progress he thinks he can detect a slight rustling. An animal in a bush, perhaps. Or the careful step of someone following them through the trees. Linus shakes his head to clear it. 'We're nearly at the road,' he tells Adam, trying to keep his voice steady. Then he sees that it's actually true. Below, through the trees, he sees asphalt.

Linus allows himself to breathe out. Nowhere is still a live scene so there will be traffic going to and fro – engines, police cars. Someone will pick them up. Adam will get help. The flush of relief is so strong that he starts forward, and Adam cries out in pain.

'Sorry,' Linus says, slowing. 'We're good now.'

'No,' Adam says. 'He's coming. I made the fire. Coming.'

'What?'

Adam slumps and pulls Linus down with him, hard. He takes Linus's head in his hands, seems to be trying to crack his head against a rock. Linus struggles. 'No,' he says, 'No ...'

Someone pulls Linus firmly upright. A man, a shape against the light. Adam grabs at their legs and Linus goes down but as he does, the man seizes Linus and cushions his fall. They roll down the hill together. Linus is aware of a pair of strong arms wrapped around him as if in love. They slide together through the leaf mould and dirt until they come to the foot of the hill. Linus's cheek comes to rest on the road. It is already warming in the early sun.

'Are you ok?' asks a voice, one he knows intimately.

Linus grins and rubs his head and says, 'I guess so,' before taking it in – whose voice it is.

'Mr Winham.' Linus scrambles to his feet. There he is, real and tired, face fine-boned and weary. He sticks out a hand for Linus to shake and he takes it, expecting it to be marble or some other inhuman substance, because that is what Leaf Winham is – inhuman. He is made of celluloid and other people's hopes. But the hand is just a hand, warm with a strong grip.

Blood leaks from Leaf Winham's ear, crimson beads trace a path down his neck.

'They think you're dead,' Linus says, blank. Then his breath catches. 'You're dead. So I'm dead.' He feels like crying. He has never thought about dead people crying but it makes sense. It is death, after all.

'You're not dead,' Leaf says. 'We're both ok. I promise.'

'You're bleeding.' Linus is reasonably upset by this – the rich red trickle leaking from his ear.

'Bleeding means you're still alive,' Leaf says, smiling. 'What's your name?'

'Linus. Where's Adam?'

'He knocked himself out in the fall,' Leaf rubs his forehead, weary. 'He was trying to break your neck, I think. So I grabbed you.'

Linus looks uphill and sees Adam stretched out, fifteen feet away. He looks peaceful, face quiet at last. 'Is he ok?'

'Knocked out, but ok.'

'He said he set the fire. Who is he?'

'My cousin,' Leaf says. 'He's sick. I take care of him sometimes because he hurts himself. Sometimes other people. He doesn't mean to, but he does. I don't like those locked-up places. He's family. But this time he went too far. You saw what he did to his throat?'

Linus thinks about how close he was to Adam as they walked, how Adam put his arms about Linus's neck to get over the rougher ground. He thinks of Adam's throat, open and smiling red.

Now, as he looks at Adam's still face, Linus thinks he can see traces of Leaf Winham. He squints. Maybe, probably. All certainties seem to have disappeared.

'Is my house gone?' Leaf asks.

'Mostly,' Linus replies. He can't stop looking at Leaf Winham. 'Did he really burn it?'

'Yes.' Leaf strides back uphill to where Adam lies prone. He kisses each of Adam's sleeping eyelids. 'It was just a house.' Leaf cradles Adam's head. 'It's ok, darling,' Linus hears him murmur. 'I'll always look after you.' He turns to Linus. 'I guess you don't have a radio?'

Linus shakes his head. 'Someone will come along soon enough. They use these back routes for sending the patrol cars home.'

'Ah. Not long then.' He pats the ground beside him. 'Come sit with us.'

'I should wait on the road,' Linus says. Exhaustion is creeping over him like a living thing, crawling up his legs and through his eyes.

'We'll hear the cars coming,' Leaf says. 'You hear everything up here.' Now that Linus listens, he hears it. Every sound, every bird, every whisper of the leaves is clear as though it were engraved. The air is like a living bell. 'Come,' Leaf says again. 'It will be all right.'

Linus gets up, feeling the mazy print of the asphalt road on his back. He can't face being alone. He makes his way determinedly, unsteadily, towards Leaf, his feet sinking into the leaf mould. In the end he crawls on all fours up the hill. Linus sits down next to Leaf, who puts his hand on his shoulder. 'Thank you for helping Adam,' he says.

As Leaf moves his arm Linus sees what lies behind it – what protrudes from Adam's side. The bright pink end of a blow dart. That was not there before Adam fell, Linus is sure of it.

Adrenaline rushes through Linus but he makes himself move slowly. He touches Leaf's hand where it lies on his shoulder as if in reassurance. He slides gently away from Leaf down the hill and starts to lift himself to his feet. Linus's senses are so alert he almost feels the deep sting in the back of his neck before it happens. He puts his hand to the place and tries to pull the dart out. But it has spurs on it or something, which keep it lodged in his flesh. He can already feel it, the poison. Ketamine maybe, or something even faster-acting. There is a soft cracking sound from behind. Slowly Linus turns.

Leaf lays Adam's head gently down on the fallen leaves. Adam's neck bends oddly where it is freshly broken. Leaf looks up at Linus. His face has become unrecognisable. His eyes are dime-bright, face pale and drawn as a skull. Linus realises that he's not a person at all but a thing. He's been playing a human being all this time.

Linus hurls himself away, sliding and falling down the hill. His legs give for good as he reaches the road. He feels Leaf catch him gently as he falls, so that he doesn't hit his head on the hard surface of the road.

'We're in *Fallen Kingdom*,' Linus says, speaking up to the pin-bright eyes that are fixed on his own. 'But we don't love each other.'

'I know.' Leaf Winham slices open Linus's uniform. The little knife is so sharp that the fibres part like butter. He cuts through Linus's cotton undershirt, baring his throat. Linus understands what will happen next, but the poison has him and he can't move. He is trapped inside his still body. Linus breathes deeply and focuses on how to keep doing just that – breathing. He closes his eyes. He doesn't want to see that face looking down at him as he dies.

Leaf tips Linus's head back and the morning air plays about his exposed windpipe, his fragile arteries. As the knife comes down Linus catches the faint scent of lilac.

Late, he thinks. Everything that's happening is so vivid. *It's too late in the season for lilac.*

There is no pain when the knife goes in. The blood smells thick, salty and dark. It pours from his severed throat, flows over his chest. Linus hears the trickle as it pools on the road by his cheek. There's a grinding, a buzzing all over and he knows that it's the last crackle of his synapses, his brain entering death. As his vision clouds over it builds to a roar – sounding just like the approach of an engine.

They find things at Nowhere after the fire. They find the remains of the secret staircase, the spyholes which look out. Hidden behind a half-melted jukebox they find a door which leads to a room with no windows. There is a gurney, there are metal trays of instruments. There is a drain in the centre of the floor, like the ones in abattoirs. There is a small darkroom adjoining, and the walls are covered with the photographs of boys who will never see the sun again. The pet graveyard is not for pets, after all.

Much of Nowhere House is collapsed – walls, roof and foundations. They don't find a tunnel.

Leaf Winham was born like that, people say down in Ault. Or maybe it was Nowhere that made him so. The mountains have their own rules and always have done, especially up at Nowhere. Others know that it was Adam Leahy who committed those acts – it was he who took the boys away from the sun. No one with eyes as kind as Leaf Winham could do that.

4

Riley

She knows they've gone wrong when they cross the snowline on the third day. The trail is just taking them higher and higher. Riley tries to believe that their timing is messed up because of Oliver's injury. But she knows that they're lost. Somewhere the deer trail branched in two and she didn't see it.

Oliver is always shivering. He is cold and hurt and thin. Peaks soar all around them, but not one of them has spurs pointed like lynx ears. Riley wishes it had been a real mountain lion stalking them instead of the boy. That seems much less scary now. She wonders how long it will be before someone finds him. Maybe they've found him already. Maybe they'll never find him. Maybe his bones will get up and walk the mountain, like in that kid's song.

Have you seen the ghost of John?
Long white bones with the skin all gone
Wouldn't it be chilly with no skin on?

Riley threw Cousin's cooking stuff down the hill, far away from the body into the brush, but her fingerprints will be on it all. Should she have buried the body? She just left it there, hoping animals would take care of it. Coyotes, maybe a real mountain lion. She had been beyond thought, at that point. Maybe she still is. *Killed a man*, she thinks, wild, *killed two*— Riley stops the thought right there. It was self-defence.

But he was holding a compass, not a knife.

'Too late for all that,' Riley says aloud.

'Riley?'

'Sorry, Oliver Olive.' He looks up at her and stumbles. She feeds him another Powerbar in fragments as they walk. But she keeps seeing the lion man's eyes – red holes in a pale face. There's a kind of sawing sound – it's her gasping, Riley realises.

Oliver stumbles and falls. He screams in pain as his wounded leg hits the hard rocky trail. Riley feels above herself, removed. The mountain-lion man is ahead of them on the path, walking. He turns and beckons. Riley sees that his hand is bone-white, skeletal. His face has no skin on.

'Long white bones with the skin all gone ...'

'I don't like that one,' Oliver says. 'It's scary.'

Riley realises that she has been singing aloud. They are no longer walking. Riley and Oliver are sitting on the ground and she is stroking Oliver's back and singing. Light snow patterns the air. Her pack starts to roll away gently down the slope. She grabs it, heart racing. She hunts through it. There are no more Powerbars. Maybe she dropped them all, maybe she left them with the dead boy, the point is that they're gone.

How could she have thought they could do this? Follow these weird instructions to a place she's not even really sure exists? *Nowhere*, Riley thinks. *It's everywhere, up here. Everywhere is nowhere.* It is big and cold and doesn't care about them. All around, the mountains peer down at her and Oliver. Just two tiny lives about to stop. Riley sees now that they have faces, the mountains – caves for eyes, crooked jagged mouths of sharp rock. Their expressions are ancient.

Riley thinks she might be screaming but can't seem to hear it. There is only the mountains. The two of them will die and the mountains will go on just the same.

Beside her Oliver is crying again. There is the scent of blood on the air. The wound in his leg gives out thin threads of crimson from under the dressing.

'I tried to make us safe,' Riley reaches for Oliver. 'It's all I ever wanted.' He is crying too hard to hear her, wet tears on his face. She tries to wipe them away but the tears keep coming so she just takes him in her arms. The temperature is dropping steadily. 'Get up,' she says, trying to lift him. 'We have to get over the pass by nightfall.'

'No,' Oliver says, head buried in her middle. 'I don't want to walk anymore.'

'Get up,' Riley says through gritted teeth. Something shifts inside and the voice that comes out is not hers, it's harsh and rasping. 'Get up or I'll leave you behind here, all on your own.' It's a gloating voice from the deep places of the earth. Riley claps a hand over her mouth. She looks at Oliver in horror. His eyes are wide with the same fear. He really believes she might leave him. Too much normal has been stripped away from Oliver. He doesn't trust things anymore. 'I'm sorry,' she whispers. 'I didn't mean it. I wouldn't.'

'Demon,' Oliver whispers. Flurries of snow land on his shoulders and dark head. 'That's your demon, Riley. It made you bring us here.'

'Oliver, we have to move.'

'You always do this, Riley, you always fight with people and make us leave, and you lie all the time ...' Oliver starts to cry.

'Oliver Olive ...'

He looks at her with big red-rimmed eyes. 'Everything was fine,' he says. 'I was beating my demon and Cousin was helping me to know god.' Riley sees for a moment the adult Oliver, looking out of his child's face. Serious. Dark eyes measuring. His voice rises to a scream. 'You had to mess it up, Riley, like you always do, like you did with Mom! I hate you! I hate hate hate you!' His voice cracks and his head hangs low again, exhausted.

Riley grabs Oliver under his arms. He struggles and yells in pain but she keeps dragging him up the slope. 'Come on.' She's talking to herself and him. 'Come on.' They will die out here if they don't walk. Riley feels it, the reality of dying. Oliver's body will fail him, his heart will slow and stop, his eyes will become red holes and he will walk around with no skin on. It will be Riley's fault because she brought them here – she thought they could cross the mountains with Powerbars and pencil directions scrawled on a dirty scrap of paper.

Riley knows she's hallucinating now, because she can hear a sound nearby. It's familiar. At first she thinks it's the wind, but it's not.

'Riley,' Oliver says. 'There's someone!'

'Shh,' Riley hisses. She knows it's the lion man come back for them without his skin. Snow clouds her vision, inside and out.

'Help!' Oliver yells and she clamps her hand over his mouth. Oliver's hands beat at her, ineffectual. He bites her fingers and she yelps in pain despite herself. She holds his mouth harder, but it's too late. The whistling stops, then starts again. Is it coming closer? Riley's heart is pounding now, the snow turns into a sheet of rippling white in her mind. She listens in horror to the footsteps of the dead man as he approaches, whistling the tune she was just singing.

Wouldn't it be chilly with no skin on ...

Riley screams. She turns and stumbles, and she hears it, the actual sound as her skull hits the frozen ground. Everything is black and white and black then gone.

Riley sways gently, tightly enclosed. Everything hurts, she can't move. Caterpillars turn into liquid inside the cocoon, she remembers that from school. She feels like that, she has no solid edges. Memory seeps in slowly. They are in the mountains, Oliver got hurt, the lion was a man and then a boy, he was coming for them and whistling.

Riley tries to sit up but she is swaddled. She struggles, gasping.

She is being carried in an old blanket, twisted up in it like a hammock. Ahead she sees a dark back, hands holding the corners, and presumably there is someone behind her too, holding the other ends. Snow hurtles out of the grey sky overhead. It settles on her face in cold fingers.

Oliver, Riley thinks and starts to struggle. 'Oliver,' she yells.

'Don't move around so much,' someone says from behind and pushes Riley back down with a firm hand. 'He's ok, they've got him.' It isn't the lion man, at least. The voice is young, she guesses he's about her age.

'Where are we?' Riley asks the sky. They are near tundra, she can smell it, the cold frozen loam of the earth.

'Never-Summer Wilderness,' the cheerful voice answers her. 'On our way to Nowhere. That's where you were headed, right? Noon told us to look out for you.'

'Let me go,' Riley says, struggling again. 'Put me down!'

She feels them come to a halt. 'Ok,' the voice says. 'But you have to take it slow. Don't fight like that or we'll all go over.'

They lower Riley to the ground. 'Watch your step.'

Riley's breath seizes in her lungs. To her left is a sheer drop down the rock face. Hundreds of feet below, a thread of silver stream worms its way through a canyon. They are descending on a narrow single-file trail, winding along the cliff. This must be the other side of the pass. To the right pine forest rears up, clinging impossibly to the nearly vertical mountainside. It feels like the trees are going to roll down over them like the sea.

The boy slings the blanket he has been carrying her in over his shoulder. He smiles at Riley, shoving his shock of straw hair from his eyes – a white, dazzling smile. Then she sees that the sides of his mouth are black and empty, missing teeth. He wears an old black velvet jacket, faded in places to green. A smoking jacket, Riley thinks they're called. It's too big for him. 'I'm Cal,' he says. 'What's your name?'

'Riley.'

'That's Everett.' When Riley turns to look at the person behind, who was carrying her feet, she sees a head encased in black wool. Flinty eyes stare out from a balaclava. There's some feeling in his look that's so strong that she can't breathe for a second.

Riley catches the scream in her throat and smiles instead. If people want you to be afraid, smile so that they don't think you're prey. Lies go deeper than words. Riley can lie with her whole body.

The black-encased head gives Riley a tiny nod.

'Everett doesn't talk.'

Riley wonders if they are going to kill her. It doesn't really matter because the drop is way worse. She clings to the cliff like a pinned insect. She feels the height pulling at her, gently, like a sucking mouth. Her breath comes hard.

'Riley's a dumb name,' Cal says, reaching for her. She gets ready to bite but she can't control anything. She is frozen. Cal gently pries her hands loose from their grip on the cliff. 'So dumb,' he says to himself, shaking his head.

'It's a great name,' she says, stung. 'Cal isn't even a name. It's just short for something. Your mother didn't love you enough to give you an actual name?' She doesn't even really know what she's saying at this point.

Cal slides into place beside her, blocking the view of the deep canyon below. 'My mother's dead,' he says. 'Have some manners.'

He sounds so like Riley when she talks to Oliver that she can't help laughing, though it comes out sounding kind of insane.

'Mine is too.' With Cal on one side and the rock on the other, the path doesn't feel so bad. She doesn't feel like she's going to be blown away.

'Where's Oliver? My brother?'

'They ran ahead with him.'

Riley is scared, and exhausted by being scared, and all she wants to do now is hold Oliver and smell his hair. Riley turns and places a gentle hand on Cal's chest. She doesn't push, exactly. She applies the tiniest amount of pressure. Behind him the drop yawns. She hears Everett move, the shift of stones underfoot. He's getting ready. She keeps her eyes on Cal.

'I don't like being apart from my brother,' she says.

'His leg is hurt. They ran on ahead because he was in pain. They took him to Noon. You're too heavy to run with. It's ok, I promise.'

It has been so long since Riley trusted anyone that she doesn't recognise the feeling at first. A homeliness, a relaxation of the mind and body. She trusts Cal, though she has no reason to.

Riley steps back. Everett lowers his raised arm, which, she now sees, holds a machete. The blade is weathered, but sharp. He tucks the blade back into its sheath in some unseen place in his clothing and she thinks, *remember that.*

'Let's go then,' Riley says. As they walk Cal keeps himself between her and the drop. She tells herself that this is good because she can attack at any time. Not because he has put himself between her and that endless fall.

Half an hour later the snow has stopped. They have walked back down through spring, then into the summer.

The sheer wall of rock to the right gentles out and the path veers onto solid ground. It's so wonderful, solid land.

Riley follows Cal along an animal track that runs through rustling summer leaves. Wild jasmine and morning glory are everywhere. The path grows fainter until it's a mere graze, a ghost through the trees.

Riley feels Everett's silence in her wake. 'One of you walking ahead of me, one behind,' she says lightly. 'It looks like you're guarding a prisoner.'

Cal turns. 'You're not a prisoner,' he says, serious. 'You're just about to be free.'

Ahead on the rise is a patch of bright sunshine. The forest is giving way to blue sky.

'Come on,' Cal says. He and Everett run towards the sunlight. After a moment Riley sprints after them.

They run out into the day and skid to a halt by an old ivy-clad oak stump which stands on the lip of a cliff.

A green basin lies below – a valley enclosed by rocky peaks. The long grass of the meadow bends in the wind, as if under a stroking hand. There are low buildings on the valley floor. They look like stables or barns. There are terraces on the distant, facing side of the valley, beds and plantings and things like that – Riley guesses vegetables. She doesn't know much about growing. To the west there is a gleam of water, showing the faint pink of the coming sunset. Beyond the rocky parapets that line the valley the hills are blue whales.

In the distance the eastern end of the valley is covered in green forest which moves gently in the wind. Occasionally through the waving treetops can be glimpsed something skeletal, black and ruined. Riley averts her eyes. If you stare too hard at a grave it might look back at you.

She sneaks a look at Cal's face. His eyes have a feeling. He's glad to be home. Envy rises in Riley. She hasn't felt that kind of happiness since she was small.

'How do we get down there?' she asks. The cliff looks sheer, a two hundred foot drop at least.

'We fly,' Cal says. Reaching into the ivy-clad oak, he produces a kind of harness. Riley sees that there is a thick braided wire running from the oak down to the valley below. It's fastened to a steel bar set between a pair of standing stones out in the meadow far below.

There is some kind of wheel attached to the top. He sets the wheels on the wire where they notch sweetly into place.

'It's a zipline,' Riley says to Cal. 'Really? This is how you get in?'

He grins, white and dark places showing in his mouth. 'This is the fly. It's safe. Watch.'

Everett grips the handlebars and pushes off. He yells, a high, cracked noise of joy. It's the first sound Riley has heard him make. His legs kick the air as he accelerates, descending impossibly fast. As the descent levels out he slows a little but the report when he hits the steel bar between the stones is audible, even from where they stand above.

Everett screams again as he is flung far ahead into the grass, laughing.

'Yeah, he loves that,' Cal says, apologetic.

'But how do you get out?'

'There's a winch at the bottom. Get into the harness, someone turns the handle, up you go.' He reaches for her. 'Your turn.'

'I can't,' Riley says firmly and simply. 'I have vertigo. I can never do that.'

Below, Everett brings the handholds for the zipline back to the foot of the cliff. They put it in a basket with the harness and Cal starts to haul it up.

'You can do it,' Cal says. 'You made it through the cliff path. I saw that you were afraid – but you did it.' Cal takes the harness out of the basket. 'We'll do it together. You hold onto me.'

'No,' Riley says. 'I'll go down another way.'

'There's no other way,' he says, holding out an arm. 'Time to fly.'

Riley thinks of Oliver and lets Cal put the harness around the both of them. She puts her arms about his neck and settles into the contours of him. He smells like warm skin, sweat.

'Ready?' he asks. 'I won't let you go. Close your eyes if it helps.'

But Riley doesn't. If she's going to die she might as well see it coming. They push off and all she can feel is her heart beating against his as they whistle hard through the air. As the speed picks up her eyes water but she still can't close them. Riley concentrates on Cal's warm limbs.

They hurtle off the end of the line, are flung into the long grass.

'I did it,' Riley says. She unbuckles herself and rolls into the meadowsweet, laughing. She finds she can't stop.

'You've got a grip like a monkey,' Cal says, rubbing his neck.

'How many monkeys hug you?' It's a really good joke. Riley doubles over, wheezing.

'Uh, none.' Cal sounds uncertain. Every time she looks up and sees his puzzled expression it makes her laugh even harder.

'Ok,' Cal says, 'whatever, let's find Noon.'

Riley follows him across the grass, lightheaded. Giggles erupt from her at intervals. It's so surprising when things go right after a bad time, it's almost as much of a shock as when they go wrong.

Riley, Cal and Everett head downhill towards the scattering of outbuildings. The ground is covered in young clover and waving grass, knee deep. Something startles as they pass – a pair of jackrabbit ears bounces away above the nodding grass. There's the sound of rushing water nearby. The sun is a fiery trace between two peaks above. It casts a narrow corridor of gold light all down the valley, a path to somewhere.

Riley can almost feel the woodland to the east, dark against the gold and green of the meadow. The giant spider of a house crouched among the trees, pulsing like a heart.

'Is that Leaf—' Riley asks.

Cal holds up his hand abruptly, cutting her off. He and Everett stop dead, grass waving about their knees, eyes trained on the ground at their feet.

They turn to the east, towards the house, not looking at it. Their gaze remains lowered. Both touch their hands to their mouths, and then the two of them reach towards the house as if releasing something on the wind. They do it at exactly the same time, like it's a dance they both know well. They stand tense and still, like they're waiting for an answer. The breeze strokes the meadow. A hawk circles overhead on spread wings.

After a moment, Cal relaxes. He brings his chin up briskly and taps Everett on the shoulder. 'It's ok,' he says and Everett nods.

Cal bends to look Riley in the eye. 'We don't say the name,' he says quietly. 'Come on.'

Riley nods. She has learned something else, now – that they are afraid of Leaf Winham, and that they think he's still alive. Or maybe they're scared of his ghost. But they think he's listening, that they can summon him with his name. It's a vulnerability, and it's good to know where those lie in people.

As they walk, Riley pinches the delicate inner skin of her elbow between sharp nail tips. The pain needles down her arm, her eyes water. Good, she has learned something important. This is a dangerous place. It makes you forget things, like caution, and fear. For a moment back there she felt happy.

The stables sit by an orchard. They have most of their roof and the rest is patched with plywood, corrugated iron and a refrigerator door. Tumbledown but not weird. It doesn't have a pulse, like the spider house Riley saw in the trees. The stable still smells faintly of long-ago hay and horses, their friendly warm breath, as if the building itself remembers them. As they go down the row of loose boxes, she peers over an open half-door. Inside the stall the floor is covered with bits of carpet like the samples you find in warehouses and showrooms. There's a bedroll in the corner. Strings of lights run across the ceiling, glowing red. They're shaped like chilli peppers. Pictures torn from magazines are Scotch-taped to the wooden walls.

'They're ok,' Cal says, defensive. 'They were for horses but they're big bedrooms now.'

'It's great,' Riley says, meaning it. 'Everyone together.'

She hears the crying then, the unmistakable sound of pain. Oliver. Everything else goes from Riley's head. She runs down the aisle towards the sound, flings a door open at the end of the stables.

Oliver lies on an old metal table. He's tied down with climbing rope and Riley's heart hammers; she can see where the rough plastic fibres cut into his legs and arms.

The girl in green, Noon, stands over him holding a needle and thread in a white-gloved hand. She starts as Riley crashes in. A smile spreads slow across her face.

'I'm glad you made it,' she says.

Riley goes to her quickly. She puts herself between Noon and her brother, making her body a shield. 'What are you doing to him?' Even though she can see what Noon is doing. But Riley can never think straight when Oliver's hurt. She unties him, fingers trembling. Noon watches, her expression sympathetic.

Oliver clings to Riley. 'Where did you go?' His throat is dry with crying. 'I woke up and you weren't there!' He sounds a lot younger than seven. Riley feels a terrible twist inside – he's hurt and tired and little and he didn't ask for any of this.

'It's ok, Oliver Olive,' Riley says. 'I'm here now. I'm not going anywhere ever again.'

Noon puts the needle down carefully in a metal kidney dish. She looks more normal in daylight but only a little. Riley finds it difficult to see what her face is really like because her expressions move so quickly, like there are lots of people in there all taking turns. She isn't beautiful or anything. She looks like a stalk of wheat. Tall, hair almost the same colour as her tan skin. She wears a t-shirt and pants, both of faded green. Noon's clothes may be old and fraying but Riley can tell that she's in charge. You learn to work stuff like that out quickly if you've been in the system.

'How did that happen?' Noon nods at Oliver's leg.

'Stray bullet from a hunter,' Riley says. 'It was bad luck.' Oliver's arms tighten on her. He hates it when she lies.

'So, what do you want to do about it?' Noon's voice is neutral.

Riley takes a deep breath. She lets Oliver hold her a moment longer. She sees that one of his feet is shoved into his sneaker, bare. From the other ankle the Nana sock dog grins, its yellow face stained with blood. Riley wishes fiercely that he had two socks. She's doing a bad job at caring for him. Riley takes a deep breath and looks Oliver firmly in the eye. 'You let her sew you up,' Riley tells him.

His face begins to collapse once more.

'You've got to be fixed. Do it brave or do it crying, it has to be done.'

He hiccups, swallows his tears. 'I'll do it brave.'

Her heart hurts but it doesn't matter. There's no time for him to be a kid right now.

'I'll hold your hand and tell you a story,' Riley says to Oliver. 'You don't look at the needle or at her. You look at me. It'll hurt. You make as much noise as you like. But if you move we'll have to tie you down again, you hear?'

He swallows again and nods, trusting her.

In the end she can't tell a story, Oliver is crying too loudly for that. Riley holds his hand tightly and listens to his pain. The needle moves, silver then red.

'You want a drink?' Noon asks, leaning on the metal table. She holds out her hand level, watching it. It was steady while she held the needle but now it trembles. 'Blood makes me feel weird,' she says, and Riley sees she's pretty close to tears too.

Oliver groans in her arms. 'I can't leave him.'

'He'll sleep now,' Noon says, and she's right, Oliver's nearly there already, eyes closing. 'Nature's anaesthetic. Put him down in the end stall. It's Danny's, he's away out on the range right now.'

Noon carries the metal kidney dish with her. There's a little of Oliver's blood at the bottom and she tips it out onto the ground as they go. She bends and whispers something to the earth that Riley cannot hear.

The last stall on the row is lit by a storm lantern. It has a camp bed neatly made, a large jar of jawbreakers, the kind they have in old-fashioned drug stores, and a shoe box of rag-eared paperbacks. Riley looks at the spines. They're all mystery and adventure. Hardy Boys, Nancy Drew. *The Call of the Wild*.

She puts Oliver down on the bed. He curls up tight as a snailshell and is instantly asleep. No blood seeps through the white gauze dressing.

'Here.' Noon gives Riley a handful of gauze and cotton wool. 'Change the dressing once a day. Clean the wound. Put some of this on it.' The tube of antibiotic ointment is three years expired.

'Will he be ok?' Riley asks. 'Will everything be ok?' She doesn't know why she's asking this person she hardly knows for reassurance. But Noon seems like she knows things.

'I hope so,' Noon says. 'I left the bullet in. I didn't think it was a good idea to dig it out.'

Noon hands Riley a flask of something from her pocket. Whatever's in it feels like flame and makes her scream-cough in silence, eyes streaming. She tips her head back and empties the flask into her mouth again. The world flickers. 'I don't really drink,' Riley says, feeling a dumb smile spreading across her face.

'I can tell.' Noon puts a warm hand on her arm. 'Keep the rest of it to clean his leg. Now come on. You need food.'

'Where's food?' Riley is suddenly so hungry it feels like her stomach is cramping and eating itself.

Noon smiles. 'Follow your nose.'

Riley can smell it now. Meat. Fire. She turns and stumbles out of the stable, towards the scent. A hundred feet away through the apple trees a fire burns. There are people, too, but they seem insubstantial to Riley. Only the meat is real. Behind the fire a large barn rises dark against the night.

'This is Home Barn,' Noon says. 'It's where everything happens, pretty much.'

Inside, the barn is lit with storm lanterns. There are plastic lawn chairs scattered round, and some other kids who sneak glances at her, but they're at least trying to do it politely, without her seeing. That's good. People who stare when they first meet you are bad news. These all seem like people from a dream, anyway. Their clothes are ragged and oddly paired. A tall thin girl wears ski pants and a Christmas sweater with reindeer on it. She could be leaning against a fireplace strung with festive stockings if it weren't for the sandals on her feet. Everett still wears his balaclava. There are other people here but Riley's fading, she can't seem to focus or count.

'Sit.' Noon pushes her gently into a chair by the big fire pit which roars red. There are rabbits on spits, eggs bubble in pans. Noon gives Riley a bowl with a rabbit thigh and a couple of fried eggs. Riley scoops up a handful and shoves it in her mouth. There are fresh herbs on the rabbit and meat juice runs down Riley's chin.

Noon kisses her own hand and points to the east. It's the same gesture, like a dance move, that Riley saw Everett and Cal make earlier. Then Noon tears the rabbit with her hands and teeth. Everyone does the same thing before they eat – they kiss their hands and release something eastwards, eyes lowered. Riley wonders why they choose to live here, in the shadow of the house, right next to the thing they're afraid of. But it's a good place, she can see that. No one will bother you here.

The food hits Riley like a drug. The night takes on a texture.

People say things to her but she's floating. She badly wants to eat everything on her plate but she forces herself to stop.

'I'll give the rest to Oliver,' she says. They must be careful, she knows that. Riley and Oliver mustn't take too much from these people. They have to give, not take – make themselves valuable somehow. That's how things work. People don't want you if you're no use to them. Riley needs to be wanted, here at Nowhere.

Riley wakes Oliver gently. He starts to cry but he stops when he sees the plate of rabbit meat. She feed him scraps with her fingers. 'Not too fast,' she says, anxious. 'Don't make yourself sick.'

His head nods with exhaustion. Riley feels the familiar stab – love or worry or both, what's the difference, really? She takes off Oliver's sneakers and strokes his bare foot. Where are they going to get him another pair of socks?

'Tickles, Riley, stop.'

'Ok.'

She curls up gently behind Oliver and there's nothing, after that.

5
Adam

The coffee he makes is really bad, bitter and undrinkable. Adam tries to clean the filter. He doesn't understand coffee machines. Christie left last night to stay at her sister's. He hopes she'll be back soon. The whole apartment seems to hold the energy of their last argument – in its corners, under the sink, in the closets. It's like black needles in the air. Adam gives up and rinses his coffee cup.

Adam is an architect. He has always wanted to make things, unlike other kids who wanted to be firemen or rock stars. He knows brick, mortar, cement – but what he really loves is wood. Adam knows what wood wants, its temper and limitations. He knows how to make it beautiful and how to make it talk. He is shy, not as good with people.

Adam tightens and loosens and tightens his tie in the mirror until it's damp and crumpled. By this time he's late, so he swears at his reflection and runs out the door, trying to remember where exactly on the block he left the car.

He breathes deeply as he leaves the city. The Mustang blows along the roads among the russet leaves. Adam tries to take it slow

– he is still a little shaky – the fight with Christie took it out of him.

The drive out to Nowhere is beautiful. Autumn is well advanced but the deciduous trees are still flush and red. Through them can be seen the land sharp beneath, the sky bright blue behind a lacework of branches.

No one has told him what is needed from him at Nowhere and this adds to Adam's nerves. He is not likely to meet Leaf Winham himself, but the thought of all the hellos and small talk with whoever it might be is exhausting. So much work to be done before he can start to have the real conversation, the only one that matters, with the wood.

Up the road goes, snaking like yarn. Adam likes driving up past the lakes and meadows. It is a different world up here – a higher level of existence, like those medieval paintings of paradise, suspended in the clouds above all the regular dirty mortal business.

He turns off the highway onto an unmarked road that winds along the mountainside. The next turn, to Nowhere, is unmarked too and he drives past it twice, retracing his steps, squinting.

The road goes up in a series of hairpin bends. The Mustang strains. At a certain point Adam realises, startled, that he is driving in silence – the engine has cut out. He steers, cursing, into a gravel turnout. The incline is too steep. Over and over the Mustang's engine roars and strains and dies – he can't get it going again.

Adam gets out of the car, into the mountain silence. The land lies spread out below. It is easy to see how someone could feel like a god.

He has only stood there a moment, wondering what to do, before he hears the sound of an engine on the cold air. A black pickup comes round the downhill turn and pulls up. 'Thought I might find you here,' a friendly voice says. The guy has a baseball cap pulled low over his eyes. Adam catches a glimpse of brown chiselled jaw. He feels his heart lurch. Old instincts, the kind that make people bend low at altars, stir. Even Leaf Winham's jaw looks famous.

'Everyone's engine stalls on this corner,' Leaf says, eyes shadowed in the brim of the baseball cap. 'Thought I'd come check.'

'You didn't have to come yourself,' Adam says. He is startled to hear how high his voice sounds.

Leaf Winham shrugs. 'It's a good day for a drive. Jump in.'

The cab of the pickup is warm, which is welcome. Adam is very aware of the man beside him, his proximity, the tiny rustling movements of his clothes and body. He can smell Leaf Winham, he realises. A spiced, bark-like attractive scent comes from his skin. *Leaf Winham is giving me a ride*, he thinks, and it's hilarious and kind of wonderful and before he realises he has coughed out a laugh.

Leaf shoots him a glance of understanding but doesn't say anything.

The road runs up the mountain. Leaf Winham asks Adam questions. Where is he from? Does he like living in Boulder? Adam answers the questions. After that initial shock he feels almost relaxed. It's such a strange conversation that he has forgotten to be shy. No big deal – just having a catch-up with the star of *Wolves in the Ruins*. Adam loves Leaf's second film. It lived behind his eyes for days after. It was about a group of runaway kids who lived in abandoned tenement blocks in an unnamed city. It was Leaf's breakout role at fifteen. Leaf and Adam are the same age. He has always found this weird – that a person like Leaf could have an age.

A set of high steel security gates looms on the road ahead. Above the arches a wrought metal sign. *Nowhere*. Adam has seen it in pictures. This is the entrance to Leaf's kingdom. 'Welcome to Nowhere,' Leaf says. 'It was called that when I bought it years ago. I kept it because I thought there was nowhere I would ever fit in. I thought it was smart, back then. Edgy. What an idiot. Never got round to changing it.'

The guy who sits in the booth has a gun. A big one. The gates part silently as the pickup approaches, and the guy with the automatic tips his hat at them as they pass. Leaf pulls over. 'Sorry,' he says. 'Paperwork.'

Adam sees a black town car parked behind the gates. A smiling man with silver hair emerges. 'Hi y'all,' he calls. He looks like everyone's favourite grandpa. 'Samuel Ross,' he says, offering Adam his hand. 'Head of security, which means I live a slow life, right?' In the other he holds a clipboard and a fountain pen.

The nondisclosure agreement is weighty. Adam starts to read it and then shrugs and flips to the end to sign.

Don't forget, Adam thinks as he gets back in the pickup beside Leaf, *who this is. Don't be fooled. This is not just some guy.*

They are in a long meadow valley, tool down a pine-scented road. There are paddocks and split-rail fences on either side; horses peer over the bars with curious faces. They enter an orchard ripe with apples. When he leans forward, he glimpses bright colours through the trees. 'Is that a carousel?'

'I bought a whole fairground and had it shipped up here,' Leaf says. 'Crazy, I know. I was using at the time. Back then I wanted everything to be unreal. Nowadays I spend all my time trying to cling to reality.' He shrugs. 'It costs more to move it, now. Plus maybe it's not such a bad thing, having a reminder of the stupid stuff I did when I was high.'

For a moment Adam doesn't know how to answer. Leaf is not what he had imagined. He seems lonely, like someone who hasn't spoken for a while. 'I think about that all the time,' Adam says. 'I'm in all the buildings I design. They're pictures of who I was at the time.'

Leaf turns for a moment with a smile of such sweetness that Adam feels dizzy. 'That's it,' he says. 'So the Ferris wheel speaks for itself. To your left,' he adds.

Adam looks and there it is, a great Ferris wheel against the sky. He snorts before he can stop it, then claps a hand over his own mouth.

‘Yeah,’ Leaf says. ‘I know.’

The house heaves into view. It’s log and shining glass, in the style of a cabin. But eight times the size. He can see an infinity pool up on the third storey. The log is a façade, Adam realises – underneath the house must be concrete, stone. Nowhere House is like Leaf – pretending to be a regular guy.

As they go up the broad steps Adam catches a glimpse of white down the side of the house. A stretch of green grass. White wooden crosses stand upright in the earth. Adam catches his breath. ‘Jackrabbit,’ he whispers. It’s what his grandma taught him to say when going past a cemetery. ‘Who’s buried there?’

‘Pets,’ Leaf says. ‘Cats. A couple of Jack Russell terriers. My chinchilla, Maxy. I find it difficult, letting things go.’

The heavy double doors swing open into a large atrium. Pairs of antlers ring the walls. A row are mounted above the cavernous fireplace. Buckskin and cowhide rugs litter the boards. Two staircases wind up to a high gallery behind. The house stretches out and above, airy. Adam sees how beautifully built it is, how each newel is turned with love. Light pours in from all angles, lighting the room gold. It’s like a cathedral. Adam catches his breath.

Leaf takes off his cap. His face, so familiar from the screen, is startling. It’s exactly the same yet completely different. Leaf has fine lines around his eyes which Adam hasn’t seen. Maybe they cover them with makeup. His hair is dark at the moment, longer than Adam expected. He is smaller, slighter than he looks in pictures. Adam realises that he’s staring, and that Leaf is holding out his hand.

‘Let me take your coat,’ he says, and Adam struggles out of it. For some reason all the holes are in the wrong places but in the end he hands it over.

Leaf takes the coat. ‘Thank you.’ Then he lingers, tapping his finger on his chin. Adam waits politely, and then he understands.

'Oh,' Adam says. 'You don't know where the closet is.'

Leaf looks at Adam steadily. 'No, I do not know where to hang it.' He peers around the room for a moment then gives up and puts Adam's coat over his own shoulders. Adam's worn-out jacket no longer looks shabby but romantic, settled about Leaf's lean frame. 'Let's go to the veranda.'

'Uh,' Adam feels awkward. 'What am I supposed to – can you show me the work?'

Leaf looks at Adam with interest. 'Ok.' He leads Adam to the far side of the hall, where there is a hatch door. He opens it. A dumb waiter shaft yawns black. It makes Adam think of stewed greens and sorrow. He feels like he catches a whiff of those things, ghosts on the air.

'There was an apple farm here once,' Leaf says. 'We used the foundations for Nowhere House. It's difficult building up here. You have to blast into the rock. Anyway, I thought since this shaft runs all the way up the house, we could put it in here.'

Adam waits. He isn't good at everything but he can tell when people aren't finished talking.

'I want a staircase.' Leaf's words seem to come with physical difficulty. 'One that runs all the way up the house. And it has to have places where you can ... look into the rooms. Cameras are no good, the mountain messes with the signal.'

'You want to spy on people?'

'Yeah. I mean, no. I have problems with guests.' Leaf scrubs his face, which is suddenly weary. 'Not everyone is a friend. I always forget. They steal things. They take photographs of my bedroom and sell them. I need help.' Leaf swipes a hand over his eyes but not before Adam sees the tears there. 'I'm sorry. I get how it sounds. This is not your problem.'

Adam closes his eyes – better not watch himself do this, it's insane – and puts his hand over Leaf's. Leaf grips it. His other hand clamps down on Adam's like iron, crushing.

Adam makes an 'ah' sound.

'I'm sorry.' Leaf lets go. 'I really hurt you.'

Adam can't think what to say. He holds his throbbing hand.

Leaf holds out Adam's coat. 'I didn't mean to,' he says quietly. 'I'm sorry. You'll want to leave, now.'

Adam doesn't reach for the coat. He looks at the walls, the height of the house, imagines its inner life. 'You could use the dumb waiter to create a false wall against this side of the atrium,' he says slowly. 'Hide the door with a bookcase that opens into the shaft. Put a spiral staircase in it which goes up through the storeys, ending in your suite.'

'Ok.' The tips of Leaf's ears are red.

Adam takes his coat from Leaf's hands and drapes it carefully over the back of the vast linen couch.

'So you can do it?' Leaf asks.

'Maybe,' Adam says. 'I don't know yet.'

'Let's go outdoors,' Leaf says. 'Everything is better outside.'

Adam follows Leaf's straight back through sunlit hallways. He stares at the man's shoulder blades, the glimpse of neck beneath his dark hair. Adam wonders if Leaf rides the carousel alone, sometimes. He pictures him alone at the top of the Ferris wheel, surrounded by sky, the child shining out of his eyes. For a moment an image crawls into his mind, of Leaf and him together on the Ferris wheel, talking, side by side.

Adam catches his toe in a fold of the soft wool runner that spreads along the corridor. He stumbles, nearly falls, but doesn't. A firm hand catches him. When he looks up his eyes meet Leaf's.

'You ok?' Leaf asks. Adam blushes, something he hasn't done for years.

'Yeah,' he says, distant.

They come into a long gallery, sunlit. 'Cool jukebox,' Adam says. Anything to shift focus. It's beautiful and neon, flush against the wall. He can tell it's expensive, vintage.

'It's bust,' says Leaf, rolling his eyes. 'I got ripped off. Doesn't work.'

They sit on the side porch looking out over a gentle rise of green. White crosses stand upright at intervals. The sinking sun makes a narrow stripe of gold on the hills.

'What's your girlfriend like?' Leaf takes a thin pack from his pocket, which produces an impossibly thin cigarette. The light flares on his face, for a moment he is clear in the narrow Zippo flame.

'She's great,' Adam says automatically.

'Are you in love?' Leaf takes a deep drag on his long slender cigarette.

'No.' Adam feels the world lift up like a physical weight. It's a relief to admit it. 'I love her but I'm not – not that.'

'Have you ever been in love?'

Adam stops. He puts his head in his hands. 'I guess if I had to think about it for that long, no.'

'I've just been in love,' Leaf says. 'Recently escaped or fallen out of it or whatever. Or maybe it's over, but I'm still in it. I don't know.' He takes a photo from his wallet.

'Is that her?' Adam asks.

Leaf looks at him with sunlit eyes.

Adam takes the photograph. It's a young guy outside an Irish bar with a hand-lettered sign. His eyes look troubled. He wears a white vest, jeans, a purple velvet belt. His hair is long, courses down his back, red as autumn leaves.

'Right,' Adam says, embarrassed. 'Ok. I mean, sorry—'

'It's not an emotion, love.' Leaf examines his fingernails. 'It's more like violence. No one tells you that.' He smokes.

'Maybe only some people ever feel it.' Adam has always known that he is not made for such things.

'How lonely,' Leaf says. 'But also, how peaceful.' He coughs and hands his cigarette to Adam. 'I can't. You have it.'

Adam holds the cigarette awkwardly. It makes him feel like he's got too many fingers on his hand or maybe too few. He starts to put the cigarette out but Leaf takes it quickly.

'Don't waste it.'

Adam says awkwardly, 'I've never liked ...'

'How unfair when I love it so much. There should be a happy medium.'

'You should take better care of yourself.' Adam is not sure what's happening to him. Maybe it's the altitude. Every moment feels lit with a brilliant intensity.

'I wouldn't be alive today if I didn't smoke. The things these eyes have seen.' He smiles. 'Does Mrs Adam bake? Does she greet you with a kiss at the door in the evening after work? Is it checkers or gin rummy after dinner? A little blond darling on the way ...'

'Ok.' Adam stands. 'Thank you for the opportunity.' It's all some kind of rich person's game and Adam has his own problems. He wonders how to find his way back to the central hall and the front door, the way out. He wonders how he's going to get back to his car and whether it will start again.

A hand falls on Adam's shoulder.

'I'm sorry,' Leaf says. 'I am – I push and push. It's an old habit. My family had nothing, when I was growing up. You learn to take things from people. My sister took purses from women at the mall. I learned to be hurtful.'

Adam sits down heavily. He puts his head in his hands. 'You're right, though,' he says through his fingers. 'Christie's pregnant. I don't know what to do. We've got no money. I'm not a father. I'm not ready, I'm not ... I feel like I'm being killed,' Adam says. 'My throat cut right through. Every night I wake up from dreams I don't remember and I can't breathe. Something terrible is going to happen. I know it.'

Leaf touches Adam's hand. 'Look.' Adam raises his head. A

butterfly is settled on the railing. It opens and closes slow wings. 'It's a purple emperor,' Leaf says. 'I had a hundred shipped over from England. For the first year after they were released, I thought they'd all died. Didn't see a single one. One day almost a year later I was up at the top of the barn. And there's this oak tree that leans in close to the hayloft. And the branches were covered with purple – there they were. They'd been living up there all the time. Purple emperors are arboreal butterflies. They live in treetops, not down here – usually in oak trees. I hadn't realised, or I'd forgotten, or maybe I didn't care. I wasn't paying much attention to things outside myself at that time. I was in a bad place.' He smiles. 'They do come down to ground level sometimes now. Maybe they've realised that it's home. But they needed that year to adjust. They needed time.'

'It's beautiful,' Adam says, hopeless.

'The point is,' Leaf says, 'this place is kind of outside time. It's like when you're on a boat at sea, or in an airport. You can drink at any time of day and you can hide from the ticking clock. Not forever – but maybe for a little while.'

On the green hill wild rabbits move in the sinking light. They are ghost-grey and gentle among the white crosses. The sky is a haze of gold and blue.

'Have I seen this before?' Adam doesn't mean to say it but the sense of familiarity has been growing in him ever since he got here. 'I can't have done but—'

Leaf smiles. 'She likes you,' he says. 'Nowhere.'

'She?'

'Don't you think Nowhere is a her?'

'Uh,' Adam says, uncertain.

'Let me show her to you.' Leaf takes a case from beneath his chair. He removes three black cylinders, opens them and spreads the plans out on the table carefully. 'This is Nowhere.'

Adam looks closely. One is a blueprint for Nowhere House. It has glass and steel and wood and metric measurements. The next one is a plan for a farmhouse, on yellowing paper. It's simple, the farmer's home when this place was an apple farm. But you can see how the builders blasted the foundations out of the mountain, the rock. The last is a crude diagram. The ink is faded to a pale taupe. It shows a small structure with six rooms, around a central courtyard.

'I'm not sure that one's real,' Leaf says, pointing at the oldest building plan. 'It's seventeenth century. People say there was a monastery up here once but it's hard to check. The other two are ok.'

'This is great.' Adam knows his voice sounds vague. His brain is lighting up. He can see all the ways the old and the new Nowhere fit together, how what came before was used again. 'They're beautiful.'

'They are,' Leaf pauses. 'Look. Would you like some weird advice?'

'Sure,' Adam says. He touches the plan of Nowhere Apple Farm with a cautious finger.

'Sometimes if you hide, you really find things. So you could stay here. Take a break. It might help you work through stuff.' Leaf keeps his eyes on the hill, the crosses, the rabbits, the ending day. 'While you build the staircase. It's much easier if you're on site.'

'That's nice of you,' says Adam awkwardly 'but—'

'It'll all still be there,' Leaf says. 'Believe me. Whatever you leave behind, it will all still be waiting when you get back.'

Leaf looks at Adam and he feels like no one has ever actually looked at him before, or if they have, they didn't see. His body floods with something. Oxygen, relief, something else he's not ready to name.

'Also,' Leaf says, 'I'm particular about work on the house. It's good to keep me happy.'

'I guess I could stay for a while,' Adam says, 'to start it all off.' He feels dizzy.

'Good.' Leaf leans into Adam's ear. 'They feed on urine and dung,' he whispers.

'What?'

'The purple emperors. They feed off bodily waste.' Leaf smiles wide into Adam's face.

Adam coughs. 'That's interesting.'

'It's why I relate to them,' Leaf says. 'It's show business in a nutshell.' He gets up from his chair. 'Come down to the stable and meet the horses.'

'Ok.' Adam's legs feel numb and clumsy. He follows Leaf as he steps off the porch and walks across the green hill, leading the way through the white crosses. Adam pauses and does not follow. He takes the longer way around the hill. The thought of walking over the dead makes Adam uneasy, even if they're just pets.

6

Riley

She wakes shaking from dreams of Cousin – his grey stiff flesh. Dreaming is a good thing though. Riley only ever dreams when she feels safe. Morning light falls through the cracks in the door, Oliver stirs warm in her arms. There are birds calling outside, so many, in rivers of rippling song.

Riley eases out of the stall, closing the stable door gently behind her. She goes to the barn, blinking in the bright daylight. It's mostly empty. A girl – tall, big-boned, strong with a ragged pink mohawk – huddles in a corner, singing to herself.

'I'm Riley.' She knows she should make people like her, if she can.

'I know. Midnight.'

'Uh.' Riley looks at the morning sun pouring in through the barn door.

'It's my name,' the girl says with exaggerated patience. 'Midnight.'

Riley sees that Midnight has a baby at her breast – that's who she was singing to. Riley looks away, uncomfortable. It's too intimate. She feels like she knows too much about the girl too soon.

On a long table in the centre of the room there are dishes, loaves of Wonder Bread and little packs of butter like you get in diners. There are bowls of tiny crimson strawberries.

Riley crams a slice of bread and butter into her mouth. She puts another slice in her pocket to take back for Oliver. When she looks up, Noon is there, close to. She puts a hand on Riley's cheek and smiles into her eyes.

Riley's mom used to call it *having the sun in your head*. When someone looks at you and they shine so much inside it comes out of their eyes. It's a gift. It makes people do what you want. Riley has tried to fake it, she does a pretty good impression but she knows it's not the real thing.

But then, apparently Riley's father had the sun in his head and look how that turned out.

'Come with me,' Noon says.

They walk through summer grass, towards the lake. The light is different here, maybe it's the altitude or sun reflecting on snow on the peaks. Maybe it's happiness. But as Riley watches the light dance on the still water she says to Noon, confident, 'I've been here before.' She stops, confused. 'I don't know why I said that.'

'You've always been here,' Noon says. 'That's how people feel, who belong at Nowhere. When I first saw this place I knew I had come home. It was like I'd just been away for a while.'

'Did you miss me while I was gone?' Riley means it as a joke but it doesn't come out like that.

'Yes,' Noon says. 'Now – we need something dead.'

The rabbit shivers in the wire trap. Riley is sorry, its eyes are big and frightened. She knows how the rabbit feels. Noon breaks its neck with one quick movement.

'You'll settle in, Riley,' she says, taking the corpse up by its long soft ears. 'But there are a couple of things you need to know right away.'

Riley follows Noon to the shore. The water is bordered by a narrow strip of sand, bright white, like a toy beach or a beach in a picture. The water gleams and the reeds dip in the breeze. Riley wants to feel the fine white sand on her feet and she bends to take off her shoes.

'Better keep those on for now,' Noon says. She puts two fingers in her mouth and whistles.

Nothing happens. Riley squints in the sunshine and scratches her elbow. Noon whistles again.

Something stirs in the reeds. It's big. It makes wide trails in the gleaming water as it comes across the lake. Riley glimpses a dark, scaled head, a dead eye.

Noon puts the dead rabbit down on the sand. 'We're going to run now,' she says comfortably. She grabs Riley's hand. 'There's a place we can watch from.'

Riley is staring at the slow thing that is coming through the water. 'But—'

Noon drags her away from the lake and Riley starts back to herself. Noon is right. She does not want to stay to meet the thing in the water. They run to a tree where a rope ladder hangs down the trunk.

'Up,' Noon says. She does sound slightly worried now. 'Hurry.'

Riley climbs the ladder, up into the heart of the tree. Noon is right behind her. There's a platform in the branches. Their arrival startles a cloud of purple canopy butterflies, which burst into the air and then vanish into the blue morning.

Noon pulls the rope ladder up after them. 'Oh, look,' she says, approving. 'There he is. Isn't he beautiful?'

Riley hisses a hard indrawn breath.

The crocodile comes out of the water slowly, made clumsy by land. Its warty hide is dark and sleek-wet on the shore. Yellowed teeth jut out from its closed jaws. It moves ponderously across the sand, lifting one slow armoured leg after another. It is fifteen feet long or so. It's too big to imagine, even though she's looking at it. Maybe it's the biggest living thing Riley has ever seen. The thick heavy tail leaves a furrow in the sand behind it. Somehow Riley finds that most terrifying – the drag of that heavy heavy tail.

The crocodile opens its jaws and takes the dead rabbit in its yellow teeth. Its entire head parts in two, because it is made all of jaws, with two tiny eyes above.

'Aren't you scared of it?' Riley asks. 'What about the kids and babies? What about if it comes in the night ...'

'Listen,' Noon says.

Faintly, Riley hears a high sound from below.

'You'll hear him coming,' Noon says, cheerful. 'I feed him a dog toy now and again, hidden in meat – something that squeaks. His stomach acid always dissolves it in the end. But in the meantime we can hear him coming.'

'It sounds like tiny people screaming,' Riley clutches the railing and watches the dark shape scrape itself across the shore on its belly, back towards the water.

'He won't hurt us,' Noon says. 'We look after him. That's how it works at Nowhere. Balance.' She shrugs. 'He sleeps a lot anyway. It's too cold for him up here. He lived in a tank back before Nowhere burned. There was a kind of zoo. I don't know what happened to the other animals. Maybe they're on the mountain, somewhere. Imagine, herds of wild giraffes and zebras roaming the mountain.' She smiles. 'They would be dead by now, of course. The first winter would have seen to that. So we leave Tinkerbell alone. Ok?'

Riley nods.

'And we don't go to the house. His place.' Noon nods in the direction of the black burnt thing in the distance. 'Except when – just don't, ok? It's not safe. And we don't say his name.' She looks out over the lake. Sun ripples on the water. 'And most importantly, we look after the children. We have five little ones here. We're lucky. We can give them the lives we didn't get. Everything we do here is for them.'

'Ok,' says Riley. Then, in a rush, 'I feel like that about Oliver. He has to be happy. It has to be better for him.'

Noon takes her hand and even though Riley isn't so good with touch, she holds Noon's hand hard for a moment.

'When did you come here?' Riley asks. 'Where were you before Nowhere?' She wants to say, *what were you running from?* But she's not sure she wants to know. And there's no need. She can see in Noon's long look that she understands what Riley means.

Noon looks back out at the lake where somewhere beneath the surface the crocodile is swimming with its prize in its jaws.

'I didn't think he'd live long,' Noon says. 'He's so far from home, in a strange place, his owner gone. I could tell he was scared. Sometimes things can get too scared to stay alive. But he found a way. He was cold and hurt and he got burnt in the fire, but he lived. It's harder than it looks, living.' She looks at Riley closely. 'You don't like him,' she says. 'I thought you might like him.' Noon looks suddenly sad and also a little sulky. Riley can't help but laugh.

'I might grow to like him,' she offers.

Noon takes Riley's hand. 'You're safe here, Riley. I want you to know that. You and your brother. Nothing bad will happen to you here.'

Noon throws the rope ladder back down the tree trunk. 'Tonight you'll see worship.'

'Worship?' Riley asks. Misery and cold rush back in. Thoughts of Cousin. It seemed for a moment or two she could be free here at Nowhere. *But all places and people are the same in the end, aren't they*, she thinks. And everywhere, in the end, there's the old man in the sky.

'No,' Riley says.

Noon turns at the top of the ladder and stares. 'What did you say to me?' she asks softly.

'I won't worship,' Riley says. 'There's no god. No one is helping us. No one cares. I won't pretend. You can't make me.'

Noon smiles a little. 'It's not like that,' she says. 'You'll see.'

Oliver is just stirring as Riley closes the stall door behind her. 'Hey, Oliver Olive. Breakfast.'

He looks at her with mistrust, remembering the pain of yesterday. But the sight of food wins out like it almost always does with hungry people.

Riley changes the dressing. The wound looks pale and dry. She thinks that's a good thing. She smudges butter over the bread, squashing the little square into softness through the foil then spreading it gently.

'Don't let it ...'

'Don't worry,' she soothes. 'I'll be careful.' Oliver doesn't like it when the soft bread tears. You'd think being half starved for months on end would make him less fussy. But when everything else has been taken away only the small things are left. Riley watches him eat a handful of tiny strawberries. He likes those – forgets to be mad at her for a moment, because they're little toy strawberries. Kids like small things because so much of the world is too big for them. It's nice for Oliver to feel like the giant for once.

She wonders if there are too many kids here at Nowhere. Kids aren't that useful, they don't work but still have to be fed. If there are too many kids maybe there won't be room at Nowhere for Riley and Oliver.

What they need is for a space to open up. Riley cuts that thought off, stops it dead.

Midnight leans over the stall door. 'Time to work.' Her baby peeks out of the swaddle at her chest.

Riley gets up quickly. 'Ready.' *Prove your worth.*

The baby smiles at Riley as she opens the stall door and she nods at it in surprise. It is cute, she supposes. She's not really into babies or children. She loves Oliver but that's because he's Oliver.

Midnight takes a step back. 'Don't touch any of the kids here, ok? Keep your distance.'

'I wasn't going to,' Riley says.

'It's just they've grown up here, their immune systems aren't prepared for all the stuff you guys probably brought in.' Midnight turns away, shielding the baby from Riley.

'Whatever,' Riley says, stung. She doesn't want to touch the gross baby anyway.

There are two smaller barns behind Home. Both are full of activity. One seems to be for vegetables – preparing them, preserving them. At each table someone is doing something useful. Riley takes Oliver's arm to help him across the grass. Midnight takes his other arm gently and Riley reluctantly likes her for that. It's weird how the bodies of the people you love can feel like your own, if they're hurt. Riley feels a slice of pain every time Oliver winces.

Outside the low barn she puts him in front of a big basket of potatoes. 'Can you peel?' Oliver nods and Midnight gives him a potato peeler. 'Not going to cut your hand off or anything like that?'

'No,' Oliver says. 'I know how to peel a potato. Riley taught me.'

Midnight takes Riley to a dim shed a short distance away where meat hangs from hooks. She points at a pile of rabbits, soft and grey on the table.

'Skin them,' she says, holding out a knife. She wants Riley to be upset.

'Sure,' Riley takes the knife.

Midnight shrugs and goes.

'Good talk,' Riley calls at her retreating back. She doesn't need to be liked. She needs to be indispensable.

Riley makes cuts along the back legs to leave the belly fur intact, then pulls the hide off the bodies. The rabbits slip out of their skins, buttery smooth. She guts the carcasses and puts the skins to one side, ready to be scraped and cured. Soon the twelve rabbits lie side by side on the trestle table, naked red things, like a neat row of just-born babies.

She hasn't seen anyone at Nowhere wearing fur; she guesses that no one here knows how to treat a hide. Riley can help with that. She touches the soft grey fur with a finger then turns the hide over and starts to scrape it free of fibres. The activity soothes her.

'I came to see if you need help.'

A girl stands in the doorway, a large cooking pot held to her left hip. She is younger than Riley. Twelve maybe. She's so thin all over, it seems like if she turns sideways, she'll disappear. A large overbite gives the impression that her mouth is pursed in thought.

'Thanks.'

'I think Midnight wanted you to mess that up,' the girl said, putting the rabbits neatly in the pot. 'But you're really good. I'm Dawn.'

'Riley.'

'If you're all done, come to the kitchen.'

They walk through the long grass, cicadas singing. The sharp peaks rear up, all around.

'How did people used to get in and out of here?' Riley asks. 'Before.'

'The main gate,' Dawn says, kicking a rock ahead of her. 'But Noon welded it shut. No one can come get us, now. The fly is the only way in or out.'

In the trees to the left, there's a large empty pit carpeted with rotting leaves. There's something naked and bad about the big hole yawning in the ground. Riley thinks, *plague pit, bodies, elephant trap.*

Dawn sees and she laughs. 'It's a swimming pool.'

'Oh.' Riley can see glimpses of shattered blue tile, now, beneath the leaves.

'And it's the prison,' Dawn says. 'If you mess up, Noon throws you in there and puts snakes in with you.'

Riley freezes for a second and Dawn hits her on the arm.

'Not really. We did keep Samson in there for a while.' She smiles. 'Samson was a piglet. He was delicious.'

The kitchen is an old shed with a hole in the roof. It's warm. In the centre of the earth floor is a pit filled with glowing embers. An intricate rigging of ironwork sits above it. There are pulleys and spits and hooks. Dawn rubs the rabbits with salt, wild garlic and herbs, and pours something into the bottom of the pot that smells like beer. Then she puts the lid on and shoves the pot out onto the rigging, over the heat. 'Four hours,' she says happily. 'Then the meat will just fall off the bone. What?' she added, seeing Riley's look. 'I like to cook.'

'Great. I like to eat.'

'I hope you like carrying trash to the compost too.'

They labour across the meadow in the sun, the bag of food waste heavy and warm between them. The compost lies at a distance in a shallow pit in the shadow of two tall crags. It reeks, healthy and humid.

Riley and Dawn work through the morning and early afternoon. There's always something to be done when you live in the wild. Riley's least favourite activity is shovelling soil into the earth toilet. *Prove your worth*, she thinks, wrinkling her nose. Despite herself, Riley is unspooling like wire. It's been so long since she did anything normal like talk to another girl. After they went to Cousin, Riley kept herself to herself at school. Cousin didn't approve of friends.

Dawn whistles really well, the sound reaching hard and high into the air and Riley scrubs and sweeps to the tune of half-remembered country songs. It feels like those Saturday mornings with Mom when Riley was younger. They would clean the house, talking all the while, Blondie pouring from the old record player in the living room. Other Saturday mornings they went to the woods together. Riley still feels her mother's hand on her back sometimes, feels her quiet whisper in her ear – showing her how to train the rifle, their hands wrapped around the stock, holding in the mist of their breath in the cold air. That was before all the mornings went bad.

'How did you get here?' Riley asks Dawn.

'My parents,' Dawn says, cheerful. 'They took me up to the pass one day. Told me to get in the car, we were going for a picnic. I should have known – they never took me out anywhere. A picnic? Plus it was winter. Anyway my dad stopped the car at the top of the pass and my mom got out and opened the back door and pulled me out onto the road. Then she got back in the car and they drove away. That was two years ago. They liked drugs. I think they couldn't afford to feed me anymore. Midnight found me.' She shrugs. 'I don't miss them. They're probably dead now.'

'It's lucky she found you,' Riley says. She remembers the cold up there, the way the white whirling air seemed both inside her and out, as if she hadn't been there at all.

'Noon sends someone to walk the trails every few days. There's almost always something on the highest part of the road through the pass. Pets, usually. Dogs. A frozen sack of kittens. Why do people always leave them just there? Maybe if the snow kills them, the owners feel like it's not their fault. So far I think I'm the only human being who's been dumped.' She clears her throat. 'Midnight found me on the road,' she says. 'But it was Nowhere that sent her there – to bring me home, where I belong.' A second later her grin is back. She squints up the sky.

'Nearly sundown,' she says. 'Time for worship.'

Riley nods.

Dawn looks at her for a moment. 'Noon told me that you don't want to worship – but it's not god, you know. It's more ... it's our own stuff.'

'Sometimes that's even worse,' Riley says.

Things with their mother had been bad for a while so when Riley walked into the kitchen and saw her bent over Oliver, she was glad, at first. She thought, *oh, good, they're bonding*. Mom was ok with Riley but she had always been a little – puzzled by Oliver. Like she couldn't remember ordering him and it was too late to send him back. Lately, Riley often caught her looking at him in silence. There were things in that look which Riley didn't like. So she was glad to see Mom and Oliver together like this. The sun lit them in a halo against the picture window.

Riley saw the board laid out on the Formica table. The letters and numbers, waiting for the dead to speak through them. That wasn't unusual. She had been spending more and more time with the Ouija board recently. Later Riley wonders if it wasn't the first step – her mother prying open the gate to death just a crack, which she would soon open fully and walk straight through.

A sound from Oliver made all of Riley alert. She saw something gleam in her mother's hand. It was a pin. Her mother was piercing Oliver's little thumb. A crimson bulb swelled up where it sank in. Mom wanted Oliver's blood for the board. She had begun to speak about this recently – how the *board* wanted blood. Oliver's face was all squeezed up, but he wasn't crying, he was trying to be brave.

'You can't use family blood,' Mom said brightly to Riley. 'If I want to talk to your father I need someone unrelated. Otherwise I would have asked you.' She said this as if Riley was correctly disappointed at the loss of this opportunity.

In this moment Riley understood the expression 'blind with rage'. It would be easy to assume it's a metaphor or whatever. Riley saw that it wasn't because her world went black. Everything stopped existing for a second.

The next thing she was aware of was her own hard breath and someone else's close by, hot and upset in her ear. There was flesh between her hands. Mom's shiny chestnut head filled Riley's vision, she smelled coconut shampoo.

Her mother hacked and wheezed, clawing at Riley's grip on her throat.

'Don't you hurt him,' Riley said. 'Not ever.'

Her mother waved an urgent hand, a rattle in her throat. Riley slowly unclenched her hands from her mother's neck. There were little dark ghosts of Riley's fingers on her skin. Her mother got up and went from the room. She wore her hair down for a week, though neither she nor Riley ever mentioned what happened. Riley watched her all the time after that. She tried to never leave her mother alone with her brother. Her mother had problems. It was difficult to be her child, her daughter. Sometimes Riley feels those problems stirring in her own mind. She gets a dark tightness inside that makes her do things. Riley looks back on her mother's sorrow and anger and thinks, *yes, I get that. I understand why.* Sometimes when Riley looks in the mirror she sees her mother looking back – the same vague, unfocused gaze she fixed on Oliver as she put the pin into his thumb.

Riley doesn't like the old man in the sky but she likes the other stuff even less. These are the reasons why, probably.

Dawn takes them up through the orchard, away from the stables. The others are already gathered, Riley can hear voices ahead.

The path weaves behind a fold of red rock into a clearing in the orchard. The Nowhere children are sitting and standing on the grass. There's talk and laughter. It's like a picnic.

Behind them there is something metal, rusted and broken like the remains of a burnt-out star. A couple of cabs are still attached to it, lying on the grass. Their chains swing and chink in the wind. It's not possible grounded as it is, but the great metal circle seems to turn slightly as she watches. Crows sit along its bars, cawing.

'It's a Ferris wheel,' Riley says, blank. Beside her, Oliver squeaks with excitement. He must have some dim memory of a fair. Riley has it too, though she can't recall exactly when – a vague impression of being allowed to stay up late, of funnel cake and cotton candy. Of Mom.

'Careful of your leg,' Riley says. 'Don't jump around like that. You can't go on that wheel. Look, it's old and broken.' The more Riley looks at the wheel the less she likes it. It's like skeletal remains.

It's so unexpected that Riley can't escape the impression that it has been hiding all this time.

The late afternoon air is still warm but the kids have got blankets and comforters. Riley sees newspaper peeking from waistbands and out of the collars of sweaters. Insulation. One small red-headed child, a boy she thinks, toddles unsteadily across the grass, wrapped in an electric blanket. The cord trails after, the plug leaving a line in the soft dirt floor. He points a tiny finger at Riley.

'Hi,' Riley says.

The little kid smiles, bright. 'Mommy,' he says.

'No.' Riley is shaken, she doesn't know why. 'Go find your real mommy.'

'Come here, Rufus,' calls Noon from across the clearing. Rufus smiles and wanders away.

There are five little children, including Midnight's baby. The oldest looks about nine. Riley worries, again, about that. She's uneasy because there don't seem to be any grownups here. Riley and Oliver need lots of working adults so Nowhere can support two new arrivals. The kids are happy and dirty. One of them grabs a cushion from another one and they both cry, pointing at each other. Midnight comes over and scolds them. Her baby's eyes go round and startled at her raised voice and Riley can't help laughing, it looks so surprised. There's another feeling in her, a painful-sweet pull. It's the first time she's been around a family in a while.

She sees it in Oliver's face too. 'Can I go play with them, Riley?'

Riley's smile suddenly feels thin and brittle. 'Not right ...'

'Hey, Oliver,' Dawn says. 'You want to come help me find some dandelions for salad? I really need some help.'

'Um, ok,' he says. Dawn takes his hand. Oliver doesn't usually like people quickly, but he likes Dawn already.

Cal is standing over by Noon. He's not smiling his white smile. Their heads are bent together and they're talking close.

They're so absorbed they don't notice Riley approach.

'He's never been away this long,' Cal is saying to Noon, pleading. 'Two full days late, now. I have to go and look for him. I can walk the trails in the dark.'

'No one moves alone at night,' Noon says.

'But—'

'Cal,' she says gently. 'I'm worried. But we don't want to lose you too.'

Cal looks like he might be about to cry, but he nods. He sees Riley and scrubs one eye with a fist. 'Maybe you saw him on the mountain, Riley?'

'Who?'

'Danny,' Cal says. 'My brother. It's his place you're sleeping in.' His words are rushed. He's got a faint, faint hope that Riley might save him. 'He went to walk the trails. He's tall. Missing his right little finger, like me.' It's phrased like a question – he is still pleading.

Riley's insides make a movement like a big wave crashing. The bitter scent of lion fills the air. She sees it all again, she is back there in the firelight, the big body like a cage over her, brown eyes turning to bloody holes. She sees the stump of a little finger twitching on the pine needles. *You seem like a girl who doesn't want to be found.* She looks at Cal's face and it's clear now, she wonders how she missed it before – the lineaments of the lion boy echoed in his bones.

'No,' Riley says. 'We never saw anyone after we left the main trail.'

'We saw the demon,' says Oliver, at her elbow.

Riley starts. 'You're supposed to be helping Dawn.'

Oliver shrugs. 'I didn't want to so she gave me a toy.' He frowns and worries the rag doll in his hands. He's not interested in adult conversation but he always likes to correct Riley when she lies. Riley should have thought of that.

Noon is watching him. 'You saw a demon?'

'Uh huh. Riley saw the demon and she killed it,' Oliver says.

'Yeah,' Riley says, smiling down at him. 'I sure did kill the demon, didn't I?' Riley throws her smile at Noon, rolling her eyes a little. *Sun in the head*, she thinks.

Oliver gives her a look of disgust, which Riley knows she deserves. He starts towards the other kids, who are piling on top of Midnight on the grass, screaming.

'Hey, Oliver Olive.' Riley seizes his hand. 'Come hang out with me, ok? You can play with the others soon enough.' She doesn't know if this is true. 'I'd better stay with him,' Riley says to Cal and Noon. 'Keep him distracted.'

'I'm going out first thing tomorrow,' Cal says to Noon. 'If I don't find him, I'll go out the day after that. And the next day and the one after that, every day until I find him.'

Noon nods and touches his shoulder.

Oliver tugs on Riley's hand. He strains towards the other kids.

'How about we climb that tree, Oliver Olive?' she says. 'See? It's so high, I bet we can see all the way to Boulder if we get to the top.'

‘Ok,’ he says, resigned, and lets Riley draw him away.

Over her shoulder Riley says to Cal, ‘Sorry about your brother. I’m sure he’ll be home soon.’

7

Adam

He has been at Nowhere for twenty-six days. His bedroom is large and light, with a floor-to-ceiling window that shows the mountains. It smells of cedar. Adam has never slept in a room as nice as this and he loves it – except for one thing. The men's clothes in the closet.

The first day he asked Leaf, 'Can I move this stuff?'

Leaf was standing by the window, lit by mountain sun, talking about the view. He turned his bright hazel gaze on Adam. 'The clothes? No.'

Adam said, hesitant, 'I could put them in another closet, another bedroom, there must be plenty of room—'

'No.'

'But ...'

'Please, let's not fight.' Leaf looked plaintive and young suddenly, and Adam felt like a bully.

So the shirts and pants and sweaters are still hanging in the closet. They're not clean and they're not his size. In fact, they are many different sizes. There are a couple of flannel shirts, which would fit someone taller and more rugged than Adam. They bear brown sweat stains under the arms and still hold the sharp odour of the man who wore them. There is a grey suit which smells faintly of cologne. There are running shorts and a singlet, marked with green grass skid-marks where whoever it was slipped. There's a Grateful Dead concert t-shirt, worn soft with use. That one smells faintly of pot.

These untenanted clothes are the only thing Adam doesn't like about life at Nowhere. At night sometimes he dreams that the past inhabitants of his room return. They materialise in the dark closet. A body fills the sweat-stained flannel shirt slowly, like a tyre being pumped up. A head grows slowly from the collar of the grey suit like a balloon. Legs descend down into the empty pants legs. Adam thinks of them as the mirrormen. They step out of the closet, grinning. They look at Adam with their mirror eyes.

Now he showers and dresses quickly, taking his clothes from the pile he keeps neatly folded on the chair beside his bed. He doesn't use the wardrobe.

Adam wipes his brow, leaving a streak of sawdust. He's pleased with the wood he chose – aged cedar to match the house. The scent of it fills the air.

'How's it going?' He hadn't heard Leaf approaching over the sound of the drill. 'Can you take a break?'

'Sure.' As Adam takes off his safety glasses he sees Leaf pass a hand across his own brow, wiping away imaginary sawdust.

'Stop it,' Adam says.

'What?'

'Stop – storing me. I'm not a character. I'm a person. You should learn the difference.' Adam strides out of the house into the sunshine. There's a light breeze and the woods rustle with life. Somewhere there's a woodpecker.

'It's my job,' Leaf says. He stands on the steps, arms folded. 'You want paying? You let me do my job.'

Adam blinks. He feels calmer than he has ever been. 'If you speak to me like that again I quit.'

'Fine,' Leaf says, mouth creased with anger. 'I'm sorry, ok, please – look, let's take a walk.'

They go up the sloping paddock. Seven or eight horses follow hopefully, ears pricked. Sometimes the horses touch Leaf or Adam with their velvet muzzles, hoping that they've brought food.

'I used to think,' Leaf says, pushing a grey horse gently away from his side, 'I'll wait a little, until I'm more famous. Until people will miss me just a little more.'

'Wait, until what?'

'Until I kill myself.'

'That's messed up.' Adam stumbles as a friendly bay noses him in the small of his back. He rights himself and turns to Leaf. 'What kind of person would say that?'

Leaf kicks a tussock of grass across the field. 'Do you want me to lie?'

'No.'

'Sometimes I feel I've given everything I am to the characters,' Leaf says. 'Maybe there's not much left.' He puts a conciliatory arm on Adam's shoulder. 'Let's go see Tinkerbell. If you understand Tinkerbell maybe you'll understand everything.'

The horses follow them all the way to the fence, nosing at their pockets.

Leaf and Adam go past the staff block, where some children are running through the long grass, chasing each other. It's nice, Adam thinks, through his anger, how everyone lives together up here. The kids get to grow up in this beautiful place.

They go through the dappled light of the orchard, until water gleams ahead.

'It's over this way,' Leaf says. 'He needs a temperature-controlled environment so I built a tank by the lake, using the water.' Leaf speaks briefly into his walkie talkie.

Leaf leads Adam to a stairway down into the earth. The entrance is nearly concealed by sedge grass. Adam follows, heart beating fast. They come out into a small chamber below the water. A bench sits between two glass walls on either side. Carefully placed lights show waving waterweed, gravel and sand, floating particles.

'I told them to feed him,' Leaf says, settling on the bench. 'I want you to see.' Adam sits too. He knows the lake water can't get in, but he feels like it might.

A silvery corpse drops from the surface above. Blood leaks in threads through the fish's gills into the water.

A great dark shape stirs in the depths, in the distance, sinuous, great body swimming.

The crocodile comes into view. Adam can see its eyes, each dark warty scale, every tooth that protrudes from its ancient jaws.

'No,' he says. 'No ...'

Leaf holds him in place, gentle but firm. 'It's ok. Tinkerbell can't hurt you. The glass is four feet thick.'

The crocodile parts its jaws and takes the fish. It turns slowly, its scales scraping on the glass, and goes back into the darkness of its tank.

Adam gasps a great breath. The water on either side presses in on him.

'I know,' Leaf says. 'I know, I know, I know.'

Adam is interested to find that he is actually trembling. His hand, when he holds it level, cannot maintain a stillness. 'What do you know?' he asks, almost absent.

'I keep him to remind me,' says Leaf. 'My family sold me to

show business. Then my mother let them eat me. Then I took control, and I decided how much they ate.'

'And me?' Adam asks. 'How much of you do you think I—'

'I'm sorry,' Leaf calls as Adam runs up the steps, into the fresh air. Leaf runs after, into the light.

Adam is leaning against a tree as Leaf stumbles out. He strokes the bark because it's real under his fingers.

'I'm sorry,' Leaf says. 'I didn't mean to scare you with Tinkerbell. I—'

'It isn't the crocodile that scares me,' Adam says. 'It's you. Stop it. Stop hiding behind all this – stuff.'

'I don't know what—'

'You say things but you don't really talk. You tell stories. I'm not interested in stories.' Adam comes close to Leaf. 'You're going away tomorrow. What do you feel about that?'

Leaf gasps like he's just come up from deep water. 'I can't wait,' he says. 'When I'm away I can be whoever I want. But also—' Leaf takes another hard breath. 'It also means being away from you.'

Adam says, quiet, 'You don't get to eat me alive.'

'It's other people who eat me,' Leaf says, 'they all take, take ...'

'None of that is happening now,' Adam says. 'You and I are both here.' Adam puts his thumb to Leaf's cheek, touches his warm skin, fingers making roads in Leaf's hair. 'Can't you see that?'

'These are easy things to say,' Leaf hisses. 'So easy.'

Adam pushes down panic and reaches for a still place inside himself. 'Either you want me,' he says, 'or you don't.'

'It's not that easy,' Leaf says.

'No.' Adam pushes down thoughts of Christie and the baby. 'But I can't go on like this.'

Leaf looks at him, cold. 'Learn to go on,' he says. 'Like everyone else.'

In the distance Adam thinks he hears the crocodile, moving dark beneath the water.

8

Riley

They sit beneath an apple tree. Riley holds Oliver close and he rests his head against her heart. They watch the sun sinking behind the peaks. Nowhere sinks into gentle dusk. Kids are running everywhere.

'I like it here,' Oliver says. 'Can we stay?'

'I don't know.' Riley has learned not to promise him too much. 'We can try.'

Noon goes to the front of the group. She stands before the fallen wheel and everyone falls quiet. Everyone who was sitting stands, so Riley does too, helping Oliver to his feet.

The sun is a finger of fire behind the western peaks. The last of the light falls like a path of gold through the valley, from the entrance across the lake and the grass, through the forest. It looks so like a path that Riley is not surprised to see that it ends at the distant, blackened ruins among the trees. Riley quickly glances down. She realises that in only one day, she has taken on the habit of averting her gaze from the burnt-out skull of a house.

Noon touches her hand to her mouth. 'We send our breath to him.' Riley had thought that this gesture was a kiss but she sees now that it's not. Noon breathes gently into her palm. Then she releases it, giving her breath towards the east. All around, the others are doing the same. Even the kids are in perfect time with everyone else. Their hands let their breath fly in the direction of the ruined house at the end of the valley. Riley feels again, through grass and trees, the pulse of that blackened thing. She looks around at the serious downturned faces.

She realises, with slow horror, her mistake. She thought that they were afraid of the house and of Leaf Winham. But what she sees in their faces as they send their breath eastwards is not fear. It is love. Beside her, Oliver is imitating the Nowhere children. He gives Leaf Winham his breath.

Horror fills Riley with a cold trickle. She clutches the locket on her breastbone.

The red finger of sun disappears behind the peaks and the valley plunges into dark.

Riley seizes Oliver about the waist and drags him backwards into the apple trees. She feels it in his body, the moment he's about to cry out, and clamps her hand over his mouth. He fights her but she keeps her hand tight and her arm firm around him, dragging him away from the clearing. She's panting by the time she thinks it's safe to stop.

'We have to go, Oliver Olive,' she whispers. He tries to shake his head. She can feel the fury running all through his body.

'It's you and me,' she says quietly in his ear. 'Just you and me, like always.'

After a moment, he nods. She takes her hand away from his mouth. 'We'll go slow, ok?' Riley looks up. In the fading light she tries to see the shape of the peaks through the leaves. Where did the sun sink? Riley turns in the direction – she hopes – of the zipline.

'Come on.' She looks behind her through the knotted branches of the trees. No one is following.

The ground is uneven, they stumble on roots and stones. Oliver is limping and crying out in pain after a few minutes of walking. Blood seeps through the white bandage on his leg, a narrow slash of red.

'Riley, I'm tired,' Oliver says. 'It's cold and my leg hurts.'

'It will be ok,' Riley says. 'Just a little further.' But reality is setting in. Can she take him out into the mountains at night, with no gear and a wound? Riley pushes these thoughts away – doesn't matter because they can't stay here. Maybe they can hide somewhere in the valley until daylight? Riley thinks of the crocodile and the bitter taste of panic fills her mouth.

'It'll be ok.' She squeezes Oliver's hand.

'You already said that.' Oliver twists out of her grasp. But she knows he'll come. The two of them are all they have.

Overhead the moon is yellow and on the wane. Riley always thinks it looks bitten, like this. It sheds enough light to see the open meadow ahead, through the trees. Up the rise, beneath the cliff face, she can just make out the posts of the zipline.

'We're here, Oliver.' Her voice is unsteady with relief. 'See?'

'Ok,' he says, exhausted. They walk across the moonlit meadow hand in hand.

As they draw near Riley sees that there is no harness, no line running up the cliff. The posts are just posts. She breathes. Maybe these things are stored nearby. *Don't panic.* But her heart is already pounding. Riley hunts through the bushes, the grass, the undergrowth. But there is no metal wire and no harness. She can't think and fear is beating like a drum. She doesn't know how close they are to the lake.

Riley yells, 'Oliver!'

'Uh?' He raises his head from where he was sleeping in the grass.

Riley points. 'Go climb that tree.'

'I don't WANT—'

'I said, go climb that tree and stay there.'

He trots off towards the lone gnarly pine she's pointed out. She watches his tired form as he climbs. He gasps with pain at the strain on his injured leg. Then he slumps down, hugging the branch he's sitting on. He might be asleep.

Riley looks everywhere for the zipline gear. She scrabbles in earth and undergrowth and combs the cliff wall with her hands, looking for openings. Every so often she glances over at Oliver, slumped on the branch. And every so often she checks the grass for the approach of a long, dark shape made of teeth.

'How's it going?'

Riley yells and jumps. She backs away from the stand of tall grass she was looking in.

Noon stands in the meadow in the moonlight, hands in her ragged pockets.

'Don't touch me,' Riley says. 'Don't come near me.'

'I won't,' Noon says. She sits down on a rock. 'I'm sad today,' she says. 'Cal's brother. Danny – he's missing. Each one of us is everything to each other here at Nowhere. But.' She swallows and Riley realises that Noon is trying not to cry. 'He and I were – well. We were happy. So if he's not home by now, there's a reason. I'm so scared he's dead and I don't want Cal to see that I'm scared. Every person here in this place is precious to me. Our families, where we ran from – they weren't families. The places we ran from weren't homes. We made this family and this home. All we have is one another. I know you understand that.'

'Ok.' Riley is so tired of lying and hiding. She is weary of it down to the bone. It might be a relief, she thinks, to confess.

Noon looks down at the ground, breathes into her palm and releases her breath into the air, towards Nowhere House.

'It makes me feel sick when you do that,' Riley says. 'Little rats worshipping a dead king rat. He killed people.'

'That was the past,' Noon says. She comes closer. Moonlight has bleached her of all colour. 'I saw you for the first time as you were walking home from school. I watch that school sometimes. Midnight watches, I watch. We look for the ones who need help. I knew right away that you had to come to Nowhere. I saw that you were one of us.'

'What does that even mean?' Riley wants to push Noon away, she wants to run or hit something.

'You have the right hunger. The cold place deep inside you. No one survives here without those things.' Noon smiles at Riley but it's sad, like she actually understands how hard it all is, like Noon truly wants the best for her. 'I asked three girls before you.'

'What happened?' Riley asks. Her heart pounds splashy and strong.

'They didn't come,' Noon says. 'They chose to stay where they were. One of them is dead now.'

Riley whispers, 'I want to leave.'

'This isn't a prison,' Noon says. 'But I mean what I say. You belong.'

Riley shakes with rage. 'Don't try that brainwashing garbage,' she says. 'This is a place. It's made of rock, grass, earth. The house is just a burnt-down house, whatever. It doesn't have feelings. It can't want me. It doesn't want anything.'

But even as Riley says the words they don't feel true. She felt welcome here – by the people and the land. She had thought for a moment that she belonged. A tear tracks down Riley's cheek like a hot needle and she scrubs it away. She was right to keep her guard up, not to trust, all these years. Trust tears a hole in you in the end. Riley swears to herself that she won't ever make this mistake again.

'That day we met,' Noon says. 'I had been watching you for weeks already. I saw what happened in that house. I listened. I knew I had to get you out of there, I saved your lives.'

Riley laughs. '*I* saved our lives,' she says. 'I got us out of there. There was just no place to go except here.'

‘You can’t leave,’ Noon says.

‘I can do whatever I like,’ Riley says. ‘Whatever is best for me and Oliver.’

Noon shakes her head in the moonlight. ‘I don’t think you can do whatever you like.’ Noon pats the space beside her on the rock. ‘Sit. What’s the worst that could happen?’

‘I’m ok here.’ Riley sinks to the ground where she is. The wet night-grass seeps through her jeans right away. She tries not to shiver.

‘I had two daddies once,’ Noon says. ‘One was good and one was bad. I found out too late which one was which. Now I can only really remember one daddy – what he was like, the things he did. It’s much harder to recall my good daddy. I wish it wasn’t like that. But the people you never forget are the ones you kill. In fact if you’re not careful all the living ones fade away and only the dead are left.’

‘You killed your daddy?’ Riley asks.

‘I did it and ran. Just like you.’ Noon raises her eyebrows at Riley. ‘Rat poison?’

Riley feels as if the ground beneath her is trembling. ‘What?’

‘Riley,’ Noon says, patient.

Riley bows her head. She whispers. ‘Is Cousin … is he really, is he—’

Noon nods. ‘Sometimes Cal brings a newspaper from Ault.’

‘Oh,’ Riley says. ‘Ok.’ She tries to figure out what to feel.

‘It was good,’ Noon says. ‘When I saw it I knew you were on your way. Everyone walked the trails every day until they found you.’ Noon draws a stem of grass from its sheath and nibbles the soft white end. ‘You know what’s waiting for you out there.’

‘We can stay out of people’s way,’ Riley says. ‘We can live in the wild. Or hitchhike out of state. We can go far away where people don’t know that story.’

‘Or you could stay here,’ Noon says.

‘I won’t stay in a place that worships him as a god.’

'Is that the problem?' Noon laughs. 'We don't worship him.'

'It looked like it,' Riley says.

'People need gods,' Noon says. 'Especially when they're often cold and hungry. Life out here isn't easy. Some of the kids don't even really know what he did, they were too young to understand before they came here. But everyone has a favourite Leaf Winham movie. It's harmless.'

Riley makes a scornful sound and Noon holds up her hand.

'But what they're really worshipping is this place, their home. They're giving thanks for being safe at Nowhere.' Noon clenches her fists for a moment. 'There were more Nowhere children once, when I first came here,' she says. 'Word spread. Kids came here wanting safety. We grew. In the end we were thirty, maybe. It didn't work. We divided into tribes, groups took territories in the valley, they started raiding and stealing from each other. The stronger ones didn't let the little ones have food. They didn't respect this place – they had no gods. There were fights, and then there were killings.' Noon takes a deep breath. 'Me, Danny, Midnight, Cal and Everett realised we had to work together. In the end we were all that was left. We made this place safe. We found out how to worship. It keeps us all as one.'

'This won't work on me,' Riley says but her voice shakes.

Noon breathes out a hard puff of frustration. 'I'm not trying to make anything work. I'm trying to explain. We live on a knife edge here – never more than one bad month away from starving, laid open to sickness, right next to death. Nowhere is all we have. She's our god and she keeps us alive. If some of them choose to think of her as Leaf Winham I'm ok with that.'

'Not many of you left,' Riley says slowly. 'What happened to the others?'

'Nowhere chose us,' Noon says. 'We did what we had to do.'

A wash of cold sweeps across Riley's skin. 'What Oliver and I have to do,' she says, 'is leave in the morning.'

‘All right,’ Noon gets up. ‘Better spend the night up in that tree, just in case our friend comes out of the lake on his night walk.’

‘I should never have come here,’ Riley says.

‘She likes you,’ Noon says. ‘Nowhere. You’re welcome and I hope you stay.’

Her mother always spoke about Nowhere with fear and hatred. ‘It took everything,’ she said. ‘Evil lives there.’ As a child Riley had nightmares about fire leaping into the night sky, the flames reflected in pools of blood on a vast floor. But it drew her too. She thought about Nowhere, imagined it. The place beat like a pulse beneath her daily thoughts. She spent hours at the library, hunting down old newspaper articles with pictures of the house.

She was sitting on the front step of their old house in Boulder when she heard the news that Mom was really dead. Oliver was sleeping inside. Riley always made sure he took his nap. Sometimes the memory is so vivid in her mind that she feels the late sun on her skin, her thin summer dress, the warmth of the stoop through the cotton.

She held the locket in her hands, brought it to her nose and inhaled the particular scent of the old silver. The car that pulled up was a Buick. Cousin got out. Riley knew when she saw him what he’d come to say. She knew that her mother was gone. She got up and went to meet Cousin, not wanting to wake Oliver yet – to give him a few more moments of peace before he knew.

Cousin said he couldn’t keep Riley and Oliver at first. Then after they had been at the group home for six months, he changed his mind. Riley remembers the relief of hearing that they could leave the home, that they would be with family. Riley and Oliver had never known Cousin, growing up. Later they understood why their mother had kept him out of their lives.

Bad things can start so slow, like they did with Cousin. Normality slipped off its axis gradually; by the time it was at its worst Riley couldn't say how they had got there. Anyway there was no one to help. Both of Riley's parents are shut away forever now, in the silver that hangs about her neck, and in the ground.

Riley stays awake, one arm around Oliver, the other wrapped around the trunk of the tree. Nowhere chirps and rustles and chatters to itself. A night bird sings high and liquid. Clouds scud across the bitten moon.

Pink light spreads across the grass and something makes a deep sound above them on the edge of the cliff. Riley starts awake. Cal is below her, holding the harness.

'Time to go,' he says. 'If you're going.'

'We're going.' Riley shakes Oliver awake. 'Come on, Oliver Olive. Move.'

His pupils are blown out large, almost to the edge of his irises. His brow feels skillet-hot under her hand. Infection.

'Help me,' she says to Cal and she lowers Oliver into his arms. Oliver cries out with pain. Above, there's a flash of tawny hide on the cliff.

'There's a lion up there,' Cal says.

'She'll move on,' Riley says.

'She's circling the valley. It's her hunting ground.'

'Just get me up there,' Riley says. 'I'll scare her away.'

'She won't scare,' Cal says. 'And he can't run.' He nods at Oliver.

'We'll be ok.'

Riley straps herself into the harness with trembling fingers, and Cal begins to winch her up. Her feet leave the ground.

Oliver starts crying. 'Don't leave me, Riley!'

'Won't be long, Oliver Olive.' As Riley ascends she sees her among the trees. The lion slinks gold between the trunks. Riley glimpses a heavy head and yawning, long, long yellow teeth.

'Bring me back down!' she calls. She can hear how bad her voice is shaking. 'Cal, please.'

Cal doesn't need telling twice. Riley hurtles backwards, downwards. She screams as she hits the grass and rolls.

'You ok?' Cal asks. He unbuckles her gently. Riley finds that she is crying, big gulping sobs.

'Hey, hey.' Cal puts his arms around her, surrounding her with his warmth.

'We've been alone for so long,' Riley whispers into his shoulder. 'Me and Oliver.'

'Not anymore,' Cal says, stroking her head. 'You've got us now. Let's get Oliver back somewhere warm where he can rest.' He whistles and Everett comes out of the trees where he must have been waiting. He unfolds a blanket and they put Oliver gently into it. They pick it up like a hammock, one at either end, carrying just like they did when they first brought Riley and Oliver here.

Cal, Riley and Oliver walk through the valley of Nowhere in the rising sun. Light glitters on millions of dewdrops as they wade through the long grass. The sky behind the mountains is turning a painful azure blue. Riley lets her chest unclench, lets the places in her she has kept closed tight all these years unfurl like a flower.

She feels that this time, they are here to stay.

Cal takes them back to their stall. 'Rest.'

'Where are you going?' Riley asks, as he turns away, back towards the west. She had been hoping, maybe, he would want to talk.

'I'm going to look for Danny again,' Cal says. He pushes the heel of his hand into his eye socket, hard.

'What about the lion?' Riley asks.

'She won't touch me,' Cal says. 'I belong to Nowhere.'

*

Oliver squints at a Hardy Boys book, mouthing the long words. Riley curls up next to her brother, holding him close, letting her warmth spread through and fill the bed of the boy she killed.

Riley asks, 'Do you trust me, Oliver Olive?'

'Yes,' he says. 'Sometimes.'

'No more talking about the demon we met on the trail.'

'Why not?'

'It's bad luck to speak of a demon after you kill it,' Riley says. 'Sometimes it brings them back to life.'

'I don't want to lie,' Oliver whispers.

'You have to,' Riley says. 'Or I'll tell the demon to come back to life and get you. It'll take hold of you in the dark with its long claws and big teeth.'

'You're mean.' Oliver's eyes fill with tears.

'I have to be.' Riley's chest turns hot. 'I take care of us. No one else will.'

'You don't,' Oliver says. 'You just get us in trouble.'

'Go to sleep.'

'I hate you.' Oliver turns away from her. He cries quietly. Riley stops herself from reaching for him. He has to take it seriously. At length Oliver's sobs slow and quieten. Eventually his breathing steadies. He has cried himself to sleep.

Riley doesn't sleep. Danny's dead face fills her mind. The curl of his stiffened lip over his teeth, the empty red tunnels of his eyes.

9

Marc

He dreams of eating a pizza. He is enjoying it but then Kimble comes in, turns the pizza over and starts spreading butter all over the base.

'You're ruining it,' he says, irritated, then comes awake with Kimble's hand clamped over his mouth. They are not eating a buttered pizza, they are in a tent in the mountains.

Kimble taps the back of her hand twice. It means *pay attention* or *red alert.* Marc nods slowly and she takes her hand away. He hears it now, too – the stealthy movements. A quiet tread outside. Whoever it is stops by the tent. Marc can hear breathing through the thin walls. A bear?

A whisper comes. It's thin and penetrating, it makes its way into his ear like a needle.

'Here,' someone hisses to someone else, sibilant. A long sound like a knife, or a nail, 'Now here, now here, now here.'

Marc tries to scramble to his feet and falls, trapped in his sleeping bag. Outside, he hears feet running lightly away. No way to tell how many. Marc fights his way desperately out of his sleeping bag. 'Wait!' he calls. 'Stop, don't go!' He fumbles for his prosthetic, cursing in the dark. When it's fitted he struggles to the mouth of the tent, grabs at the zip at the entrance of the tent, yanks it down. Marc crawls into the night air. He knows it's too late. They are gone.

Kimble is right behind and seizes him, pulls him up by the back of his t-shirt. 'Chill, Marc,' she says very quietly. 'They're armed, remember?'

'They were—' Marc's breath comes fast. 'Kimble, they were so close, right on the other side of the canvas ...'

'I get it,' she says. 'But we need to plan and be smart, ok? What we don't need to do is follow voices into the forest in the night.' Marc sees she is wearing her head torch and GoPro camera.

Marc nods, rubbing his brow. 'Did you get anything?'

'Mostly you freaking out,' she says. 'So no.'

Linus is kneeling at the entrance of his one-man pop-up. He clutches the shotgun so tightly that Marc can see all the bones in his knuckles.

'They're gone,' Kimble says. She goes to Linus. 'It's ok,' she says. 'You're ok.'

He nods briefly, as if he has been waiting to be relieved of duty.

'We should set a watch from now on.' Kimble checks her phone. 'It's two hours until dawn and I've slept. So I'll sit up.'

Marc doesn't sleep much after that. He watches the light bloom through the canvas. It's good to know Kimble is just outside, watching the dawn too.

In the morning they move slowly, starting at imagined movements in trees. Marc eats fistfuls of Honey Nut Cheerios from the box, staring at the gate to Nowhere, a small patch of grey between two high walls of rock. At his feet two chickadees quarrel over a fallen Cheerio.

Linus spreads a topographical map out on the ground. 'This is the road where I got picked up,' he says. 'Where Leaf Winham tried to kill me and where he then killed himself. It was exactly here.' He circles it on the map. 'The road is disused now. That's where we start. And I suggest following a grid system from there, covering all the ground uphill, or west of the road.'

Marc nods.

'Watch out for bear traps,' Linus says, folding the map into a neat square. 'Take a stick. When the leaf litter is deep, sweep ahead before you step. If you step in one they'll take your leg off.'

'Too late for me,' Marc says, shouldering his pack. He used four extra linings when he put on his prosthetic this morning, to cushion his residual limb. It will be a long day. 'Lead the way.' As they go Marc notes the shapes of the peaks, the position of the sun. He winces and adjusts the GoPro on his head. It gets heavy, after a while.

Dappled sunlight falls on the narrow road. Its surface is cracked and cratered, half hidden beneath pine needles, fallen branches and broom pollen.

'It was here,' Linus says.

'How can you tell?' Marc asks.

'I've thought about it a lot,' Linus says. 'You do, when someone cuts your throat.'

'Right,' Marc says quickly.

'And I've looked at maps,' Linus says, 'and read the police report. It was a hairpin bend and there aren't so many of those on this road. Also, I remember that.' He points to Lion Mountain, which lies on the other side of a tree-filled valley. 'The two peaks – the ears. See? It looks like there's only one because they're perfectly lined up. If you lose your bearings sight your course along the ears to head back to this spot.

'So I'm east,' Linus says, 'Kimble north, Marc west. We're looking for some kind of entrance. It might be in a cave, it might be in the ground. There might be some kind of structure around it. They never found it, so I'm guessing it looks natural. It will be concealed, probably overgrown. But animals will almost certainly be using it.' He pauses. 'Hopefully not large predators. So look out for animal trails that lead into undergrowth and don't come out the other side. OK.' He hitches up his pack. 'Let's go.'

They go up the bank and head in their assigned directions. Marc soon loses sight of the other two among the trees. The sounds of their voices fade and now he is alone in the forest.

Marc doesn't look for the tunnel. He takes his bearings, glances at his old compass, the one he's had since he was a kid. Marc sets off west around the hill towards the far end of the valley. He gives the gate a wide berth, following narrow deer trails through the trees. Below Lion Peak he steps over an old chain which lies among the pine needles. Hidden in the brown and gold of the forest floor is a dented sign: DANGER – ROCKFALL.

The ground is covered in Indian paintbrush and mountain violets. The air is filled with wild thyme.

Branches rustle ahead and Marc stops dead. He stands motionless, listening. Through the trees to the left of the path, something is coming with a slow tread. He thinks of Leaf Winham coming through the forest through shadow and light, back of his head a red crater lined with white bone splinters. They say he nearly took his own head off before they shot him, cut a gash in his throat like a yawning mouth, like a canyon in his flesh, so they say, yes, that's what they say ... Marc can almost see him now, the lithe figure in the green shadow. He can smell rot and the salt of blood. I *might faint*, he thinks. *If I faint I don't have to see him.*

Something is moving, beneath the busy noise of life and insects, sun, sky, air. A tawny shape emerges from the trees. Marc catches his breath.

The puma is muscled, summer-healthy. She turns her head and looks at him for a moment, before padding back into the trees in the low afternoon. Mountain lion.

It's some minutes before Marc starts to breathe again. He shakes himself and runs up the magnolia path, fighting the heat and his hacking, laboured breath. Too many cigarettes. Clouds of pollen hang in the air and he wheezes, eyes watering. The sky is warm and golden, air still fresh with morning. Marc goes faster, cannoning off tree trunks. A hummingbird keeps pace with him for a few moments. In the distance above the treeline, the high peaks are pale blue, just as they are in his dreams, white-capped, almost blending with the sky. He runs faster along the narrow cliff path, faster and faster, coughing, slipping on shale, trying to keep close to the rockface.

He jogs through the forest, slipping on fallen pine needles. The missing half of his leg aches, it will be sore tonight.

Marc bursts from the trees and slides to a stop, arms windmilling, at the edge of the cliff. For a moment he thinks he'll go over and adrenaline fills him with its electric touch. He stumbles back, away from the drop. He can see the stump where there was once a pulley or zipline or something similar. Below, the meadow is stroked into different colours by the wind. A rabbit bounds through the long grass.

Marc hunts through his pockets. He finds a broken pen and a tattered gas station receipt. He scrawls quickly on the back of the receipt, wraps it tightly around a stone. Then he hurls the stone into the air. It arcs high then falls down, down into the valley where it bounces on the turf then comes to rest. Marc waits and watches, every muscle held. He doesn't know if he wants someone to come or not. The breeze moves in the grass in the valley below. No one comes.

Marc turns and runs back through the forest. His heart pounds heavy and bitter. Maybe no one will find it, maybe the note will lie there in the wild grass, the thin paper driven to pulp in the next rain. Or maybe it will be found and read.

When Kimble and Linus make their way back to the hairpin bend opposite Lion mountain, Marc is already there, leaning against a tree which grows from the rutted asphalt. He is eating an apple.

They come back to camp in the pink dusk. Linus hands over the SD card from his camera to Kimble.

'My battery glitched,' Marc says. 'Nothing from today.'

Kimble shrugs. 'It wasn't a very interesting day.' She hums. 'And we do it all over again tomorrow.'

It's quiet around the fire. The three of them are lost in thought. 'Let's do something else tomorrow,' Marc says suddenly. 'Let's hike to the gate instead.'

'They might shoot at us,' Kimble says.

'Exactly.'

Kimble looks at him with a slow smile. 'Ok.'

'We're five hours from the nearest hospital,' Linus says. 'You're welcome to a gunshot wound. I'll watch tonight and sleep tomorrow.' He gets up and lumbers away from the fire.

'I'm hungry,' Kimble says. 'Is there another burger?'

'No more vegan ones,' Marc says.

Kimble takes the patty from the grill with her bare hands and eats it in three mouthfuls.

Marc stares. 'I've never seen you—'

'I only eat meat when I'm afraid,' Kimble says. 'And I'm never afraid. But this place scares me.' She gets up and wipes her hands on her pants leg. 'I'm going to bed.'

They creep through the resin-scented pines, bent double. It's a mountain summer's day, sky aching blue through the branches above, the sun a white disc overhead. Crickets sing and somewhere a woodpecker drums.

When the gate comes into view ahead Marc and Kimble come to a halt, keeping to the shelter of the trees. Close to, the gate looks worse – dead animals impaled on metal, faces shrunken into snarls. An orange t-shirt flutters in the wind, worn to rags by wind and weather. One lone child's shoe swings by its laces. Broken glass and razor wire gleam in the sun.

Kimble looks at Marc, hand outspread, palm up. That's not really one of their signals. It's universal. *What now?*

Marc stands up and walks out of the trees. He stands in the open before the gate. 'Hey!' he yells. 'Come out. I want to talk.'

He waits, squinting up at the gate in the bright air. The cicadas sing. Sun beats down on his head.

Marc sees it before he hears it. The bullet hits the tarmac beside him, throwing up a spurt of fine dust. Then the sound of gunshot comes, echoing through the stone passage behind the gate.

Marc turns and runs into the trees towards Kimble. From behind them comes the clamour of metal on metal and a cracked voice screaming, 'Run! Run!'

They run through the forest, sliding, scrambling away from the screams and the shots. Marc feels the gate at his back like an eye.

They don't stop until they have left the gate far behind. Marc bends double, hands on his knees. His breath comes in long wheezes. 'Have to get the leg off,' he says briefly to Kimble between gasps.

She looks around. 'Here.' She leads him to a fallen tree and helps him sit.

Marc eases the prosthetic off with a groan, leaning it carefully against the pine trunk. The stump burns and aches. He massages it, head hanging low. His back heaves. High sounds come from him.

'Sorry, Marc,' Kimble says, awkward. 'I always forget. I shouldn't have gone so fast, should have helped you ...'

Marc raises his head and looks at her. His eyes are full. 'That was fucking great,' he whispers, before collapsing into high laughter once more.

Kimble releases a long whoosh and sits beside him on the fallen tree. 'It really was.' Her hands clench on the pine bark. 'And I got it all.'

Marc wipes his eyes. 'Run, run,' he repeats, thoughtful. 'Was that the same voice?' he asks Kimble. 'The one we heard in our camp the other night?'

She nods.

10

Riley

The day is glaring bright again. Riley watches through the trees as Cal approaches across the meadow. The smoking jacket hangs loose on his frame. He is thin and drawn these days. Riley hears him sometimes at night, crying through the wooden stable wall. At first he went out on the range every day looking for his brother. Then it was every other day. Then once or twice a week. He is losing hope. Riley winces as her stomach cramps with emptiness. They are all hungry.

A blight has come over Nowhere. There has been no rain for weeks. There are no apples or little strawberries, no eggs in the birds' nests. The vegetables have soft black patches all over and the sweet potatoes are filled with worms. For a moment when she saw them, Riley considered eating the worms. She's always cold now, even in the fierce sun. Sometimes her eyes go weird.

Riley backs further into the shade of the trees as Cal approaches, his feet dragging through the grass. If Cal goes out on the range she likes to watch for his safe return. She doesn't want him to know.

It's thin eating again today – graham crackers with water and dried apple slices, packets of jelly with no bread to put it on. Oliver limps away from Riley to talk to Midnight. He prefers almost anyone to Riley, these days.

They scrape the green off the crackers and eat them slow in little bites.

After, the others stay in the shade of the barn, sheltering from the heat. No one is working. Riley understands why lions spend all their time lying around waiting for the hunt. Only the children seem cheerful. One of the smaller ones, Peach, sings a song to herself, staring at a blade of grass she holds in her hand.

Riley finds Noon behind Home Barn, staring at the trees. Hornets swarm over the apples that hang rotten on the branches. The smell of spoiled fruit is heavy in the air.

Noon looks at her, asking the question with her eyes. Riley shakes her head. 'No rabbits in the traps.' The only one they caught this week was sick. Patches of fur were missing and it shook. They burned the corpse. That was difficult. Even through the smell of burning hair Riley could smell the meat and it took all she had not to pull it out of the fire. It's not just the traps. Riley hasn't seen another rabbit for a week. They don't play on the green hills at dusk. They don't bound through the long grass or nibble young shoots in forest clearings.

'There were fish floating belly up in the lake yesterday,' Noon says. 'The crocodile didn't come to be fed. And now I have nothing to feed him. Maybe he's dead too.' Riley finds herself rubbing her aching stomach and wondering what crocodile tastes like. Her hip bones have that same sharp edge they used to, when she and Oliver first got here.

Riley puts her hand on Noon's shoulder. 'The rabbits and the fish will come back.' *But when?*

Noon puts her hand on Riley's. 'I know what must be done.' She doesn't seem to be speaking to Riley. She looks so sad. 'Blood in the land,' Noon murmurs. She talks like this sometimes, like someone in the Bible or maybe an old tree, if trees could talk.

Riley shakes her hazy head. Hunger brings strange thoughts with it sometimes, vivid and dreamlike. The boy who tasted like Clearasil sometimes had weed and Riley feels like that now, images and ideas streaming brightly through her mind without sense or order.

Noon cups her hands at her mouth. 'We go to Ault,' she shouts. Her voice echoes off the valley walls. 'Raid.'

Dawn waits for them at the edge of the meadow as they come out of the apple trees. She gives them each three sugar cubes. Riley shoves hers into her mouth, crunching hard. The sugar courses through her.

Dawn holds a Tupperware box. Noon takes off something that hangs around her neck, under her shirt. Riley sees that it's a little bag of washed leather. Dawn holds out the Tupperware box and Noon puts it in gently. Noon says quietly to Dawn, 'You'll have everything ready?'

Dawn nods. Cal watches them with an unreadable expression.

Midnight says, fretful, 'I don't like leaving Una.'

'I'll take care of her,' Dawn says. 'I promise.'

Midnight nods. Her necklace is kind of goth, strung with shining silver lug nuts and chicken bones. She puts it in the Tupperware. Cal does the same. His necklace looks like finger bones – maybe raccoon. Dawn closes the box reverently.

Riley looks away, embarrassed. She feels like she's been caught looking at someone undressing or something. She lingers behind as the others go towards the fly. 'Why do they do that? Leave those behind.'

'It's like a promise,' Dawn says. 'You're saying that you'll come back. Plus,' she adds, 'Cal loses literally everything. If you haven't crawled around on a forest floor in the dark helping him look for his pen, you haven't lived.' She smiles. 'See you later.'

Riley follows the others towards the fly. The long grass kisses her knees. The golden line of light lies along the valley – the sunlight road. The others walk ahead, leaving trails behind them in the green-gold meadow. Midnight says something to Cal and touches his shoulder. He shrugs, not looking at her. He doesn't look anyone in the eye these days.

Riley turns back and runs after Dawn. 'Wait!'

Dawn pauses, startled. Riley closes the distance and quickly takes her mother's locket from around her neck. She presses it into Dawn's palm. 'Keep this for me.'

'What is it?'

'It's a picture of my father, I think,' Riley says. 'I don't know. I've never been able to open it. It's my promise to come back.'

Dawn nods. Then she flings her arms around Riley and hugs her, hard. Riley hugs her back, throat closing. 'You won't tell? It's personal. It's my most precious thing.'

'I won't tell,' Dawn says, holding Riley tightly. 'I swear.' After a moment Dawn steps back. 'You better catch up with the others,' she says. 'They get so crazy when they're raiding. Don't get left behind.'

Riley runs through the low afternoon light.

They go south through the woods. White gnats move in clouds over tall nettles, honey-scented mountain alyssum. The scent of lilac lies on the dawn air sweet like death. A fly crawls up Riley's nostril and she snorts.

'Quiet,' Noon says softly. 'We're near the main trail.'

They tread light and soft down the mountain, through the woods. If they pass close to a campground or a trail they drop to all fours and crawl in single file. Riley smells the meat on grills, hears children playing ball. But she is a ghost, travelling by unseen. She's not here. She is nowhere.

*

The town of Ault comes into view, low buildings scattered across the valley floor. The sunlight has gone and thick clouds are massing to the west. They walk down through scrub, seeing occasional rusty bedsprings or an abandoned washing machine.

'Once,' Midnight says in Riley's ear, 'we saw a dead girl up here. There was rope around her neck. Her face was like bad fruit.'

'What did you do?' Riley's skin is crawling up and down her back.

'What were we supposed to do? Next time we came by she was gone, no bones or anything. So someone probably found her.'

They emerge behind a Denny's. It's all so weird – the feel of asphalt under Riley's sneakers. It seems like years since she lived in a place like this. It is impossible that it has only been two months. They pull their ski masks down over their faces.

Above the mountain lightning flickers through the cloud.

Behind the supermarket they fill their backpacks with out-of-date baby formula, cans, dried pasta, flour. They find vitamins, disinfectant.

Riley points up to the corner of the building where a camera sits winking like a shiny black eye.

Noon shrugs and pats Riley's shoulder. They go. To her surprise they don't head back towards the Denny's and the narrow trail back up the mountain. Instead Noon beckons them along another street. They are heading into town.

Noon whispers to Midnight, who nods and jogs away in a different direction.

'Where is she going?' Riley asks.

'To the veterinarian,' Noon says.

'Great,' Cal says. 'Let's go home, she'll catch us up.' There's a tightness in his body, a waiting.

'We're not done yet.'

'No,' Cal says. 'You promised, Noon.'

'We have to get off the road.'

The drainage ditch is deep and grass-lined, and dry at the bottom, for which Riley is grateful. Grey storm light falls in, making their faces wax-pale.

'Stop, Noon,' Cal says. 'I won't. I can't, not again.'

Noon puts a hand on his face. 'Whatever choices we had,' she says, 'they're done. We made them long ago.' She grips the back of his neck. 'Do you understand?'

After a moment he nods. Noon kisses his cheek gently. 'It will be ok.'

They crawl along the ditch in single file. A street sign looms above. *Snow Line Rd.* Noon climbs out and beckons. Riley and the others follow her at a jog. They go into a backyard via a gate with a broken latch. Then they go down through the small neat yards, hopping fences, until they come to a pretty green garden and a clapboard one-storey house with flowers in boxes at the windows. A shape detaches from the shadows and Riley catches her breath.

'Did you get it?' Noon breathes at Midnight, who nods and raises the plastic bag she holds tight in her fist.

'What are we doing?' Riley's voice comes out louder than she meant. She doesn't like this.

Noon puts a finger to her lips. 'We're waiting,' she says, softly. 'And watching.'

The drapes are open and the inside of the house is as neat as a pin. A window is cracked open, it's a warm night, and bugs slam themselves against the bug screen. Cute things are everywhere inside. On the counter sits a mug saying insert coffee here and an upward-pointing arrow. A kitten calendar hangs on the wall. Everything is pink or baby blue – pink rug, pink tablecloth, baby-blue apron hanging on the hook by the pale-pink tiles.

After a few minutes of watching the empty room, Noon whispers, 'Are you sure—'

'She does it the same time every night,' Midnight says. 'I found her last year. I watched. I knew we'd need her.'

Riley crushes a mosquito against her neck. Its full sac of blood bursts on her skin.

A woman comes into the kitchen. She's blonde and delicate. She looks right among the pastels and prettiness. 'Come on, kids,' she calls.

Two children come into the kitchen. The girl wears a pretty, very clean dress with flowers on it. The boy wears shorts and a collared shirt. They're around six and eight years old, maybe. Their hair is perfect. The girl's looks like it has been styled with curlers. The boy's is smooth, parted to one side, shining.

The woman pulls a kitchen chair out into the middle of the floor. She takes a bottle out from under the sink. 'Alicia, you first.'

The girl sits on the chair. Her mother soaks a pad of paper towel in whatever is in the bottle, and then puts it in front of the girl's nose. 'This will make you better,' she says, and puts a plastic bag over the girl's head. She struggles, inhaling fumes. The bag concertinas in and out with her breath. Her mother holds her firmly down on the chair. When Alicia starts to sag, she takes the bag off her head and kisses her. 'Good girl. Go lie down, now. We'll go to the doctor in the morning.' She beckons to her son, 'Come on, Benjy. Your turn for medicine.'

He holds back, mouth pursed with fear.

'Daddy will be home tomorrow,' the woman says. 'You want to be all better for when Daddy gets back, don't you?'

The little boy nods.

'What are we doing here?' Riley whispers at Noon. Her body convulses with disgust. Noon strokes her back, puts a finger to her lips. *Wait.*

Riley can't watch it again, so she stares at the flower beds, the cutely dressed gnome fishing from the ornamental pond.

Bedtime is early, 7 for the kids, 9 p.m. for the mother. At last, through the window, the warm glow of the bedside lamp goes out, but they wait an hour longer to give everyone time to fall asleep.

Noon lifts Riley up from where she's crouched. 'This is the time to go,' she says quietly. 'If you don't want to be part of this – it's now.'

'What are you going to do?' Riley feels sick, like it was her who breathed in the fumes, her head inside the plastic bag. She takes a deep breath. 'Actually it doesn't matter. Let's go.'

'Are you sure?' Noon holds her at arm's length. Riley feels her measuring look.

Riley nods and pushes Noon gently away. She follows Midnight through the dark.

Midnight picks the lock on the kitchen door easily. There's no deadbolt, it's a simple mechanism. This neighbourhood is like one of those places you see on TV, Riley thinks, where everybody says nothing bad ever happens and nobody locks their doors. They're wrong of course: bad things happen everywhere all the time and always have.

They go through the dark kitchen along the hall to the bedroom. The woman sleeps peacefully, one arm thrown over her head. Her hair is in curlers.

Midnight goes softly to her. For a moment she looks down at the woman's sleeping face. In one swift movement she clamps a cloth pad over the woman's nose and mouth. The woman wakes for a moment, struggles and then sinks back down.

'Horse chloroform,' Midnight murmurs, quiet as a wind in the trees. 'Quicker.'

Cal and Midnight bind the woman's hands and feet and roll her up in a blanket, tight as a swaddled baby. Cal bares his teeth as he does it, not a smile but a fixed grin of distress.

'We're going to be fast,' Noon says. 'Out the front gate and right down the road, through the strip mall to the Denny's. Ready?'

'Hold up,' Midnight says. She moves quickly from the room and is back within a minute. 'I locked the back door,' she says. 'Don't want people walking in here with those kids all alone, sleeping.'

Noon nods. 'Let's go.'

Midnight takes the head, and Cal her feet. Midnight is careful to make sure the front door locks behind them.

In the road Cal and Midnight walk fast, perfectly in step. Riley hurries behind, heart pounding. She turns back once to look at the dark house. Later, she is never sure if it was her imagination, the sight of two small heads at the window watching their mother being carried away.

The run back up the mountain passes in a blur. Riley isn't conscious of feeling tired or sore. They are like one animal, all of them together, travelling through the night. The air has colours, she breathes them in.

The woman lies like a cocooned caterpillar on the grass on the Nowhere valley floor. They are all panting, bent. It was a hard rush. Riley hardly remembers the journey back, they were all so high. Spying, breaking in, taking the woman – it was like electricity running right through her. As she looks around, Riley sees in the others' eyes the same unearthly light that fills her.

'What are you going to do with her?' Riley's not sure what answer she's hoping for.

'Take her to the house,' Noon says. 'Blood in the land.'

'To kill her?' Part of Riley does want to kill the woman. Maybe it's this easy – getting used to killing.

'No,' says Noon. She presses a pointed finger on Riley's shoulder. 'Why, do you want to?'

'Stop it,' Riley says. The finger is making her feel weird, like Noon is reaching inside of her.

'No one is going to die,' Noon says, removing her finger. 'Well, not today. Everyone is going to die in the end. Nowhere needs something from her, that's all.'

Noon flicks a finger and Cal and Midnight pick the woman up. They all jog together through the meadow, the orchard, past the barn, into the deep forest that surrounds Nowhere House. Lightning pierces the dark to the east.

They follow narrow deer paths, winding through the thickening trees. The forest changes around them as they go, fruit trees giving way to older pines, oaks, some hung with grey ribbons of moss, brown bark covered by soft vivid green lichen. Something large flies past Riley's face, beating the air with powdered wings. It's too big to be a butterfly, surely? But everything's wrong here, it doesn't seem like a place where people belong.

At times the house crawls into view between the trees and then retreats, its blackened gaps like toothy holes. Even though they're heading straight towards it Cal, Noon and Midnight keep their faces averted, don't look at the house directly.

The house seems to know. It plays with them. Again and again Nowhere House slides in and out of view, getting closer through the dark branches. It's hard to throw off the impression that it's coming to them, rather than the other way around.

The going gets more uneven underfoot, Riley stumbles. Lightning forks across the air. Through the leaves Riley sees the broken white crosses, the green hill cast grey in the stormlight.

Nowhere House rears up dark and sudden before them. It's blackened, roof missing in some parts. Ivy and creeper winds all around it, bright green moss growing in some places on the burnt-out shell.

Noon goes to the vast front door and takes up a crowbar that lies there. She levers the boards up with a crack.

'In.'

The door swings closed behind them. The outside world blinks out.

They are in a big high hall where a fireplace yawns large at the end. There are deer antlers mounted above it.

Riley takes take a deep breath and gathers herself. She can't lose it now. If you panic, use all three senses. Look at something, listen to something, touch.

There's old yellow tape strewn on the floor in dirty coils and arcs. She knows what this is, the TV shows have all taught her that. POLICE POLICE POLICE POLICE POLICE POL ... it says in shouting letters. Nothing stirs.

She follows Cal and Noon across the high hall. She tries to listen, to focus on sound. There's the faint hushing of the wind in the trees outside. Water drips somewhere. Dry leaves blow across the floor. Through the ruined roof of the high hall, the stars are out.

Riley shivers. The air is dank and chilly. There's a rotting leather couch to her left. As she glances at it, the surface writhes and Riley stifles a scream. A whiskered snout peeps out and disappears. *Rat*, she thinks, though it could just about be a possum. The dripping sound goes on, *plink, plink, plink*, in uneven plosive sounds. Something white and broad sails through the high roof and out into the storm-lit sky. The owl glides out into the dark on silent wings.

They go behind the vast stone chimney that houses the great fireplace and turn down a long hallway. The remains of blackened shattered mirrors gleam from the walls.

Plink, plink, the drops keep falling. She shakes her head, irritable. It's both hypnotic and unsettling.

As they go, she feels the house take them all in its arms. When Riley looks up she sees that the fireflies are out. They dance green overhead, darting in and out of the shell roof of Nowhere House. Riley follows Cal's straight back through dark passages. She can imagine hands reaching for her from the shadows.

They come out into a long room at the back of the house. Stars peer through the bare rafters, but some roof cover remains towards the back. There is something else there too – a darker scar in the blackened floor.

The woman is beginning to stir in her swaddling. She moans, low and pained.

'Quickly,' Noon says.

The dark scar is a circular place, sunk into the floor and through the foundations. The fire didn't make this, a person did. The floorboards have been hacked away to show the stone foundations at each side, the ground below. It's like a window let down to the earth. An indoor garden. There are rocks and earth and small trees, everything covered by a riot of vines. Some night flower has opened with the dark and its light fragrance hangs in the air, over the old scents of char and ash. Patterns of rocks are traced around the plants in whorls, in geometric shapes, making wandering paths through the scented plants. Five smooth round stones form a circle in front of a lilac tree which spreads its branches against the bare stone foundation. Someone took care with this, Riley realises. It is a place with great meaning.

There is a tall wooden chair at the edge of the sunken place. It has wizardly pointed turrets on its back. Cal and Noon put the woman in the chair. There are restraints on the armrests and at the foot – thick cracked leather straps, solid as steel. Cal fastens them about the woman's wrists and ankles. One of the armrests is set out at an angle and slants curiously downwards. When Cal fixes the woman's left arm it dangles in space, hanging above the drop, the window down into the earth. Meanwhile Noon takes a piece of cloth from her pocket and binds it about her head, covering her eyes tightly.

Dawn appears through the dim air and Riley starts.

'I'm glad you're home.'

Noon hugs her.

Dawn takes out the Tupperware box and puts Noon's necklace once more about her throat. Midnight takes hers with a visible give of relief. Noon touches her shoulder.

'You did well,' Noon says. 'Go and see your daughter.' Midnight nods and runs into the dark.

Riley holds out her hand to Dawn, waiting. She's glad to see it doesn't shake. Cold thoughts dart through her, crazy thoughts like – *maybe she won't give it back. Maybe I dreamed that I gave it to her, she might have dropped it in the woods, could have lost it.*

Dawn smiles and reaches into the Tupperware with delicate fingers. The chain and locket pool gently in Riley's palm, a slight gleam on the old silver.

'There's a well out back,' Noon puts her hand on Riley's shoulder. 'A pail next to it. Bring water.'

Riley jumps, heart pounding then nods. She makes her way towards the place where she can see the largest pattern of stars, where the wall gives way to the land.

The well is protected with a solid wooden cover and when Riley draws the bucket up the water tastes good – clean, almost sweet.

The moaning is louder now, Riley hears it as she makes her way back. Noon takes the pail from Riley and puts the lip very gently to the bound woman's mouth. The woman sputters and coughs, then drinks eagerly, her throat moving up and down like a piston.

When her gulping slows, Noon takes the bucket away. She nods at Cal.

He comes forward and the moon and starlight gleam on the blade in his hand. He makes a small nick in the woman's arm, the one that hangs out into space. She moans and struggles. Cal's mouth is rigid and thin. He holds her forearm firmly, widens the incision a little so that a narrow trickle of blood runs down her wrist, her hand, and then falls into the dark place below. The woman's moan builds to a scream. It shatters the air, broken and high.

'Blood in the land,' Midnight whispers.

Noon murmurs, 'Blood in the land.'

Beside her Cal hangs his head. His lips hardly move but Riley feels the words, his warm breath on her bare arm. 'Blood in the land.'

Riley opens her mouth. She hadn't meant to. But the words come as if they've always been waiting in the depths. 'Blood in the land,' she breathes. 'Blood in the land.'

The blood trickles from the woman's arm. Most falls directly onto the earth below. Blood spills onto the broken boards at the edge of the sunken place, fast now, *plink plink plink*. It drips down onto the earth.

Riley understands that she heard the sound of the blood dripping as they walked down the corridor. Even before they tied the woman up and cut her, she heard it dripping, because here time doesn't matter. The blood is always feeding the land.

Noon cleans the woman's wrist with a cotton ball and antiseptic. She binds it with gauze.

'Hungry?' Noon asks, kind.

The woman shakes, then nods her head. Her eyes are full of fear.

Riley had been sure they were going to kill the woman, despite what Noon had told her. For some reason what they are doing feels almost as bad.

Riley tries to keep this thought down – it's more important than ever that she keeps her mind clear – but she could have sworn, just now, as she watched the blood fall through the air and patter gently onto the earth below – Riley could have sworn she saw the earth gently rise and fall. It looked like Nowhere was breathing. *Or swallowing maybe. Yes, like something drinking,* thinks Riley, hazy, *after a long drought.* She pinches her arm. She's so tired that her vision stutters. It's easy to get confused.

The house speaks and ticks around them, alive in the night. It would be easy to imagine a ghost here. But Riley sees that Nowhere House doesn't remember anything human. It doesn't care enough about people to hold on to them in that way. Riley will not see her father in this place.

Noon strokes Riley's head. 'Thank you for today.' Noon sways. Her eyes close with tiredness. Dawn puts her arm around Noon.

'I have to watch,' Noon says. 'It's my place, it's my job.'

'Then I'll stay with you too.' Dawn brings out a container. The scent of mushrooms fills the air. Riley's stomach cramps. It has been some time since she ate well.

'Eat,' Noon says softly to the woman. 'We're not going to kill you.' Noon inserts a spoon gently into the woman's mouth. She chokes and spits out the contents. She slumps forward, head hanging like a broken flower.

'No,' Cal hisses at Noon. 'I won't do it again.'

'Then go.' Her voice is gentle.

Cal picks up his flashlight and turns. He goes fast back through the broken hallway. Riley runs after him, following his light.

Cal is out of the front door ahead of Riley, his light moving away through the forest. Riley peers through the dark searching for the dancing beam. 'Cal!' she calls. 'Please, stop.' The light stills.

He is leaning against a tree, face hidden in his arms. His back heaves. His flashlight lies on the forest floor, lighting the briar leaves brilliant green. Riley puts a tentative hand on his back, one, then the other. His heart beats right through his ribs.

Cal raises his head. There are tears on his cheeks but the lines of his face are fixed with anger. It's all through him, comes off his skin like static. 'Sometimes I wonder if that's where Danny went,' Cal says. 'Whether she took him and put his blood in the land. Maybe she put all his blood in the land.'

'She wouldn't do that,' Riley says.

'Where is he, then? Where's my brother?' He clenches his jaw and hits the tree with a closed fist.

'Cal.' Riley feels it coming, like something that needs expulsion from her body. She is going to do it. She will tell him the truth, now, she owes it to him, and whatever happens afterwards she will at least be free of this weight, the leaden knowledge she carries in her depths every moment.

'What do you think happened to the others who were here?' Cal says, loud and bitter. 'There were more of us. So much blood went in the land.' He strokes the tree as if saying sorry to it and breathes deeply. 'No, that's not fair. I shouldn't have said that. Noon did what had to be done, back then. It was bad, before. We didn't have any rules. We didn't worship. There had to be a leader. I know that. I miss Danny, that's all. I don't know who I am without him. We protect each other. You know the foster homes you have to be careful of? The ones who make you call them Mom and Dad, like, right away.'

Cal straightens up. 'Sometimes I get so scared that Danny's dead. But I know,' he taps his chest, 'in here, that he's not. I would have felt it if he'd died. I just would. It's a brother thing. I don't know what's happening to him but Danny's out there somewhere. If I keep looking I'll find him. He's my brother. Of course I will.'

Riley can't answer. She sees that there will never be a time when she can tell him the truth. Instead she kisses him on the cheek. His skin is warm and rough with stubble under her lips. She kisses him again on the corner of his mouth, and then again, touching his lips with hers. His body loosens with surprise and Riley slips in close against him, into his warmth. His mouth parts and she feels the edge of his warm tongue. All of her is lighting up.

Riley keeps her eyes open because she doesn't want to miss any of it. The delicate skin of his lowered eyelids. The dark fringe of his eyelashes.

The other reason she doesn't close her eyes is that when she does

Danny is there, staring at her with the ruined, bloody tunnels of his eyes.

Riley wakes stiff and cold in the sunrise. They are curled together under Cal's jacket. The ground is hard and uneven, every part of her aches. Both she and Cal are covered in fallen leaves as if the forest has given them a burial.

Close by, something soft and grey moves. The rabbit hops into view and sits on its hindquarters. It looks at Riley with its deep dark eye. Its ears and nose tremble. Then it moves off, leisurely, and is gone into the tangled undergrowth.

Riley shakes Cal and he groans. 'Cal,' she whispers. 'The rabbits are back.'

The first drops of rain patter lightly on the forest floor.

11

Adam

Two walls of the dining room are sheer glass. It's like eating in the sky, among the mountains, the treetops. Candles burn and flicker, reflected in the clear panes. In the distance, the Ferris wheel turns, lit by flashing red lights.

Leaf glances up only briefly as Adam sits. 'Did you have a good trip?' Adam asks.

Leaf smiles and returns his gaze to the paper. Adam feels like he did when Daddy got fired from the plant, all those years ago. He and Mommy sitting quiet, the room saturated with the scent of meatloaf. They knew what would happen if there was noise when Daddy wanted no talk.

Leaf's housekeeper brings in quails, roasted to the brown of parched grainfields. Leaf stands to kiss her on the cheek. 'Thank you, Ada.' She smiles and leaves in silence. Leaf goes back to the paper. Adam struggles with the tiny bones in silence.

'It's good to be back,' Leaf says suddenly, and Adam jumps. 'I hate leaving home.'

'What were you promoting?' Adam asks. He finds Leaf's schedule dizzying.

'I wasn't. I went to see about some stuff with the Foundation.' Leaf's foundation helps young men get off the streets. And I had to see Rick again.'

'Rick, who you're in love with?' Adam asks.

'It's over,' Leaf says, gently. 'Has been for months.' He puts down the newspaper. 'I can always feel it coming,' he says. 'The end. My fingers start itching.' He rubs the tips of his fingers and thumb together. 'It's like being bitten by mosquitos.' Leaf gestures towards his rejected plate. 'What is this? Roasted mice? It's like chewing on a pincushion.'

'It's great,' Adam says even though he hates it.

Leaf cracks a quail leg, sucking the marrow out.

'That's gross,' Adam says mildly.

Leaf pushes his plate away and lights a cigarette.

Adam coughs.

Leaf shrugs. 'I can't stop.'

'You stop by not doing it,' Adam says. 'It's just action.'

Leaf narrows his eyes and clears his throat. 'You stop by not doing it,' he repeats. It's eerie how accurate the impression is. It's more than tone – Leaf has captured tiny hesitations and rhythms that Adam never knew he had.

'It's just action,' Leaf says in Adam's voice. 'It's just action.'

'Stop it,' Adam says.

'Why?'

'I don't like it.'

'You don't like it,' Leaf says in Adam's voice, and now he smiles with Adam's smile – shy, the tiniest bit lopsided, turning up at the right-hand corner. If you stayed around him long enough, Adam thinks, he might steal all of you. You'd look in the mirror one morning and there would be nothing.

'Why are you doing this?'

'It's the itching in my fingers.' Leaf releases a long stream of smoke through his nostrils. 'You'll leave soon too. Everyone does.'

'Sure, if you make them.' Adam pushes back his chair and leaves the room.

In the hall firelight flickers, throwing the shadows of antlers giant against the walls. Adam stares at the fire. He takes long, slow breaths, trying to calm his mind and body.

Someone comes down into the hall. Adam keeps his gaze on the fire and doesn't look. It might be Leaf or it might not, and he can't face it if it's not.

A hand touches his shoulder, tentative.

'The thing is,' Leaf says, 'I lash out at the people I like. I grew up poor and then I got rich and I grew up way too fast. I got lazy and spoiled and now I've forgotten almost everything that normal people know.'

'Ok,' Adam says. 'Go on.'

'I'm so afraid that I'm a monster, then I act just like one.'

'That was almost an apology.' Adam turns. 'I can show you now.'

'Show me what?'

'It's done,' Adam says.

'Really?'

'Look,' Adam says. 'You didn't notice when you came in that you had an entire new wall and a new bookcase?'

'Sorry,' says Leaf, meekly.

'Come.' Adam leads him to the new bookcase, reaches behind the books and touches the lever. 'They're all real books,' he says, 'except *Pride and Prejudice*. That's fixed, to hide the switch.'

The bookcase slides neatly back to reveal the dark yawning mouth of the secret stair.

They go inside and Adam closes the door. It's not cramped, they're not touching, but it's not a large space and he's aware of their two bodies, he can feel the warmth of Leaf's skin. Adam takes the flashlight from where it hangs from a hook on the wall and flicks it on. The spiral stair leads on upwards, snaking through the space he's made between the false panelled walls of rooms on either side.

He points to the places in the walls on either side, which are studded with light. 'These are the peepholes. On this level they look into the hall on the right and into the den on the left.

'Most are hidden by bookshelves. One or two holes are set into the friezes carved on the pillars in the wood panelling, or the eyes of daisies. I designed some to look like screws in the corner of the antler mounts.' Adam swallows. He wants Leaf to like it – to love it.

Leaf puts his eye to a pinpoint of light facing the den. Adam starts to talk again but Leaf grabs his wrist strongly and puts a finger to his lips. Adam peers through an adjacent hole. Samuel Ross, Leaf's head of security, is in the den. He's not doing much. He stands, staring, blank face handsome. He has a pen in one hand and a notebook in the other. Both arms hang loose by his sides.

'Looks like he's powered down for the night,' Adam whispers.

Ross's head turns sharply towards them. He stares at the blank wall. Eyes narrowed, he approaches. He peers; it feels like he's looking directly at them. His blue eyes are piercing but apparently Adam concealed the holes well. Ross makes a sound that's somewhere between a sigh and a cough. He makes his way slowly out of the room. Adam and Leaf shake with laughter.

'Are they on all the floors?' Leaf asks. He's trying to sound neutral but Adam hears that edge in his voice, the sharp excitement.

Adam leads, flashlight picking out the spiral staircase. There are small landings on each floor. 'Viewing platforms,' Leaf says. Together they peer through the peepholes at the quiet library, the screening room, the study. Only the library is occupied. Leaf's housekeeper, Ada, stands, dust cloth in hand, reading a leatherbound edition of *The Man in the Iron Mask.* Her burnished curls shine in the low light from the sconces. They're designed to resemble Victorian gas lamps.

She looks up sharply. Like Ross, she seems to feel their eyes on her, though the staircase is soundproof. She closes the book with a snap, replaces it carefully on the shelf and goes from the room.

'She wanted to read more,' Leaf says. 'I'll give the book to her tomorrow. I want her to have it.'

'If you do that, she'll know,' Adam says. 'That you were watching.' He takes a deep breath. 'Ok. Last one.'

Three storeys up the staircase ends. There's a short passage with another viewing platform at the end. Adam ushers Leaf ahead of him. He holds his breath and watches Leaf's back as he leans down to peer through the peephole.

'Oh,' Leaf says. He covers his mouth with his hand. 'What did you do?'

He knows what Leaf is seeing. Adam's unmade bed, the door of the wardrobe containing the mirrormen clothes. The vast plate glass window, reflecting back lamplight and his clothes strewn across the floor. These holes give onto Adam's bedroom, so Leaf can watch him any time he wants.

'You should leave me,' Leaf says.

'I'm not afraid of being seen,' Adam says. 'Look anytime you want.'

'But what if my fingers start to itch?' Leaf's voice is a child's whisper.

Adam finds Leaf's mouth with his. He strokes Leaf's jaw. 'Let me make you happy.'

Leaf is still. He neither returns Adam's embrace, nor pushes him away. In the dim light Adam can't see what he's thinking. 'Ok I give up,' Leaf says. 'You win.'

'You go back and sleep in your own bed,' Leaf says. So Adam gets dressed as Leaf watches. He fingers the collar of Adam's button-down. 'You're pretty scruffy, aren't you?' His voice is fond.

Adam is stung. He loves this shirt, it's Fred Perry.

'You need new clothes, anyway,' Leaf says. 'We'll get you everything you need.' He gets out of bed and heads towards the shower. After that first passionate scuffle in the staircase, the bedroom part wasn't a success. It was awkward, nothing fitting or flowing easily. *But it doesn't matter*, Adam thinks. *We have the rest of time to get it right.*

He realises that Leaf is looking at him with understanding. Adam is bad at hiding his thoughts.

'That wasn't great,' Leaf says. 'That's my fault.' Adam starts to protest but Leaf stills him. 'No, it's ok. I've got issues. From when I was a kid.'

'Anyone would,' Adam says. He touches Leaf's cheekbone.

'I want to change,' Leaf whispers.

'Don't,' Adam says. 'You're perfect.' He winces inwardly. He understands all those songs on the radio now, all those movies he made fun of when Christie made him watch them. Love makes you say ridiculous things.

'Lonely people get into bad habits,' Leaf says. 'But I want to break them.'

Adam's feelings are so strong they resemble terror.

'How long can you hold your breath?' Leaf asks.

'What?' Adam laughs. 'I don't know.'

'You could time it,' Leaf says. 'I want to know.'

'I don't understand.' To Adam the conversation feels surreal, like joke or a story, not a real person talking to another.

'It doesn't matter. Time for you to go.'

Adam feels a cold wash of fear. 'What did I do?'

'Nothing.' Leaf's crooked smile makes Adam's heart fit to break. 'I get bad dreams.'

'What dreams?' Adam has a need in him, to drink Leaf in like water.

Leaf shakes his head.

'Please,' Adam says. 'I want to know.'

Leaf breathes. 'Fine,' he says. 'In the worst one I'm a Russian doll. I'm inside myself. I'm trapped, screaming to get out. It's dark inside all those layers, weird versions of me, keeping the real me inside.'

'I'm sorry,' Adam says.

'I know you are,' Leaf says gently and pushes Adam out of the bedroom. The door closes behind him with a click.

Back in his room Adam feels elated and lonely. He sits on his bed and stares at the wardrobe. Before he can change his mind he goes over and flings open the door. Shuddering, he pushes the mirrormen's clothes as far down the rail as he can. Adam hangs his Fred Perry shirt carefully on the end of the rail.

Is he ready for this? But it's done, now. The die is cast.

For a moment Adam could swear he hears someone crying. A child. But it's gone; it was the wind, maybe, whistling its mournful way through the valley.

He looks at the centre of the rose where the spy hole is hidden. He smiles a little and waves, in case Leaf is watching.

The next couple of days are happy. Adam and Leaf take long runs together. Leaf is encouraging Adam to get fitter. They swim in the lake at the head of the valley. It is shockingly cold but they have to, Leaf says. Cold is good for you.

'You have a heated pool,' Adam complains, teeth clicking together.

'Just because you *can* have something doesn't mean you always need it,' he says. 'It's good to deprive yourself occasionally.'

'Only rich people say stuff like that.' Adam tosses water at him.

They swim in icy water, shouting. They make out at the top of the Ferris wheel. Ross operates it from the booth below. They pass him on each revolution – he stares at the controls, deliberately not looking up. It's strange at first, this intimacy before strangers. But Adam gets used to it surprisingly quickly. The people who work here are part of Nowhere – the land, the house. There's no need to feel anything about their opinions. But the attitude of the staff towards Adam shifts subtly, too. They are more attentive. He has stopped being one of them.

Leaf pulls Adam underwater and kisses him there. The romantic parts go well. They are working on the rest. Adam wants to accept Leaf as he is, he really does. He knows how hard it is to escape childhood. But he feels so lonely sometimes when they're together. He feels furthest away from Leaf when their bodies are closest.

He puts his hand on the back of Leaf's head, on the place where the seam of the scar rises from his skull. It's an old scar, maybe very old. Adam has seen it through the shining golden hair. Leaf doesn't talk about how he got that.

'What can I do for you?' Adam asks. 'I want to make you happy. Tell me what I don't know.'

Leaf's face closes in thought. It's unnerving, his ability to become blank, untenanted. It's an acting thing, Adam supposes. Leaf can show feeling so he knows how to hide it too. Leaf strokes Adam's shoulder, slick and cold. This is something Adam has asked him to do, when he vanishes. 'Let me know you're still in there somewhere.' Now Adam wishes he hadn't. It's like being stroked by a machine.

'Hey,' Adam says. 'Hey.' He pokes Leaf gently in the ribs.

'Darkness is like a disease,' Leaf says, dreamy. 'You can be inoculated. If you let in a little, Adam, you won't get sick.'

Adam looks at him, measuring. 'What does that mean?'

Leaf takes a deep breath and tells Adam what he wants with averted eyes. 'Underwater is the way to practise. You work up to it.'

Later Adam will remember Leaf's voice telling him his desires, mingling with the call of loons in the reeds, their long mourning notes.

12

Riley

It's Riley's turn to bleed the woman. She flicks on her lighter and passes the flame along the blade. The woman jumps when she hears it and starts to cry.

'Stop it.' Riley speaks in a whisper, like Noon told her, because voices are less identifiable that way. They don't want the woman to recognise who's speaking or know how many of them there are.

There's not much room left on the woman's arm, which is covered in band aids. Riley finds a patch of bare skin, making sure it's far away from the blood-rich blue veined places on her wrist. She tries to think of it like the cut she makes in rabbit hide to skin it.

Riley cuts neatly into the woman's forearm. The woman cries out. She shakes with sobs. The blood runs down her white flesh and drops into the sunken garden. Riley doesn't look down. She doesn't want to see it again, the ground breathing in and out.

'Are you all going to kill me?'

'I don't know,' Riley replies honestly. 'But I saw what you did to your kids and I wouldn't care if you died.' Riley shakes the bottle of baby formula and puts the nipple to the woman's mouth. The woman sucks hard, she's hungry, takes too much and chokes. Riley removes the bottle and waits for it to pass.

'My name's Alison,' the woman says through tears.

'I don't care about that either.' Riley pushes the rubber nipple back into the woman's mouth. 'Drink.'

Dawn is shaking Riley's shoulder, gently, speaking to her. She holds a piece of summer carrot in her other hand. Riley startles up. How long has she been sitting here? She's by Home Barn, the afternoon is low and golden, and the air is warm. Dandelion clocks blow over the meadow in the long light. Riley looks down at the rabbit trap in her hands. Right, she's supposed to be mending it. But the wire has got loose somehow, the end has cut Riley's hand. Blood trickles down her finger.

She stares as the drops fall, coating the sleek blades of grass at her feet. Does the earth tremble a little with pleasure?

Riley, Midnight and the little ones are by the lake when the men come to the gate. The summer sun beats from the blue sky, the meadow is tall and bleached gold, alive with grasshopper song. Riley smells the warm earth on the wind.

Midnight, Oliver and Riley are in the sandy shade of the rocks. Oliver sits playing with the sand and Midnight lies back with her baby on her chest. Una stares at Riley with her round dark eyes.

Riley can't sit. She paces, watching the water as it gleams under the sun. The kids crouch in the shallows, building pebble castles and digging holes.

Oliver fidgets, restless. 'Can't I go in the water, Riley?'

'No. You stay here.' Riley says to Midnight, 'I don't understand, how can you let them swim in the lake? The crocodile ...'

'The crocodile won't hurt them.' Midnight yawns and turns over. 'You always hear it coming. It makes a squeaky noise.'

The little red-haired boy, Rufus, drops his electric blanket on the sand and wanders towards them. He smiles a shy smile. 'Mommy,' he calls. That's all Rufus ever says. *Mommy.*

'No,' Riley says as kindly as she can. 'We've talked about this.'

Rufus smiles and turns away back to the gleaming waterline. He always seems so happy. He and Hallie scream and run along the shallows, water scattering in diamonds.

Everyone seems to take care of the kids together. Apart from Midnight and Una, who's always wrapped tight to her chest, there's no indication of parents. There's the very blonde-headed one, Whitey. She's a little older than Rufus, six maybe, and one of her eyes has been injured in the past. The eyelid has healed wrongly, the skin too tight, so that her eye never opens fully. A thoughtful, serious child. She doesn't talk much. Whitey wades out into the lake.

Riley can't take it anymore. 'Come back,' she calls. 'Come back in right now, Whitey!'

Whitey turns and looks at Riley, then drops and swims out into the water.

'I'm going after her,' Riley says. 'I'll bring her back.'

Midnight clamps an iron hand around Riley's wrist. 'You don't touch her. I've told you again and again, you outsiders don't touch the children until it's time, you might contaminate them.'

'So I'm more dangerous than that thing?' Riley's breath comes fast. 'We won't hear it coming – who can hear a squeaky toy underwater? You're insane.'

'You have to calm down,' Midnight says. 'I'll get her out of the water, if it means that much to you.' Midnight stands and yells. Whitey turns around and swims back towards the shore.

'Listen,' Midnight says to Riley. 'At a watering hole at dusk in

Africa, all the animals gather to drink. All of them together. Antelopes and lions and hippopotamuses. Not everything is hunting each other all the time. There's a balance.'

'It doesn't make any sense.' Riley tries not to yell. 'Why would you take the risk? Are you – are you trying to give one of them to the crocodile – to Nowhere? Like,' she lowers her voice to a whisper, 'like that woman in the house? Is it another kind of sacrifice? Are you raising them for the blood?'

Midnight slaps Riley so fast that her hand is a blur. 'Don't you ever say that.' Her voice trembles. 'Everything that every single one of us does here is for them. Every single thing.' Midnight stops, and Riley sees that Hallie is standing a few feet away. Hallie is thin and dark – nine or so. She seems lonely. The younger kids are too young to be her friends, and the rest of them here are too old. She's only three years younger than Dawn but it's a world away.

'It's ok, honey,' Midnight says. 'Riley and I were just talking.'

Hallie holds out her hand, looking at Riley. There is a cricket in her palm. Hallie never says anything at all. She smiles though, a lot. She's smiling now.

'Thank you,' Riley says, not moving. She's not allowed to touch. Riley sees that Hallie has torn the legs off the cricket.

'Hallie!' Midnight says. 'That's not nice. We don't hurt things unless we need to eat them.'

Hallie nods, serious like she's just learned something. She puts the cricket in her mouth. Then she spits it onto the ground, still wriggling, and wanders away.

Noon feeds the kids separately, at odd times of day. Riley understands it. She must have been giving them extra food during the bad time; they didn't lose weight. Oliver eats with Riley and the others but Noon always tries to give him something extra, even if it's only a little something – a boiled pigeon egg, a rabbit heart.

Something flashes, blinding bright in the distance.

Midnight tenses. 'We have to go. Come on, kids,' she calls. Over the meadow, the point of light flashes again.

Riley takes Oliver's hand, holds it tight. 'What's that?'

'It's Noon,' Midnight says. 'She signals with a mirror when people come to the gate.'

Noon, Everett and Cal are in Home Barn. 'How long have they been there?' asks Midnight.

'Cal saw them about an hour ago,' Noon says. 'They came up the road then went into the tree cover. I think they're trying to decide what to do.' She shoulders a ragged canvas backpack. 'Let's go.'

The road to the gate is overgrown, not travelled much. Brambles and creepers spill all over the ground. Riley feels asphalt under her trainers, ridged and bulging like a frozen sea, full of holes and craters.

The road passes into a narrow defile between the high red rock on either side. It feels like being inside something breathing. Riley can't help the feeling that the cliff walls on either side are moving gently in and out like flanks, or like a birth canal. Nowhere seems to breathe, everywhere. At the end, there is the gate. It's solid steel, rearing up fifteen feet high. Rusted, greenish lettering stands above it, flaked gold spelling out the name of the house. It's backwards, of course, from Riley's point of view. There's curlicue on the 'W' which sets it apart from the H, makes it look like there's a weird gap in the middle of the word.

Now here.

It's like a word game or a joke. Now here, the opposite of nowhere.

The base of the gate is shored up with rocks and boulders so it can't open inwards. It wears a winding crown of coils of rusting razor wire. Wicked shards of green glass gleam in spikes along the top, glued there somehow. On top there are the remains of animals. A gleaming green spike pierces the body of some bird, a blackbird perhaps. It has been impaled. There are others. A rat, a possum, a rabbit, a blue jay – dried-out old remains. It's a warning. This is what happens if you try to cross. Riley can't look at the gate without feeling it in her flesh, how it could hurt her.

Noon holds up a hand to signal silence. They creep closer to the metal, the carrion. Wind whistles through the struts and wire, singing on the steel. The gate is welded shut. There must have been electricity here when it was done, or at least acetylene gas or something. Noon motions them forward and they climb the slope of boulders. There are small gaps in the structure of steel. Riley looks through.

Beyond the gate the sun-warm road runs on down the mountain, a sheer drop to one side, scattered pine forest lining the gentle upward slopes on the other. It ripples in the breeze. At first she thinks, *but there's no one there*, and then she sees it, a gleam in the green shade. Metal or maybe a camera, winking in the sun. Something stirs. A dark head, an arm. Their face is in shadow. Noon hands Riley a claw hammer. Very quietly, she takes other metal tools out of her backpack and gives them to the others. A crowbar, a wrench, a rusting cast iron bell.

'Hello?' a voice calls. 'Hello?' The man hesitates. 'Is there anyone there?' He seems to feel their presence, silent behind the metal. 'Uh, is this Nowhere – the place Leaf Winham used to live?'

'Fans,' Midnight breathes. She smiles like she's about to have a good time.

Noon holds something above her head. It's an old .22. Riley breathes inwards. She hadn't known there was a gun at Nowhere. She longs for her own gun, tossed down the hill after – well, never mind that.

'Cover your ears,' Noon breathes. She squeezes her eyes closed, points it skywards and fires.

The sound is deafening in the narrow rocky cleft. It shatters her eardrums even though her palms are clamped over them. Everything seems to be shaking – Riley's heart, her bones, the gate. Her head is full of ringing song. Everett, Cal, Noon and Midnight start beating on the gate with their tools. Riley is still partly deaf from the shot, but she does it too, screaming and pounding the reinforced steel with the hammer. She glimpses, through a gap in the steel, two figures, both men she thinks, with backpacks and some kind of equipment.

Hot joy and anger course through her. Seeing them run makes her feel so good.

They beat on the metal until they're sure the men are gone. They lean against the warm rocks and pant. Riley sees her grin mirrored on the others' faces. They won. They're a castle with the drawbridge up. *Now here* forever.

'Sometimes they come back,' Noon says. 'Someone should keep watch today.'

'I will,' Riley says. She kind of wants them to come back, to pound the metal gate and scream at them like a ghost, to see the fear in their faces.

'Can you use this?' Noon asks. Riley nods and takes the gun.

She leans against the warm rock in the sunshine. Home, she thinks, yes. She has found it at last. She can't suppress the thought – will a day come when the men at the gate are not fans – when they are looking for Riley? No one knows she's here. Why would they look for her at Nowhere?

The high voices fade into the distance. Everyone's a little delirious as they head back to Home Barn. Riley sits, but her senses are alert. Beyond the gate, the wind rustles in the leaves. The air is still as a pond, there's no breeze. She bends silently and looks through the gate. There is movement in the undergrowth opposite. Something is coming. Riley reaches for the pistol.

A deer moves out of the shadow of the forest and stands in the ruins of the road. It must be a buck, its antlers are graceful and pointed – on one side, anyway. When the buck turns its head, Riley sees that that on the right side, the top half of its antlers have been snapped off. It's horrible, somehow, this maiming, the disfigurement. Riley's breath catches in her throat. The deer raises its head and bounds away back into the dim forest.

13

Marc

Kimble and Marc lie staring at the dark like children who can't sleep. Crickets and frogs sing in the forest. They just finished the last of the tequila they brought. It has been another day of searching. The woods seem endless. Marc is starting to wonder if everyone has imagined this tunnel. But they got some good B-roll and Linus told a story about how he saw the fire that day so it was kind of ok.

'Marky Mark?' Kimble asks, drowsy.

'Mm.'

'We're here because we want to understand them, right?'

'Right.'

'Not because we are them. Not because it wants us here. The house.'

'What do you mean?' But cold thrills are already crawling on Marc's skin.

'You know what they say. Nowhere draws lost kids to it. Are we lost kids too?'.

'Wish I'd had a camera on you for that,' he says. 'Poetic.'

She laughs. 'I am that.'

Marc drifts, everything blurring through his eyelashes. 'You're my best friend, Kimble,' he says, half into his pillow. 'You're like my sister. I wish you were my sister.'

'Thank you, Marky Mark.' Her voice trembles with amusement but it's not mean.

'We love each other, me and you,' he says, sliding towards the dark.

'Maybe we do.'

'I wish you'd forgive me,' he whispers.

'Don't,' Kimble says, sharp. 'Do not ask me to comfort you, not about that and not when you're drunk.' All the warmth is gone from the air. Marc stares at the spinning dark. A dull ache begins to throb at the back of his head. He waits, mouth dry and heart pounding, for this to pass.

Kimble and Marc had the idea for the documentary on the Nowhere children at exactly the same moment. They were in Vegas covering something terrible, like always. People had died.

'It can mean something, right?' Kimble says, stirring her drink with her straw. 'This job. It doesn't have to be bullshit. Or not all of it.'

'I used to think that.' Marc tosses back his third tequila shot. He takes out a cigarette, feeling a rush of joy at the knowledge that he can smoke it right here, indoors. He misses the tip of the cigarette with the lighter on the first pass but gets it on the second, squinting.

'It must be hard,' Kimble says, 'being away from Silvie.'

He nods, because it is. 'I love her so much. I didn't believe in love before her.'

'People think romantic love is the only kind,' Kimble says. 'Or at least the main kind.' She snorts. 'It's so reductive. Romance is totally overrepresented in books and film and the way we talk ...'

'Ah,' Marc says.

'What?' Kimble sucks on her frozen margarita. 'Why are you looking at me like that?'

'Because I see.'

'What's that now?' Kimble asks, an edge to her voice.

'You're in love,' Marc says.

'What? I don't know what you mean.'

'Ok.' Marc shrugs and swirls the tequila in his glass.

'Jesus, Marc,' Kimble's voice rises. 'You can't just say stuff like that.'

'It's not an insult.' Marc pats Kimble's arm. 'We can talk about it if you like. But we don't have to.'

'The times,' Kimble says, 'that you pick to be insightful are demented.'

'I am annoying,' he says, wagging his finger in her face. 'But I am correct.'

'Fine.' Kimble rests her head in her hands. 'Ok, why not? No reason you can't know. She and I have been friends for years. We went to NYU together. She just got divorced from her husband. I had never thought of her like that. But one night we drank too much and I cried about – doesn't matter – and she comforted me. And I saw her. I really looked at her for the first time. The weirdest thing is that I could see her getting freaked out, because she was seeing me too.' She shrugs. 'It's not so comfortable, being seen. It's excruciating actually. But I can never go back to who I was, now. See, *that's* demented. I was just living, going about my business, then everything turned on a dime. Now I'm always scared because so much of me depends on that person. On Margot.'

'We have to put it all somewhere,' Marc drops his cigarette into his empty glass. 'It's an achievement – to love.'

'Love is a rock face.' Kimble chews a toothpick. 'If you put a foot wrong there's a long way to fall.'

'You won't fall,' he says.

'We never talk like this,' Kimble says.

'I know. Do you like it?'

'I think so. Do you?'

'I think so too,' he says but it's hard to tell. Marc has a fear of abandonment that's nearly as old as he is. He feels him stirring in the deeps, the lonely child he once was. 'I'm happy for you, Kimble,' he says. 'You deserve to be happy.'

'We're going on our first vacation together,' Kimble says. 'Margot and me. Mauritius. It's paid for, non-refundable. Next month.' The toothpick in her hands snaps into two neat pieces. 'It's good to have something that can't be changed. It's freeing, weirdly. She wants us to spend real time together.'

'Real time?' Marc asks. 'As opposed to fake time?'

'I guess she just means – being with her, instead of always on the road with you.'

'I see,' says Marc.

Kimble takes the salt shaker and pours it into her palm. The salt makes a little white mountain in her hand. She stares at it.

'What do you want most?' Marc asks. 'If you could cover anything, make any doc on any subject, what would you make?'

Kimble throws the salt over her shoulder (to keep the devil away, Marc remembers that). She crunches an ice cube in her teeth. 'Don't you already know what I'd do? What would you make?'

'That's cheating,' Marc says. 'You can't throw the question back.'

'I can do anything I like.'

'We'll both say what we want to make. On three.' Marc taps his empty glass with a spoon. 'One, two, three.'

'The Nowhere children,' Marc says as Kimble says, 'Leaf Winham.'

They stare at one another. 'I didn't know you were interested in that,' Kimble says. 'I mean – I've always wanted to go out there. When did you ...' She shakes her head. 'Let's drink more.'

'Yes.' Marc's body hums with feeling and tequila.

*

'We could,' Kimble says dreamily, head resting on her folded arms. She's very drunk and nearly asleep. They're in a different bar now. It's full of mirrors. Marc doesn't remember getting here but it seems ok.

'Could what?' Marc lights the wrong end of his cigarette and coughs, taking a mouthful of whiskey to get rid of the taste. They're going to get moved off the table soon, he can see the waitress giving them that resigned look. But she'll wait a couple more minutes, he knows, hoping that they'll leave of their own accord.

'We could make something about Nowhere.' Kimble runs a wet finger around the rim of her glass, making it whine.

'Mmm,' Marc says. 'The lizard tail comes off, is the problem. It's all rumour, no facts. No reliable witnesses. And mountain people don't like flatlanders.'

'They haven't met us yet,' Kimble says. 'We're good at sliding through the cracks.'

'That's true,' Marc says, delighted. His head is full of bees.

He gets up, swaying only a little. 'Ok,' he says. 'I need to be unawake. Seven a.m.?'

Kimble nods.

'You ok on your own?'

'I thought I was,' Kimble says, thoughtful. 'But I was wrong.' She gets her cell phone out with slippery fingers. As Marc walks away he hears Kimble say, 'Margot?'

Marc has never heard that voice from Kimble before – the warmth, the hope. It makes him feel very drunk and afraid.

Marc collapses on the bed but his mind keeps turning like a windmill. He thinks and makes a phone call and thinks some more, as the bed weaves under him, swimming in liquor.

Marc and Kimble leave for Salt Lake City at 7 a.m. There's been a murder in a conservative Mormon family. Marc feels sick of everything. He doesn't want to ask another grieving parent about their dead child. But he does it anyway and Kimble pushes in close on their tears, and the job feels even more terrible than usual.

Afterwards they sit, shaking, in a diner. Marc orders too much food then stares at it, revolted. Kimble glances at him then slides his onion rings and grits over to her side. Marc closes his eyes and feels the white travel up his face.

'Are you going to puke?' Kimble asks, interested.

Marc shakes his head but he doesn't know. He takes a trembling sip of iced water and breathes deeply.

'So,' he says. 'Do you want to do it?'

'What?' Kimble eats an onion ring in one mouthful and Marc winces.

'Make the show about Nowhere,' Marc says. 'We've got a shoe-string budget. We've got a short window of time.'

Kimble chews slowly. 'How did you do that so fast?'

'I caught them in a receptive mood,' Marc says. 'And I used my last favour.'

Kimble nods. Everyone has a final favour that they save up – to shoot you to the top or save you from the bottom. 'And I was drunk,' he adds. 'Tequila confidence. Anyway I booked an interview.' He takes out the hotel envelope covered in long scrawls of ballpoint. 'I wrote it all down. Annie Lyons, who says she was taken by the children for some kind of bloodletting ritual.'

'Give me that.' Kimble takes the envelope, annoyed. 'What a mess. I'll start a schedule. When do we go?'

'End of this month,' Marc says. 'We need to be there until September.'

'But—' Kimble stops herself. 'Are you sure? We couldn't wait?'

'We need to catch Annie before she goes to Cancun for the

summer,' Marc says. 'And you know how it goes. The longer they think about it the more often they cancel.'

'Yes,' says Kimble. 'I do know how it goes.'

'It's our chance.' Marc shrugs. There is no budget, of course, he's funding this all by himself and deciding the schedule. He won't need his retirement fund anyway.

'You're sure,' Kimble says, 'about the timing? It has to be next month?'

'I know.' Marc shakes his head. 'It conflicts with your vacation.'

'It's not just a vacation.' Kimble stares ahead at something Marc cannot see. 'That is bad luck,' she says quietly. 'What are the odds?'

'Take a day, think about it,' he says lightly.

'Ok, Marc.' Kimble's voice is controlled and low. 'Why now? Tell me that.'

Marc shrugs. 'That's the wrong question.' If he wasn't so hungover Marc would be afraid of Kimble now; her eyes are like broken flint. He keeps his body loose to hide his fear. Marc forks grits into in his mouth, meeting Kimble's gaze. 'Do you want to do it?'

Kimble slides out of the booth. 'I'm beat. See you tomorrow.'

Marc watches her leave the diner and then through the big window which gives onto the street. Kimble stands perfectly still for a moment. Then she takes out her cell phone. She presses her lips together in a tight line and makes a call.

Kimble suspects what Marc has done and he knows that, and she knows that he knows. Neither of them will mention it. They will go to Nowhere. They will put all the rest aside and work.

Marc spits the grits into a paper napkin. Guilt surges through him but the wave of relief is stronger. Only Kimble can get him through what comes next.

14

Riley

The apple trees have shed their rotten fruit and new green boles are appearing among the leaves. The hornets are gone. The grass everywhere is growing long and glossy. Flowers are coming out, the meadows and woods are starred with wild roses and horsemint. The cicadas sing furiously and plump rabbits and wood pigeons find their way into the snares every day. There seem to be birds' nests with rich-yolked eggs in almost every tree.

'Time for her to leave,' Noon says. They're in the Home Barn, eating roast pigeon for breakfast. 'We've put enough blood in the land.'

Cal nods. 'I can—'

Noon touches his hand. 'Everett and Riley can take her.'

Cal nods. He spends most of his time out on the mountain, searching for his brother.

The woman's head hangs, her chin resting against her chest. Her eyes are slitted, seeing something other than Nowhere House around her.

Her arms and legs stick out pale from her filthy nightdress, covered in band aids and dots of taped-on cotton wool. Her hair is a greasy mat and she smells of her own bodily waste. The odour, combined with the scent of the chloroform, makes Riley gag. She doesn't think they even need the chloroform; the woman seems to be unaware of her surroundings.

'I saw him,' Alison slurs.

'Ignore her,' Midnight preps the cloth. Riley's eyes water.

'Leaf Winham,' the woman says. 'He's still here. He came to me.'

Midnight claps the cloth over the woman's mouth. 'Shut up,' she says, comfortable.

'Gentle,' Noon's voice is stern.

'She doesn't deserve gentle,' Midnight hisses. 'Everett and I watched her through the window those nights. The things she's done ...'

Noon puts a calming hand on Midnight's wrist. 'She has taken in all our hunger – she has put her blood in the land. We treat her with respect.'

Noon, Midnight and Everett give their breath to the house. The woman's mouth hangs open and a slow string of drool drips from her chin. When they lift her into the blanket she feels as light as a bundle of sticks.

Rain begins to fall as Riley and Everett carry the woman down the trail.

'Are we taking her back to Ault?' Riley asks, panting. Everett just shakes his head without turning. 'Good talk,' Riley mutters to herself. She has never heard Everett speak a word, and she has never seen him without the black ski mask. Sometimes she wonders if he has a mouth at all under there. She imagines pulling back the wool to find only a smooth blank surface where his face should be.

The mountainside is wooded, there is plenty of cover, but Riley still feels exposed. She realises that she has gotten used to being enclosed in the valley, cradled by the surrounding peaks. The sky is too big out here; she feels like an ant crawling across a stone.

They pass along narrow deer trails, along a high ridge, then start to descend. Below, Riley sees it snaking along the hillside. A road.

They crouch in the undergrowth by the roadside. Everett motions for Riley to stay still. Every part of him is alert, listening. There's no sound but the rain and a wood pigeon somewhere, softly mourning. Everett nods and they dart into the middle of the road, their burden swinging between them. The road over the mountain pass is a dark river cutting through the trees. Riley stares at it for a moment, the bright yellow lines and smooth black tar. The woods and the road are side by side, but they are like things from two different universes. Everett waves at her, impatient. She starts and nods. They lay the woman down gently on the asphalt, right in the middle, on the painted line. As they're rolling up the blanket, there comes the distant sound of an approaching engine.

Everett claps Riley on the shoulder. It's impossible to be sure, but she thinks he's pleased. Together they run back into the forest, back up the mountain, through green leaves dripping with fresh rain.

Tonight there will be a fire by the Ferris wheel. Riley helps Oliver through the orchard, which is green and alive with birdsong. The evening air has a hint of autumn chill in it, and Riley pulls her rabbit-skin cap down over her ears. She has made one of these for everyone at Nowhere.

The wound in Oliver's leg is somewhat better – it seems to have settled into a constant dark angry red. It refuses to fully heal. Riley thinks the recent bad nutrition is partly to blame. She hopes it will be ok now. Oliver says it doesn't hurt much. Riley tries to keep it clean. Sometimes she can smell the wound, its sweet rotten odour.

*

A bonfire of pine crackles at the base of the cliff. Sparks rise red in the night. Firelight plays on the rusting metal of the Ferris wheel.

The children are seated in a circle on the grass. Light dances on their uplifted faces. They are looking at the stars.

Noon gets up and draws Riley and Oliver into the centre. Riley feels a stab of fear. What if her blood is to feed the land? Maybe the woman's blood wasn't enough. But Noon touches her cheek and smiles. She takes something from her pocket, and puts it around Riley's neck, where it sits alongside her locket. It's a rib, a small one, from a baby deer maybe, pierced at either end, strung on a red cord. The bone is pure white and polished by age. Riley puts her hand over it. The bone is very cold to the touch. *Just been dug up*, Riley thinks.

'You've been patient,' Noon says. 'I know it wasn't easy. But you have proved yourselves, and you have waited long enough.'

Noon gives Oliver a necklace of small vertebrae that click together like beads.

'You are both part of us now,' Noon says. 'No more doubt or fear.' A hard lump rises in Riley's throat. She nods.

Around the circle, everyone claps and whoops. They crowd in to hug Riley and Oliver.

'Welcome,' Noon whispers in Riley's ear. 'You will always be Nowhere and Nowhere will always be you.'

The children turn to the east as one, towards Nowhere House in the distance, and Riley finds herself turning too. As the others put their hands to their lips, she follows suit. For the first time, Riley gives Nowhere her breath too.

Now here.

They laugh and drink small sips of burning liquor from a bottle, something that tastes of liquorice, with weird lettering on the label. It's old, the neck of the bottle crusted with white sediment. Each mouthful lights up their bodies like fireworks. Midnight does an impression for the kids, of the men running away from the gate. The children scream with laughter, jumping up and down in the light of the flames.

Noon comes to Oliver. 'Do you want to go play with them?'

'But it's not allowed,' Oliver says.

'That was before. Now it's allowed.'

Even so he looks to Riley for permission. She smiles and gives him a little push. 'Go on, Oliver Olive.'

The children scream and chase each other, Oliver panting with his odd hobbling run. Riley watches with a painful twist in her heart. She looks at Cal, sitting across the circle in the firelight. His head nods and sinks to his chest every so often. He's always tired from walking the mountain, looking for his brother. But as she watches he looks up and meets her eyes.

Riley quickly looks away but she still feels his gaze, which sends blood coursing through her cheeks.

She realises that Everett is standing in front of her. He holds a hand out and after a moment Riley takes it. He shakes it twice, up down up down, then turns smartly and walks to the other side of the fire where Dawn is talking to Midnight about something that makes them laugh. Everett sits down cross-legged nearby. He is still. He keeps his eyes on Dawn.

'I'm sorry.'

Riley starts. Noon's face is close to hers in the firelight. 'Sorry for what?'

'It's hard, to take the blood sometimes.' Noon's words are a little slurred.

'I saw what she did to those kids.' Feeling and conviction well up. Riley hesitates. 'Is it real?'

Noon smiles. 'Depends what you mean.'

'Does bleeding her make the land better?'

'I think so,' Noon says. 'I think it makes the world better.'

'Me too,' Riley says, fierce, and Noon takes Riley in her arms. They hold each other tightly for a moment. Midnight strides over, singing, something out of tune about hills and pipes calling. She takes the bottle from Riley with a flourish. 'I'm older than you, you shouldn't even be having this.' Noon follows her, leaving Riley alone.

'Come for a walk,' Cal says in her ear. Riley nods.

They go into the dark, leaving the voices and the firelight behind.

Cal and Riley sit on the platform above the lake. The white moon ripples on the surface of the water. Above, the sky is velvet. There are night sounds of frogs, cicadas. Fireflies dance in the woods behind.

'Does that happen often? People coming to the gate?' Riley asks.

'Sometimes. They want to see where he lived. Nowhere House.'

Cal salutes to the east and Riley does too. By the light of the moon, his missing finger makes his hand look claw-like.

'How did that happen?' Riley asks.

'We tried to kill someone,' Cal says. 'Me and Danny. We got the same punishment.'

'Is that why you ran away and came here?'

'Nope,' he said, throwing an acorn at the lake below.

From the far side of the lake, in the distance, Riley hears something that could be the squeaking wheeze of a dog toy.

'It happened here,' Cal says. 'At Nowhere.'

'Who did you try to kill?' Riley asks. Her heart is beating fast. 'Who took your finger?'

'Noon,' Cal says. 'Before she became leader I tried to stab her with a knife. Danny and I didn't realise, yet, that she could make things so much better here.'

'How—'

'She did it with a machete on a tree stump. Cauterised it after, then sewed it up.'

'How do you live with her after she did that to you?'

'Noon saved our lives,' Cal says. 'I'd be dead if it weren't for her. I'm just glad she has such good aim.' He hurls another acorn down into the dark lake.

Riley starts. Is something moving under the moonlit water?

'Scared of heights,' Cal says, 'scared of the crocodile ...'

Riley wants to say, *I've killed two people, I'm not scared.* She finds these moments of possibility exhausting. Every time she could tell Cal the truth she has to make the choice again not to. It wrenches all the strength from her. Instead Riley says, 'Those are normal things to be scared of.'

'You know you can't ever leave, now,' Cal says. His arm slips about her waist.

'No?'

His hand is warm, it strokes gently. 'No. Those are the rules. Nowhere has you.'

'Ok,' Riley murmurs into his mouth. He tastes of liquorice. She imagines Leaf Winham's shadow looming over them, blacking out the stars and sky, a giant. She imagines his arms wrapped around the valley, holding them all in. She's a murderer too, she belongs here.

Riley slips into the stall. Oliver is already asleep. She strokes his head gently.

'I know what the demon is, Riley,' Oliver whispers, half dreaming.

'Oliver, there's no demon here,' she says. 'We're safe.'

'Hallie told me. The demon is growing up.'

Cold runs up and down her. 'Oliver, did you tell Hallie about what happened on the trail?' Riley shakes him awake. 'About the demon?'

He starts to cry. 'Don't be mean,' Oliver says.

'Did you?'

'No!'

'I mean it. If you say anything to anyone about the demon again, I won't let you play with those kids anymore. I'll lock you in here all day on your own.' Riley looks into his eyes. 'Do you understand?'

'But—' he says, fresh tears welling up.

Riley shakes him again. 'Tell me you understand.'

After a moment, he nods, scrubbing his eyes with a fist.

In the morning he won't speak to her. He looks at her with resentment over the rag doll he's shoved into his mouth. Riley lets him be. He gets over these things eventually.

Noon sets Riley to watch the gate again.

'They sometimes come back,' she says. 'Nothing like human optimism.'

Riley sits yawning by the gate in the warm afternoon. Her body remembers the places Cal touched her last night, and where she touched him. The sun and these thoughts join together and she drifts.

There's a sound from the other side of the gate like the scratching of wood on wood. Riley sits up slowly and puts her eye to a hole in the gate.

The broken-antlered deer stands in the centre of the road. He rubs against a low branch, scratching. The antler is growing back, Riley thinks, but it's thin like a question mark. She's glad to see he's doing ok.

'No want go,' says a little voice behind her. The deer leaps away. Riley turns. Whitey is there in her long white dress. The hem is brown and tired, it drags on the dusty road.

'Hey,' Riley says. 'Pick up your skirt, keep it out of the dirt.' The dress has intricate embroidery at the neck; it's linen, Riley thinks, long and flowing like an old-fashioned nightdress.

Whitey doesn't seem to hear. She shuffles forward, dress trailing. She reaches longing arms towards Riley and makes a little peeping sound. 'Up.'

'I'm not carrying you.' Riley doesn't care about the dress that much. 'What are you doing here all by yourself?' She's not keen on kids in general but Whitey makes her sad. Even her name is odd, like someone forgot to give her one then looked at that white hair and thought, *that'll do.* Riley thinks, at times, that she can see Noon in Whitey's serious expression.

'No go,' she says in that reedy voice. Riley realises that she has never heard Whitey talk before. Whitey lunges towards Riley, reaching with both arms. Her foot catches in the billowing white gown and she lands on all fours on the cracked asphalt. She crouches there, back heaving. She starts to cry.

Riley climbs down the stack of boulders to the road.

'Hey,' she says to Whitey. 'It's ok. We just get up again.' She picks her up out of the dust.

'No go away,' Whitey whispers.

'No,' Riley says, looking into her forlorn face. 'I won't.' Whitey makes to put her arms around Riley's neck and she feels a strange warmth. But it's not a hug. Whitey's hands close about Riley's neck. They squeeze. It's impossible, the strength in her little hands. Riley chokes and grabs at them, but the small fingers are like steel. Her vision starts to cloud. Riley shoves Whitey away hard, so she falls again on the dusty broken-up asphalt, hitting her back hard. She bursts into tears. Riley goes to help her up again but she jumps up and runs. Her scream is high and cracked; it sounds like it could pierce the rock.

Riley watches her run up the overgrown road back towards Home

Barn, heart pounding. Riley can't help thinking – what if that had been Oliver, whose throat she had her hands around?

When Riley reaches Home Barn, Whitey is hugging Noon's legs and crying. She whispers into Noon's ear. Noon's gaze is on Riley like a dagger.

'Why would you hurt a child?' Noon's voice is cold. Riley has never seen her angry.

'I didn't mean to,' Riley says. 'She was – I guess she was playing. She had her hands around my neck, I couldn't breathe. I was just trying to get free.'

Noon takes a deep breath. 'Have you been struggling recently, Riley? Mentally?'

'No,' Riley says. Noon's face changes under her eyes; now it is so full of disappointment, as if Riley has just told her a lie.

Oliver is looking at her from the corner of the barn. Riley hadn't seen him there. He comes forward slowly, eyes big. Riley holds out her arms to him, but he reaches for Noon instead.

'Oliver,' she says blankly. 'Oliver Olive, what are you doing?' He looks like he's scared of her.

'You don't like children, do you, Riley? Midnight told me.'

'I guess not,' Riley says. 'But I don't want to hurt them.'

'Everything we do here is for the children,' Noon says. Riley sees that Peach, Whitey, Rufus and Hallie are standing in the doorway of the barn. They look on, silent.

'Everything,' Noon says again.

'I understand.' Riley looks at Whitey. 'I'm sorry.'

After a moment Whitey nods.

Noon comes close and looks Riley deep in the eyes. 'You can't do that again.' She puts her arms around Riley and breathes in her ear. 'Don't make them angry.'

‘I’m sorry,’ Riley says. The shock of Noon’s displeasure is awful – she feels like she has been left outside a warm-lit window, looking in, shivering in the cold.

‘It’s all right.’ Noon touches Riley’s cheek. ‘Nothing can stay the same forever. It’s one of the signs of change – that Nowhere is getting ready to transform. We are becoming ready.’

‘What do you mean?’

‘No one grows up, here,’ says Noon. ‘This is a place for the children – for them to be safe. So we must leave, or we must transform. Midnight is almost too old for Nowhere already.’

‘You’re scaring me.’ Riley is held – she cannot take her gaze from Noon’s pale eyes.

‘Change means fear and loss,’ Noon says. ‘But it is the only way.’ She leans in and embraces Riley. ‘Children are sacred,’ she murmurs. Every hair on the back of Riley’s neck thrills. ‘Growing up is a demon.’

15

Adam

He's sitting in the sunshine drinking lemonade, thinking about Leaf's return tomorrow. He chews on his lip, almost drawing blood. He starts at the tap on the shoulder. Lemonade spills from the rim of the glass onto the slate paving. Adam realises that no one touches him these days, except for Leaf.

It's Samuel Ross. 'There's someone here for Mr Winham,' he says, flat.

'Well, he's not here,' Adam says.

'I think it would be good for someone to talk to this person.'

'Ok,' Adam says. He has a terrible fear that it's Christie, that she has come to mess it all up, to take him back or tell Leaf that Adam is a terrible person. The child is due in a month.

They drive the golf buggy down through the falling leaves to the Nowhere gate. Standing by the guard booth is a uniformed police officer.

'I'm Adam Leahy.' He offers his hand. The officer shakes it with both of his.

'Officer Lloyd, Boulder PD.' He's probably only in his forties but looks older, as people tend to do around here. He has a thick grey moustache and a constant look of mild surprise. 'I wanted to talk to Mr Leaf Winham regarding a police matter.'

'He's not here. You can talk to me.'

'It's regarding Rick McFadyen.'

'Oh.' Sourness creeps through him at Rick's name. 'What did he do?'

'Mr McFadyen has been missing for six months. According to his datebook, Mr Winham was one of the last people to see him. Here, at Nowhere.' Officer Lloyd looks around at the peaks, the wooded hills. 'Beautiful spot,' he says politely.

'Rick and Leaf don't speak anymore,' Adam says, distant. 'Rick moved away.'

'If so he moved without his passport or his ATM card. Both were still at his apartment. Why would be leave those behind?'

'I don't know, I never met him,' Adam says. Jealousy spikes in him. Rick takes up more of his thoughts than he would like.

'I thought maybe you had run into one another,' says Officer Lloyd.

'Leaf stopped speaking to him before I came here.'

'Well, if you or Mr Winham think of anything—'

Samuel Ross appears silently at Officer Lloyd's shoulder and hands him the usual wedge of paper. Surprise crosses the officer's face as he reads the cover page. He says, with dignity, 'I'm a police officer. We don't agree not to disclose things.'

'Of course,' Adam says. 'I'm sorry—'

'We would be most appreciative of any help in finding Mr McFadyen,' Officer Lloyd says. 'He has a mother, sister, brothers – family who are very anxious to find him.'

Adam feels a spike of guilt for his unkind thoughts. 'Ok. I'll ask Leaf to get in touch.'

Samuel Ross is at Officer Lloyd's elbow again. 'Mr Winham will cooperate fully with any police investigation. Please contact our office to schedule an appointment.'

'Thank you,' says Officer Lloyd. 'I will.' He puts the NDA firmly back in Samuel Ross's hands. Ross takes it. He melts away, is gone so quickly that Adam looks around for him in bemusement.

'Mr Leahy?'

Adam starts. 'Yes?'

'Walk with me to my car, why don't you? It stalled a little ways down the hill.'

'Ok,' Adam says. It seems impossible to say no.

The gates part in silence and they walk through. Adam is suddenly unnerved. He realises that he hasn't been outside Nowhere in months. Sounds are different out here, the crickets louder. The wind is harsher on his cheek, the sun unrelenting as it beats the top of his head. He misses the valley walls.

'I hope the engine starts,' Officer Lloyd takes off his hat and wipes his brow. His hair clings to his skull in wet strands.

'I'm sure it will,' Adam says. 'These inclines are hell. Downhill is easier.'

'Smart,' Officer Lloyd says. 'I'll remember that. Downhill is easier.' He laughs a little.

'How far is it?' Adam asks. The space all around is getting to him.

'Not much further,' Officer Lloyd says. 'I heard the engine working hard a ways back and I thought I'd pull over to let it cool but then it quit anyway.' He pauses. 'The only turnout I passed, there was a car already. Been there a while, if you ask me. A blue Mustang. Covered in leaves and so on. A shame. It's a nice car.'

'Yes,' Adam says. 'That's mine.'

They round the corner. The cruiser is at an angle across the road. 'Blocking the way,' Officer Lloyd says, apologetic. 'But I couldn't help it.'

He opens the door of the cruiser and backs away from the wave of heat that escapes from the car. 'Woah,' he says, cheerful, leaning on the door. 'Give it a minute. You know, Mr Leahy, you seem like a nice guy.'

'Thank you,' says Adam, cautious.

'You were reported a missing person,' Officer Lloyd says. 'But I found you I guess.'

'I was never missing,' Adam says.

'Your girlfriend doesn't agree,' says Officer Lloyd, swinging down into the driver's seat. He winces. 'Damn, this seat is burning hot. Anyhow.' He pauses before closing the door, squints up at Adam. 'Don't you feel guilty for leaving her like that?'

Anger starts to sing all through Adam. 'What the hell gives you the right?' he asks. 'I told her I had a big job to do. I told her I'd be away.'

'Two months ago,' Officer Lloyd says. 'You think that's ok?'

Adam gasps. Pain crawls up his chest. 'No,' he says. 'I know it's not.'

Officer Lloyd nods, thoughtful. 'I used to think there was no such thing as real good people or real bad people.' He pauses. 'Then I started in the force. And now I know that isn't true. Fair enough, most fall somewhere in between, but there are truly good people and bad ones. And,' Officer Lloyd takes a card from his wallet, 'there's also another kind. The really bad ones. Monsters and gods are the same thing, I guess. Neither are human anymore. You're not one of those monsters, Mr Leahy. You messed up. If I were you, I would call your girlfriend and go home. There's still time to make it right.' He holds out the card. 'If you decide to stay here,' he says, 'you could need this. It's my number. It will find me night and day.'

Adam takes the card with numb fingers.

Officer Lloyd turns the key in the ignition and the cruiser growls to life. 'Well, would you look at that,' he says happily.

Adam watches the police car disappear down the mountain road.

*

That night Adam can't sleep. He tosses, irritable. Everything seems flat and tiring without Leaf. But he will be back tomorrow. Adam can't get Officer Lloyd out of his mind. The encounter bothers him more the more he thinks about it. He fingers the card with Lloyd's number on it, turning it over in his hands.

Adam lifts his head at a faint sound. At first he thinks he's imagining it, but it draws nearer. It is a car engine. Maybe it's staff driving home or something, he tells himself. But surely they would all be gone by this hour. The engine comes closer and he's sure – someone is driving up to the door of Nowhere. Leaf must be back early. Adam gets out of bed. He can't find shoes and he doesn't care but then he stubs his toe on the side table and hops in agony for a moment or two. He can hear the car pulling up. Adam tosses his clothes here and there (he does not open the closet, he does not go near the mirror-men). Adam hears the vast front door creaking – it's so loud, audible even on the third floor. He finds sneakers, shoves them on his bare feet and runs down the grand staircase.

The hall is quiet. The alarm console flickers green on the wall. It is disarmed. Adam peers out of the window. He can't see a car, but Leaf may have parked round back. Somehow Adam has missed him. He runs up to the master suite on the second floor. Leaf will be there, unpacking. He likes to deal with his own clothes.

Adam opens the door to Leaf's room, eager. The lights are off so he flicks the switch. Everything is cool and white and beautiful; the linen canopy on the four-poster bed flutters in the gust from the opening door. The room is empty. The door to the palatial bathroom is open. He looks at the pristine room for a moment then shakes his head, turns the light off and leaves.

Adam searches Nowhere House, wandering like a ghost. Maybe Leaf fell asleep somewhere. Maybe he's in the den. Maybe the gleaming steel kitchen. Maybe he's gone out on the porch to smoke. But these places are untenanted. The rooms are all dark. Leaf insists that all lights are turned off at night. He is very environmentally conscious.

Adam paces to and fro before the fireplace in the hall. The dead antlers cast shadows on the walls. He's worried that there has been a burglar or a home invasion.

Adam notices a faint glow. It's from the hallway which leads to the long sunroom. Adam goes to the hallway. It is empty. The dimmer is on low, soft uplighting leading away into the house. None of Leaf's staff would forget to turn off these lights.

Adam goes down the hall, heart beating in his throat. The sunroom is dimly lit, too. It is also empty. Adam walks around it three times, looking for a hidden intruder. But there is no one. Eventually he turns the light off. He goes back to bed.

Adam is finishing his breakfast on the terrace when he hears the front door creak. He throws his napkin down.

Leaf is standing in the hall. He looks up and sees Adam. They run to each other and hold tight.

'There was a police officer at the gate,' Adam begins.

'Ross told me.' Leaf runs a hand through his hair. He looks tired. 'He probably just wanted to look around. Maybe he wanted an autograph.'

'It didn't seem like that,' Adam says.

Leaf smiles, a little grim. 'He left when I found out I wasn't here, didn't he?'

'He was asking about Rick.'

'People will use any excuse.'

Adam feels a surge of guilt. Leaf is always being watched. He understands why Leaf wants the secret staircase. With all these eyes on him all the time, who wouldn't want a private place where he can be quiet and watch in turn?

*

They walk among the apple trees. Leaf likes to say hello to Nowhere when he's been away. It's good to be outside in the sunshine. The air is full of the scent of green and growing things. Leaf bends to stroke the grass. 'She's happy today.'

Adam smiles. He likes Leaf's insistence that Nowhere is a person.

'How did you two meet?' he asks. 'You and Rick.'

'Through the Foundation,' Leaf says.

'He worked for you?' Adam asks.

'No. We helped him.'

'So he's – homeless?'

'He was,' Leaf says. 'We got him back on his feet.'

'Isn't that a little weird?'

'What?'

'You have—' Adam waves his hand around him, taking in Nowhere, the peaks, the valley, the house of warm wood and gleaming glass. 'All this. He doesn't have anything. You know what I mean?'

'I don't,' Leaf says. 'Explain it to me.' His eyes are warm and his tone is level. But Adam suddenly feels cold. He can't say why.

'Isn't it kind of unethical to date someone who the Foundation is – helping?'

'You tell me,' Leaf says politely. 'You seem to know.'

'Where were your bags?' Adam says suddenly.

'What?'

'I met you at the door when you got back this morning. You didn't have any bags.'

'Ross brought them in from the car,' Leaf says.

'I didn't see—'

'It's his job for you not to see him.' Leaf stops. 'I can't stand jealousy.' His voice cracks. 'It ruins everything. It spreads like rot.'

Leaf thrusts his fists against the trunk of an apple tree. He punches it hard, making small noises of pain.

'Hey, hey.' Adam takes hold of Leaf's wrists. 'Stop it.' The grazes on Leaf's knuckles ooze blood. 'I didn't mean to—'

'Everyone wants things from me,' Leaf says. 'Even the police just want to get in here and poke at me and look and pry. Before I put up the gate and hired Ross, people found their way in here all the time. They would take branches from the apple trees. One woman tore hair from the horses' manes.' Leaf leans against the apple tree. He tips his head back, eyes closed. 'You're just the same as all the rest of them – you want to own me.'

'That's not fair,' Adam says. His heart pounds hard at the pace of disaster. 'I was just asking. Last night I heard the door. The alarm was off. Who else knows the code? And there were lights on in the house. I thought you had got home early.' He swallows. 'I looked for you all over. So when you came in this morning, and I didn't see your luggage, I just thought—'

'What? That I was hiding from you somewhere in my own house?' Leaf's voice vibrates with anger. 'What you're saying makes no sense. Where do you think I was?'

'I don't know,' Adam says. 'But I also don't understand.'

'Do you know why I work with the Foundation?' Leaf asks. His voice vibrates with anger. 'They say that long ago five children were kept here, back when it was an apple farm. They were murdered and the town covered it up. Maybe that's why Nowhere wants me to help young people in trouble. She's trying to make up for it.' Leaf breathes. 'And maybe it's time you went back to your girlfriend.'

'I'm sorry.' Adam feels everything receding. He imagines a world where he doesn't see Leaf or touch him ever again. Adam takes Leaf's hand and kisses it gently, avoiding the bloodied knuckles. 'I don't want that,' he says. 'I want you.'

Leaf gives him a smile. Adam's heart swells and almost stops. 'I don't want my fingers to ever get itchy with you,' Leaf says. 'I want you to stay forever.'

‘I will, if you’ll have me.’ Adam feels he’s lifting right out of his body.

They come out through the trees. In the distance, beside the house, is the green hill mounted with white crosses. ‘Jackrabbit,’ Adam murmurs.

‘What?’

‘Nothing,’ Adam says. He squints. He had thought there were twelve graves on the hill – now he counts thirteen.

‘Did something die?’ he asks, anxious. ‘Is that a new grave?’

‘Just some tropical fish,’ Leaf says. He trails a finger down Adam’s cheek. ‘Did you swim yesterday?’ he asks. ‘How long did you hold your breath?’

16

The Lilac Boy

Big Bobby Sullivan tells the story at the bar of the Dew Drop Inn sometimes, when they'll let him, and when he's had his third or fourth drink.

He was shooting grouse out of season one early fall when he saw the face in the tree.

It had been a poor day for grouse, but Bobby hadn't come up here for the kill, more for the crisp air and to be alone on the mountain with his thoughts and the whispering trees. And away from his wife, with whom he'd had an argument that morning. There had been snow a couple of days before. It hadn't stayed; the weather warmed straight after and everything smelled fresh-turned, like the earth was alive.

Bobby stopped by a lilac tree to eat his sandwich. It was a meatball sandwich; his wife made the best meatballs in Ault. Everyone said so. He ate it sitting by the lilac tree, which was in full bloom. The scent was heavy, making him kind of sleepy; lilac always did that to him for some reason. There was a rustling in the tree and Big Bobby took up his gun again, thinking of bears. They travelled this way around this time of year. He peered into the purple and green but couldn't see anything. But he had the prickle in his skin that told him eyes were watching. The sun went behind a cloud and it felt later in the day, suddenly, than it had a moment before. He realised that his watch had stopped. Bobby felt very alone all of a sudden. He thought about home and a beer and these seemed like great things. Just because he needed a little while away from home didn't mean he didn't love it. And he wanted to get off the mountain. He couldn't remember why he'd wanted to come out here so badly. He struck out through the forest back towards the main trail.

A few moments later he stopped. He realised he had left half his meatball sandwich on the ground by the tree. He groaned aloud.

Bobby was raised near the mountain; he knows that you never leave food out like that, not in wild places. The bears find it. They learn to like human food. After that they are unstoppable. A couple of years before, tourists had got into the habit of leaving food out in clearings by parking spots, and then retreating to their cars to watch the bears come. The bears learned quickly. When tourist season ended and there was no more food they started coming closer to town. Some of them learned to knock the lids off trash cans. Eventually a black bear was caught on camera, delicately letting herself into a kitchen by turning the handle on the porch door. After that of course the Park Service had to shoot her. Bears cannot start to like human stuff. Just like people mustn't let the wild get inside them or it might take over.

Bobby likes a bear, in its place, and he didn't want his sandwich to lead to all that so resignedly he began to retrace his steps to retrieve it.

He pushed through some scrub and the lilac tree was there, ten feet or so away. Bobby caught his breath. There was a face in the blossom. It looked up and its eyes drove holes into him. *I never got so close to screaming like a girl*, he said later. The eyes he looked into were black tunnels. The small face was scarred with smears of orange-red blood. The thing opened its mouth and screamed. Bobby saw pieces of half-chewed meatball on the pink tongue. A scent of caries and decay filled the air and he clapped a hand over his nose and mouth.

Then the face disappeared, and there was a commotion of blooms and leaves and a thump. A small body fell to earth and Bobby heard, unmistakably, the sound of a child crying.

His fear vanished – he had two boys himself and he recognised that tone – just a hungry child who had been pushed too hard. Bobby said, gently, 'It's all right, son.'

The boy looked up at Bobby. Tears made tracks through the dirt on his face. He clutched Bobby's sandwich to his chest. The red stuff on his mouth was meatball sauce. 'You hold on to that now,' Bobby said. 'I've been looking for someone to help me finish it, so I'm glad you came along. Now, why don't we get somewhere warm? Maybe brush your teeth and give you a bath. How about some pyjamas?'

He offered his hand. The boy looked at it and bared his teeth. Big Bobby held his breath; he thought about that rotting mouth closing on his tender palm.

'Dead,' said the boy, fast and low. 'All dead – dead, dead, dead.'

Bobby was shaken. But he held his hand out still, in offering. After a moment the boy put his small filthy hand in Bobby's and they walked slowly, carefully through the forest and all the way down the mountain.

'So I knew someone had loved him, once,' Big Bobby says always, at this point in the story. Someone claps him on the back and they all pretend not to see as he quickly wipes his eyes.

The little boy was never identified. Bobby took him to the police station and he seemed ok with that. He could read, Bobby thought, because he gave a little nod when he saw the 'police' sign at the door. But he wouldn't talk. His injury was substantial. Who would do that to a child?

His clothes were in tatters. Some of the labels were from

companies that went out of business years ago. No one had reported a boy missing matching his description. In the local paper they called him the Lilac Boy.

'I know how it sounds,' Bobby would say. 'But I think he came out of the mountain.' He'll sometimes pause here and wipe his eyes again. 'How long had he been up there? How many years?'

The boy was taken by the state, and later Bobby heard he was adopted. Somewhere far away. That was good, he thought. Get him away. Give him a chance to get the mountain out of him.

Big Bobby could never find that particular lilac tree again though he looked and looked. He was never the same after that day. Though who is exactly the same after any day that passes? Still, the mountains do things to people, mind and body.

It's because of stories like this that in Ault they say, *don't go nowhere alone*. It's kind of a pun, but it's not a joke.

17

Riley

She's pulling carrots in the meadow. She likes carrots; they always feel like a surprise. They grow wild at Nowhere, come out of the ground thin and bright like shoelaces. She shakes the dirt off one and eats it. Fresh, sweet, crisp. 'Blood in the land,' Riley murmurs. She slips one into her pocket as a peace offering to Oliver. He's still upset. He fixes her with dark-green judging eyes. But he'll come around.

She sees a figure at the top of the cliff. Her heart fills with light; Cal is back from the mountain. Riley still loves to be here when he returns. He's always sad but it makes him hold her so tightly and makes her feel so needed.

She runs to greet him.

Something is wrong, Riley can see that as she gets closer. Normally Cal has a sure, clever step like a cautious deer but today he's unsure, stumbling a little. When he's near enough she sees that he is crying.

She breaks into a run. He does too and they seize one another hard as they meet at the foot of the slope. 'What is it?' Riley asks, heart pulsing with worry. She strokes his forehead like that could help. 'Are you ok? Are you hurt?'

Cal shakes his head, mouth wrung out. 'I found him,' he says. 'Danny.'

A hum begins in Riley's ears. 'That's great,' she says. 'Where was he? Is he coming back now?'

Cal shakes his head.

Riley takes his hand. She holds it as hard as she can. Grief is a solid thing, she knows. It will fill your body right up.

Cal takes her face in his hands and looks at her, searching. 'I don't know what to do,' he whispers. 'Help me understand. Tell me what happened.'

'What happened when?' Riley meets his eyes, bewildered. *Sun in the head.*

'Don't, Riley.'

'Cal, I don't know what you're—'

He shoves her away, hard. 'I have to talk to Noon.' He runs from her through the meadow, down towards Home Barn.

Riley follows. She walks, doesn't run. She needs to think. The humming in her ears builds to a roar. She weighs up all the options quickly. Can she get to Oliver? Maybe she can take supplies, and Oliver, and be gone by the time ... Then she remembers that Oliver is helping Dawn repair the hinges on the doors to Home Barn today. She curses inwardly.

Maybe this is nothing, she thinks. Cal's upset. There's no reason to connect his brother's death to Riley. How can there be? She breathes, bright, drawing all the sun she can into her head.

'He was four miles down the magnolia trail,' Cal says. He stands upright as a spear at the front of the barn. Riley slips in at the back. She can see Oliver is seated on a stool right at the front, looking up at Cal. Oliver worships Cal a little.

There's a tremble in Cal's frame which makes Riley's heart sore.

Noon shakes too, her whole hand in her mouth. Riley knows that this can't be true, but that's what it looks like. Her white fist is shoved hard in, almost down her throat.

'He was by the tree like a ship,' Cal says. 'He was off the trail, down the hill in the deep brush. Or what used to be him. Animals had been but his jacket and boots still held some bones. His skull was there. I thought maybe snakebite, or he ate the wrong kind of mushroom. But there was all this stuff thrown around.' Cal swallows; she can hear the dry click of his throat. 'A cooking pot, clothes. Not his stuff. Someone else had been there. There were two holes ...' He covers his mouth. 'Bullet holes in his skull.'

He takes a deep breath and reaches into his pocket. 'Then I found this at the edge of the clearing.' He opens his hand.

So that's where the other one got to, thinks Riley, blank. The stupid Nana dog looks up from the worn-out grubby cotton.

'It's my Nana sock!' Oliver is so happy. 'Can I have it, Cal?'

'In a minute,' Noon says. She says gently to Cal, 'Let me deal with this.'

Noon helps Oliver up. He stands, looking at her with trust.

'We're so happy that you and Riley came to live with us,' Noon says.

Oliver nods. 'Me too.'

'We're a family now. And that means we tell each other the truth. You want to stay here with us, don't you?'

'Yes,' says Oliver. His eyes are wide.

Noon kneels and puts a hand on his shoulder. 'Oliver, how did your leg really get hurt?'

'Riley shot me,' he whispers.

Noon says gently, 'How did that happen?'

'She was shooting at the demon,' Oliver says. 'She shot him in the eyes.'

Riley stares hard at Oliver. Heat and cold race up and down her frame. A roaring builds in her ears.

Oliver turns and looks straight at Riley. 'She says it was a demon,' Oliver says, high and thin. 'But it was a boy. I saw. He had a hand like that.' Oliver points.

'Like this?' Cal raises his maimed hand, shaking.

Oliver nods. 'Riley said not to tell. She said to lie. But I didn't want to.'

'Did you come here to kill us all,' Noon asks, 'like you killed Danny?'

'I don't think so,' Oliver says, worry creasing his brow.

'No,' Riley says. 'It was an accident. He attacked us—'

'He would have never,' Cal's voice shakes. 'Ever.'

'Oliver?' Noon bends and strokes his cheek gently. 'Did the boy attack you and Riley?'

Oliver turns his eyes up to Noon's. 'No,' he whispers. 'Sometimes Riley lies.'

Someone seizes Riley from behind, a hand closes about her neck. She's pressed against black wool. Everett's breath is hard on her cheek. She sees the gleam of metal. The machete kisses her throat. All Riley can think is that she has been waiting for this all her life, to be murdered. It runs in the family after all.

Noon whispers, 'You killed Danny and then you came here. We welcomed you. You slept here and ate our food and made yourself one of us.' Noon stops. 'What is that you're holding?' she says gently. Riley realises that she's clutching the locket at her throat. The old silver gently grazes the edge of Everett's machete.

Noon unclenches Riley's fist from around the locket.

'Don't,' Riley whispers.

Noon pulls hard, snapping the chain. 'Who's in here?' she asks. 'Who do you keep next to your heart?'

Dawn steps forward. 'I know.'

'Dawn,' Riley whispers.

'You killed my friend,' Dawn shakes her head. 'You killed and lied.'

'I didn't mean to,' Riley says, eyes fixed on the locket in Noon's hand. 'Please.'

'I liked you, Riley,' Dawn says. 'That's worst of all.' To Noon she says, 'It's her father and her mother in the locket, or so she thinks. It doesn't open, but it's her most precious thing.'

'You kept this from me, Dawn,' Noon says, kind. 'We will talk about that.'

Noon puts the locket on a rock. She takes up a stone and raises it high above her head.

'No.' Riley's voice sounds like someone else, she is outside her body.

'It's not nearly enough payment,' Noon says, 'for the life you took.'

'Please,' says that strange voice from Riley's body.

Noon brings the stone down on the silver. Once, twice, three times. On the fourth blow there's a sharp crack. The locket springs neatly open.

Noon holds up the picture so that Riley can see.

It's not a photograph of her father, or not exactly. It's both of them.

Riley's mother and father stand under a cherry tree in bloom. Her mother looks young. She has terrible hair, a fluffy fringe. But she's smiling, happy in a way Riley rarely saw her in life. She has her arms around a man. Just some goofy young man. Riley stares at him, the father she never knew.

Noon gazes at the picture. 'Oh,' she says, 'Riley you lied about so much. I know who that is.'

Riley shakes.

Noon raises the rock above her head and pounds the locket into nothing. Riley's parents' faces vanish under her blows. Noon takes the mangled remains of the locket and stamps on them until they are flattened in the dust.

They carry Riley back to the stall. She writhes and struggles and twists her head, trying to bite. It's no good. Everett raises the machete and Riley screams. He brings the handle down on her head. Everything bursts into light and stars, the world swims. She is faintly aware of being put down in her stall.

The doors slam shut. Darkness falls. Outside Riley hears Noon say, 'Do you want to shut the bolt?' She hears a small peeping sound of pleasure. That's Whitey, Riley thinks. Then the bolt slides home.

Adam Leahy was killed by Leaf Winham three days before Riley was born. There had been hope, deep down inside her, about Nowhere. Riley acknowledges this to herself with a wash of bitterness. She wondered whether by coming here she might understand something about her father – why he abandoned his family for this high lonely place. A part of Riley had hoped that here at Nowhere the locket would open and she would know her father at last.

Light traces the outline of the door, thin pencils of daylight. Riley feels around the edges of the door, touching the light, but there's only a raw patch of wood where the catch once was.

Time starts to bleed into itself. If you're in the dark long enough you start to wonder if you exist. Her head throbs and she might vomit. She breathes deeply and it passes. She has to be ready to charge at the door the next time it opens, to get away. Otherwise they're going to kill her. The world swims and she tries not to drift, pinching the thin skin of her wrist hard between her nails.

She starts awake at the sound of the door opening. Riley drags herself onto all fours and crawls towards the light. She's unsteady and she retches. A hand reaches in and puts down a bowl. The door crashes shut and she's back in the dark. Outside the bolt slides home. Riley feels for the bowl with delicate shaking fingertips. She follows the scent – savoury, salty. Her hands find the bowl's edge. She dips her finger in and licks it – it's a stew. The strong odour of mushrooms fills the air.

Riley knows what it is, and that this is all the food that she will get. She scoops it into her mouth with a clawed hand. When it's gone she licks the bowl and fingers clean. She feels a faint gleam of hope. If they're feeding her, maybe they're not going to kill her after all.

The light is blinding and the rope is around Riley's neck before she can think. She claws at it but Midnight has already pulled it tight. She drags Riley out of the stall, into the dusk.

The Ferris-wheel fire is burning bright. Midnight drags her to the circle.

'Please,' Riley says to their averted faces, serious in the firelight.

Dawn begins to cry. Oliver hides his face in her shoulder.

'Please.' Not one of them will look at Riley. 'I didn't mean it.' She feels like a ghost. 'Don't—' she pleads again, looking around, hoping, seeking. She is invisible. When Riley's eyes light on Cal she stops. She drops her head to her chest. Riley can't look at Cal.

Noon stands and hands something to each person – two small objects. After a moment, with a rush of fear Riley realises what they are. They are human teeth. One is painted black, the other left white.

'You know what we're voting for,' Noon says. 'Riley has killed one of our own.'

Noon points at a tree stump. Everett goes to stand beside it. His machete gleams at his belt. Riley has seen this stump many times at firelight nights. She has even sat on it, talking and laughing. Now she sees the brown stains that spread across it. *This is where they take the fingers*, she thinks, hazy. She assumes that this time it's for her head.

'It's the worst punishment we have,' Noon says. 'So I want us all to agree.'

The faces around the fire bow, and offer their breath to Nowhere. Noon takes up a leather bag. 'White is no. Black is yes – for the house.'

'What does that mean, for the house?' Riley's throat is so tight she almost can't get the words out.

'You've no right to ask questions.' Noon's face is grim and stony. 'But I will answer. It means that all the blood goes to the land.'

Noon moves around the circle. One by one everyone drops a tooth in the bag.

Riley sees it, the flash of black in Cal's hand. She watches Oliver carefully, but she can't see what lies in his palm. 'Oliver Olive,' she whispers. He does not look at her.

Noon spills the contents of the bag onto the bloodstained tree stump. Black teeth, all.

Cal's throat moves hard. 'Wait. Maybe we ... Hold on a second.'

Noon comes close to him and puts a hand against his cheek. 'Do you want to change your vote?'

Cal's mouth hardens. He shakes his head just once.

The firelight is rocketing into the sky, Riley sees, and sort of mingling with the stars.

'Is this what you did to the others who lived here, before?' Riley struggles to get the words out. They seem to be solid in her mouth. 'Did you give their blood to the land?'

'We made ourselves safe,' Noon says. 'We made Nowhere safe.'

'What's happening?' Riley's mind is floating outside of her body. The faces in the firelight are drifting, fading in and out of the dark. She thinks of the mushroom stew she ate. It's too late, she knows, but she retches, bends double, trying to throw up. She can't and spits uselessly onto the earth.

Noon's face stretches and contracts, shadows and light writhing across it like worms. 'It's time for you to go. We're giving you as an offering.' She turns to Cal. 'It's your right to offer her. But first we take her bones.' Riley wants to scream but her mouth seems to have grown beyond a usable size.

'And this is for all.' Noon raises her voice. 'I have taken down the fly. I have cut the cable into pieces. We don't leave Nowhere anymore. We trust the land.'

Around the circle heads nod.

'We have discovered the penalty,' Noon says, 'for inviting outsiders in.' Noon comes close and reaches for Riley's throat. Riley waits for the blade, the cut.

Noon unfastens her bone necklace. 'You are no longer one of us.' Her breath smells like a warm meadow; it brushes across Riley's cheek.

Noon nods at Cal. 'You can take her now.'

He nods, pale. Riley struggles and pulls at the rope around her neck, but it's no good. As she goes, she sees Oliver's face, his mouth a round 'O' of horror. She wants to tell him it's ok, but it's not. 'Riley!' He starts to run to her but Dawn catches him. She holds Oliver back as he struggles.

'You did the right thing, Oliver,' Riley hears Dawn say. Dawn strokes his head.

Oliver's high cracked voice follows them, calling her name, as Cal takes her towards the woods.

With her last glance backwards, Riley sees Noon spreading her arms and tipping her face up to the night sky. Cal tugs on the rope around Riley's neck and she stumbles. But just before that, she could swear she glimpses Noon rising into the air, arms wide, taking flight.

The world gets stranger as Cal and Riley go through the trees. The rope about Riley's neck has become a live thing like a warm animal. The ivy and stinging nettles are crowned with whitish-green blooms and some of the flowers rise into the air and dart like gnats. The moss and leaf litter are a rich carpet beneath her feet.

Riley feels Cal's presence beside her like a sun but she can't look him in the eye. 'I'm sorry.' Riley can see her voice in the air. The words hang there in the dim forest light.

'I trusted you,' Cal says. 'I wish I'd never met you. But soon you won't be here anymore. You won't be anywhere. That's good.' He walks faster and tugs. Riley coughs and pulls at the rope about her throat. 'The sooner we do this the better. No one will miss you. Even your little brother hates you.'

'What did they give me?' Riley asks. 'In the mushroom stew?'

'The mushrooms,' he says. 'You know.'

Nowhere House rears up in the clearing ahead like a blackened tooth. Cal drags her towards it, the rope tight and choking about her throat.

As he shoves the door open with his shoulder, Riley thinks how quickly she could bend and seize a stone, of the report on his skull. But she hesitates and he feels the thought and turns.

'There's no point,' Cal says. 'I meant what I said. You can't leave Nowhere. The gate is sealed, and Noon has taken apart the fly. This is our valley and we would find you wherever you hid.' He leans in close. 'Also, if you run, I'll take your brother to the lake, tie him up and whistle for the crocodile. That would be real justice. Then you'd know how I feel. How it is to lose him.' He leans back, eyes cold. 'Are you going to run?'

After a moment Riley shakes her head.

They walk through the house, disturbing a pair of crows and a fox that turns and looks at them with golden eyes before slipping into the shadows. The walls and everything are pulsing. The house is alive, all right. Riley sees lights dancing in the air, all around. Each glowing orb surrounds a tiny person-shaped thing. Their dragonfly wings beat fast, a blur.

The sunken garden is green and dim. The chair looms, high and pointed. The wood is dark with blood – Alison's of course, and the blood of many others. The blood glows bright; Riley sees every drop, each stain on the wood. She struggles again, a river of fear rushing through her. She knows that once she's fastened into the chair, everything ends. The orbs of light are everywhere in the dark air. The tiny people watch, expectant.

The straps close about her arms and legs. Cal stands back. For the first time, he looks hesitant.

'Do it,' Riley says. She feels vicious, at this last moment. 'Why wait?' She was a fool to have imagined she could find a place in this world.

Cal takes out his pocketknife and slides it in, not quite into her vein, but nearby. The pain is not as bad as she expects. Adrenaline, probably, and the mushrooms might be helping. Riley's main sensation is heat, the warm gout of blood running over her wrist. The orbs of light dance through the air towards Riley and her wound. The small people hover by her wrist on their dragonfly wings. They dart delicately in and out of the red stream of her blood. She knows it's the drug they gave her but it's so vivid, the sensation of little lips sipping at the cut. The skin between all worlds seems worn very thin, here.

'Leaf Winham will come for you,' Cal says. 'You'll see him soon enough.' For a moment his anger gives way. He looks worried and sad. In that moment Riley believes him. Then she remembers that she is feeling fairies drink her blood.

She smiles, white-lipped. 'No I won't,' Riley says. 'Because he's dead.'

'When you've had the mushrooms,' Cal says, 'that doesn't matter. Normally we give them baby formula too. We don't want to make it too bad for them. As for you, all you get is mushrooms. We punish you inside as well as outside.'

'Cal.' Riley's body is singing.

'You probably won't die today,' Cal says, 'so someone will be back again tomorrow. Not me. I don't want to see you ever again.' Riley watches him walk away. His back heaves; he's crying and she wants to call him back but she can't, and she won't, and it would do no good anyway. Cal is lost to her.

His footsteps fade. Riley is alone in the house, now. She tries to think, to make a plan, but the bobbing lights fill her vision, and all that will run through her mind are two words, over and over. *Now here Now here Now here.* It mingles with the rhythm of her blood, dripping onto the earth.

When next she surfaces, Everett is there. His eyes look pin-bright against the black wool mask. He has just opened her up again, she can tell, because there is a hot rush passing across her wrist. He holds out a bowl. Riley's stomach clenches. She can smell the mushrooms.

'No,' she whispers.

Everett tips his head and nods at her slowly. He offers the bowl again. Food is better than no food, she thinks, when she is losing so much blood. Time has folded into itself, but she recalls from her time watching the Alison woman that the mushrooms' effects seem to last around four hours. Riley nods. She can handle it. Everett feeds her with a spoon, gently.

Riley eats. But halfway through her mouth purses out and her body collapses into sobs.

Everett offers her the spoon again. She shakes her head, tears running down her face.

He nods at her. The spoon clicks against Riley's teeth.

'I don't want to die,' Riley says. 'I know what I did. It was a mistake. I shouldn't have to die for a mistake.'

Everett shakes his head at her, slowly.

'Why do you wear that on your face?' Riley asks.

He shrugs.

'I don't believe you,' Riley says. 'Everyone does things for a reason.'

Everett puts the bowl on the floor. He goes still, so still that he almost blends with the night behind him. Or maybe it's daytime; Riley's not sure.

'Tell me,' Riley whispers. 'Why?'

He draws a finger diagonally across his face, transecting his eyes, his mouth. Then he does it again, and again.

'Show me,' Riley says.

He shakes his head.

'Doesn't matter, does it?' she whispers. 'I'm not going to last long. Do it for the dying. I'm giving all my blood to the land.'

Everett looks at her for a long minute. Then he raises his hand and draws the mask slowly upwards.

Riley tries not to make a sound when she sees, as more and more of his face comes into view. He puts the mask down beside him and just looks at her, brown eyes wide and beautiful among the scars. His skin is crosshatched with pale seams, all razor thin. A person made each scar with slow purpose.

'I'm sorry,' Riley says.

Everett shrugs. He covers the rutted landscape of his face with the black ski mask.

'Did you ever like me?' Riley asks.

Everett shakes his head. Then he nods.

'That's what I thought,' she says. 'Will you tell Oliver something for me? Please?' She coughs and sags in the chair. 'Please.'

Everett comes close and bends his head. She whispers into his ear, 'Tell him I won't let the demons get him.' He looks at her. 'Thank you.'

Everett nods and goes.

Riley lowers her head to the strap on her wrist. She grasps it in her mouth and gnaws, teeth grinding on the leather. Time moves on, she seems to be fading in and out of the world, but she doesn't stop. The leather is so thick she can't tell if she's making any difference at all. Shadows grow longer or maybe the sun rises. Riley swallows, jaws aching, dry lips gripping the strap. She thinks longingly of the well outside. She can see her blood on the patchy grass below, in the sunken garden; the dark slick stain spreading outwards. It drips gently from her wrist onto the grass.

At some point she becomes aware that footsteps are softly approaching across the long room behind her. Dry leaves flurry out of his path. He carries his own weather with him.

Riley shivers. She knows who it is – who is coming. Of course she does. His power touches everything, fills the ruins of Nowhere House. The light turns silver, every sound is etched upon the air. He comes to a halt just behind her. Riley twists and cries out, struggling against her restraints. She can smell the fresh earth on him; he is newly risen from the grave. His breath touches the back of her neck.

'You're not real,' Riley whispers. She knows it's a hallucination born of blood loss, the mushrooms and exhaustion. She knows all this but she doesn't believe it.

'Close your eyes if you like,' he says, gentle in her ear. 'You don't need to look upon me.'

Riley obeys, tears leaking hot from between her eyelids. She feels his every movement as Leaf Winham bends and puts his lips to her slit wrist, drawing the blood from her like a lamb feeding from its mother. Riley doesn't cry, she will never give him that. She thinks, *you killed my father but you will not kill me.* She goes inside herself. Even in the dark of her mind, the tiny people still dart, enrobed in light, hovering on dragonfly wings. She breathes and breathes. At length she feels the mouth leave her wrist and he's gone, or the hallucination has passed – whichever it was.

The light has fallen though it's too early for dusk. Time seems to be slipping out of place; Riley is afraid that all the rules of the world are breaking. But when she looks up through the ragged roof, she sees it is a storm which has been gathering overhead. Rain begins to fall in fat drops. Thunder rolls so loud she thinks she'll die and a jagged snake of white splits the air. It feels close, so close, the electricity of it grazes Riley's skin. Through the holes in the burnt-out house it rains like swords falling. Thunder cracks the world.

There's no point, Riley thinks. *Leaf Winham is real, he's here.* She heard his voice and felt his touch. Riley tips her head back, lifts her face up to the scattered rain that falls through the ruined roof. Cool drops pattern her face. She opens her mouth to drink the rainfall. The glowing lights dance in the air around the wounds in her wrists, darting through the downpour, sipping from her.

Riley closes her eyes. Let them have it. Maybe this is what it was supposed to be. She came here to find a home, to find her father. Maybe this is how. Maybe it's time to accept, at last, that she's not the kind of person who makes it out alive.

Something hurtles past her, shutting out the falling rain and electric sky. The thing charges away from the storm, flying down the length of the gallery into the shelter of the house. Riley recoils, heart pounding. As it goes, she sees the outlines of antlers and delicate legs. Then the deer is gone in a flash of fawn hide. As it vanishes into the dark Riley sees that one of the deer's antlers is thin, broken, just beginning to regrow.

Riley stares. She wishes that her hands were free so she could pinch herself. It's hard to tell what is real. But she felt the deer's passage, smelled its wet hide, heard the drum of its hooves. She has to hope.

'Have fun while you can,' she whispers to the dancing lights. 'Because there's another way out of here, and I'm going to find it.'

Riley bends her head to her wrist and takes the thick leather strap in her mouth once more. Grimly she gnaws, working the iron-hard leather between her teeth.

She doesn't think about time, she just chews until her jaws are sore. Occasionally she rests, teeth singing, but even then she keeps her mind working.

Houses are logical, she knows this. So Riley thinks about the house, goes through it room by room. She makes maps in her mind, soaring over the valley, looking down on Nowhere from above. She thinks about rock formations and caves and secret passages. She lets the dream take her, lets Nowhere wash over her, trying to summon every inch of it in her mind.

Riley judders awake to find Noon at her side, holding a bowl.

'I'm sorry,' Riley says.

'Eat.' Noon pushes the spoon against Riley's mouth. It clicks against her teeth.

'Please,' Riley says with her jaw locked shut. Keeping her eyes on Noon she works the leather cuffs around her wrist so that the bitten part is hidden on the underside.

'Did you see him?' Noon asks, tapping the spoon against Riley's set teeth.

Riley shakes her head.

'Yes, you did.' Noon forces the rim of the spoon between Riley's jaws and forces them apart. 'Eat.' The thick mushroom taste makes Riley gag. She thinks grimly of the hours to come. The blurring between real and unreal both terrifies and exhausts her. There is no way to know how much blood she has lost.

'You'll want to kill yourself, you know,' Noon says, conversational. 'But you won't be able to. We decide when you die and what you believe.'

'Mommy?' Rufus peeps around Noon's legs.

Riley tips her head back and breathes. 'You brought a kid to—?'

'Kind of late for morals,' Noon says, taking the opportunity of Riley's open mouth to shove a spoonful of mushrooms in.

'Mommy,' Rufus says brightly.

Riley chokes. All she can smell or taste is mushroom; the thick meat-earth scent fills her nostrils like mulch, gathers at the back of her throat.

Noon makes a new cut in Riley's arm, vertical, following the line of the vein. It's the kind of cut you use to end things for real. The blood is a pulse, it is a solid thing making its way out of her flesh.

Rufus watches the thin stream of blood as it falls through the air. He puts out a pink finger to touch it.

'No.' Noon pulls him gently away. 'Let it go to the land.' A peep comes from behind her. Three small shapes come out of the shadows. Hallie, Whitey and Peach look at Riley with serious faces.

'You're sick,' Riley says.

'They want to watch,' Noon says. 'It's not often someone gives all their blood to the land anymore.'

'Who are you people?' Riley whispers. 'You call yourselves the Nowhere children but you're demons.'

'Haven't you guessed yet?' Noon asks. 'We're not the Nowhere children. They are.'

'I don't understand.' There is a warm blaze of light on Riley's cheek. It must be sunset, she thinks, vague.

'Their lives were taken,' Noon says. 'We wear their bones around our necks. That's how they recognise us. They know we'll look after them, protect them. We owe the Nowhere children that.'

'Look,' Noon says softly. She shines her flashlight down into the sunken place. 'Leaf built this place over them. He had a trap door that went down here. But I wanted them to be open to the sky. So we broke open the floor and opened it. We made them a garden. We cleared away the remains of the wall that collapsed, down there. It took nearly a year.'

Riley blinks.

'Really look,' Noon says. 'You're always so busy watching out for danger, Riley – you never actually see things.'

Riley looks, following the torch beam as it tracks through the green, across the earth and stones. It comes to rest on a twisting lilac tree. Five round stones are set in a circle at its foot.

'That's not real.' A feeling is building in Riley.

'Yes, it is. You know what those are.' The smooth round shapes set in a circle are not stones. The skulls are small, almost fully buried in the earth, only their rounded tops are exposed. The bone is old, worn to a smooth sheen. The upper rim of one eye socket is just showing above the earth.

'Cal, Everett, Danny, Midnight, Dawn, me – we were never the Nowhere children,' Noon says. 'We take care of them.'

Riley closes her eyes. She understands that Noon wants her to lose her mind. It's part of her punishment. She won't let it happen. 'That's not true,' she says again.

'Isn't it?' asks Noon, gentle.

'You're just trying to make me crazy.' But Riley feels panic rise. The line between *is* and *is not* will not stay put, it wanders to and fro.

Noon smiles. 'You decide.'

'Please,' Riley murmurs. 'Just let me see Oliver.'

'No,' Noon says. 'We can never see the person we love again – so neither can you.'

'Have you seen the ghost of John?' Riley mutters to herself. It's the only song she can think of. 'Long white bones with the skin all gone. Wouldn't it be chilly with no skin on? Have you seen the ghost of John? Long white bones with the skin all gone ...' She focuses on the words, the rhyme.

A small hand touches her face. Riley opens her eyes. Peach strokes her cheek. She looks at Riley with large brown eyes.

The feeling hits Riley like a wave. 'They're sad,' she whispers. 'Why are they so sad?'

'The worst things you can think of were done to them,' Noon says. 'And they never get to grow up. So we look after them, love them – the way people should love children. And,' says Noon, 'we find unforgivable people and we give their blood to the land in their honour.' Noon leans in close to Riley's ear. 'In case you were wondering, you are unforgivable.'

'No.' Riley closes her eyes to shut out the children and the house and Noon. The world is beginning to pinwheel, she tries to hold tight to herself.

Leaf Winham's face hovers before Riley, his voice brushing her ear like velvet. 'They need the blood in the land.'

'Leaf Winham did it by accident,' Noon says. 'He put blood in the land and it kept him safe. We're way better than him. We don't kill for pleasure.'

Leaf Winham smiles at Riley and licks her, tongue dragging up and down her cheek. His breath smells of lilac.

'Why,' Riley wonders aloud or in silence, 'can I see so many ghosts in this place but not my father?'

'He was weak,' says Noon, unconcerned. 'Only the strong survive death.'

'You're lying.' Riley is not sure if she's speaking out loud or not. Maybe it doesn't matter. 'You must be.' Then it all comes up like a hurricane and swings over Riley's mind, covering everything in darkness.

18

The Nowhere Apple Farm

Once upon a time, at the turn of one century into another, Nowhere was an orchard. Sweet mountain apples grew there, ripe on the branch. Hundreds of trees basked in the sun and drank the rain. In mid spring the blossom was a thick carpet of white across the valley floor and the scent filled the air for miles around. Even on the lower trails people swore that they caught faint traces of that sweetness when the wind was right.

Nowhere Apples was owned by the Dunnings, a married couple who had been settled there some eleven years. They had built a farmhouse at the end of the valley; men from Ault and Fraser and Boulder dug the foundations and raised it. Thomas Dunning worked alongside them most days, sharing the sweat and the toil, and making sure there was beer at the end of the day. In time, they raised a flourishing orchard.

Jane Dunning had young eyes and smiled as if she meant it. When she came down to Ault for paraffin or sugar she asked after people's children and remembered their names. Her husband Thomas was rarely seen in the low towns, but he had a kind way about him, it was agreed. And he was a generous soul – if there was something you needed storing for example, which you did not quite care to keep at home – certain deliveries, items which had somehow escaped the eye of the authorities – why, Thomas stored it in the cellar, and you collected it when all was well.

The farm flourished, Nowhere apples became a delicacy and Nowhere cider was famed for its crisp flavour. The farm made work for men and women in the region. Jane joined a luncheon knitting group which took place in Ault each week on a Wednesday, riding her pretty warmblood bay mare down the mountain and leaving by mid-afternoon to make it back home by dark.

In due course Jane became one of the heads of the knitting group. Jane and another of the founders, Angela, took a particular liking to one another. So though they lived up on the mountainside, the Dunnings quickly came to be felt to be part of Ault. Jane's health was not good and she often had bouts of illness lasting some months when she did not come down from Nowhere. But in the end she always reappeared, smiling and calm and ready with her knitting needles.

One day at knitting circle, when Jane asked eagerly, as she always did, after the families and relatives and children of the other women, her friend Angela raised her brows.

'Why, Jane,' Angela said gently, 'you are so attentive to the families of others. I am sure that you look forward to having a family of your own.'

Jane smiled and tipped her head, with the light in her eyes that all women know.

'No!' Angela kept her voice low.

'I'm sure it's a girl,' Jane said. 'I'm going to call her after my sister.' She rested her hand for a fleeting moment on the place.

Angela slapped Jane's arm lightly then threw back her head and laughed. The other women looked at the pair with interest, wondering what was under discussion.

Jane quailed noticeably under the many eyes. Her face drained abruptly of colour. 'I should not have told,' she breathed into Angela's ear. 'Please, please do not repeat it.'

'I would not dream of repeating it,' said Angela, puzzled by her friend's distress.

'Only,' said Jane, 'I have lost so many, you see. I have become superstitious about it all. I can't bear to tempt fate once more.'

Angela took Jane's hand in hers. 'I have forgotten it already.'

Jane sent word down the mountain by her husband soon after that she could not attend knitting group. She was once more struck down by illness. There was much tutting and sympathy and it reminded the ladies that they should each have a glass of wine to preserve their own health.

Angela waited for word, good or bad. Nothing came which was an answer in itself.

In the spring Jane was there again at the pre-knitting luncheon, pale and wan. Angela looked at her, and Jane bit her lip and shook her head and Angela bit hers too and that was all that needed saying on that matter.

'Let us lower ourselves to crochet, for once,' Angela said brightly. 'We deserve a respite.'

But there was something subtly wrong about Jane's body – it sat and moved and stayed still in all the wrong ways. Angela knew this well, the rhythm of fear.

'Your crochet is very elegant, Jane.' Angela laid her hand on Jane's for a brief moment.

After that Angela watched her friend closely. She saw that Jane knew some of the same terrible truths about the world that she herself did. She would never ask Jane about it, of course. Everything depended on not remembering [those things hands in the dark].

Occasionally members of the knitting circle brought gifts to the lunch – delicious preserves or candies or a set of intricately embroidered handkerchiefs. After that day it always seemed to come about, by consensus, that Jane should be the one who took home the preserve or had first pick at the candy.

One Wednesday Jane was not at the lunch – but she had not sent word. The group waited the poached chicken for twenty minutes, but she did not appear. Nor did she arrive afterwards to knit. She had always sent word in advance when she would be absent, always, the ladies said to one another, but life is life. So they went on with their work.

The next Wednesday Jane did not come again, nor was there any communication from her. There were some pursed lips but everyone knitted and talked as usual and no one made a business of it, because mountain people hate a business.

On the third Wednesday, the women assembled and ate their cold beef. All of them glanced, at intervals, at the empty place where Jane should be.

Usually after lunch had finished and the table was cleared they picked up their knitting and began the real talk. But today everyone lingered, meeting each other's eyes. No one took out their knitting and there was a burdened silence in the air.

At length Angela cleared her throat. 'Is there any word from Jane? No one has seen her?'

There was a chorus of 'no's' and a flurry of shaken heads.

'And Mr Dunning?'

'He has not been in town these three weeks,' said Juniper Nailey. 'He buys tobacco from my Andrew at the store each Wednesday without fail. But he has not come the past three.'

'And no one has seen or heard from the Dunnings in all that time?' Angela kept her voice level.

Again, the company shook their heads.

'Very well,' said Angela. 'I am sorry to say it, but I fear that we must involve the men.'

Around the circle, the women nodded. They gathered their gloves and hats and knitting bags and filed out of the front door. They dispersed through Ault, fetching husbands and brothers and sons from the mill and the convenience store and the sheriff's office and the bank.

Ben was splitting logs behind their house. *Crack*, went the axe, opening the wood's white flesh to the air. *Crack*. He stopped and smiled when he saw Angela.

'They need our help up at Nowhere,' Angela said to her husband.

He looked at her for a moment. 'All right.'

A mounted expedition of twelve set out. Angela rode her old grey cob to the square, where the search party had assembled.

'Are you—?' asked her husband.

'Yes, I am coming with you,' she replied.

Angela leant forward, patting her horse on the neck. 'Quick as you can, Storytime,' she whispered in his flickering ear. Storytime turned and gently bit the folds of her riding habit.

They went up the mountain, pushing the horses hard.

The party pulled up as the approach to Nowhere loomed ahead. The cliff walls looked high and menacing, and the narrow way was cast in shadow. It seemed like a vice, meant to close on them. The horses curveted and ducked their heads, sensing unease.

'Tsk,' said Angela. 'No time for all that.' She nudged Storytime into a canter and rode into the crevasse.

*

The valley was quiet in the low light, and Angela rode the track fast through the apple trees, Storytime's hooves throwing up clouds of dust. She looked to either side, hoping for signs of life. A pair of pigeons burst from a treetop but there were no people.

When the farmhouse came into view, Angela pulled Storytime to a halt. He blew and huffed, expressing his disapproval of all this rush. Angela hitched him to the post. She could hear the hooves of the others approaching but she did not want to wait.

She knew, deep down, what she would find. The message was on the air already. Sweet sick rot, decay. When she opened the door to the farmhouse it rolled out in a wave. But it was unthinkable that Angela should not go in – she owed that much to her friend.

Angela spent two or three minutes inside that place, then came out hand to her mouth. The men had arrived and were dismounting. She stood on the step, shaking like a reed. Her husband came to her and placed an arm around her waist.

'What?' he asked briefly.

'I don't know how to say it.' She stared ahead then turned her face upwards to him. Her eyes were wide, wider than human eyes should stretch, showing rims of white around the iris. 'They did have children, Ben,' she whispered. 'There are five children in there, with her.'

Jane Dunning had tried to protect them from the knife but it had not been possible. She took all the blows that she could. After he ended his family Thomas Dunning put the knife in his own throat. It was still lodged there.

'Why would he do it?' asked Angela, pressing her handkerchief to her mouth. The men were inside now and she could hear the sound of retching. 'Who would do that to children?' Angela was almost grateful for the stench – it made it easier to believe that this thing had truly happened. 'She never said a word about her little ones – to me or any of us.' She turned to her husband. 'Did he ever mention them?' she asked, imploring. 'The children? Did you know?'

Ben shook his head. 'Dunning never said a word.'

'Five children kept up here in secret.' Angela's mouth set hard then trembled. Her eyes stared at something he could not see. 'And the little baby, Ben. She had the baby.'

'Sometimes,' Ben said, taking her hand, 'you only know what you know. We cannot always know the reason why.'

'I know,' Angela said. 'The reason why.' He looked at her uncomprehending, and she saw it then – the distance, the great expanse between his past and hers. 'Your parents were kind to you,' Angela said. 'They always protected you from harm.'

'They were,' Ben's expression was sweet and puzzled. 'They did.'

Angela smiled and hung her head and tried to breathe.

The search party filed out of the farmhouse. Their faces were white, brows laced with beads of sweat. One man went to the trees to vomit and another quickly stumbled after him.

'The sheriff must be informed,' Abel Manton said, wiping his brow. 'We ride for Boulder.'

Angela drew a deep breath. 'No.'

'He must,' Ben said, gentle.

'You know what they think of mountain people. They have been waiting for something like this to happen, all this while.' She turned to Abel Manton. 'And do you wish to be asked to explain some of the goods you keep up here in their cellar from time to time?'

He looked at her, mouth gaping.

'Oh, yes, of course I know. Everyone knows.' Angela's mouth tightened, but she held her tears at bay. 'She was my friend. I mourn her deeply. But her murderer is dead, and there is nothing to be gained from outsiders coming in and poking into things. Whatever happened here, she was an innocent and I want her memory preserved as such.'

'But, Angie—'

Angela crouched down and put her hands over her ears. Her scream rolled all down the valley, high and ragged. Storytime threw up his head, wild-eyed. 'Questions just unsettle everything,' Angela said, breathing fast.

It seemed after some discussion that most of the rescue party had at one time or another stored goods which to the law did not exist, in the apple cellar at Nowhere. It was well known in the town that things that did not exist travelled through Nowhere. Did they all want to be associated with these deaths? People make all kinds of assumptions. Someone might suggest that there was a disagreement about the stored goods. Someone might suggest the disagreement became violent. And now Angela had put it like that, they decided, what was the good in sullying the family's name? They didn't know what had truly happened here, after all.

'Better that it was bandits or convicts,' said Angela. 'Who is to say it was not? These things happen every day.'

After a moment, everyone nodded. It was agreed.

Angela went through the house, taking away the childish things. There were not many. There were no toys and the children seemed to have all slept together on one straw mattress in a small room. There was one set of clothes for each of them in a dresser. The drawers were labelled with their names.

Angela scrubbed the labels off each drawer.

She helped swaddle Jane's and Thomas's bodies in linen and bind them over the back of the sturdiest horse, to be taken down to Ault.

The men buried the children in the earth floor of the apple cellar, along with the knife that took their lives. Angela could not be inside the house for this so she stood in the orchard in the light mizzle and turned her face up to the rain. Storytime bowed his head at the hitching post, blinking at the cold drops. He was angry with her, she knew, and would blow out his stomach in revenge when she put the saddle back on.

Abel came out of the house, dusting earth from his hands. 'It was Indians,' he said, confident. 'No doubt about it. They never rounded up all the Ute. Some still live wild up here. No one will do anything about it, despite my letters ...' Angela saw that he had already begun to believe this, and for a moment she was so envious of his conviction that it took the breath right out of her chest.

Angela knows that if she works hard enough, if she trains her mind to the thought, she can cleanse the memory of that day at Nowhere from her mind – the sight of the red and white pile of flesh and small faces, the crisp linen of the nightgowns, the purple-white skin, the small, outflung leg, the tiny foot, all that old, dark blood.

Sometimes on long nights when the wind comes hard down over the mountain, and sleep eludes her, memory breaks the surface and Angela wonders, for the length of a gasp or a heartbeat, whether she did the right thing. Her friend Jane's kind eyes and those five small lives are gone and the truth is hidden forever. There will be no reckoning and no justice.

They must have all been born at Nowhere, those children. It seems they never left in all their short lives. They had never known anything but Nowhere and never would.

Angela puts these thoughts away and closes the door on them with the firmness of long practice. She knows all too well that some recollections are best left behind in the dark. Angela hardly retains any memories at all of her daddy or [those things] that happened back then and she lives a truly happy life, so she knows that this is the best way.

Angela thinks, with another of those surges of envy which are so familiar to her, that at least those children never had to grow up to carry [those things] with them. They will not spend years with [those things] sitting on their shoulders like a demon, weighing them down until they are bent double with the pain and the questions, growing older and wrestling with the fact that no one seemed to see, at the time, or perhaps no one cared. The Nowhere children are beyond such questions; they do not carry the pain of [those things]. They are free.

19
Adam

Adam pounds up the track. He has run seven miles this morning. The pool is shaded by lemon trees. There are fluffy towels and a robe already laid out on the sun lounger. Everyone here knows Adam's routine by now. He wonders, uneasy if it's what Leaf encourages all his guests to do. The exercise, and the other thing with the breath.

Adam kicks his sneakers off and dives. The water closes over him. It's so quiet down here. Nothing but cool blue. He's getting better – he can hold his breath for almost five and a half minutes now. He'll be ready for Leaf when he reaches six.

They're in the master bedroom; the moon lights up the treetops through the vast window. Adam brushes the hair out of Leaf's eyes. He worries he's crowding Leaf but he can't stop. It's strange being close to someone so beautiful. Adam feels the constant need to check, with glances and small touches and adjustments of Leaf's collar, that he's real.

Leaf asks in a neutral tone, 'How are you doing with holding your breath? Are you ready?'

Adam says, 'I'm ready.'

If he had any doubts they vanish at the sight of Leaf's expression. He is almost shaking with excitement.

Adam goes to prepare.

The bathroom is flagged in Italian marble. Adam turns off all the heating and opens the windows. The fall night cools the room quickly. There's a solid marble table along one wall big enough to lie on.

The bath is filled with cold water. Some ice cubes still float in it. Adam gets in. The cold is like an assault; he gasps at its ferocity. As he lies there he breathes quickly and deeply, trying to oxygenate his blood as fully as possible. He has even brought a white sheet to cover himself. This was not specified but Adam thinks it will add realistic detail.

Once he is fully chilled, he gets out, quickly dries himself and gets up on the table. To his cold skin, the marble feels almost warm. Then he goes utterly still. He even tries to slow his heart rate. Thanks to months of practice, he can hold his breath like this for up to five minutes. It has to be perfect. He has to be cold, unmoving. The rubber balls make uncomfortable lumps in his armpit. He squeezes them tightly to his body. This is to block the brachial artery, to weaken the pulse in his wrists to almost nothing.

He pulls the white sheet over himself, so he is just a shape on a slab. Adam takes one last deep breath, closes his eyes and calls to Leaf.

Every sound is vivid as he lies in the cold dark. The door handle's wheezing turn, the quiet hush of feet on marble. He feels rather than hears him approach. The living coming to see the dead.

Leaf's hands tremble as he pulls back the sheet. His inhale is long and wondering. Adam feels warm lips on his cold ones. Leaf begins to cry, Adam hears the wet sound of his breath. Warm hands stroke his chilled chest. Leaf holds Adam's pulseless wrist. Adam hadn't known what to expect, but it wasn't this. Leaf lies down gently beside him. He strokes Adam's cold flesh, nestles his head into the crook of Adam's shoulder, kisses his still throat.

Adam holds his breath for almost six minutes as Leaf continues to cry.

They lie together in the warm bedroom, radiators on full, Adam wrapped up in an electric blanket. Leaf is solicitous, worried, so caring. Adam feels like he's bathed in light, the focus of Leaf's whole attention.

Adam's fingers grip the soft whorls of chestnut hair at the back of Leaf's neck. 'I felt like my soul left my body. Does it feel like that for you?'

'Maybe it would,' Leaf says, 'if I had one.'

Adam unwinds his fingers from where they have been clenched in Leaf's hair.

'Time for you to go,' Leaf says.

Adam should be used to it by now but it still feels like being struck across the face, at the end, when Leaf tells him to go.

In his room Adam trembles. He does not sleep until pink touches the sky.

Adam walks through the woods to the stables. He goes there to think, sometimes. It's peaceful when there's no one but the horses, like right now. The top doors to the six loose boxes are open. The horses move leisurely in the dimness. Adam glimpses shining hide, dark eyes, pricked ears, soft muzzles. He likes it. The horses don't care about people business. They carry on with horse things.

His favourite is Daria, a clever chestnut with a bright yellow mane. The mare bows in Adam's direction over her stall door. She knows him and wants a carrot. He strokes her velvet muzzle. She nudges his pockets, hopeful.

'Sorry,' he says. 'I forgot, today.' He frowns, shaken by thought. Adam's finger traces a name over and over again in Daria's copper hide.

Adam still shakes a little when he thinks about last night. He hadn't understood what it would be like. He thinks about Leaf's face hanging over him, grieving over his cold body. Adam felt dead. He saw, with a terrible wave, that Leaf liked him dead.

He thinks about Officer Lloyd. He thinks about a deactivated alarm and rooms that should not have been lit at that time of night.

He thinks about Leaf's question. 'Where do you think I was?'

Leaf was in the house that night, Adam is sure. Maybe Adam also knows how to find it, Leaf's secret place.

Leaf, Leaf, Leaf, he writes on Daria's sleek coat with his finger. She tosses her head, annoyed, then moves into the depths of her stall.

Adam feels the great give of fear in his heart. He had thought there was nothing more terrible than love, but he is beginning to realise that this is not true.

Adam sits on his bed staring into space. He realises he's staring at the wardrobe and turns away. He feels that the strangers' clothes look back at him, even through the wood. He knows he is being watched, not just by the clothes. He feels Leaf behind the wall.

Adam made Nowhere House into a many-eyed monster. He should not be surprised that it feels monstrous. Sometimes horror comes on him, a suspicion that there is no person at the peephole but something else, crouching in the walls, breathing gently in its great leathery chest, red eye fixed to the peephole.

He readies himself for bed, giving no sign that he's aware of Leaf's presence. Adam crawls under the sheets and turns the light off. He gradually makes his breathing heavy. He lets his body go still. After a time he feels the eye move on to another part of the house – searching, always searching.

Adam stares ahead, wakeful. The trouble with darkness is that it lets your mind roam free. His child may have been born now – might be out in the world. Adam has hurt the people he should have loved. He has thrown away his life. For a moment he can actually see it in his mind's eye. A sheet of paper held in his own hand, abruptly crumpled to nothing in a closed fist. Waste.

That doesn't matter right now, he tells himself. *All that matters is the truth.* He has been under a spell but the spell is broken.

He waits until the house is quiet and there is only the sound of wood relaxing after the heat of the day. From the forest can be heard the faint call of an owl.

Adam lowers silent feet to the floor.

You could not find them without the three plans for Nowhere House in front of you, without studying them carefully with knowledge – almost with love. But there are spaces on the blueprints that do not exist, which lie between past and present – which are nowhere. Few people can read architectural blueprints properly. It is like a superpower. You can find panic rooms, safes, even bodies buried in drywall – if you know how to read a building. Adam has studied all the plans of Nowhere. He knows its bones, its foundations. He probably knows more about Nowhere House than anyone else in the world.

Adam knows where Leaf's secret place is.

The long gallery is quiet. The jukebox stands against the wall, glowing neon in the night.

There are two things in this house that are not marked on any plans, but their existence is clear, if you know how to look. The way the foundations are structured and arranged don't make sense – unless these two places exist.

The first one is a room. The second one is a tunnel.

Adam's first concern is the room. He needs to see the secret heart of Nowhere, the one that Leaf keeps hidden.

He feels gently around the back of the jukebox. There is something, a space, behind this wall that should not be there. Adam's fingers brush against something on the jukebox and there is a click. The jukebox swings aside to show a doorway, spilling warm light.

Adam goes in quietly, heart thrumming.

The room is clean and clinical-looking. It has the appearance of a mortuary, or maybe an operating room. The walls are shining white tile and the cement floor slopes to a drain at the centre. There is a metal table like a gurney. Metal instruments gleam there, neatly and evenly spaced.

The tile walls are covered with photographs. Adam looks. His heart stops. He takes another look and then another. Time and space rearrange. He feels as if it were his own body, what's happening to the young men in the photographs. Flesh, bone, wide mouth, a glossy terrified eye. The person who took the photographs loves eyes.

All the pictures are the same. Red and black and white – teeth parted, mouths stretched wide and screaming. In some of them Leaf's face is visible. In some of them he holds a little silver knife. Adam knows he should run but he can't.

Adam sees a river of auburn hair, the colour of fall leaves. He reaches for the photograph. Adam last saw him in Leaf's wallet. Rick McFadyen's eyes are so wide that Adam can almost see the image of the photographer reflected, the flash of the camera. How can a person have so much of their insides laid open to the outside, and still live?

Adam starts to cry. There are other things mounted on the wall – Adam's mind will not understand them.

So he feels it too late, the movement of air. Arms wrap around him in a strong lover's embrace. Leaf isn't holding him hard enough to hurt, not yet.

'Hi,' Adam says, quiet. 'It's ok, you can let me go.'

He feels Leaf's indecision. He wants to believe Adam. His arms loosen.

Adam turns. He looks at the beautiful face and his heart does that *tap tap tap* it always does, even now.

'I wanted to tell you,' Leaf says. 'I want to share everything with you – I didn't know how.'

'I understand,' Adam says. He looks around the room. 'It's impressive.'

'If they do want to live,' Leaf says, 'the Foundation helps them. The ones who want to live do what I did. They work and get clean and make a life. But so many of them want to die. That's why they were on the street in the first place. They were trying to kill themselves as fast as possible. In the end, does it really matter whether it's me or an overdose?'

'I don't know.' Adam tries to keep his face still, as still as Leaf's. Inside, his brain spins.

'I love you, Adam. I never wanted my fingers to itch with you.'

'I have never felt such love for another person as I did for you,' Adam says.

'Good.' Leaf's sigh of relief takes up his whole body. 'I don't enjoy it,' he says. 'Please believe that.'

Adam smiles. 'It will be ok,' he tells Leaf.

'Will it?'

'Yes.' Adam nods. 'We love each other.' If he makes a mistake, he will become a photograph on the wall.

Leaf starts to speak and then stops. His face twists. 'You said "did".'

'What?' All of Adam's skin comes alive.

'Before. You said, "I have never felt such love for another person as I *did* for you."' Adam sees it now, in the eyes – the thing that looks out from behind Leaf's face.

Leaf moves like a spider, fast and sudden. He takes aim at Adam with his tiny gleaming knife. Adam stumbles, grabs at something mounted on the wall. It's pale and graceful and slender. Even as he reaches for it he thinks, *what a strange place to put a handle.* It comes free easily from the brackets that held it.

Adam sees that he holds bone. It is an adult human femur, bleached and polished to the sheen of ivory. He grips it in his fist, staring for a moment. Then Adam throws the bone at Leaf's head.

Adam runs out of the passage, past the jukebox, along the passages and ways of Nowhere, through the high-ceilinged rooms, up into the library. He slides a hand along the bookshelves, sweeping a couple of books into his arms. When he reaches *Decline and Fall of the Roman Empire* he reaches behind. His fingers find the lighter fluid and firelighters he left here earlier. He had to be sure, he told himself as he did it, he had to prove it. But Adam realises that he had already been sure.

Adam's fingers grasp *Pride and Prejudice.* The staircase door opens without a sound – he had been so proud of that, the utter silence of its passage.

Adam slips into the staircase. The door closes and he flicks the security lock, which means no one can get in through this door.

Adam leans against the secret walls he built, panting. He thinks about Christie and the baby. He cannot lie down and do nothing. He has to try – even if he fails and Christie and his child never know, he has to. What are fathers for – except to try?

Leaf is powerful. Officer Lloyd knows what he is, everyone who works here must know too. No one will do anything against Leaf Winham. The police will not charge him, courts will not convict him.

But if it is all laid bare, if people see the pictures of those young men and boys, see that terrible wall, that room – maybe there is a chance. Adam knows that as a plan, it's not great. The house will burn. Leaf might die. Adam could die too. But he doesn't want to live in a world where Leaf walks free.

'Ok,' he whispers to himself. Everyone knows that there is one thing that always brings help.

Fire.

Adam tears pages from the books he grabbed from the shelves and makes a pile of kindling. He layers the firelighters carefully through it all, making sure it will take. The staircase should function almost like a chimney. He never treated the wood to make it fireproof. That's not like him. Why didn't he? The spell, Adam thinks, bitter. But his mind was trying to tell him. It was always working underneath.

Adam lights a match and throws it onto the pyre. The bright yellow flame starts small, a cautious tongue licking. Then it rears higher and higher, hungry for it all.

Adam ducks out of the staircase, closing the bookshelf door quickly behind him. Smoke seeps through the gap at the bottom. Adam can very faintly hear the crackle as the staircase draws up the flame. It's working just like he hoped.

He doesn't know where Leaf is. Maybe it doesn't matter now. But his skin ripples on his flesh anyway.

Adam treads quiet through the house. He goes to the north-west corner of the long gallery. He drops to his hands and knees, runs his fingers over the smooth boards, searching for a seam. He finds the release and opens the hatch down into the foundations of the house. He slips in, and pulls the trap door down behind him. This is the second secret that the blueprints told him.

Adam goes through the struts and supports and boulders that shore up Nowhere House. The floorboards creak overhead and Adam freezes. It could be the natural conversation of wood at night. It could be Leaf walking through the long gallery.

The earth rises on a gentle slant and the space between the

foundations and the ground grows narrower and narrower. Adam puts the flashlight in his mouth. He bends then crawls. The house feels like it's pressing down on his back. He is flat on his stomach now, edging ahead on his elbows and knees. Maybe he was wrong. Maybe there is nothing down here but dark.

Adam catches a scent which seems impossible. It's October, not the right season. But it's unmistakable, filling the air with its delicate perfume. Lilac. Adam gasps and sinks his fingers into the earth, pulling himself forward. Suddenly the beams and foundations above his head are gone. He rolls out into an open place.

This is the deepest part of the house. It is made of old stone, rock walls which glisten with mica. A young lilac tree clings to one side. Before the tree, five round stones are circled like some kind of magic. Adam breathes. He doesn't like them, those five stone-like things. And who would plant a lilac tree underground? How does it stay alive down here?

He shines the torch through the heavy blossom and sees it – a glimpse of dark through a lilac. An opening yawns in the rock wall. Adam takes a deep breath and goes into the night-scented flowers. He pushes his way through into the dark. The scent tickles his nostrils, fills the back of his throat. His flashlight dances on the tunnel walls; they glitter, a million tiny points like stars. Who made this? Adam touches the tunnel wall with a marvelling hand. This was already here, as far as he can tell, in the seventeenth-century plans. He goes through the gleaming passage – the tunnel of stars. It makes him think of the water reflecting back the sky when he and Leaf swam in the lake that night. Then it makes Adam think of the beast beneath the lake. He can't breathe, suddenly. He stops and bends, hands on his knees. Adam wonders what Christie has named or will name their child. He wonders whether, if he lives, she will ever speak to him again. Thinking of his life before Nowhere is like raising a wrecked ship from the deep. Is it too late to travel back, between the worlds? Adam doesn't know. He is not sure who he has become.

Leaf's approach is soft-footed, silent; Adam doesn't hear a thing. The first he knows about it is the knife in his throat, so fast that he doesn't even feel pain. He does feel the blood coursing hot down his chest, though. Leaf holds Adam close, as if with love.

'I can't let you go this time,' Leaf says sadly. 'You're a liar.' Leaf's mouth is on Adam's neck; he kisses near the edge of the wound that stretches across Adam's throat. Adam thinks through the pain and shock, *is he drinking my—* But that's not important.

Adam breathes and slides his hand very slowly into his pocket. *Fingers*, Adam commands. *Move.* They don't, probably because of shock. Adam puts everything he has into it, to force his hands into purpose. He nearly shouts when his fingers twitch. They graze the corduroy of his pants pocket. Adam feels with gentle touch. His pocket seems empty; maybe he didn't take it from the top of the dresser this morning, maybe he left it in the shorts he wore yesterday. Leaf is still kissing his neck, lips gentle. He presses his face against Adam's nape. His eyes are wet, he must be crying. His mouth is also wet but Adam can't think about that. Leaf's arms hold him like bands of iron. Adam is almost crying too. He left it on the table this morning, he must have done, and he is going to die.

Adam's thumb brushes the smooth cylinder of the ballpoint pen. He feels the violent shock of hope. Adam's fingers fold about the pen in a gradually tightening grasp. His body is trying – it wants to help. All or nothing.

Adam whips the pen from his pocket – backwards, upwards, point first. He's working blind but his aim is true. He drives the pen into the cavity of Leaf's ear. Adam feels it puncture the eardrum. The sound is worse, like a boot torn from sucking mud. Leaf's arms loosen and release. Adam twists out of Leaf's grasp.

Adam pulls himself upright on the rough stone walls of the tunnel and makes his way clumsily down into the dark, feeling the wall with one hand, clutching his throat with the other, blood trickling hot over his fingers. His legs and hands seem to be floating away from his body. Blood from his throat spatters in his wake. He sinks to the ground. There's no way to tell how much time passes. When he comes to, he feels how badly he is hurt. The slash in his neck is terrible.

Adam groans and drags himself a little way along the rough stone floor. He wants to live, he realises, to see his child. Maybe he doesn't deserve it but life is rarely about getting what you deserve. He forces himself to his feet and half hops, half limps along the rocky floor. Slowly, with gritted teeth, step by step.

There's a hint of fresh forest in the air ahead and Adam tries to hurry. He laughs, which is a mistake: it really hurts. He might just live. He might make it home to see his baby.

The tunnel ends in a narrow hole, a steep incline which turns from stone to earth. Above Adam hears leaves rustle, he hears open air and stars – can you hear stars? He thinks in this moment he can. They pulse overhead.

Behind him something stirs in the long dark. Adam turns and stares down the tunnel, his breath caught like a ball in his throat. He listens, every nerve straining, but now there is only silence. The sound of nothing, of the tunnel. Adam makes a rasping sound. Enough with looking behind. Forward now. He reaches and pulls himself up towards the open air and the night.

He crawls out of the earth. Another lilac shields the mouth of the tunnel and he pushes his way through, spitting leaves, breathing its mineral scent. The forest is cool; a nightjar calls nearby. Adam crawls on, hands clutching at the forest floor, moving on foot by agonising foot. He doesn't know how much time passes. But he knows when he won't make it any further. His body is stopping again.

He finds a friendly tree and props himself up, gasping, against its trunk. He can't control the noises he's making. Pain is undignified.

The tang of smoke is in the forest air. There's a glow on the horizon. Adam thinks, *good. Burn.*

He is not safe, not at all. Adam knows who (what) follows him. He tries to move again, to get further from this place. Leaf will be coming.

The world cants to one side, black bursts and flowers over everything.

When Adam opens his eyes a man is looking back at him. It is not Leaf. It's a young firefighter with a kind face. 'He's coming down the tunnel,' Adam tries to tell the man. He can't speak, has no wind. Maybe Leaf got his trachea; his breath seems to be coming from his open throat. 'Have to go. Coming. Murderer.'

20

Riley

When Riley opens her eyes she is alone. The long room is quiet. It's day, late afternoon, she thinks.

Riley starts, her senses singing. The sound could anything – it could be trees speaking in the forest or rain falling or distant deer hooves drumming the earth – but in this moment it sounds like small feet running somewhere in the depths of the burnt-out house. *No*, she tells herself. *Ignore it.* The drug must be wearing off; the cuts in her arms throb with pain.

There is a movement, a shift of air at the end of the hall. Riley stills.

The deer with the broken antler walks delicately out of the corridor, into the light. He looks at her, every muscle poised for flight. Riley tries to be a stone. She doesn't even breathe. The deer advances a step, just one, foreleg poised. Riley clears her mind, so the deer won't even hear her thoughts. She becomes nothing.

The stag walks towards her, gathering confidence. It breaks into a trot. Riley is lightheaded from holding her breath as it comes close. The deer pauses on the edge of the sunken place, then leaps down into the garden. It approaches the lilac tree and then it is gone, into its depths. It does not come back.

The five skulls are there, planted in a circle before the lilac. Riley tries not to look at them; it won't help.

Riley bends to the leather cuff at her wrist. She tears at it, feeling her teeth move in the gums with the force of it. If Riley doesn't get free she will lose everything she loves. And same if she does.

When she feels the gnawed ends of leather fall away she can't actually move for a moment. Hot tears fill her dry eyes. She lifts her wrist from the arm of the chair. She unbuckles her other hand and the straps about her ankles. She rubs her hands and feet, letting the circulation return.

Riley remembers the directions that first brought her to Nowhere. Lilac is an entryway. She sways as she stands. She lowers herself down into the sunken place, fingertips clinging. She staggers as she reaches the ground, falling to her knees. Riley breathes and gets herself up. She goes towards the lilac, shivering as she steps gingerly over those five round shapes. 'I'm sorry,' she whispers.

Pushing her head into the lilac, the scent fills Riley's nostrils like sickness. Through the leaves and blossom, in the stone foundation, she sees darkness. A hole, a tunnel. The entrance is large enough for a deer to walk upright, antlers and all.

It takes Riley a few minutes to haul herself back up over the lip of the sunken place. She lies on the floor of the long room, leaves shushing above her in the breeze. Her head swims. She breathes deeply. She's going to need all her focus for the next part. When her heart has settled and the world has more or less stopped dissolving, she gets up slowly and makes her way through Nowhere House, leaning on the walls at intervals to steady herself.

The walk back through the woods is like a dream; sometimes she finds herself sinking to the ground and struggles back upright. As she goes she thinks of the first time with Cal, under the tree, of waking shivering in the dew, his jacket spread over them for warmth. She remembers how fresh the world smelled that morning and the warmth of his skin.

When the woods begin to thin, Riley draws into the shadow of a spreading oak. She fits herself neatly behind the trunk. A cloud of purple butterflies scatter past on the evening air.

She can see Home Barn in the distance and the huddled shape of the stable block. Figures move about in the dusk. A fire burns in the pit outside, and Riley shivers, imagining warmth. She can just catch the faint scent of roasting meat on the darkening air, even the kerosene in the lamps that hang in the barn. Riley's stomach growls. She clings to the oak trunk and waits, watches as they eat and talk. She sees the familiar hobble of one of the smaller figures. Riley can't make out Oliver's face at this distance but she knows how he stands and walks in every mood. His head hangs, despondent. He moves slowly.

Riley waits, shivering as darkness falls. Slowly the fire dies to red coals, and the faint sound of talk dies too. She waits until there is nothing but quiet and trees and frogs and crickets. A bat crosses quick in the night.

When she thinks enough time has passed Riley slips out from under the trees. She moves slowly, alert all the while for movement from the stables.

Close to, someone snores in one of the loose boxes. Everett, she thinks. Riley has to hope that Oliver is still sleeping in the same stall as before. The moon is clouded over and she moves forward in small grim steps. She needs things – light, for one, food for another. Riley feels her way around the barn walls and takes a kerosene lamp from its hook and lights it with an ember from the fire. She goes to the compost bin and digs through it. She eats quickly – turnip ends, a foot discarded from the roasted pigeon. The claw crunches in her mouth, savoury. She finds a crust of bread someone didn't want, with butter still clinging to it. They must be eating well, to throw so much away. But there has been a great deal of blood in the land, lately.

Riley creeps to the stall and opens the top door. Oliver is asleep on the camp bed with his thumb in his mouth. He hasn't sucked his thumb in some time – since they left Cousin's. Riley sits by him, silent as a ghost. She doesn't know what he'll do. He might still be angry with her. He might bring the others and then she'll go back to the chair. She winces as she pulls her sleeves down over her forearms to cover the wounds. Whatever happens she doesn't want him to see that.

'Wake up, Oliver Olive,' Riley breathes into his ear.

He starts up and makes a muffled sound against her palm. Riley puts a finger to her lips. Above her hand, his eyes are dark and serious. He nods and she takes her hand away. They look at each other for a long moment. Then Oliver throws himself into Riley's arms. His tears wet her shirt, his back heaving silently. She can feel his mouth moving, pressed against her shoulder. 'Sorry,' he says silently, over and over. 'Sorry.'

Riley strokes his head. 'We have to go,' she mouths into his ear. He nods frantically against her neck.

Riley helps Oliver up and pulls all the clothes she can find onto him. She takes a flashlight from the bedside. There's a compass, too – who knows where he got that, but she puts it in her pocket. Best be prepared. It feels so like the night they ran away from Cousin. Another flight in the dark. When does it end? She hopes that Oliver, at least, can find a way to stop running.

Riley turns to close the stall door behind them when she feels it – eyes, a presence on the back of her neck. She turns slowly. Midnight's face is golden in the light of the lamp.

'I'm going to put every part of you in the land,' Midnight says quietly to Riley. 'Right now.' She gathers herself to yell, to summon the others. Time slows and stutters. Without a thought Riley turns and throws the oil lamp back into the stall. It arcs through the air before hitting the back wall where it shatters in a gout of flame. Oil and fire lick the wooden wall, down to the sawdust that covers the floor. Midnight throws herself into the stall, grabs a blanket and tries to smother the fire. Riley flings the stall door closed, shutting Midnight in.

Riley seizes Oliver's hand and they run into the night. Behind them there are shouts and commotion. But no one follows. Fire beats everything.

'Riley,' says Oliver, panting and stumbling through the grass, 'I can't see.'

'I know,' she says. 'No flashlight yet, ok?'

Their eyes adjust slowly. Riley can make out the forest ahead. Once they're safely in the trees she risks pausing to catch their breath. When she looks back, half the stable is alight. It has caught like tinder.

'Will they get hurt?' Oliver asks.

'No.'

'Why did you lock Midnight in the stables?' Oliver sounds tearful. Riley gets that, she feels like that too.

'I didn't,' she tells him, stroking his head.

He twists away from her caress. 'But—'

'Hurry up, bud. Ok? Just walk.' Riley adds this night to the deep place where she keeps all the things she can't acknowledge, all the lies she's told. *Getting crowded down there.* 'Come on. We can use the flashlight now.'

The beam dances over the long beards of Spanish moss and clouds of tiny white moths swarm in its light. Riley feels exhaustion dropping on her like a hammer, but she shakes her head and keeps walking. When she looks back there is a narrow red halo in the sky over the stables. The blaze rises higher, stabbing upwards into the black night.

Oliver balks at the sight of Nowhere House. 'I don't like it. It's scary. Riley ...'

'It's ok,' Riley says. 'It's just a place that's been through some stuff. You know? Like us.'

Oliver thinks about it. 'Well,' he says. 'I guess we *have* been through some stuff.'

Riley hugs him.

'Ow,' he says. 'Too tight.'

'Sorry.' Riley lets him go. She presses the heel of her hand quickly into each eye to stop the tears. 'Let's keep going, Oliver Olive.'

There are fireflies high in the ruined ceiling of the house and Oliver shouts and points at them. It's wonderful that he still feels like that every time he sees a firefly.

When they reach the sunken garden she turns his head away from the bloodstained chair. 'We just got to get down there, ok?' She lowers him gently by the arms then hands him the flashlight. She tries to let herself down slowly but her fingers go weak and lose their grip. Riley falls hard to the earth.

'Riley? Riley?' Oliver's face is shadowed and worried as he trains the flashlight on her.

'It's ok,' she says, recovering her breath. 'We just get up again, right?'

'Right,' he says. 'This place is fun. And it smells nice.'

'It sure does,' Riley says after a moment. She pushes herself upright with a grunt. 'Give me the flashlight and hold my hand. Don't let go, ok?'

Oliver nods. Together they push through the lilac and into the tunnel. The walls are rough, carved through limestone. Mica glitters in some places on the walls. It's probably the course of a long-gone river. Riley sees a pile of deer droppings on the rock floor and feels another wash of relief. Whatever this passage is, living things use it.

Oliver and Riley walk for a time, hand in hand. It's good just to be together. The torchlight moves in a ball of yellow on the path ahead.

'Riley,' Oliver says, eventually. 'I didn't mean to—'

'Oliver Olive,' she says. 'You didn't want to lie and that's a good thing. Promise me that you'll never worry about that again. You didn't do anything wrong. Ok?'

'Ok.' He holds her hand even tighter.

'I want to tell you some things,' Riley says. 'They're really important. Are you ready?'

She feels him nod.

'Firstly,' Riley says, 'I should have taken you to a doctor, to look at your leg. It's still not good. I can smell it. So the first thing you have to do is go to a doctor. Ok?'

'Ok,' he says. 'Yeah, it does kind of hurt.'

'You've been really brave.' She swallows. 'Secondly, Mom loved you very much, and it wasn't her fault, all the stuff that happened at the end. She was sick. All she had for you was love. As for me, I love you so much that it takes up my whole body. Ok?'

'Ok.'

'Sometimes, in your life, people will tell you that they can save you. They can't. They just want something.'

'Ok ok ok!' He kicks a pebble.

'Stop that. And never,' says Riley, 'never ever smoke. Ok? Never.'

'I won't!' Oliver says, wounded.

Riley swipes her eyes again. 'And never buy anything from the top shelf of those small non-chain grocery stores. The top shelf is always out-of-date stuff. You'll be able to tell from the dust. Always buy at eye level. That's the stuff they replace. Ok?' She is shaking now. She can smell fresh air ahead, the woods. They are nearly there.

'Riley,' Oliver whispers, 'is it going to be ok?'

'Of course,' she says. 'Let's get out of here. You want to look at some stars?'

The tunnel entrance is lined with rough briar and tree roots. 'Hold tight,' Riley says. 'Up we go.' She boosts Oliver up and hauls herself up after. She thinks for a moment she won't make it, but she does, just.

Above, through the rustling canopy, the stars are spilled burning across the sky. Riley feels lighter and lighter, like she's about to float. Or fly.

'We can take some time,' she says. 'Let's wait 'til dawn.' It's not far off, she can feel it in the air. She sits on a boulder. 'Shall we tell stories?'

'Yes!' Oliver sits beside her and lies in her lap. 'The one about how I was born!'

'Yes. That's a good one. Ok. Once upon a time, there was a woman who wanted a baby so much, it filled her every moment and thought. She wanted a little boy with green eyes ...'

Oliver listens, eyes closing. Riley puts her arms around him, holding him steady at her side so that his sleep is deep and undisturbed. The east turns pink and pale blue. Riley waits until there's good light, enough to walk easily by, then she wakes Oliver gently.

'It's time.'

'Ok.' He rubs his eyes and yawns.

'This is the last thing.' Riley takes the compass from her pocket and presses it into his hand. 'Forget all of this. I mean it. Everything. Tell them you've lost your memory. Don't ever think about this place, or me ever again. Forget Nowhere, forget the name Riley and especially the name Oliver. Become new. You can have a wonderful life and be happy. I know it.'

'Riley,' Oliver whispers, 'what are you doing?'

'I had my chance,' she says. 'It's done now. Too many people have died. I'm going back and you're going on without me.'

They were still just within hearing when it began, so Riley caught the sound as she and Oliver walked through the woods towards Nowhere House – the screams from the stables. She knows they're all dead.

She accepts it, now, that death follows her. Not her own it seems but that of others. Riley spreads death wherever she goes but she won't let it touch her brother.

She shows Oliver the compass. 'You follow this. When it points here, you go this way, ok? Follow this part, to the left of the arrow. You'll get to the main trail. Find a grownup. A good one. There are good ones. You'll be able to tell.'

'No.' Oliver's face twists. 'I won't go! You're not allowed to leave me alone!'

'It's the only thing I can do.' She holds him one last time as he beats at her with his fists.

'You come!' he screams. 'You and me together, like always ...'

'I'm a murderer, Oliver. Do you know what that means?'

He nods, swallowing. 'Yes. The lion man. Cousin. And—' his voice catches, wet. 'All of them in the stables.' He claws at her, grasping fistfuls of her hair, hanks of her clothing. 'I don't care, Riley,' he whispers.

Riley strokes his head. 'But someone has to look after them.'

'Who?' he asks. 'There's no one left.'

'The children. They don't have anyone else.'

'They DIED,' Oliver shouts. '*I* need you!' The hurt in his small face is so strong that Riley staggers.

'I'm no good in the real world,' Riley says. 'I'm hardly a person anymore. I can make a difference here.'

'You've gone weird, Riley. Please, no. Please.'

'Oliver Olive.' She reaches gently to the nape of his neck and unfastens his bone necklace. She ties it around her own throat. It hangs so heavy that she can hardly breathe. 'You need a real life. It's over, you and me.'

'It's supposed to be just you and me,' he whispers. 'Like you always say. Just you and me.'

'Time to go.' If he doesn't, right now, she might change her mind.

'I don't love you anymore, Riley,' Oliver says. 'I don't love you at all.' He waits for her to take it all back.

She shakes her head. Tears spill hot down her cheeks.

'I hate you,' Oliver says quietly. 'For real.'

'I know.' Riley turns him about and gives him a gentle push to the north-west.

Oliver stumbles then rights himself. He walks away, back hard, head hanging low. Riley watches until he's out of sight, his slight figure lost among the trees. She can almost hear it, the sound of her heart cracking in two. She turns and goes back down into the earth, into the dark.

They are waiting for her just inside the mouth of the tunnel, the five of them. Their eyes each have a green glowing firefly at their centre. Hallie holds baby Una against her shoulder.

A voice says, 'Mommy?'

'I'm here, Rufus,' Riley says. She takes Una gently from Hallie, holds her in the crook of her arm. The baby smiles up at her. 'I'm going to look after you.'

They reach for her with eager arms.

21

Marc

His father comes to Marc in his sleep – the gentle man who raised him. He pushes his glasses up his nose and says, 'You watch out for Tinkerbell, ok, son? You be careful.' Marc knows it's a dream because his father always preferred to speak French with him. But he reaches out for him anyway. '*Papa*,' he says. '*Tu me manques*.' I miss you.

Marc wakes, aching, with the memory of being loved. It takes him a moment to understand the sound that's everywhere, pounding on the canvas above. Storm. The tent flap is open. Through it the world flickers. Everything is lit for a moment in white stark detail. Then the thunder comes. It's more than a sound, it shakes the earth. It's like they are inside thunder, made of it. He fumbles, breathing hard, with his prosthetic. Then he crawls out to join Kimble.

Kimble's hair is blown everywhere, lifted by the wind, and she's yelling, he can see that by the stretch of her mouth, her bared teeth, but he can't hear anything over the screaming gale and the thunder.

Something sails through the air overhead and lands lightly on delicate hooves. Another deer charges through the firepit, which is a puddle now. Its legs kick a spray of ashy water into their faces.

Suddenly the deer are on all sides; they flash past, flowing to the right and left, dodging and parting ways in alarm, leaping over the collapsing tents, over Marc and Kimble where they cower, arms protecting their heads. Then they are gone, away down the mountain. Marc reaches for Kimble's hand and she takes it hard and tight.

Linus appears through the onslaught of rain and crouches beside them. Marc catches his words faintly under the tumult. 'We have to go.'

'What the hell is going on?' Marc yells back.

Lightning divides the sky, hot white. The thunder is so loud that they all cower. Linus's mouth makes the same shapes over and over again. He grasps Marc's arm. *Landslide*, he mouths. *Storm. Earthquake.*

Marc moves his hand through the rain; it is like pushing into a solid substance, breaking a surface. Hail is beginning to fall, too. Icy marbles bounce off the ground.

A tall wave of mud topples and pours through the campsite, drenching them in a river of slick brown. A fork of white cracks the night sky and even though he's prepared for it, the thunder, the shaking, the noise, it still stops Marc's heart when it comes – the roar.

'Time to go!' yells Linus.

They run together, wading, slipping in the torrent.

When they reach the treeline Marc stops.

'What are you doing?' Kimble yells. 'We need to go. Now.'

'I'm not leaving,' Marc yells back.

'This place is being washed away,' Kimble yells and Linus nods, grabbing Marc's arm for emphasis. The sky is being torn open by jagged light. The slope is bare, exposed to the great turmoil of the sky. Marc feels like a gnat clinging to a leaf. They're so fragile in their human bodies.

'Back to the van,' Linus yells.

Between the hills, in the distance, Marc sees that the road to the gate of Nowhere is running, a river. Another crash shakes everything.

He watches as the gate crumples like paper under the landslide. The road into Nowhere lies open, under a fall of rock.

'What about them?' Marc points down at the gate.

Kimble shrugs.

Marc proffers his hand, palm up, and lifts it gently. Rain beats and bounces off it as he shows it to Kimble. *Help.*

She shakes her head.

Linus yells, 'Let's go!'

'They might die,' he says to Kimble through a mouthful of rain. He knows she can't hear him but he knows she understands. 'I need her.'

Kimble shakes her head. He sees her mouth shape the word – *idiot.*

Linus is in Marc's ear, he yells something about search and rescue. He tightens his grip on Marc's arm. Water and mud sluice down around them.

Marc tears free. He had wanted more time before seeing her. He didn't want to do it in a storm in the middle of an earthquake. But there is no more time.

'Get the van,' Marc yells at the two of them. 'I'll meet you at Leahy's turnout.' He's almost sure that they hear him. Marc tightens the hood about his face as Kimble lunges for him. He ducks away from her grip and is gone into the driving rain.

The boulders have crushed the steel gate under their weight. Marc climbs. A slick weal of red spreads across his wet hand where it drags across the razor wire and he winces, shakes his head and goes on. No time to be careful.

In the narrow channel of the pass beyond the ruined gates, the water rushes fast. He was right; the valley is flooding. It's hard to push forward now. He thinks about a figure perched in the rocks above, the ricochet of gunfire off the narrow walls in the rain, thunder hiding the shot. She wouldn't. He's almost sure.

Marc runs down the cracked asphalt road which is now rushing water, ankle deep, into the meadow. Even with storm clouds boiling overhead and almost blinded by rain, Marc sees how beautiful it is, this green valley protected in the teeth of the mountains. He had hoped he would remember the way and he does.

He passes evidence of the life the children lead. A pink tricycle, handles carefully mended with duct tape, lies upended, one wheel gently turning. A teddy bear with no eyes lies bloated and sodden in a patch of flattened grass. He passes the burnt-out skeleton of the stables, roof patched with sheets of plywood and rusting metal.

He thinks of the children who live here and play with these things – he feels fear that is not to do with the rain or the storm. It's the fear that comes when you touch the edge, the places where life and death meet.

He runs through the woods. Thunder cracks overhead, or was it something else? Did it come from above, or below in the earth? Marc speeds up, slipping and running through the pine forest. He feels the furry texture of the air that means lightning. Marc pushes himself on, panting. He just needs a little longer.

Nowhere House rears up before him, roof partially caved in, a hulking skeleton in the flickering light. It is boarded up, seemingly abandoned. But he guesses it's not. *Now here.* There is a door of sorts, layers of plywood. He puts a testing hand against it. Firm, solid. A bolt on the other side?

'Did you get my note?' he yells through the door. There's no answer so he hurls himself against the plywood, throws his weight at it again and again until the wood gives with a splintering scream.

The house is dim, quiet, the assault of rain suddenly muted.

She lies in front of the fireplace. She must have been caught in a rockfall or hurt herself somehow. Her shoulder is covered in blood.

'There you are,' he says, wiping rain from his mouth.

Her hair is plastered to her head. It's in a neat, though wet, ponytail. She wears a flannel shirt, jeans, boots. Practical. Ordinary. She looks like a regular woman in her forties who lives quietly by herself in the mountains.

'Get off my property.' Her voice is scratched from disuse. She takes the gun from the holster at her hip and trains it slowly on him. 'I mean it,' she says. 'You're trespassing.'

'Hi, Riley,' Marc says. A hot lick of rage strokes his throat. It's not fair that she can still hurt him. 'You don't recognise me?'

'I don't know any people,' she says. 'Nice try.'

Marc remembers that slight smile like a blow to the heart. He takes a deep breath and leans against the wall, takes a cigarette from his inside jacket pocket. His hand shakes a little as he lights it.

'I smoke now,' Marc says. 'Sorry. I took most of the rest of your advice. I always buy things at eye level, on the shelves. And I have a pretty happy life.' He is startled to find that this actually feels true.

Her mouth opens in a silent 'o'. She bends a little at the middle as if she's been dealt a blow. She stares at Marc, her eyes rake his face. 'No,' she says quietly. 'It can't be, because he would never come back. I told him to never.'

'He didn't.' He smokes and looks at her. 'But once, a long time ago, I had a different name.'

Riley pushes herself upright. 'You can't be him,' she whispers. 'If you're lying or it's a trick, I think it might kill me.'

'You told me to forget Oliver,' he says. 'Oliver's gone. So yes and no.' Marc takes a deep drag on his cigarette. 'Riley,' he says. 'The girl who was hatched from an egg.'

'Oh,' she says. 'Oh, oh.' Riley gives a hacking sob and her hand clamps over her mouth. 'Hello, Oliver Olive.' She comes towards him, wincing at the pain in her shoulder. Marc tenses. She might shoot him after all.

Close to her wet hair carries the scent of woodsmoke. Riley throws her armd round him. Marc hurtles back in time. He's there again, clinging to her for warmth as the lion stalks them across the mountain. Riley was all the safety he knew, once.

He could say, don't call me that name, or you abandoned me, or how could you how could you. Instead he whispers back, 'Hi, Riley.'

Her grasp tightens. He puts his arms carefully, slowly, around her. He holds his sister gently, after all this time.

Oliver found his way from the tunnel to the lilac. He didn't know what to do; he was hungry until the man came with the meatball sandwich.

He did just what Riley said and told them he didn't remember anything. Even as Oliver cried at night with rage and hatred for what she had done, he never told other people. For a time, he was just the lilac boy.

Oliver was in hospital for a while. By the time they had debrided all the infected tissue in his leg they decided it wasn't worth saving so they took it off neatly below the knee.

Oliver went into the system but Riley had been right, he was a cute kid. A family in Arizona wanted him, even without half his leg. He got a new name, Marc Villeneuve, and a new language. He was happy about those things. As time went by Marc realised it was too difficult to keep two selves in him at once. He had to erase the boy who once had a sister who chose an empty mountain over her living little brother. So he put Oliver down into the dark deepest places of himself. Marc was easier to live with than Oliver. Marc had no past. The next year the family moved to Quebec and Oliver was gone.

Marc holds Riley gently at arms length. It's hard to look at her, but he can't stop. 'I came for a reason.'

He takes the photograph from his wallet. Silvie looks out, serious, from the garden. He feels the usual tug and horror of it all. Her small face, upturned, the field daisy in her hand.

'This is my daughter.'

'You have a daughter?'

'Yes.' Marc's hands won't stop trembling.

Riley takes the picture with gentle, careful fingers.

Her name is Silvia, really, it's from the Shakespeare play. Her mother Claude likes all those things. Marc met her on a shoot for a reality TV series in Germany. She is very French and lives in Paris in a studio near the Marais. She makes fun of Marc's Quebecois accent. Marc fell hard while they were on location and then he came up for air. When the project ended he did what he always did and left. Then he thought better of it. By the time he came back she had given birth to Silvie.

Marc has only fallen in love once in his life and it happened the moment he saw Silvie. Even as a baby her gaze was mistrustful yet direct, as if she already knew that life was a slippery thing. Her dark eyes are Riley's eyes and the shock of that was terrible, at first, like a ghost walking in from the night. But Silvie isn't Riley at all. Silvie is just herself. He and Claude became friends. Their daughter was the sun and they revolved around her.

Silvie was diagnosed with Berger's disease when she was seven. It was already advanced. Her kidneys were failing.

'It's ok,' he kept telling Claude over the phone. 'It's ok.'

'Shut up,' Claude said. 'You have no understanding of ok. You're the most damaged person I've ever met.' There had always been an edge to their talk but since Silvie's diagnosis it has become stinging and hurtful. Marc and Claude give one another their anger because there's nowhere else for it to go. Sometimes Claude calls and just screams, and Marc understands that. It's how he feels too.

Claude donated her kidney first. It lasted a year before Silvie's body rejected it. Marc gave his next, which lasted two. There was a donor but that didn't work out. She needs a third transplant. Claude's parents are dead and Marc's parents are not related by blood. They were running out of answers.

'Are there any other family members?' her doctor asked.

'No,' Marc said automatically and then he stopped.

It had been so many years since he had been Oliver that he sometimes thought of it as a dream. But he knew, whenever he allowed the memories of Riley to surface, that she was real. So the rest of it probably was too.

Marc went back and forth. It felt like being split in two. Maybe it was all irrelevant anyway. Maybe she was dead. Riley never seemed like someone who would make it to old age. But anything was worth it for Silvie.

He was frightened of seeing Riley again in the way you're frightened of childhood nightmares. Riley killed people. She left him on his own. He was scared because Riley has something he desperately needs and she could say no. He was terrified that maybe she was in fact dead. Most of all Marc was afraid of what he would feel if he saw her. Love doesn't die just because you stab it in the heart. It can walk around, wounded and bleeding, for years.

The documentary Marc is making is not about Leaf Winham or the Nowhere children, although those things are in it. It is about his daughter. This story is about finding a donor for Silvie.

The camera is supposed to look at its subject down the lens. Marc knows it actually points the other way. Everything you film is really about you.

Riley is still staring at the photograph wide-eyed.

'You want me to know your daughter?'

'Yes.' Marc shuts down all other thought. He has to get out of here.

'It's hard to be a parent.' Riley hands the picture back. 'I know about that.'

'I saw you on the CCTV at the dumpster,' he says. 'All the baby formula. Blood in the land?' He wonders how Riley, with her wasted frame and stick-like arms and legs, took Annie Lyons all the way up the mountain on her own. But she might have a cart. Maybe she even has someone helping her in Ault.

'Yes,' Riley says. 'And Una likes to pretend to eat.'

'Riley,' he says, hopeless. 'They don't like anything. They're gone.'

'You don't know who they really are, Marc.' She shakes her head. 'They're my responsibility. All of them. Hallie, Whitey, Rufus, Peach and Una.'

Something gives on the peaks above, a cracking yawn like the world opening. Through the window, the valley tosses like the sea in a gale. A tree falls across the clearing, a tall pine, graceful and slow. Lightning makes a white crack in the sky.

'Riley,' Marc grabs her hand. 'The way out, the one we took last time. Where is it?'

Riley looks up at the shattered sky. She turns, pulling him into the depths of the house.

Riley and Marc run through the dark halls. Memory rears up strong. Marc is suddenly seven again, he is Oliver and he's scared of Leaf Winham whose ghost roams here.

As he runs he sees a bright unicorn blanket thrown over a rotting couch. A Barbie with no head on the mantlepiece, a basketball in a dark corner, plastered with leaves. He feels the sick punch of sadness.

They come to the long gallery. Marc looks at the broken floor, the sunken place. 'It's down there, isn't it?' Memory and time are sliding together.

Riley puts her arms around his neck. 'I can't go with you,' she says into his ear. 'I can't leave them alone.'

Marc takes her bony shoulders in his hands. 'You have to.'

She shakes her head. 'They need me.'

'They're not here, Riley,' Marc says, desperate. 'They would all be adults by now. They're not real.'

'They're here,' Riley says, confident.

'Where?' Marc can't stop his voice rising.

'I don't know exactly,' Riley says. 'But trust me.'

'No.' Marc shakes his head. He takes her face in his hands. 'Have you ever heard five children be this quiet? There is no one else in this house.'

'You're wrong,' Riley says, smiling.

Marc takes a long breath. 'Don't make me say it.' He can hear the pleading in his voice.

'Say what?' Riley asks

'Those children died in the fire you set,' Marc says, 'along with all the others. Did you think I didn't understand, even back then? I saw you do it.' His throat catches when he thinks of it – walking away from the flame and the screaming. He feels a stab of anger – imagine if someone tried to do that to his Silvie. 'No one survived.'

'The children didn't die,' Riley says. 'They were already gone. They lived here a long time ago, they were killed by their father.'

'You're talking about the apple farm,' Marc says slowly. 'That woman confessed on her death bed that they had covered up the deaths of five children. So you think that's who they are? Hallie, Rufus, Whitey, Peach and Una? Ghosts of the children from the apple farm?'

'They live here,' Riley says. 'It's their place.'

'No.' Marc's voice trembles. 'Those were real kids, who I knew. I played with them. I touched them. They were not ghosts.'

'You could only touch them because of this.' Riley fingers the leather thong at her throat. A glimpse of bone against her clavicle. 'It's their bones. That lets them know you.'

'I thought I could do this,' Marc says. 'Speak to you. But maybe

I can't.' He covers his eyes with his palm. 'The night we ran, Noon put the kids to bed. She locked them in the stall to stop Peach wandering. I saw her do it. Then I woke up and you were there. You set the stables on fire. No one got out. They died, Riley.' He takes a deep breath.

'The five children at the apple farm,' Riley says, patient, 'are—'

'They are nothing to do with this.' Marc almost wants to hurt her now. 'Angela Smith talked about taking the children's names off the chest of drawers at the apple farm. Those children were called Harriet, Elijah, Sarah, Anne and Charlotte. No Peach, no Whitey ...'

'I know,' Riley says. 'They don't use their given names. They call themselves by new ones they made up themselves.'

'When do you see them, the children?' Marc asks. 'Why can't you see them now?'

'You wouldn't understand—'

'Do you only see them when you've eaten those?' Marc points at a dirty bowl which sits against the wall. 'This whole house stinks of mushrooms.'

'The mushrooms are just a doorway,' Riley says. 'The children showed me that.'

There is a rumbling from below. 'We have to go,' Marc says. 'Both of us, now.' It might already be too late.

'I know you don't understand,' Riley says. 'But they're my children.'

'Fine.' Marc throws his hands up. 'If you're right, they can't be killed. But you and I can die, and I won't leave without you.'

Riley wipes her eyes and nods. 'Ok.' She avoids his gaze. Marc sees her eyes glisten with feeling as she jumps down into the hollow place in the earth. Riley thinks he came back for her. She doesn't understand yet why Marc needs her.

He brushes that thought aside as the house flashes up white with lightning.

Riley leads Marc past the five round, smooth skulls, through the lilac and into the dark. The blossom is sodden with rain and clings to Marc's face; he's soaking wet and blinded by leaves and flowers. It's like being born. He has been born so many times in this life – as Oliver, as Marc, and lastly with the arrival of his daughter. He doesn't know which, or how many parts of him had to die to make room for the new. There's no way to tell; change is like that.

The tunnel is smaller than he remembers, the ceiling lower. Marc can only just stand upright. Riley grabs a torch from her pocket. The beam dances on the rocky floor ahead. It's quiet down here after the raging storm above. There is only the faint sound of water, rushing somewhere behind the walls.

The world cracks and breaks overhead.

'Was that—'

'Yes,' Riley says. 'I think it was the house falling.' Her torch beam dances on the cave wall. Her face is ghostly. 'It will hold,' she says. 'Solid mountain stone.' But Riley doesn't sound sure. 'Come on.'

Marc and Riley walk faster, faster and then they run, and somehow he finds that he's holding her hand. They run down the rocky passage, through the mountain, just as they did all those years ago. The flashlight plays on the glittering walls.

'I remember this,' Marc says breathless. 'It sparkles.'

'Yes.' Riley slows and runs a finger down the gleaming wall. She turns to Marc. Her fingertip glistens in the torchlight. 'Wet,' she says. 'Oliver ...' The mountain shakes. The earthquake is moving the world.

'Run,' Marc says. 'Really run, now.'

The rock wall splits and a fissure opens boiling white. More cracks appear with sounds like gunshot, spewing foam and water into the tunnel. The water bursts through, reclaims its ancient path, becomes a river again.

Marc and Riley wade through the water which races about their calves. As it rises to their knees they slip and stagger, panting. He stays close behind Riley, trying to shield her.

Riley cries out and grasps frantically at her neck. 'My necklace,' she shouts over the water. 'It's not here!'

'It doesn't matter,' he shouts.

Riley clings to the rock. She shakes her head and cries.

Marc seizes her. He's not leaving without Riley – her living body. He pries her hands from the wall and she screams and beats him with her fists. He feels how thin and fragile she is. Marc lifts her above the racing current and carries her on.

The water creeps higher and higher; it's thigh deep, then at their waists. Marc fights through the frozen torrent. Riley struggles in his arms and twice Marc stumbles and is dashed against the wall. He rights himself, heart pounding.

Marc thinks at first it's hope or a hallucination, the faint grey light ahead. But it's there. He shouts and pushes on faster. The way out is still open. Maybe they won't die here after all, drowned or buried in the rock. *If we hurry*, he thinks. *Maybe.*

He shoves Riley hard out of the mouth of the tunnel, forcing her up out of the dark earth. He hoists himself out after, into the forest.

Coming out into the storm is like being beaten. The air screams. Wind batters his ears, rain falls in long freezing needles battering the earth. Lightning makes the world click white, grey, white, black. A roll of thunder shakes everything.

'We have to go back – my necklace,' Riley shouts into his ear.

There is the distant crash of rock. The mountain is falling into the valley of Nowhere. Riley lunges back towards the tunnel entrance.

'No,' he yells.

'You don't understand,' she says. 'I have to ...'

'It's too late.' Marc takes Riley by the waist and drags her down through the trees. The hillside is flooding; water flows around them, calf deep, yellow and brown with topsoil. Lilac blossom floats past on the racing current. Lightning flickers.

Riley claws at him, 'I need their bones to see the children. Noon told me, she told me ...'

'She told you that while she was torturing you,' Marc spits in Riley's ear. 'While you were high.'

She shakes her head, mouth crushed with sadness.

Marc gestures around at the black and white world. Rain falls thick and hard, the trees whip back and forth like grass in the wind. He is so cold he has to lock his jaw to stop his teeth from chattering. Marc looks at Riley, pleading.

After a moment, Riley closes her eyes and nods. Marc puts his arm around her and half lifts, half pushes her on. They will both get out of here alive. There is no other answer.

A dark shape rears out of the undergrowth to their left and leaps away, racing the hurtling current. Marc glimpses antlers, slender legs. More deer flee down the mountain, ghosts in the rain, legs flying.

Marc peers through the thick grey air. He has studied the maps of this place until he knows every peak, every gully. But the storm is a pelting veil, they can hardly see a foot in front of them. A fresh wave of silty water hits their ankles like a blow. Riley staggers. Marc decides that any direction will do. Riley says something he can't hear over the crashing of rock and earth and water. The storm is rising. Thunder shakes everything.

'What?'

Riley shouts, gesturing at the torrent that rushes down through the scrub. He leans in, trying to catch her words, but they are drowned out. It sounds like, 'Did you see the inky hell?' Marc shakes his head, pointing to his ear.

Together they slide and stumble downwards, blinded and gasping with cold. Every so often the world goes white and crackling and thunder rolls through, shaking their very bones. They are in the heart of the storm. Plants are uprooted as the water gathers force; rivulets from across the incline join together and feed into the torrent, strengthening the current. Riley slips and he lunges for her, catches her hand. Her weight pulls him earthwards – they both roll and slide down the slick incline into a narrow gully where the water rushes fast through its deep channel. Marc fights his way to his feet, spitting frozen mud. He pulls Riley up. The sides of the gully are steep and almost liquid. Even as Marc watches, the earth lip dissolves and slides down towards them. They can't get out without bringing the slope down too.

Riley points downstream and Marc nods. They turn and wade, panting. Above them, the solid banks dissolve and crash down into the racing current. The water level rises above their knees, the torrent pushes them forward, harder and harder.

Maybe they will drown like this, Marc thinks. If not they'll die of exposure on the mountain. He doesn't know how far the road is, or if they're going in the right direction. Maybe the road is gone. Maybe the van got washed away and Kimble is dead.

At last the gully grows shallower and begins to level out. Around them, the trees are thinning. The thunder falls behind. When Marc shouts, 'Are you ok?' he can hear Riley when she yells, 'Yes!'

A scree of boulders looms to their left.

'Climb out that way,' Marc shouts. 'You first.'

Riley nods. He lifts her out of the water onto the rock. Marc reaches, searching for purchase. He's trying to pull himself up when he hears it. 'What's that?' he shouts at Riley.

'What's what?' she shouts back.

He shakes his head. 'I don't know,' he yells. 'A kind of squeak.'

Riley's eyes widen and she lunges down, grabbing for his arm, trying to pull him up. His wet flesh slips through her fingers.

It hits Marc like an avalanche, the vast thing in the water. He glimpses hooked teeth, a yellow hooded eye. The crack of its old jaws is horrifying as they close on his leg like a vice. The crocodile yanks and drags with terrible strength. Marc is plunged into the brown icy roar, face up to the pelting sky. He splutters as earthy water fills his mouth and nose.

Marc doesn't know how long the crocodile pulls him through the water. Eventually it slows. It drags Marc into the shallows, hauls him up in jerks, tussles him onto the mudshore.

Now or never, Marc thinks. He reaches for his prosthetic leg and pulls down hard. His limb comes out of the socket. Marc flips over and crawls away down the current, leaving the prosthetic behind. Water batters his face and body. He looks over his shoulder for an instant. The crocodile stands on the muddy spit like a stone, titanium protruding from its jaws. Marc scrambles up the shallow bank on the other side and crawls fast across the forest floor. When he looks behind again he sees the prosthetic in the mud, abandoned in the rain. It is warped and bent, marked by great teeth. The crocodile is gone.

Marc gasps and crawls to the base of a pine tree. He grasps the lower branches and pulls himself upright. Maybe he can support himself on branches, pass from tree to tree. He makes it two steps before the next branch is just out of reach. His fingertips graze its leaves as he falls. Marc's face hits the mulch. The sound of the storm and the water in the gully roar in his ears.

Marc turns his head.

The crocodile is fifteen feet away. His yellow eye glows in the downpour. The slit pupil is fixed on Marc. It holds the memory of millennia. The crocodile is like the mountains. Marc is a tiny speck meaning nothing.

I've been waiting for you, Marc thinks. He knows the crocodile can hear him. *I just didn't realise it.*

'All right,' he says, spitting rain. He hopes he did what he could with his life. Maybe he was a good man at times. He hopes Silvie will forgive him. He hopes that they will meet as gnats or planets or meteor dust one day, out there in the black expanse. Marc doesn't mind dying so much. But he wanted his daughter to live.

The crocodile's eye explodes in a mist of red. It judders in agony.

Marc turns his head. Riley looks back at him. The barrel of the old revolver steams a little in the cold. Riley blinks rain from her eyes and sights again. It's best to make sure. She pulls the trigger and it clicks. 'Gun's wet,' she shouts, eyes wide. She pulls the trigger over and over and it clicks uselessly. Marc and Riley keep their eyes on the still form of the crocodile as blood pours from its eye socket. 'Is it dead?' Riley shouts.

The crocodile stirs and Marc catches his breath. A sound comes from its vast depths like a sigh or a low growl. The crocodile backs away, turns its great weight slowly uphill, back into the storm. Its thick black tail drags behind, clearing a swathe on the forest floor. Marc hears a faint squeaking as it retreats into the distance.

Riley helps Marc slowly upright. 'Here.' She puts his arm over her shoulders. 'Put all your weight on me.'

'We're lost,' he says. 'Riley, we lost the way so long ago ...'

'It's ok, Oliver Olive.' She strokes his wet hair. 'We're nearly at the road.'

Ahead through the trees Marc sees the black sheen of wet asphalt. He must be dreaming because he sees their van pulled askew into Leahy's turnout. He thinks he hears Kimble yelling.

Marc stares at a thick, corded neck. He has never been so glad to see an ugly rose tattoo. The van shudders and jolts down the hill.

'It keeps burning,' Marc says. He meanders between consciousness and unconsciousness, between English and French.

Linus hushes Marc, cradling his head. 'Nothing is burning. You've got hypothermia, I would say. Both of you.'

Riley is belted into the seat beside him. She bounces like a ragdoll with the van. Marc takes her and holds her steady. He pushes her pale face. 'Wake up.' He is afraid that she's dead but she stirs and looks up at him with those eyes – his daughter's eyes.

'Riley,' he says.

'Oliver Olive.' She reaches a trembling hand. 'Did I really do it, to the children that night?'

'You know you did,' Marc says. 'The night you made me leave.'

'No,' she says. 'They are with me in Nowhere House. Hallie, Rufus, Whitey, Peach, Una ...'

He wonders how often she has recited these names to herself in the dark. 'I can't help you, Riley,' Marc says. 'But you can help Silvie. She's sick. You need to consent to donating your kidney. Say it now. Tell me you constent.'

'Why?' her voice wanders.

'In case you die.'

'So you didn't come back for me.'

'No. I came for her.' Marc is exhausted. 'Please.'

'Is she like you?' He can't read the feeling in her voice, maybe he never could.

'She's not like anybody else in the world.'

Riley touches his cheek. 'I hoped you'd have love. But I have to get back home as soon as I can. To my own little ones.'

Marc steels himself. He holds her hand tightly. 'You were a child,' he says. 'We were both just children when it all happened. It wasn't your fault. But this is now. You can save my daughter's life.' Marc takes a deep breath. 'Your children would want you to help,' he says softly. 'I know they would.'

Riley's face goes still with shock. She turns away from him, stares at the window, the driving rain. Her mouth moves silently, in some unheard conversation. He has lost her, Marc realises bitterly. He judged it wrong. Or maybe she wouldn't have helped anyway, no matter what he said. He sees now that Riley herself is beyond help.

Marc lets himself collapse at the waist. He stares at the juddering floor of the van. It was all for nothing, in the end. The world is soft at the edges now and pointless. Nothing is real without Silvie.

A hand lifts his chin gently.

'Don't touch me,' he says into her palm.

Riley raises Marc's face to meet her gaze. 'I'll do it, Oliver Olive,' she whispers. 'I consent.'

'Thank you.' The relief is almost more than his body can take. Marc surrenders to black. But he sees that there is fire in the air, encircling them both in flame. It will never stop burning.

'Linus and I agreed it was insane,' Kimble says. 'But we still came to get you.' She shifts, trying to get comfortable on the plastic hospital chair. 'Couldn't see a thing, rain falling like park railings. And then the van stalled, just by Leahy's turnout. Can I have your pudding?'

'Sure,' Marc says. He makes to pass it to her but his hands still haven't lost their shake.

'It was Linus who realised,' Kimble takes the pudding and peels back the foil. 'He said to me, "Marc knows this place. You realise that, Kimble? Marc is keeping things from you."'

'And I said—' Kimble puts pudding in her mouth and closes her eyes. 'I said, Marc would never lie to me like that. He would never trick me, persuade me to do a fake project for his own selfish reasons—'

'Kimb—'

'I told him,' Kimble says, raising her voice over Marc's, 'we trust one another, he and I. We're a team. He would never do that.'

'Kimble ...'

'I'm still talking.' Kimble spoons pudding into her mouth. 'The road was basically a river. We couldn't move. Then you came out of the trees, with her. We got you into the back seat, and then the engine started again right away. That place is so weird.' She pauses. 'You weren't wounded, there wasn't any blood.' She is disapproving.

'Sorry,' Marc says. Kimble appreciates blood: it means that the situation is serious enough to deserve her attention.

'So.' Kimble focuses on the spoon and the pudding. 'She's your sister?'

'Yes.'

'And you lied to me about this whole thing. About the documentary, about who you are.'

'Yes. The first part. The second part – no. I didn't lie about who I am. You know who I am.'

'Ok.' Kimble rises from her chair.

'Kimble.' Marc closes his eyes. 'I messed things up for you with Margot,' he says. 'I made you miss your trip. I did it on purpose. I was scared you'd leave me. That you wouldn't be my friend anymore.'

'Marc,' Kimble says. 'You can't keep people around like pictures on the wall. One day we might not be friends anymore. I can't promise that won't happen. But we're friends now. Ok?'

'Ok.' Marc swipes a hand across his eyes. 'I'm such an asshole.'

'That's true,' she says, taking the edge of his blanket between finger and thumb. She stares down at it. 'Try not to be too much of an asshole when you meet her.'

'Who?'

'Margot. She's coming out to Boulder tomorrow.'

'Oh,' he says. 'That's great.' After a moment, he says, 'I've got to check on—'

'They're still doing tests,' Kimble says. 'Scans, tissue typing, I don't know, to see if she's a match. I asked as I came in. Why haven't we talked about that?'

'I thought,' Marc says carefully, 'that I should stop putting my problems on you. I'm trying to learn boundaries.'

'Jesus,' Kimble says. 'There are boundaries and boundaries, Marc.'

'This one has to work, Kimble. It has to.' He can't stop the tears.

'Um,' Kimble says. 'Ok. Do you need a—?' She leans forward and puts her arms stiffly around him. They stay there for a moment.

Kimble sits back. 'I didn't like that.'

'No,' he says, shaken. 'Why did you do it?'

'I don't know.'

'Ok,' Marc says. 'Let's not do it again.'

Kimble nods and there is a stretched silence. 'So can I get you anything before I go?' she asks politely.

'No, thank you,' Marc says. 'I have everything I need.'

She pokes the spoon into the empty pudding pot. 'There is something else, actually. You should know that I'm editing the footage.' Kimble licks her finger. 'In fact, I'm making the documentary. By myself. If you want I can credit you as an exec or whatever. I've wanted to produce and direct for a while and this feels like a good opportunity. I'm assuming you have no problem with that.'

'No problem,' Marc says after a moment. 'Good idea.'

'Great. My agent will be in touch. Also, I'm paying Linus ten thousand dollars, if we can get it.' Kimble stands. 'Bye, Marky Mark.' With her pointing finger she quickly traces a circle on the back of his hand. *Love.* 'I'm glad you're alive.' She walks away quickly down the ward.

22

Marc

On the day that Silvie has the transplant, Marc chews on his hospital bedsheet. He sits and sweats and chews. It will be hours before she comes out.

After much argument the hospital consented to one parent observing from the glassed-in gallery. Marc and Claude agreed it should be her.

'You did the first part.' Claude put her hand on Marc's. Her nails were ragged, bitten down to the quick. The red polish was almost all gnawed off. 'Now it's me.'

Marc kissed her hand, careful not to hurt the raw places where she chewed her nails and cuticles, and for once neither of them could find anything biting to say. They argue, he and Claude, but they're part of each other too.

Marc shakes at the thought of what's happening now, Silvie's tender flesh, the scalpel moving on her unconscious body.

He levers himself out of bed and takes the clunky wooden crutches from where they lean against the wall – his new prosthetic will not be ready for some weeks – and makes his way across the hospital. It takes him a while to get to Riley's ward, step by clumsy step. The crutches feel like using roller skates after years of ice skating. But there is something comforting about the solid wood under his arms, the reality of it.

Riley is awake. She blinks slowly, eyes still unfocused from the anaesthesia. She is so thin that she almost blends in with the bed. Marc feels the fall of terror. What if she dies because of what he has asked of her?

Riley catches her breath when she sees Marc. Her smile is awkward, unpractised; he supposes she hasn't had much call to use it over the years. 'They're doing it now,' she says. 'For Silvie.'

'I know,' he says. 'I guess I came to see if you were ok.'

'I'm ok,' Riley says. 'So long as you know it's not two for one.'

Marc snorts quickly, covering his laugh with his hand.

'Does it hurt?' he asks.

'No.' She winces even as she speaks.

'Don't lie to me, Riley,' Marc says, furious, 'not now.' He's shocked at the sound of his voice which is not his own. It's the other one he gave up years ago. Marc is scared of letting Oliver back in. It means too much.

'I don't know what's going to happen, Oliver Olive,' Riley says, 'but I know you're doing everything you can and so am I. So is everyone. Ok?'

He nods. The fear is so strong it's hard to form a thought.

'Let's wait together.' Riley holds out her thin hand and he takes it quickly in his. They sit like that for a time.

'I miss my children,' Riley whispers.

'Why do you keep saying things like that?' She constantly provokes him with these fantasies, it makes him furious. 'You understand reality, Riley, I know you do—'

'So do you, Oliver Olive.'

'Don't call me that. I'm going outside for a cigarette.'

A doctor appears in the doorway. The doctor opens his mouth and Marc forgets everything else.

Marc and Claude get balloons and cake. They get pointed party hats and soda and buttons saying 'You're the best!' They make their way up to the ward clutching big plastic bags of these things.

Silvie is asleep. Marc and Claude sit down on the hospital chairs as gently as if they might break them.

Silvie stirs. 'Hi.' She sounds so small. 'I feel sick.'

Marc leans over her anxiously. 'Are you ok, you want a nurse?'

'Is that cake?' Silvie points. 'Can I have some?'

Claude quickly cuts a piece for her. Silvie nibbles at the frosting, leaning back against her pillow. 'Mm,' she says. A moment later she is asleep again.

Claude and Marc sit by her bedside, talking in whispers and moving forkfuls of sheet cake around on paper plates. At their feet plastic bags spill party hats and streamers onto the white linoleum floor.

Silvie has banned all crying, so even though she is asleep Marc leaves the room to do it. He puts both hands flat against the tiled wall of the hospital bathroom and presses hard, harder, down until he is empty.

Marc finds Riley staring out of the window as usual. She is healing slowly. A week ago they moved her to this rehab room on the fourth floor so she could move about some. She doesn't move, though. All Riley does is stare down at the small patch of grass they call a garden, or out at the parking lot. She hasn't been in a city for thirty years.

Riley doesn't seem to hear Marc come into the room.

'You have a visitor,' Marc says.

Her head turns as quick as a snake.

'She wanted to thank you in person.' Marc is scared now. Maybe this isn't a good idea.

Silvie pushes past Marc, impatient. 'Hi.'

'Hi,' Riley says, grave. They look at one another.

'My dad says not to upset you because you're crazy,' Silvie says. 'But you don't look crazy.'

'Your dad's right.' Riley bares her teeth in a snarl, snorting hard through her nostrils, crossing her eyes. 'I'm completely crazy.'

Silvie shrieks with laughter.

Riley glances once more at the window.

'There's not much green out there,' Silvie says. 'It must be hard. You're used to having grass and animals and stuff.'

'Where I live,' Riley says, 'there are tons of rabbits. Sometimes there are hares. Do you like rabbits?'

'I loved my rabbit,' Silvie says. 'He was called Snow Machine.'

'Snow Machine is a great name for a rabbit.' Riley sits down on the bed and pats the chair beside her. Her cheeks have taken on a faint pink.

Silvie sits and casts a baleful glance at Marc. 'I know.'

'What kind was he?'

'He was a lop-eared rabbit,' Silvie says. 'They look a little dumb but Snow Machine was not dumb. I even taught him to come to his name ...'

Riley nods, eyes wide, listening.

Marc hovers. He wonders, uneasy, how Riley knows how to do this. To talk to children, after all those years alone.

Marc takes Silvie to bed. Then he comes back to Riley's room. She is alert, waiting.

Riley says, 'She's a great kid.'

23

Marc

The late afternoon is low and golden, giving way to desert twilight. Marc sits in his wooden chair, waiting for the first stars. The world is an expanse in all directions, bare and beaten by the sun.

Silvie makes shapes in the sand with her toe and hums. She's learning clarinet and the same flat notes constantly fill the house.

It has been good for them, the desert. They came out here after Silvie's surgery then Marc stayed. The desert is as different as you can get to mountains. Though Marc's heart still stutters when he hears thunder.

Silvie stays with Marc during the school semester. She goes to Claude for Easter, for the summer, for Christmas. When she's away Marc feels her absence like a deep cut.

'Chips,' Kimble says, curt, emerging from the house. She tosses the bowl lightly onto the table. Corn chips leap out onto the sand. 'And beer.' She puts the can in Marc's hand. 'And root beer.' She kisses Silvie's head. 'You better eat your dinner, you rotten little potato.'

Silvie nods hard.

'We're going out,' Kimble says to Marc. 'Margot wants to drink.' Margot and Kimble come to stay sometimes.

Marc gives Kimble the sign for cool, a circular rotation of the wrist. She gives it back and goes.

He sees it in his dreams sometimes – the lightning-bleached moment when the crocodile came from the water. Other things have been surfacing lately too. His mother. Oliver, Cousin, Riley.

My child is not dead, Marc reminds himself, looking at the desert sky. *Kimble is not dead. I am not dead.* He feels a deep grateful shock for these things at various times of day. Sometimes Marc catches his reflection in a store window or in the mirror while shaving and thinks with a start, *still here*.

Silvie taps Marc's forehead with a firm staccato finger. 'Can I have a popsicle?'

He squints up at her. 'After dinner. After the stars.'

Marc and Silvie used to watch the stars come out together most nights. They do it less often these days – she is growing up.

Silvie continues to tap Marc gently, humming as her finger drums his eyelids and ears and head. The kidney transplant has held, so far. It has been three years since Riley gave it to Silvie. Maybe this one will last.

Silvie stops tapping. She kicks up dust with her heel. 'Dad.'

'Yes.'

'Can I have screen time?'

'Watch the stars, for god's sake.' Marc's voice rises, exasperated. 'Just for a moment. Watch the goddamn st—'

'Fine. *Fine*.' Silvie rolls her eyes. She's getting to that age. She thumps down onto the seat beside him.

Marc wraps a blanket around them. He holds Silvie close, breathing her hair. Her hand steals into his. He tries not to hold it too tightly.

Riley is a question that Marc will never stop asking. Some days he feels her loss all over again. Other days he wants to weep with gratitude for what she did and then there are the days of anger, of rage so deep that he cannot speak her name. Marc feels Riley in a different part of his body each day.

He has lost his sister so many times, it doesn't seem possible that she is gone. And then it does, and then it doesn't again. Maybe he will never believe it. Maybe Riley is nowhere. Maybe she's somewhere she belongs.

Silvie tightens her grip on Marc's hand. 'Dad.' They look up.

Venus has appeared above, gleaming like a silver stud. The sky darkens slowly and there they are, the stars, puncturing the night one by one, burning down on everything.

Acknowledgments

I wrote this book at a difficult time and relied heavily on the kindness of many, many people. I could never have done it without the great compassion, talent and support of the following:

To Jenny Savill – my wonderful UK agent and fierce champion, who texted me every day when I was trapped by the California wildfires, who rearranged everything last year when I was incapable and grieving – thank you is not enough. Even so – thank you. I'm immensely grateful to the team at Andrew Nurnberg Associates, from founder Andrew Nurnberg, whose support has been a godsend since the beginning, to Managing Director Michael Dean who brings my work to the screen. I owe huge thanks to the ANA foreign rights team for taking my books out into the world – Barbara Barbieri, Benedetta Ciavarro, Juliana Galvis, Halina Kościa, Ylva Monsen, Sabine Pfannenstiel, Naomi Sankaran and Alex Stephens – you are marvels. Many thanks also to Siobhan Kelly, Rosemarie Mills, Saliann St Clair and Saskia Willis for always having my back.

Robin Straus, my US agent, fields all travails with great grace and kindness and is always ready with advice on anything from contracts to the best place for lobster rolls. I am very lucky to have you on my side, ably assisted by Danielle Matta. Thank you for putting out all the fires (except this one).

I am so grateful to Miranda Jewess for all her patience, ingenuity and gimlet editorial eye. Viper is a powerhouse and it's a privilege to be a snake. Thank you for giving my books so much care and thought. Drew Jerrison has managed publicity for four of my books now – I am endlessly grateful, Drew, for your support, creativity and dedication. Thank you to all the Viper team, especially production editor Sarah Kennedy, Emily Jarman and the marketing team for their imagination and flair, and to Charlotte Greenwood who does so much to smooth all processes. Steve Coventry-Panton designed the beautiful, dramatic UK cover which perfectly evokes the feel of Nowhere, bringing it to striking visual life. Nowhere Burning was copy-edited by the wonderful Hayley Shepherd, who catches everything.

Across the pond at Tor Nightfire in the US, fervent thanks are due as ever to Kelly Lonesome, my amazing US editor, for all her time, patience, and help. To president and publisher Devi Pillai for her endless support of my macabre books, to senior marketing manager Jordan Hanley, VP of marketing and publicity Lucille Rettino, director of publicity Alexis Saarela, to managing editor Lauren Hougen who coordinates with the UK for book files, production editor Sam Dauer for shepherding this book into its final form, Sarah Weeks and Hannah Smoot for their invaluable support in publicity and editorial respectively, and to Valeria Castorena for heroically managing the social media side. Last but by no means least, I am so grateful to art director Jess Kiley and to Nicole Lecht who are responsible for the fantastic cover art for the US edition. I could not have asked for a more haunting cover image with which to send Nowhere Burning out into the world.

To my wonderful family – to my darling dada Christopher Ward, to my sister Antonia Ward, Sam Enoch and my ebullient nephews Wolf and River, you are the lights that guide me – my pilot fish – and I am so very, very lucky to have you. Thank you for, well – everything.

I am fortunate to have wonderful friends who listen, who pull me back to my feet when it all gets too much, who are always at hand with wise counsel and wine. To (deep breath) Emily Cavendish, Emma Campbell Webster, Theo Cross, Oriana Elia, Alexene Farol Follmuth, Virigina Feito, Frankie Frascatore, John Harris Dunning, Belinda Stewart Wilson, Stark Holborn, Caroline Kepnes, Liz Kerin, Sarah Langan, CJ Leede, Francesca McConchie, Andy Morwood, Nora Noone, Thomas Olde Heuvelt, Gillian Redfearn, Alex Rooney, David Samwel, Alice Slater, Jamie Vaulkhard, Holly Watt, Anna Wood – thank you. You may never know how badly I needed you or how much you helped me.

To my godmother Jo Hawkins and to Ann English; thank you for your care and kindness and for delicious lunches – in dark times and in times of light.

To my beautiful mother, Isabelle Ruth Learmont Ward, no words can express how deeply you will forever be missed by me. You gave me everything; so this is all for you. I hope to see you again, one distant day, out there among the stars. For now, it has to be enough to have known you, to have loved and been loved by you, for all those years.

ABOUT THE AUTHOR

Robert Hollingworth

CATRIONA WARD was born in Washington, DC, and grew up in the United States, Kenya, Madagascar, Yemen, and Morocco. She studied English at the University of Oxford and later earned her master's degree in creative writing at the University of East Anglia. Ward is a three-time winner of the August Derleth Award for Best Horror Novel: for *The Girl from Rawblood*, her debut; *Little Eve*; and *The Last House on Needless Street*. *Little Eve* also won the Shirley Jackson Award for Best Novel. Ward is the international bestselling author of *The Last House on Needless Street* and *Sundial*.